KT-479-535

Also by Tricia Sullivan from Gollancz:

*Occupy Me*

# SWEET DREAMS

Tricia Sullivan

GOLLANCZ

LONDON

First published in Great Britain in 2017 by Gollancz
an imprint of the Orion Publishing Group Ltd
Carmelite House, 50 Victoria Embankment
London EC4Y 0DZ

An Hachette UK Company

1 3 5 7 9 10 8 6 4 2

A CIP catalogue record for this book is
available from the British Library.

ISBN 978 1 473 21299 2

Typeset at The Spartan Press Ltd,
Lymington, Hants

Printed and bound by CPI Group (UK) Ltd,
Croydon, CR0 4YY

www.triciasullivan.com
www.orionbooks.co.uk
www.gollancz.co.uk

For Marion J. Sullivan
world's greatest mom

**Secret Diary of a Prawn Star**
**Entry #46**
**Codename:** Chaplin
**Date:** 12 September 2027
**Client:** Bettina Haugh-Wombaur
**Payment in advance:** Yes
**Session Goal:** Resolve recurring anxiety dream
**Location:** Collingborne Road, Shepherd's Bush
**Narcolepsy status:** Nice nap at O's place beforehand
**Nutrition/stimulants:** None
**Start time:** 11:32 p.m.
**End time:** 12:27 a.m.

Mrs Haugh-Wombaur blows off a lot in her sleep. It sounds like she keeps a foghorn under the duvet. Of course, to look at her daylight life you'd never guess. She has ruffles on her bedding, and her pillowcases always match. She keeps her socks and knickers in separate drawers. None of her bras are tangled up. Even her Rabbit lives in a special velvet case with lube in a zippy bag alongside. Everything in Mrs Haugh-Wombaur's life is under control – except her colon in the middle of the night.

Oh, and of course: her dreams.

That's what she hired me for. Normally I wouldn't snoop around people's rooms to see what kind of vibrator they have in their drawer, but one time I had to make a lightning search for throat sweets when I had a coughing fit in the middle of the night. That's when I noticed that Mrs H-W's tidiness extends right down to alphabetising her make-up: blusher, concealer, eyeliner, foundation, lipstick, mascara. (I snipe because I'm jealous. I've had most of my make-up since I was seventeen and

1

it's spread over the bottom of my saggy H&M carryall so that all the containers are covered with a greasy light brown dust like fallout from an explosion.)

At the moment, I'm in the middle of Mrs H-W's recurring nightmare. I know it inside-out; it's become something of a thorn in my side. Every session I do my best to get in there and change the trajectory, but no matter what I do, it always seems to end the same way. Mrs Haugh-Wombaur is invigilating a History A-Level exam in the nude while jeering students launch plastic Angry Birds piggies at her using catapults made from protractors and rubber bands.

For some people, this would be just the beginning of a hot sex dream. Or a funny sex dream, at least. Not Mrs H-W. She's genuinely humiliated by her body, and the Angry Birds thing apparently goes back to her student-teaching days when an eleven-year-old secretly recorded his friend shooting Green Pig into her bum crack during a lesson on the Roman Empire. The video went viral.

I know I can help her get over it. On this particular occasion, I have a dressing gown all ready. I'm lurking in the dream at the back of the exam room, where she can see me smiling and being encouraging. I'm like a dream coach. In Mrs. H-W's dreams I always present like my real self, because she's insecure and I'm unthreatening. But technically I can change myself into anything I want when I'm in someone's dream. Once I changed myself into a horse so that my client could gallop off into the sunset alone, leaving his mouthy ex-boyfriend behind.

Mrs. H-W doesn't need a horse. I really don't think there's much wrong with her; she just needs a bit more confidence and less body shame. When all her clothes vanish, I'm going to rush forward and cover her up, then inform the offending History students that they've failed their tests. I am going to use my mean voice.

But before I can act, the dream is filled with the sudden gong of church bells. I startle awake.

She's farting again.

# Body confidence

Mrs H-W is thrashing around in the big bed she used to share with Mr H-W before he ran off with an estate agent he met at the gym. This evening she's been out with friends and got to bed late and a bit drunk. The drinking and/or the late-night pancakes at My Old Dutch have disagreed with her, and now the room is stifling and foetid thanks to Mrs H-W's overactive gut flora.

I shift in the armchair beside Mr Haugh-Wombaur's now-empty wardrobe. This is where I work. My debilitating narcolepsy has certain advantages, and one of them is that I can fall asleep anywhere. I have to get back in the dream because I promised Mrs H-W we'd find a way to beat this thing, and I sense she's growing impatient with our lack of success. But holy guacamole, Batman, the room smells revolting. Gagging, I stand and creep out into the hallway, listening carefully for any sign she might be waking. The hall air isn't much better, so I pad down to the lounge and crack a window. A cool shaft of night air falls into the room and I suck it in greedily. Ah. It's the little things.

My earring's internal display is discreetly informing me I have new messages. I'm kind of hoping that my next client will cancel. It's a new client who booked me for 3 a.m. on the other side of town, for a sex dream. I hate doing these – scraping together an induced orgasm out of someone's personal kinks isn't therapy and it's rarely even fun – but I've taken it out of financial desperation. I don't think I'm going to be so good at this after Mrs H-W. But the first message is just a check-in from O, making sure I'm OK. I start to compose a reply to the effect that we need to charge danger money for olfactory hazards, and then a little flag in my visual field informs me that the second

3

message is from Antonio Silva. O has forwarded it from the business line. My pulse starts flying north.

I go to the foot of the stairs and listen. Mrs H-W's breathing suggests she has fallen into a deeper sleep and is probably dreaming again. I need to get in there and do what she's paying me for. Damn. What does Antonio want? Why do I care? Well, we know why I care, that's obvious, but I don't want to care. I start up the stairs and open the message on a small internal screen in the corner of my vision. I decide I'll read one line. Just one line.

*Hi Charlie*

That doesn't count as one line, OK?

*How are you? I am fine. I need a favour and I hope you will forgive*

That's it? He's so formal. Where's the TLDR? He hasn't told me anything. Forgive what? Forgive him for being such a jerk? I mean, seriously, I'm not interested in Antonio's alleged condom phobia.

I climb a few more steps. Mrs H-W unleashes another whopper and I stop. OK, just one more line.

*me if this request is inappropriate, but I don't know where else to turn. Would you*

Would I? Would I? Would I what, Antonio? Quit beating around the proverbial.

*consider taking on my girlfriend as a client? She is seeing a psychiatrist but*

Grrrrrrr. I decide that, just for now, I'm going to pretend I didn't read that. Deep breaths of the cool air, Charlie, and let it go. Really, I don't know what possessed me to open a message from Antonio Silva of the too-giant-for-condoms dick. I do not ever learn.

Snarling a little, I close the app and tiptoe back into Mrs H-W's bedroom. I flop down in the chair, ready to take on her hostile A-level students. I can do this. I can help her. Body confidence. Body confidence. Body confidence.

Mrs. H-W blows off once more with feeling.

# TRANSCRIPT

**DC:** This is Donato Cruz interviewing Charlotte Aaron with Doctor Roman Pelka also present. We recommence at 1.53 p.m. on 17th September 2027 in Location B, Leytonstone Road, Stratford after Ms Aaron requested a toilet break. She has been advised of her right to legal representation during this interview and she has declined.

**CA:** Legal what? Er, thought I was just here to help.

**DC:** What exactly is your job? Your business card says *Dreamhacker*. Do you mind explaining?

**CA:** Oh, you must want my elevator pitch. OK, just a second, let me remember what I'm supposed to say... OK, ready?

**DC:** As ready as I'll ever be.

**CA:** I'm so glad you asked, Donato! I guess you could think of me like Billie Piper in that old TV show — damn, what was it called again? You know, where she goes to people's hotels and does dirty stuff to them. But without the sex in my case.

**DC:** I don't watch TV.

**CA:** Oh, never mind. Seriously, there's nothing sexy about dreamhacking. I sleep in armchairs and on settees and sometimes on the floor while people snore and grind their teeth and... stuff...

**DC:** How many floors does this lift stop at?

**CA:** What they do in their dreams is their business. And it's my job to help them do it in a more healthy and proactive manner.

**DC:** Your formal qualifications are...?

5

**CA:** I just remembered the elevator pitch! *Secret Diary of a Call Girl* meets *Inception*! That's it.

**DC:** OK, got it. And your formal qualifications?

**CA:** Um... well, it's a new field. There are no actual, like, governing bodies.

**DC:** But you went to — let's see — Excelsior-Barking University. You have a lower-second-class degree in Psychology. Online.

**CA:** Yeah, and look where that went! I couldn't find any proper work after I graduated, so I had to temp for an agency. Office work.

**DC:** You temped for a marketing company, apparently. Arguably some psychology there.

**CA:** Not really. What I do now *is* psychology. Sort of. In an unlicensed, rogue sort of way... That came out sounding bad, didn't it?

**DC:** And the money for... er... *dreamhacking*?

**CA:** It's not what you'd think given the size of the alternative-health community. The trouble is, dreamwork is time-intensive and it has to be done in person. The only way to make money is to charge people a lot. O has been trying to get me clients. She's posh and has loads of contacts. But it's not easy money. People want fast results or they're off to NLP and quantum healing instead.

**DC:** So you're trying to tell me there's no money in what you do. Why don't I believe you?

**CA:** Maybe you're a naturally suspicious person.

**RP:** [unintelligible]

**DC:** Is there something you want to say, Roman?

**RP:** Sorry. That wasn't a laugh, honestly. Frog in my throat.

**CA:** At least I'm employed. And I'm registered with the Council of Alternative Therapies. I pay National Insurance. You can check.

DC: We did. So you invented this profession for yourself.

CA: I didn't have a choice. I got sacked from my temp job.

DC: And why were you made redundant?

CA: Sleeping on the job. But I couldn't help it. I was ill.

DC: Your medical records show that you applied for sickness benefit and were denied. You claimed narcolepsy.

CA: It was because of the medical trial. My mate Shandy contracted typhoid so she could pay back her decorating-addiction debt. She said it was easy money.

DC: You contracted typhoid for money?

RP: What's a decorating addiction?

CA: I didn't contract typhoid, Shandy did. Mine was this other experimental infection, I'll just look up the name in my files while we're talking. Bear with me. So, Shandy's decorating addiction. She gets paid now to decorate, but before she was hired at BigSky she racked up a lot of debt buying virtual furniture. She's really hooked. She has a full-time unicorn to stop her being run over by cyclists.

RP: So she's a virtual-space designer.

CA: Trainee, but she gets a wage. It was through Excelsior-Barking's nanotech department. They were compensating trial participants. The medical study, I mean, not the unicorn. I'm still looking for the name of the infection, sorry if my eyes are rolling back. I know it's not my best look.

RP: It's OK, it suits you.

CA: Shandy says I look like a dead body.

DC: We can get the files later. We will need specifics

about this work you did. Not Shandy or Shandy's unicorn. You.

CA: Sorry, I'm a little disorganised. But hey, I'm just wondering what this has to do with... with what happened to Melodie Tan. I mean, why are you so interested in me?

RP: You'd be surprised how important these little details can be. The more you tell us, the better we can do our job.

CA: OK, but can't we take a break? I'm knackered.

DC: [laughs] We just had a break.

CA: [yawning] I'm not faking the narcolepsy, you know.

DC: You use headware. Did you check to see if it was related to your illness?

CA: Oh, my earring? The doctor said not to worry. It couldn't do anything like that. Anyway, I only use it for social media. And movies. And a bit of shopping, not that I can afford to buy fresh food, even, let alone shoes or hair products. I mean, you haven't seen my hair but since the infection it's pretty much beyond repair.

DC: Yet the piece you use is late-model. Well beyond most people's budget.

CA: My grandad handed it down when he bought himself the latest upgrade. He's... you know, he's from *that* generation. With the money.

DC: So you're not into tech?

CA: Me? No. I'm more of a people person. If I were into tech I could get a job with BigSky and then I wouldn't have to sign up for medical trials just to raise the cash to get out of the cupboard under the stairs, do you see what I'm saying?

DC: About your friend O — her real name would be...?

CA: Sorry, but I'm getting a bit hungry. How long will you need me for?

DC: We can take a short break. But we'd prefer no calls, no outside contact. Roman, sort some food.

CA: Uh... can you just tell me how long you're likely to need me for?

DC: I would clear your calendar, Ms Aaron. The police are treating the death as suspicious and you're a witness.

RP: Ms Aaron, are you all right?

CA: [unintelligible]

DC: We can't understand what you're saying. Could you speak up for the recording, please.

CA: Am I a suspect? Because the constable at the scene told me I could talk to you if I wanted but I didn't have to. No outside calls doesn't sound right to me. I mean... in films they get to make one call, or is that just America?

DC: This isn't a film. You have the right to leave. You have the right to contact anyone you wish. I merely stated what my colleague and I would prefer.

CA: I think I should go.

RP: Excuse me, Donato. Er, Ms Aaron, my colleague can be a little... intense. Let me get you a kebab and a drink. You go ahead and call anyone you like. We're not the *police* police. We only ask that you be... discreet. This is a sensitive matter.

CA: [crying] Sorry. Freaking out. I mean... it's just been so... right off the roof... I mean dead as in just gone... and it's not my fault his dick is so big...

RP: Whose dick would this be, precisely?

CA: [unintelligible]

DC: Just stop crying!

**END RECORDING**

**Secret Diary of a Prawn Star**
**Entry #47**
**Codename:** Chaplin
**Date:** 13 September 2027
**Client:** Martin Elstree
**Payment in advance:** Yes
**Session Goal:** Sexual gratification, client
**Location:** Trump Metropole, Room 819
**Narcolepsy status:** Crashed on Tube for 10 mins. Seriously
   overtired
**Nutrition/stimulants:** Takeout curry & energy drink
**Start time:** 2.56 a.m.
**End time:** 3.27 a.m.

RECORDING DELETED

Material on this recording violated terms of service for the AR
provision of Charlotte Aaron.

   To store material of this type, please reset your system
parameters to include use of power tools for sexual violence,
olfactory triggers, penile enhancement and systemic bias.

# The first cut

Gah! Only a dream! Only a dream! WTF was that sick business – ugh, can't unsee, can't unhear, can't unsmell... eww, got to get a grip.

Pull it together, Charlie.

I'm awake. I'm awake. I'm literally pinching myself.

I think I can safely say I've never helped a client build a dream where their kink turns out to be attacking their boss with power tools. Thank god the recording system censored it. Let's pretend it didn't happen.

Where am I, again?

Let me think. I did Mrs H-W and then I got that text about Antonio and then I came here. Hotel. New client, Martin Elstree. Sex dream. Well, I think calling what just happened in his head a sex dream is stretching the definition. I need to wake up properly but it's not easy. My body wants to keep sleeping.

I locate myself in the cushy chair by the TV. I drag my eyes open just in time to see Martin Elstree bucking under the super-king-sized bedspread across the room. He lets out a satisfied groan. All my arm hairs are standing on end and my skin is burning with that fast-creeping-adrenaline sensation you get when you've narrowly escaped being hit by a phalanx of e-bikes travelling at speed.

I watch Martin Elstree out of the corner of my eye. He thrashes a bit, then subsides. His breathing settles as he slides into light sleep.

I'm alert enough now to realise that the curry I wolfed at the station was a mistake. I'm going to spew. I put my hand over my mouth and lurch out of the chair, relying on the hum of the air con to cover the sounds of me sneaking into the hotel bathroom. I shut and lock the door, keeping my gaze on the tile floor. There's a mirror the size of Lancashire over the sink. I lift the toilet seat and kneel in front of it. Complimentary bath products are all lined up on a shelf in the shower. They're high-end, just like the hotel – even though Martin's booked one of the smallest rooms in the place. At first he gave me the keys to his posh flat in Convoys Wharf but I am glad now that I held to my policy of no house calls for first-time clients. Now that I know he's a fucking psycho, I may have to rethink my whole client-vetting system.

Deep breaths, Charlie. It's OK. See? Aromatherapy bath oil. Fair Trade shower gel. I fix my attention on the calligraphy of the labels so that I don't have to remember the sound of Martin Elstree's boss's croaking voice as she apologized to him for being a nasty authoritative bitch. So I won't smell her flesh burning as he—

My stomach clenches and the curry comes up in a yellow-brown roar. Vomit hits the water and spreads in clouds, like really ugly watercolours. I spit, flush, rinse out my mouth straight from the tap. Keep the water running. Splash my face with my eyes closed. I want to hide somewhere inside myself, but everywhere inside is the sense of Martin Elstree's revenge-porn dream. I thought revenge porn was just being a jackass and showing people naked pictures of your ex. I never realised it could be about taking revenge on someone you hated. With a hedge-trimmer and a blowtorch. The human imagination— No, I'm not going to think about it.

At last, to steady myself, I look up at the mirror.

*There we are, love. You idiot, look at you. Bloodshot eyes. Wet, scruffy eyebrows that shadow dark green eyes. Your skin's normally sienna but in this light it looks more like mustard, and the violet headscarf that hides your alopecia is none too flattering – remember to wear the green one next time. Earring looks OK, discreet and simple. Remember, we're supposed to be professional. When you're a professional dream therapist, you might vomit but then you carry on.*

*And you don't talk to yourself in the mirror, OK?*

I'm not sure if I said any of that aloud. Maybe a little. Things get blurred. Always takes my brain activity a while to stabilize after I've been working on someone.

There's a soft knock on the door and I jump several kilometres into the air with a squawk, then glance at myself sidelong in the mirror as if to make sure I really heard what I heard.

*Knock-knock.*

'Charlie? Are you OK?' Martin Elstree has a posh accent and one of those deep, scruffly radio voices, the kind that people instinctively seem to trust.

I try to answer but nothing comes out. I clear my throat repeatedly, putting my palm against the door even though it's locked.

'Yeah, I'm fine. I'll be with you in a minute.'

The headache is starting. It doesn't usually come on so quickly; but then, I don't usually upchuck. I flick open my contact window and check the time. I've got maybe twenty minutes before the narcolepsy hits, and there is just no way I can risk going down with Martin Elstree in the room. I might wake up with a power saw up my vaj.

I open the door and he's still standing there, in his jimjams and bare feet like a normal guy. I don't want to see his feet.

'That was fantastic!' Martin Elstree blurts, pumping his fists in that repressed middle-class way, like he's cheering for a football match in a phone booth. 'So very very empowering. I don't know how you did that but you're a genius.'

'I need to go now,' I say. He's blocking me, and even though we're about the same height and I probably outweigh him, his dream scared me so thoroughly that I can't bring myself to go any closer to him. I try to turn on my bodycam so everything he might do will be on record, but the stupid firmware is in the middle of an upgrade and won't load. Fuck.

Before I know what I'm doing, I've hit the yellow warning button on my emergency link to O.

O's voice comes straight into my head, a sleepy growl. '*Problem? Turn on your bodycam, I can't see.*'

'*Arsehole client blocking me in bathroom.*' I'm not good at carrying on internal conversations without giving away what I'm doing. Martin must notice that I'm talking to someone because he steps back with a flickering look of offended honour even as O responds.

'*Throw a glass of water on him, darling. Shower hose. Flying headbutt. Do what you must.*'

Flying headbutts are Shandy's department, not mine. I shrug past Martin without saying anything and grab the door handle.

'It's only three-ish,' he says smoothly as I open the door. 'I booked you until eight. Just need a little time to recover, you see.'

Now I'm out in the hallway, on CCTV and with O in my ear, I feel bolder. I turn back and square up.

'I don't do deathporn. I don't do gratuitous dismemberment. I'm a therapist.' My voice is shaking and I'm wanting to hurl again. If only I still had something in my stomach, maybe I could hit his feet.

He acts shocked. 'You must be joking, you don't do deathporn? You have a great talent for it. You know, I could smell *everything*—'

I let the door go and stride fast for the lift. Head feels like it's being squeezed in one of those machines that you put a minivan in and press a button and get out a little chunk of metal the size of a pepper shaker. He doesn't seem to be following me, but by now I'm staggering.

'*Are you safe, darling? Should I send Muz?*'

'*Yes, please, O.*'

Muz is a bouncer for a club in Soho. He's approximately eighteen metres tall and made of titanium. He and O are both motorbike aficionados, and he takes care of her 'hog' for her. He would squash Martin Elstree like a gnat.

'Where shall I have him meet you? Room eight-nineteen or the lobby?'

'O, I'm sorry, I think I'm going to fall asleep in public.'

'Don't do that. Put on a bit of Anthrax or something.'

I hit the button for the lift and lean on the wall. The hallway is empty and it seems to stretch on for ever into the distance. Like a dream hallway. So tired. My headache has moved into my wisdom teeth, which I was supposed to have removed last year but I was dating Antonio and couldn't face the chipmunk-cheek after-effects, and . . .

'Charlie! Wake up!'

The lift is sitting on the 27th floor refusing to move and I'm on the eighth.

'Don't think . . . I'll make it out . . .' I spot a laundry cart full of sheets.

Now, let me make it clear that under normal circumstances I would never be tempted to curl up in a pile of sheets potentially loaded with other people's body fluids, bacteria and stray pubic hair. But when I've been working, I become quite unable to control some of my primitive instincts. Right now the need for sleep is overpowering. I have to get somewhere safe and cosy before I pass out, and suddenly those sheets are looking too inviting to resist. I wonder if this is how dogs feel about lamp posts.

'Eighth floor,' I tell O. 'Laundry cart near the lift.'

Then I climb in. Last thing I notice is how the dirty sheets smell like Chanel Number 5.

**Secret Diary of a Prawn Star**
**Entry #48**
**Codename:** Chaplin
**Date:** 13 September 2027
**Client:** N/A
**Payment in advance:** N/A
**Session Goal:** Find a way to wake myself up
**Location:** Laundry cart, 8th floor, Trump Metropole
**Narcolepsy status:** CRITICAL
**Nutrition/stimulants:** Fear
**Start time:** 3.28 a.m.
**End time:** 5.47 a.m.

Before I got sick there was no particular order to my dreams.
When I could remember them, they were set in my mum's house,
or school, or sometimes in a mall or a friend's place. Or maybe
a car. They were a lot like real life, although things were stitched
together in funny ways, of course, and nothing made much sense.

But during my narcolepsy days, I started visiting the Dream
City on a regular basis. Usually I'm looking for something there,
but I can never remember what.

The Dream City isn't anything like real London unless you
count the Square Mile – and then only in that both are full of
swerves and unexpected openings. Making your way around it is
like playing a video game where the designers are having a laugh
at your expense. There's no map of it, no overview, and very little
concession to reality. Streets can turn into canals and canals
into bridges, and occasionally roads go around corners that are
greater than 360 degrees with no apology. Yet somehow it all
holds together.

For architectural chutzpah, the Dream City is like Singapore. Showy, extravagantly futuristic. There are neon bridges connecting the tops of buildings. There are fleets of cyclists riding point to point in transparent tubes. But when you explore on foot you find old parts underneath: mossy cloisters of pitted stone with broken statues, canals that smell like ditchwater and plunge unexpectedly underground. You can ride through these dark tunnels poled by animal gondoliers who use recycled smartphones to light the way.

If you look, you can find railway-siding houses with piles of junk rotting in their back gardens, just like in real London. But the back gardens in the Dream City are overshadowed by mysterious honeycomb towers whose structure looks like a cross section of bone under a high-powered microscope.

One gleaming skyscraper has a sideways restaurant, where people sit at a ninety-degree angle to the ground eating seafood while the updraughts from street-sweepers stir their hair. They appear to be living in a different gravity from the rest of us. I seem to remember being told that to get up there you have to offer certain bribes to the concierge, but I never asked what.

(The concierge, by the way, is a tulip.)

Sometimes there are snorting horses drawing carriages over cobbles, and steaming reeks rise from manhole covers as if an underground machine is gearing itself up for a very rude belch. Sometimes the buildings are square and shiny plastic, as if they've drifted in from the archetypal sleeping Lego Republic.

Sometimes the city is muted to utter silence.

Sometimes the streets are metal grates over jungles that release a fume of fruit and rot and animal smells. You can't get down there or see beyond the top of the canopy, but you can taste the moisture in the air of all that trapped life and you can hear the birds and insects in full cry. Once I saw a tiny drone fly down between the bars and amongst the leaves, and there was a crunch of metal being snapped and the sound of a motor wailing and then cutting off, and the birds went silent, just for that moment, before beginning to shriek.

One of the city's more curious features is the way you forget most of it on waking, yet when you return in a future dream, you find you can recall everything that ever happened here in vivid detail. Sometimes these memories unfold in several layers like an accordion fan; you see a certain doorway or staircase and it's like you clicked a hyperlink that offers up its long backstory in your own dream history – or maybe (I suspect) someone else's.

You never know what you will find around the next bend. Once I was in someone's flat and stepped out onto a balcony only to be confronted by a vast plain of water, apparently without waves, stretching out for ever, in all directions. It appeared to surround the building; yet when I went back inside the flat and looked out of a different window, I saw only a multistorey car park complete with two drunks having a pissing contest against the wall.

This time I'm picking my way along the bank of the swollen river, one hand on a slimy chain-link fence that separates the crumbling bank from the frontage of buildings. Sodium lamplight turns the droplets that collect on the links to gold, and they shower down on me every time I grab the fence for balance. On the landward side there are Plexiglas flood defences, but these have big holes in them as if giants have been chucking rocks at each other. Up ahead I can see a place where someone has taken wire-cutters to the fence and ripped back a panel.

In the Dream City, everything is in colour except for the people. They are in greyscale. As I get closer to the gap in the fence, I see that greyscale people are queuing up to climb through a hole in the floodgate and then stepping through the chain-link fence. They appear to be adults and children, but they are all wearing masks so I can't see their faces. One at a time, they climb through the gap in the fence and keep walking, right off the edge of the bank and into the river.

Their heads disappear beneath the turbulence.

There are no boats in sight. There are no life rings.

I hurry forward. I shout, trying to get people's attention, but no one even turns their head. When I reach the gap, I stand there and try to block the next person from coming through, but I can't.

'Hey!' I cry. 'Don't go through here. You'll fall in the river. Look where you're going!'

The person ignores me and steps around me. I even grab his arm to try to stop him.

'Don't touch me,' he says in a dull voice. 'It's assault.'

Startled by the accusation, I hesitate – and in that time he walks straight off the edge of the muddy bank and into the deep water. He disappears.

I try to block the next person. They are wearing a plastic doll mask with eyes closed. I grab the edge of the mask and rip it off. Underneath is another mask with eyes closed.

What the hell? There is no way these people can see where they are going because the masks have no holes where the eyes should be.

'Wake up!' I scream. 'Wake up!'

The person faces me and tries to walk through me.

'Where are you trying to go?' I say. 'This is the river. You're going the wrong way.'

In a tinny voice, she says, 'I'm going to a Sleepwalkers Anonymous meeting. This is the right way.'

Then she reaches out and pushes me. I fall.

There's a muddle of sky and lights and reflections before I hit the water and go under with the whole river punching down my throat like a cold fist.

# Cardboard box in Wandsworth Town

I don't so much wake up as crash into reality. My mouth tastes like rancid goat and I can feel the headache still lurking like a bank of thunderheads on my internal skyline. Sometimes I get a touch of synaesthesia, so when I smell nail-polish remover I expect it's connected to the headache. Until I open my eyes.

I am home in Finsbury Park on the sofa. O is sitting on the recliner opposite in her dressing gown, her hair in rollers that she must have slept in. Her wheelchair is parked nearby and she has put her bare feet up on it. With her reading glasses on the end of her nose, she looks like a plump, wrinkled elf as she paints her toenails a lovely turquoise. Outside, the sun is coming up over North London.

'I hope you're not hungry,' she says. 'I don't think I could make a piece of toast.'

I sit up, fuddled. My voice comes out faint and harsh at the same time, like I've swallowed sandpaper.

'How did you get me home?'

'Called Muz. He located the laundry cart just before the maid noticed you. Fireman's carry into the lift. Bribed doorman to look the other way. Minicab. Then up the stairs. Our lift's out of order again.'

She ticks off points in the air with the nail-varnish brush as though keeping score.

'Muz carried me? All that way? Oh my god. I'll have to bake him some cookies...'

I'm not totally clear on the relationship between Muz and O. He does jobs for her involving the hog and heavy lifting, but they are also friends. A bit like O and me, I guess.

'About the cookies. He did hint you could stand to lose a

stone. He said getting you out of the cab was like moving a dead tuna.'

'He *what?*'

'By the fourth floor he was winded. It's a lot of stairs, darling. But don't mention it. It's just lucky he wasn't working last night. I couldn't have helped, otherwise. I'm more of a Mycroft type, really.'

O's hand trembles as she carefully paints her little toenail. I don't know how old she is. Wrong side of eighty, I reckon. But Mycroft? I snort at the comparison.

'You think I jest?' she says archly. 'If Mycroft had lived in our time he would have been a white-hat hacker. He would have had a flat like this, and he'd have stayed in all day and solved the world's cyber-mysteries and had lots of naps.'

'Mycroft rebooted, with a taste for throw pillows and florals,' I say. 'But are you really a white-hat hacker? Because if you are, you're too cool to be Mycroft.'

O leans over and blows on her toenails. 'I wear many hats, darling.'

She gives me the slitted look she always gives when she thinks I'm being foolish, then lies back in the recliner and closes her eyes.

'I know you wouldn't have panicked over nothing, my dear. I hope you're all right.'

I shudder. 'You have no idea. That horrible person, Martin Elstree. It was a revenge dream, against his boss – who happens to be a woman. I don't ever want to work with him again. Ever.'

'I thought you might say that. He left messages on your business line.'

'Just delete them, please.'

'Are you sure?'

'His dreams . . . what he wants . . . O, it's not just kinky, it's evil. I won't do it, I don't care how much he pays.'

'I sent him your way because he pays fifteen times what Mrs Haugh-Wombaur pays.'

I cover my eyes. 'Please. Don't say her name right now. I've got a touch of Smell-O-Vision and I don't want to be sick again.'

'Sorry, darling. Look, fine, whatever. Only trying to help. All I'm saying is, I booked you with him because if he likes you he'll recommend you.'

'To all his other nasty friends.'

'He's a solicitor. His friends are other solicitors, and business executives, and tech speculators. I've worked with him myself – in fact, he's doing a really important piece of intellectual property litigation for me at the moment. He's very well-connected.'

'He seems so normal on the outside. You would never guess he's so pervy to look at him. There's something really wrong there.'

'I'd never have let him hurt you physically. You know this. I had my eye on you the whole time.'

'I'm not afraid of him physically, it's the— Look, it's hard to describe what it's like being in someone else's dream. It's as if I'm orchestrating it but I'm also the thing that's being orchestrated. It's passing through me, it feels totally real. It was horrible.'

'It must have been. Usually you try to make people better, no matter how unpleasant they are. And I note, most of these ultra-violent-fantasy men are afraid of their own shadow.'

I snort. Shandy says the same thing, but neither of them has a clue what it's like to be *inside* one of those fantasies.

'But what do I know?' she continues. 'You've got the psychology degree. I don't even have a degree.'

'You don't have a degree?'

'Nope. MI5 recruited me straight out of primary school.'

I flop back on the sofa and close my eyes. Whenever she makes fun of me, I act like a child. Stupidly, I'm actually fighting back tears.

'I just want you to say I don't have to do it.'

'Of course you don't have to do it. Who am I to tell you what to do? And darling, you know I enjoy having you here. It just seems a shame for you to be stuck living with a little old lady like me when there's money to be made out there.'

I open one eye. 'Are you sick of me, O? Because I can find another little old lady. Or a cardboard box in Wandsworth Town.'

'Don't be ridiculous! I'll be sad when you leave me. One day this business of yours is going to take off. Why do you think I help you?'

'You don't have to, though,' I tell her urgently. 'If it stops being fun for you, you need to say so. But no more dream sex. From now on it's straight therapy, bit of ASMR on the side.'

'Fine. You know I support you, whatever you decide. It's been a long night. I'm going to bed. Get some sleep. Your eyes look like old tyres.'

'Thanks heaps, Mycroft.'

**DC:** Donato Cruz once again with my colleague Dr Pelka as we interview Ms Charlotte Aaron of Seven Sisters Road, Finsbury Park. Resuming our discussion at Location B after Ms Aaron lost consciousness. It's now 4:08 A.M. Ms Aaron, given that we've just witnessed your narcolepsy in action, can you give us a bit more of the timeline with respect to your condition?

**CA:** Well, let's see. I was just going on with my normal life, temping to pay the bills and living in a cupboard under the stairs in Canning Town. Like you do.

**DC:** Cupboard under the stairs?

**CA:** Flat-share. My mate Shandy and her friends rented out the cupboard under the stairs as a fourth bedroom. Just big enough for a bed and a power socket to record my ASMR. No good if you're claustrophobic, but I'm not.

**DC:** Tell us about that. ASMR.

**CA:** You know what it is? Do you get tingles?

**RP:** I do, yeah, the sound of scissors and shoes on wet pavement, mostly, but sometimes—

**DC:** Just to clarify, Ms Aaron. By 'ASMR' you mean 'autonomous sensory meridian response', which it must be noted has only a flimsy scientific basis—

**CA:** That's not true, they've done actual science and it's a thing!

**DC:** —but is a cult phenomenon originating on You-Tube and more recently recorded on BigSky's AR sub-platform, Sweet Dreams. So, Ms Aaron, do you listen to ASMR, or do you record it yourself?

CA: Both. I have a channel, but I've not updated it for ages. Since I got the narcolepsy I haven't been able to do it. I fall asleep while I'm recording.

RP: It's not funny, Donato.

DC: I wasn't laughing. So tell us about this narcolepsy. When did it start?

CA: After the study at Excelsior-Barking. So... summer last year.

RP: While you were taking a break, I looked up the paid studies in the nanotech department but couldn't find anything that matched your description. Unless you mean the AR one. 'Enhancing peripheral nervous system response to AR triggers through internally delivered feedback.' There was no infection as such, it was a neural booster.

CA: That's the one. You took a drug, they monitored you and put you in an AR simulator to see if your experience was more convincingly real.

RP: And that study concluded in April. Your illness started in...?

CA: June. The narcolepsy started in June. But the dreamhacking started the day I took the drug. I was on a coach going to see my mum and I fell asleep and wandered into the dream of the person sitting next to me.

RP: Walk me through that. How did you know you were in their dream?

CA: Well, it obviously wasn't my dream. The dreamer was busking in the tunnel under the Natural History Museum, collecting money from tourists. There was a flood and he was up to his waist but still playing.

DC: You could have been dreaming that yourself.

CA: Dreaming in vivid detail that I was a violin

player performing Paganini? Ha! You've obviously never heard me sing in the shower. My mate Shandy says she's heard dying walruses with better pitch.

DC: OK, moving on...

RP: No, please continue, Charlotte. What happened after the bus?

CA: Just so we're clear. The guy's name was Piotr, which I knew because I was in his dream and I could hear his thoughts. After Piotr and I both woke up on the bus, he and his violin case got up and changed seats. He looked straight at me and said, 'Stay out of my head.' We were both right freaked out, but I can't understand why he was hostile. I actually materialized a rubber dinghy in the tunnel to save him, which I thought was pretty resourceful considering I'd never even been in anyone else's dream before. He just didn't appreciate it. Maybe he had a death wish.

RP: And after this incident — it happened other times? What can you tell us about those first instances?

CA: Well, I've always been a lucid dreamer, but after the drug or infection — I'm calling it an infection because I got sick, you understand — after that, I started wandering into other people's dreams on the regular. It mostly seems to happen if I'm physically close to the person, but I did test it once with Shandy when we had half of London between us and I was able to find her dream in the end. It just took longer.

DC: You got sick. What were the symptoms?

CA: Falling asleep everywhere. By which I mean *every*. *Where*. When it first started, I was visiting my mum but she ended up bringing me back to London and paying for a private doctor. I tried several drugs, nothing worked. I couldn't keep taking her money.

RP: And the people who were running the AR study — you talked to them about your problem?

CA: [snorts] They were all, 'Nope, not us, our thing couldn't have caused it plus you signed this thingie exemplifying us—

DC: Indemnifying?

CA: Yeah, exempt, condemned, that. Where they wash their hands of you. This is one reason I felt so sympathetic to Mel when she came to me... we are still talking about Mel, right?

DC: You lost your job in July?

CA: Yeah, they couldn't sack me right away, but I was fairly useless. So, like, I thought we were talking about Melodie. Am I under investigation here?

RP: Never mind my colleague. We're just trying to establish the facts.

CA: I didn't go to work because I couldn't wake up. I slept for four days solid.

DC: Four days solid? Were you in a coma? What about your... er... biological needs?

CA: I woke just to go to the toilet, take a drink of water. Then back to sleep. My room-mates couldn't get me up.

DC: Just to clarify. Where was O at this point?

CA: I've no idea. I didn't meet her until after I got evicted from the cupboard under the stairs. New definition of low point, that.

DC: You didn't know O before?

CA: Not in person. She was one of my ASMR subscribers, but we'd never met. Who is this about? Mel? Or me? Or O?

RP: We don't know yet. So you're saying you didn't meet O through a service? Like Granny Flat or something?

CA: She hates Granny Flat. Says she's not a granny.

RP: But she does take in younger women as housemates? You're not the first?

CA: She's had a few over the years. She uses a wheelchair off and on since the cancer. To be honest, she could afford to hire people to help her so it's not like I'm her carer. I think she enjoys the company. And she said having cancer made her want to give back.

DC: OK, bringing this back on topic. You slept for four days. And what happened when you woke up?

CA: I didn't, really. Shandy got scared and called the doctor, and the doctor said to call 999, and the paramedics came and took me to hospital. I was there a week with a mysterious fever. Eventually I got better and was discharged. Then I was sacked.

DC: Your employer dismissed you because of illness, then? That's illegal.

CA: Oh, they didn't dismiss me right away. Nobody believed I was sick. The doctor couldn't find anything wrong with me. She said it must be a virus. But I had problems staying awake, and I had problems telling the difference between being awake and being asleep. And the dream thing was happening all the time.

DC: Which brings us to the subject of Ms Tan. You saw her as a client.

CA: I saw Melodie Tan as a client. Yes.

DC: And what a bad move that was for Ms Tan.

CA: I don't see the need for you to be so nasty. I didn't cause this. I didn't ask for any of this! I really—

DC: What is happening? Hey! Snap out of it.

RP: Ms Aaron? Charlie? Are you... Donato, is she asleep *again?*

**END RECORDING**

# How not to be a doormat

'You did everything you could,' Mrs Haugh-Wombaur says when I call her to follow up on our session. 'Don't blame yourself. You've done more for me than any other therapist. We're down to one recurring nightmare, and I've even taken up Pilates thanks to the insights you've given me on posture and self-esteem. The vegetarian diet is working out really well, I feel ever so much better. I think I can take it from here. I'll ring you in a few months, OK?'

I don't know whether to be crushed or relieved. I stammer some polite response, careful not to say anything about the effects of the vegetarian diet. (But I'm surprised. It smells like she's dining on raw meat.) Then we ring off.

I yawn. Two clients in one night was a bit much, although Mrs. H-W won't have known the difference because I always leave in the early hours. My clients don't feel so invaded that way. I need to sleep nearby in order to enter their dreams, you see – ideally I like to be in the same room – but it's important to keep everything professional. So I stay elsewhere in the house until I'm sure they're asleep, then slip into their bedrooms and work nearby. In the morning, I slip out again before they're awake. Needless to say, I carry a lot of keys.

Speaking of keys, that afternoon I drop by Martin Elstree's office and leave the flat keys he gave me with the receptionist.

'You'll see he gets them?' I say. I don't want him turning up at O's place looking for them.

'Don't worry, love. They live in my drawer when he's not lending them out.'

She gives me a faintly pitying look and I recoil a little, flustered. People think sleeping together means sleeping together. When actually it only means sleeping together. Mind you, after

Elstree's hedge-trimmer dream, I'm no longer sure what it is I do.

I leave his office with my tail between my legs. So much for Martin Elstree being my ticket to a better class of customer. O has refused to refund his deposit, but that doesn't take the sting out.

I know I'm upset because after I drop off the keys, I don't go home but instead to the knitting café in Camden, where I eat four cupcakes and drink a tall skinny latte. I don't know why I order a skinny latte when the four cupcakes would totally overpower any dietary benefits of low-fat milk. All around me, people are knitting decorously, reading books, taking occasional sips of health-promoting green tea. I'm scoffing and slurping and scowling.

After the second cupcake, I realise I am angry. I'm good at what I do. Yet here I am, my oldest client sacking me and my newest expecting me to entertain his most disgusting, violent fantasies for money. If I say no, the fact that he's a powerful and influential person means I'll also lose the possibility of any referrals, which I now realise I was counting on.

Picking up the third cupcake, I decide it's unprofessional of me to take all this so personally. But by the end of that cupcake I've fallen into despair because apparently I can't even make a go of the flakiest career in the Alternative Therapies Handbook, and how sad is that?

Halfway through the fourth cupcake, I open Antonio's message and read the rest of it.

*She is seeing a psychiatrist but he just gives her drugs and they interfere with her work. My girlfriend is a professional musician. She's in town as a guest artist with the Philharmonic and she is having a breakdown.*

Now I'm stuck between being jealous of a professional musician and greedy for the sliding-scale fee I can charge her.

*She's a sweet person. Very focused. Maybe a little high strung. But now she thinks someone wants to kill her. She's dreaming about a stalker and she's afraid to go to sleep. It's starting to affect her work.*

I belch and get a dirty look from one of the hardcore knitters. 'Sorry, love,' I say.

I'm feeling a little sick now. I frown, reading the last few lines. *I know we didn't end in the best way. I hope we are still friends. I need your help.*

Yeah, right.

Also in my messages: a notification that my overdraft is nine pounds away from its limit. I hear an odd snorting noise, something between a whine and a sob and the sound of a pig at the trough. The hardcore knitter picks up and changes tables to get away from me.

I wish I could get away from myself.

It's coming toward evening again and O is asleep on the sofa when I finally let myself in. I can hear the whuffle of her snores over the rain that tiptoes across the skylight. The skylight is one of the few advantages of living on the top floor. O refuses to leave this flat even though she has used a wheelchair off and on for the better part of three years. It's because of the birds, she says. She keeps pigeons on the roof terrace. When I moved in, one of the conditions for living here was that I'd help look after the birds and do a bit of shopping for her. She rarely goes out; says it's because the lift's dodgy but I think she's a touch agoraphobic.

The flat is stale. In the kitchen, I find the remains of reheated lasagne and half a carafe of coffee sludge. After feeding the pigeons, I dump the lot, wash up in O's huge, scarred Belfast sink and take the rubbish out. By the time I've climbed three flights of stairs a second time, I'm so tired that I lurch like a sailor on my way over to O's workstation, which is open to my dreamwork calendar. O is a Virgo and loves to organise people. After she took me under her wing and started setting me up as a proper business, I offered to pay her but she just looked at me with those chilly eyes of hers. She's loaded and says she believes in paying it forward. I never intended this to happen, much less to go on this long, but there's no doubt she has the contacts I so desperately need.

My diary looks bleak. O has managed to book me with a regular client on Sunday the 19th at 2 a.m. She's written: 'One of the hairdressers downstairs, can't remember which one, having anxiety dreams. They never go to bed before 2. OK?'

I sigh and sign off. I get obscene amounts of sleep, but hardly ever in my own bed.

'Hope the new bookings aren't too much,' O says, making me jump.

'I thought you were down for the count.'

'Only napping. Turned in a draft of the Damselfly report today. Bit of a press to get it done.'

'Ooh, excellent! Nice one.'

O makes an obscene amount of money doing something incomprehensible with IT. I gather that she's some sort of security consultant, but she's cagey about it and I'm sure I wouldn't understand anyway. Given that she owns the entire building and rents out the flats below, she has no real need to work; according to Muz, her motivations are all internal. 'She's packing so much brainpower that she has to keep her mind active or she'd go mad,' he said the day I met him, as he helped me carry my stuff up three flights of stairs. Muz is in his early fifties but hard as a rock physically, and even that first time I met him, being around him made me feel safe. When we paused on a landing for me to catch my breath, he added, 'Keeping busy takes her mind off being sick. A word to the wise, love: she hates talking about it.'

Muz also told me that O uses cutting-edge biofeedback systems to fight the cancer that has spread to her bones, in addition to the more usual immunotherapies. That's why now, when O stretches and yawns and says, 'I have outdone myself. Sorry about the mess,' I wave my hand theatrically and say, 'Oh, pfft. I'll have the butler tell the housekeeper to tell the maid to polish all the door handles *tout de suite*.'

Then she says, 'Antonio called.'

I try to keep my tone casual. 'Yeah, he left me a message.'

'He said he was calling to book an appointment. He wanted to Spacetime you but I played guard dog.'

'You disapprove. I get it.'

I'm sure she's right, though. Antonio unexpectedly popping up in my augmented reality would probably have proven a little too... *augmented* for my own good right now.

'I don't know this person, Charlie. I only know what you tell me.'

'Oh, you mean his schlong.'

'I wasn't necessarily referring to anatomical details.'

'Details? A tool like that is *not* a mere detail, trust me. It's too big for condoms.'

'Indeed.' She is so dry.

'I bought some XXXL ones online, I think they were made for porn stars. But Antonio broke two of those just trying to put them on, and when we finally managed to fit one he said it acted like a cock ring at the base and he'd never be able to get his erection down. Then he complained about loss of sensation and said, *I am physical, everything I do has to be the best or it's not worth doing!* He was such a diva about it.'

'At which point you walked away, obviously.'

I make a face at her. 'You know I didn't. I was an idiot. I got the implant, gained the better part of a stone and started crying over dog-food adverts. Then he dumped me for not being the same fun person I was when we met. All because he's so "physical".'

I realise that I'm becoming sexually aroused just thinking about him. O clears her throat.

'And...?' Clearly she's waiting for me to recall the moral of the story.

'Oh. And I learned an important lesson about my boundaries and how not to be a doormat.'

'Good. That is all, then.'

O throws off the afghan and begins the slow process of getting into her wheelchair. I check my messages, trying to be discreet and not watch as she positions her legs and rearranges her robe. She's been working too hard, that's for sure. But if I say anything—

'Don't say anything, darling,' she gasps as she begins to wheel herself to her room.

'Not. Saying. Anything. Up to you if you want to blow yourself out. Your funeral, et cetera'

'Start writing my eulogy now so I can check your syntax before I pop off.'

I wait until her light's out, then open the windows to let in fresh air, plump the sofa pillows, put the room more or less to rights before I go, at last, to my own bed in the little second bedroom. My old schoolmates have proper jobs in sensible towns that aren't London. They are getting engaged and going to Cambodia on holiday, and I live with an old lady whose other best friends are pigeons. Most of my current friends are anxious people I met on the Internet because my ASMR helps them go to sleep. And nowadays you may as well call me a sex worker for all I try and pretend otherwise.

It's time I got real.

*Hi Antonio*, I message. *Happy to see Melodie. When is she free?*

After that, my self-pity is such that I want to say I cry myself to sleep, but thanks to the narcolepsy I actually just pass out without even trying.

# ASMR

'I can't believe you're standing me up,' Shandy moans into my Spacetime. 'I could have gone to board-game night with work people, but I chose *you* because you're so squidgy and cuddly and I miss having you in our cupboard under the stairs. Now I'm going to be stuck scraping mould off cheese and listening to room-mate grievances. Hey, where you at? Looks posh.'

'The new Hilton,' I subvocalize because I'm in a lift with well-dressed people. 'Antonio's girlfriend has invited me to her suite there. How actually bad do I look, Shandy?'

I expand the Spacetime field of view so she can see me fully. I'm wearing a manky old Spoon Bandit shirt from their first festival, shorts over dark tights, and trainers. I have proper shoes in my backpack but couldn't find anywhere around London Bridge to put them on without getting knocked down by the grey and black tide of business suits just let out of work. I have a green rag wrapped around my head, which makes people think I'm on chemo and causes weirdness but hides the fact that only random chunks of my hair are left after the trial.

While Shandy stares at me, I can see her curled up in a bean-bag in her room. She has perfect skin and an eye-catching figure, and her hair sticks out in all directions aggressively. When she takes in my look, a big white smile zaps across her face like a lightning bolt. She covers her mouth with both hands, laughing so hard that her feet paddle up and down like she's dancing flamenco.

'Bugger,' I say under my breath. 'I had it all sorted. I was planning to wear my special going-out jacket.'

'The one with the mustard stain?'

'The grey one, you know, that makes me look more young professional and less underemployed house cleaner. I had my whole outfit laid out on my bed, but then O somehow sprained her wrist trying to open the pigeon cage and I had to take her to A and E.'

Shandy stops laughing.

'Oh, that sucks. Is she OK?'

'I guess, I don't really know with her condition being what it is. I would still be there waiting if she hadn't told me to push off and do some paying work. So then I had to hustle from the Tube station, and you know how BigSky are running a promotion for Spacetime Gold and you can't walk two metres without tripping over an AR-bot trying to wheedle you into an upgrade.'

The lift lets me off at the 23rd floor and I stand in the hallway uncertainly.

'On behalf of my employer, I am so sorry,' Shandy says. 'But I thought you said O gave you some blockware for free.'

'She did. You know how she hates BigSky.'

'This is why I never come to your house.'

'I tried the blockers but they just make the narcolepsy worse.'

'But everybody uses blockware! I work for BigSky and I use blockware to block our own stuff. Otherwise you just get over-stimulated and start to hallucinate. Couple of days ago I thought I was talking to a 3D ad, but it turns out I just had feedback on one of my design apps and I told a perfectly innocent crash-test dummy to fuck off.'

'You have crash-test dummies in virtual-furniture design?'

'I got assigned to an AR human-flight project. People go up in the Cairngorms and fly in those suit thingies, but with AR they can be on other planets. Did you at least take the earring out?'

'After being waylaid a few times by AR, I took the earring out. Then I just ran through the rain, which I thought was making me wet until a Green Bus drove through a puddle and I got fully soaked. I'm so tempted to blow off this appointment and come to yours.'

Shandy and friends have a new room-mate-under-the-stairs, a New Zealander. Shandy's been trying and failing to get into his pants for a while, so he must be terribly hot and standoffish. It would be so entertaining to be there and not here.

'Don't even think of changing your mind, Horse. You need the funds. And Antonio called you. Hold your head up high, go in there and show them both what you're made of.'

'But I'm made of wet spaghetti.'

'Cut the shit and get in there. I expect a full report.'

She snaps her fingers and disappears.

Melodie lets me in so quickly that she must have been standing right inside the door waiting for me. That's her name. *Melodie Tan*. The harpist.

'I know, it makes me sound like such a joke!' She's Canadian, with a strong accent. 'My friends call me Mel. You should, too.'

Here's the problematic thing about Mel. She's really sweet. I mean that. She's got lovely warm skin, she's got hair like those shampoo adverts where the model's tresses fall like a satin sheet and absolutely no flyaways. And instead of resenting her for what looks to me like an unfair excess of overall gorgeousness, I find myself liking her and wanting her to like me. Oh, and get this: she plays the harp. It couldn't be the bassoon, could it?

She offers me a seat on the couch of her suite. She pours me a glass of wine, but I notice she's drinking sparkling water herself. On the other side of the floor-to-ceiling window, Central London spreads out looking dignified and romantic – *Nice trick, London*, I think to myself. I can still smell bus fumes on my clothes.

Melodie confides that the room is paid for by a Russian patron who insists on putting her up in the best suite in the hotel; she looks embarrassed. I of all people don't judge. I get out my AR stylus to take notes in an effort to appear professional. It is held together with sticky tape like Harry Potter's glasses, but never mind.

'So... Mel... tell me what's going on. Antonio hasn't explained anything properly.'

'I like your voice,' she says. 'It's lovely. Have you ever thought about going on the radio?'

That catches me off guard.

'My mate Shandy says I sound like I just smoked a cigar and killed some big game.'

'Yes! Exactly. It's wonderful. I have this squeaky little-girl voice and nobody takes me seriously.'

She isn't at all what I expected. I feel an urge to reassure her, so I reach out and put my hand on hers, which is trembling.

'I'm here to take you completely seriously,' I tell her. 'Everything you say I keep in strict confidence. Just go ahead, whenever you're ready.'

I remove my hand and she takes a shaky breath.

'OK.' She lets the breath out. She laughs nervously. Then she stands up and starts pacing back and forth, talking very very fast.

'See, I'm the kind of person who attracts stalkers and creepers and stuff like that. It's been happening all my life. You know, I get a lot of flowers and anonymous gifts, I get weird stuff online. Sometimes people wait around to try to catch me when I leave the theatre. I had to take out a restraining order once on a guy in Rome. They're men, usually, but one time I had a death threat from a female musician who was jealous of me. She said I slept my way into my job even though I only got into the orchestra on a blind audition – I know for a fact the director would have preferred a guy from Malaysia, but never mind. She didn't do anything in the end. At least not to me; I heard she had some other trouble with the law. I think she married a furrier. Anyway –' about here, she pauses for breath and then hurtles on '– what's been happening lately is that I seem to have a creeper in my dreams. And I know it isn't a real person, not *really*. I've even read that every character in your dreams is actually an aspect of you, which I find a little disturbing, but I digress. The point is, he's there almost every night. He hasn't tried to . . . do anything bad to me. Yet. But . . . well, OK, I'm looking at your face and you probably think I'm crazy already. Should we forget it?'

All of this comes out so fast that I find myself blinking and going, 'Uh . . .' into her sudden, loaded silence. I can't keep up.

'No! We shouldn't forget it!' I say as quickly as I can. 'That's fine. I'm just taking in the information.'

'Because, I mean, I know I sound loony—'

'You don't. Not at all. Is it OK if I ask you some questions?'

'Sure. Hit me.'

'Tell me what you can remember about the dreams.'

She sits back down and from her supple leather satchel she draws out an exquisite leather-bound journal. She starts flipping through the smooth, creamy pages. The sound is pure ASMR and it triggers me. My scalp begins to tingle and my eyes go half-lidded before I remember that *I'm* supposed to be calming *her* down, not the other way round. I step on my own foot, hard, to jolt myself awake.

'OK. I wrote everything I could remember in here. Let me look at my notes. So, here we go. In the dream there's a room. It's like a practice room, with soundproof walls and a piano and some music stands. Like the ones they had in Toronto where I trained. I'm in there tuning my harp, but the low D won't stay in. The tuning peg is wobbly, even though in the dream I can remember having it fixed recently. I've got this big canvas tote bag that my mom bought me from the Smithsonian gift shop, with all my music and stuff in it, and for some odd reason I have pitch pipes – which nobody uses any more, but it's a dream. So I go to get the pitch pipes and there's a—'

She stops and an abstracted expression comes over her face.

'No, it's not like that. Well, I can't quite remember how, but suddenly this guy is just there, he says he's going to fix the harp but he tries to steal my bag.'

'Your bag with your music in?' She nods. 'All right, go on.'

'So, at first I let him take it because I'm so surprised, and then I think hang on, I need those scores because we're rehearsing tomorrow – and in the dream somehow I'm still in school, and if I lose the sheet music I'll be in trouble, and I'm getting really upset.'

'Of course.'

'So I run out of the room after him, but we're not at the conservatory any more, we're outside on this scaffold, like a . . . what do you call it? Like a gangway. Up in the sky. I look down and I can see all these canals with boats on them, and instead of roads there are these scaffolds way up high with walkways made of boards. The city below us has so many lights, and the architecture is sort of futuristic, a bit like Singapore – but it isn't any real place that I've ever been, and I've been a lot of places. The buildings are much taller. So he's running ahead of me with the bag, and I have to chase him. And I'm wearing heels.'

'Oh, I hate that,' I say. But Singapore? A city with canals . . .

'I know, right? So I was kind of mad by then. Well, not really mad, but more panicked because I had no clue what I was going to do if I didn't get my scores off of him. I chased him and he was just about to go into this tall building with a giant tulip out front, and I grabbed the back of his jacket and stopped him, and the bag of sheet music spilled. It went everywhere. It floated down into the canals and it blew around in the wind— Oh, I've got a note here – there was this hot wind, like a blow dryer, or when you walk over a subway grate in New York.'

'Did you say a *tulip* concierge?' I'm shocked that she's been in the Dream City. I'd assumed it was my place, part of my psyche. The idea of a client going there feels out of order to me.

'Yeah, I know, so stupid, you probably think—'

'It's fine, just carry on, Mel. What happened then?'

'Well, somehow in all the confusion I found I had the score I needed in my hand – it was Debussy – and the Creeper gave me a shove and I fell off the edge of the scaffold, and he shouted after me, *You're weak. What makes you think you can survive in high places?*'

'And then you kept falling?'

'Yes, but I woke up before I hit the water.'

'Well, obviously he's lying to you. You're not weak, you've earned your success. I hope you know that.'

'Thanks. I have no idea what part of me could be undermining me so much. I feel ashamed that I have such bad thoughts about myself.'

'It's not your fault,' I tell her. 'We all have cultural introjections. We absorb messages from our environment without even knowing it, and they get assimilated into us and cause trouble. Can you describe the guy to me? How old, what did he look like?'

'That's part of the problem – he was wearing a mask. It was a white plastic mask, really shiny, but it had no eyeholes and the whole surface of the face was covered with these chemical symbols. You know like in organic chemistry when they diagram molecules and they have the element and then the little lines connecting each element to the others? One line for a single bond, two lines for a double bond... I could draw it for you.'

'No need,' I say. I was rubbish at chemistry in school. The fact that Mel knows what a double bond is means that she must have studied it at some point, which makes her even more freakishly perfect, like a Miss World contestant. During her gap year she probably built an orphanage using eco-sustainable materials.

'Just one more question. Do you dream in colour?'

'Oh, yes, definitely.'

'Can you recall if the Creeper was in colour? Or was he in black and white?'

I'm off-script now, but the talk of the Dream City and the mask makes me remember my own dream in the hotel laundry cart. The people sleepwalking into the river.

'No, he was definitely in colour. He wore green trainers, I remember that clearly. I have an excellent memory.'

'I'm sure you do.' I write down *Chemistry mask*. It might be something from the pop culture symbol base. Everybody knows Jason and the hockey mask from *Halloween*, even if they've never watched those old movies.

'So what about other dreams? Is this the only one?'

'There are variations. He only stole my music in the first one.

41

But all of them are set high up above this futuristic city, and in all of them I find I can't control anything but he can.'

'Ah. Control. OK. Could you give me an example?'

'Well, one time I dreamed I was out on a walkway over this same city, and I was looking for something important. Can't remember what it was. And the sky started changing colour. First it was orangey, like a sunset. Then it went green, then brown, then red . . . it was like when you set your desktop screen saver to cycle every five seconds. Except that each time the sky changed, I felt my emotional state shift, too. I mean, dramatically. Like in music, moving from major to minor. And this guy in the mask, he was standing there orchestrating it. Like a conductor.'

'A conductor. That's interesting. Could it be a pun? A musical conductor could be an electrical conductor, in a dream. Was there lightning?'

She smiles. 'Ah, that's cool. No, no lightning. Well, I challenged him. I said, Why are you doing this to me? And he said, I want you to know that everything you see around you is of my making. If I say we're on a boat, we're on a boat.'

'And were you? On a boat?'

'Yes! It was like a cruise ship but it was staffed by people with donkey heads. He said that was his doing, too. It was really creepy. I probably sound insane.'

She puts the journal down and hugs her knees.

'Not at all. It's just the way dreams work. So, can you tell me what you're hoping for me to do for you?'

'I'll be surprised if you can do anything, honestly, because I've never heard of dream therapy, but Antonio insisted. The thing is, it's starting to affect my work. The dreams are exhausting and on top of that, I dread going to sleep so I have to use an app, but then it's hard to wake up so I use stimulants in the daytime, and then I get palpitations and my hands shake and I can't concentrate properly. I'm starting to fray.'

'What app do you use to go to sleep? If it's buggy, it could trigger nightmares.'

She nods. 'Antonio says I shouldn't use Sweet Dreams, but I have various apps that help me with my playing, plus liminal programming that I need to use to be competitive with other musicians. There aren't enough hours in the day to do the work otherwise.'

I feel myself gulping. Liminal programming enables you to learn skills as you fall asleep and as you wake up. I can't imagine being that focused, that dedicated, to anything, as to have even my sleep programmed.

'Anyway,' she adds, 'I've tried swapping apps but nothing changes. Please don't tell me I have to quit using Sweet Dreams. I don't think I have the strength to do that right now. I could lose my job.'

Her eyes are dark and full of tears, pleading. Wow. This palatial suite, her beauty, her talent – and she's a wreck inside.

'OK, well, I'm not here to boss you around. I'm here to help you work on your subconscious mind. Is it possible this Creeper character is a manifestation of your anxiety about... well, about being so overworked?'

She shakes her head. 'No. I love my work. I've sacrificed so much to get to this point. I want this career with my heart and soul, Charlie.'

I'm nodding, making sympathetic noises.

'Antonio says you've been sleepwalking. I have to tell you, I don't know how to help you with that and you might want to see an actual doctor. I only deal with the stories that are happening in your dreams. What I do is enter your dreams and rearrange things to make them turn out better. You could think of it like me planting suggestions so that you'll dream different things, you'll be able to wake up in your dreams and take control of them. And from what you're telling me, I think this might help you.'

'See, I was afraid you'd say this Creeper guy is just some complex in my head and then we'd be all into stirring up my childhood looking for causes and I don't have time for that—'

I cut her off with a hand gesture. 'I'm not an analyst. The way I work, it doesn't really matter what kind of complex the Creeper is. What matters is how you deal with it. Maybe we'll try transforming it into something less upsetting.'

'Ooh, could we turn him into a potted plant or a really ugly shoe?'

'That's the spirit,' I tell her.

There's a knock at the door. I'm not surprised to see Antonio. I force myself to look at him, even though I'm well aware it would be better not to make eye contact. His eyes are just as dark and knowing as before, and his eyelashes are just as long, and his mouth is just as curved. I bite the inside of my cheek so that I won't lean into his faux-European kiss-on-both-cheeks greeting.

'I hope I don't intrude,' he says, with a half-bow towards each of us. 'I just wanted to make sure everything is going OK and you don't need anything.'

I watch their body language. He looks at her like she's a goddess and there's a field of sexual intensity between them even though they barely touch. On any other occasion I'd probably be withering into a dry heap of despair at everything they're getting that I'm not, but I'm still wondering whether Mel could really have found the Dream City. Because if she did, then the greyscale people aren't just manifestations of my subconscious, they are other dreamers who are blundering around the Dream City blind. Users of Sweet Dreams, maybe – after all, I use my earring to make my recordings.

Mel wasn't masked, though. She could see where she was going in the Dream City. And so could the Creeper. What does it mean?

'I am going to sleep here on the sofa if this is OK,' Antonio is saying. 'I stay out of the way unless you need me.'

I must have startled or something, because Mel glances apologetically at me.

'Let me just catch up,' I say. 'You want to start . . . now?'

'Only if that's OK,' Mel says. 'It's just that I haven't had a good night's sleep in so long.'

Antonio reaches over and touches her hair, very softly. I see his nostrils flare as he looks at her, and I flush with embarrassment just watching them.

'Getting to sleep is difficult for Melodie,' he says, gazing at her. 'But you have the wonderful ASMR. We both listen to your channel.'

I'm a little surprised, because of course I do ASMR as part of my therapy, but I've let my channel lie fallow for months. I didn't think anybody still followed it.

I started making ASMR recordings in my second year at uni when my parents were splitting. It's not supposed to affect you so much when you're technically an adult, but I didn't deal with the break-up well. Everything seemed to be melting down. To comfort me, Grandad gave me my first wearable – it was a necklace – and although he said it was supposed to be for researching papers, I used it the same as everyone else: to go on BigSky. I got good at surfing free introductory offers to play games and hang out, and sometimes I paid for a little Reality Therapy just to shock myself and put my problems into perspective. Then the gangland guy I was following in Reality Therapy got stabbed in the bathroom of Penn Station in New York, because the BigSky neural interface made it feel like you were really there. It was a little too much reality for me, quite honestly.

I ended up focusing on ASMR because it's peaceful and friendly. Such an improvement on reality.

I made my own recordings for self-therapy, but then people started following me and I got interested in helping others. I didn't talk to the camera, or offer Spacetime sharing. Unlike most of the big ASMRtists, I'm not beautiful, and I wouldn't feel comfortable putting my face out there. I worked strictly in audio, creating sound spaces full of triggers. I prided myself on being able to get tingles out of people who otherwise don't experience them, and even though it wasn't about the money, I made a nice little side income from website donations my last year of uni.

The narcolepsy put an end to all that.

Now the only time I can do ASMR with people is live and in person. I use it to help them fall asleep for our dreamwork sessions. Of course, I fall asleep, too. Then I slip into their dream and do my thing. That's my gift, the blessing that comes with my drug-trial narcolepsy curse. I don't know anybody else who can hack dreams, and when I tried to tell BigSky about it, they didn't believe me and wanted me to sign a bunch of stuff and submit to vague 'tests'. Then O told me not to trust BigSky because they are backed with criminal money these days – and I guess she would know, because that's why she stopped supporting them even though she was one of their original crowdfunders. When I started my dream therapy business, O insisted I go out on my own, and here I am.

I can tell that Melodie is beyond exhausted. She's been weirdly overanimated, and at the same time in between sentences she gets that vacant look. Sleep is calling her. She and I go into her bedroom, leaving Antonio in the main room. While she's in the bathroom, I message O to let her know I'm staying here tonight. There's a small sofa in the bedroom, and in the closet I find a pillow and blanket for myself. Mel comes out dressed for bed and props herself up on about four hundred hotel pillows. She pulls a silken sleeping mask down over her eyes. I sit with one hip on the foot of her bed and hoist my trusty bag onto the bedspread, where it looks cheap and nasty. But it sounds delicious.

'This is going to be really easy,' I tell her in a soft voice as I start rummaging very deliberately in my bag. 'All you have to do is move the first finger on your left hand when you hear a trigger you like, and move the first finger on your right hand when you hear one you don't like. If you get any misophonia, just kick me.'

She smiles, with dimples. 'I'm not going to kick you.'

I tell her that I'll be talking to her, that she'll be able to hear my voice the whole time, and once she's dreaming, she'll be able to see and hear me in the dream environment. But first we're going to find out what kinds of sounds she finds relaxing.

Then I get out my props, carefully and with my full attention on the sounds they make. One reason I keep using my ancient bag is that it makes lovely noises when you rummage in it. It has various snaps and chains that jingle softly, and there are rumbles and scratchy sounds when I pull things out of it. Mel is a musician, so naturally she's sensitive to sound. But the thing about ASMR is that what may trigger one person's tingles can be irritating to another person. I plan to run through many different triggers: the sound of pouring water. The sound of tissue paper crinkling. The sound of my nails tapping on different objects. My voice whispering. The tinkling of little beads on my bracelet. I have dozens of them that I can cycle through until I find something the client likes. I don't personally get actual tingles when I'm performing ASMR, but because I have to be so calm and calming for the listener, I can't help but get trancey. Paradoxically, I'm in more danger of a narcolepsy attack when I'm stressed than when I'm relaxed. That's how I'm able to avoid falling asleep before my clients.

On this occasion, I don't have to do much at all. Mel must be completely exhausted, because I scratch my nails on some cardboard and crinkle a few dried rosebuds in a little bowl and she goes down like timber falling.

**Secret Diary of a Prawn Star**
**Entry #49**
**Codename:** Chaplin
**Date:** 15 September 2027
**Client:** Melodie Tan
**Payment in advance:** Yes
**Session Goal:** Get rid of creepy malevolent dream character
**Location:** Hilton Excelsior, Room 2329
**Narcolepsy status:** Giant afternoon nap. Feel good now
**Nutrition/stimulants:** Donuts and celery
**Start time:** 11.35 p.m.
**End time:** 12.01 a.m.


In all dreams, there's a feeling of disjunction at first. I find myself in someone's dreamspace. If it's their house, then in the beginning it looks like my house. Usually but not always my childhood house. And then, dimly, with a slipping sensation, the shapes of rooms and furniture and smells will start to morph until I can see what the client sees. Same thing with the people. They start out being people I know, but over time as I synchronise with the client, the dream people transform so that I'm seeing the world through the eyes of my client.

I start out in the auditorium of my school in Wapping. It's dim and empty and I'm sweeping up behind the seats. On the stage I can see Mel's harp. It sits in a single spotlight, all golden; it's practically radiant. She walks across the boards and I can hear the hollow sound of her footsteps. She's wearing soft slippers and Hello Kitty pyjamas. I'm down in the fourth row, bent over behind the seats, sweeping up with a little dustpan and brush

48

like a movie usher. But there's no popcorn here. I'm sweeping up something else. Can't quite see what it is.

She sits down on the stool and puts her hands on the strings. She takes a shaky breath, and even from here I see her throat move as she swallows nervously. She starts to play.

I know this is a dream – her dream – but it seems to me that the sound of the music is more beautiful and more real than any music I've ever actually heard. It sends ASMR tingles across my scalp, then down my spine and into my extremities. I'm supposed to be doing the ASMR on Mel, but it's the other way around. I'm melting into calm.

Bugger. I can't melt. I'm working. Mentally pinching myself, I crouch behind the seats, literally keeping my head down while we wait for the Creeper to show itself. As I sweep up debris under seats, I notice that the auditorium is changing to a proper theatre, with gilded seventeenth-century boxes and red velvet. There's a lot of mess on the floor for such a fancy hall, and I wonder what the nature of the trash beneath the seats says about Melodie's dream.

The sound of the harp rises into the upper levels of the theatre and hangs under the ceiling like smoke. The air is warm with it. I glance down at my dustpan. The contents are not popcorn or chewing-gum wrappers or crumpled programmes. In the dustpan are tiny bones, hair, a desiccated eyeball or two and a decaying human finger.

Fighting nausea, I hold the pan at arm's length and look around the theatre again. Now I can see the Creeper. It's standing in the doorway of the left-hand aisle, silhouetted against a reddish light from the foyer.

She sees it, too. Her playing falters.

It starts to walk towards the stage. It's just as Mel described it: a man wearing a simple black suit. The proportions of the body change slightly as it moves, so it's hard to work out its physical size. The mask has no eyes but is covered in chemical symbols with a complicated bonding pattern. I can't see the face except for the mouth.

'You're not welcome here,' I tell the Creeper. 'This is Melodie's dream. I need to ask you to leave.'

But it doesn't address me or even acknowledge that I'm here. It keeps going towards her. I'm not really surprised. I get ignored a lot. I'm small and not well dressed and obviously I can be a bit timid. But this is dreamland. I can be whatever I want to be. Besides, Melodie is clearly terrified of this wanker, and we can't have that. I need to go bolder.

I change myself into the Incredible Hulk. With a big hammer. I'll be lucky if I come off like that diminutive chef who threatens people with her spoon on those new Bisto ads. I'm sure I could have done better if I'd had more time to think up a plan, but in the heat of the moment it's easy to go for the default that you have in your head.

With my giant hammer in one hand and my little dustpan full of bones and whatnot in the other, I stomp down the aisle to intercept the Creeper before it gets to the stage. But the same dream logic that lets me turn into the Incredible Hulk lets the Creeper teleport instantly to stand right over poor Melodie. She gives a jolt of fear. Her super-shiny hair swings back as she leans away from the Creeper, her face drawn, eyes showing a lot of white.

This is my moment. It's going to be excellent. I'll get to have new cards printed: 'Dream Bouncer'. I will *so* enjoy throwing the Creeper out of this dream.

'Hey, oi!' I yell and stomp onstage, breaking a few boards. I swing my hammer menacingly, and it just misses taking out the harp.

The Creeper turns to me. 'Stay out of this,' it says. 'This line of work isn't for you.'

It has an American accent. That's interesting, since Mel is from Canada.

'I won't stay out of it,' I say in my deep Hulk voice. 'Melodie asked me to protect her, and that's what I'm going to do.'

The thing grabs my arm and suddenly I'm normal-me again, wearing an old tracksuit that smells a little murky. I have braces on my teeth, just as if I'm thirteen again.

What is happening?

'You can't do that,' I snap. 'I'm the Dream Bouncer! You're just an ugly shoe! So take *that*!'

And I transform the Creeper into an ugly shoe: specifically, a size-six loafer with tassels, used. I turn to catch Melodie's reaction, already thinking how gracious I'll be when I decline the bonus she's going to offer me – and the man-form of the Creeper is standing over her again.

'Charlie, help!' Mel squeaks.

'You're an amateur,' the Creeper tells me. 'Is that really the best you can do?'

Melodie has slid off the stool and is edging towards the side curtain at the back of the stage. I'm aware of her, but I don't let myself look her way because I'm busy getting up in the Creeper's face. I kick it in the shins, and it laughs.

I throw the contents of the dustpan at it. Dust and finger bones come flying out, and scraps of dried skin hang in the air like tiny parachutes. A shrivelled-up eyeball bounces off the mask. Now the Creeper's mad. I can tell. The mask quivers with rage.

Melodie slips through the curtain.

'You're an idiot,' says the Creeper and disappears.

My heart is racing. I look around the empty theatre. Where did it go? How did it do that? If the Creeper is just a psychological complex, it sure is a slick one. It's not acting like it's out to get Mel half as much as it's out to upstage *me*.

I run backstage, calling Mel. It's a maze of passageways, and the farther I go the more I see body parts lying around on the floor. At first I think they're stage props, but there is a smell, too. It's nothing like Mrs Haugh-Wombaur's farts. It's primitive, blood and faeces and fear.

I find the orchestra's dressing room. There's another door inside, left ajar. Cold, fresh air comes in from outside. I open it expecting a fire exit, but when I step out I find myself on a scaffold. I reel to a stop, grabbing a support pole.

Somehow we've got somewhere very high up. Higher than any theatre, higher than the hotel where Mel dreams. Higher than anything in London; but I shouldn't be surprised, because we're not in London any more. This is the Dream City for sure. I'm nervous to find myself here while responsible for a client. I guess there's a first time for everything.

I need to be careful now. The Dream City's a tricksy place. Must orientate myself. I look around, straining my senses for some hint of where Mel has got to. The scaffold looks down on a neon-lit flyover with cars spooling silently across it, and below that a network of canals and lesser buildings sprawls. The skyline is aggressively broken by the silhouettes of cranes, like praying mantises.

'Mel?'

Where has she got to? What is this place? If it's really some kind of collective entity, then who built it? And where is it really located?

What's hardest of all to describe about the Dream City is the way it takes hold of your imagination. I know I should be looking for Mel but I'm distracted by the architecture. I see gardens set on the sides of buildings. I see hang-gliders drifting in slow spirals from the highest towers towards the water below. I see tiny windows all lit up. There must be millions of people here.

'All of this is mine,' the Creeper says in my ear. 'If you come here, you're at my mercy. Remember that.'

I snap out of my reverie and try to turn around because I want to know if the Creeper is greyscale or colour out here in the Dream City. If it's greyscale, then I'm dealing with another dreamer using the Sweet Dreams platform – which I'm now starting to suspect may be the case. If it's colour, then it's just some part of Mel's consciousness. (Unless the Creeper is bloody lucid like me, which I don't want to think about because bad implications.)

I need to know more about this entity; I need to make myself look. But while its voice is in my ear, I can't seem to move. I'm still standing in the doorway, and now from the dressing room behind me I hear water running. Then a muffled soprano cry. With a great effort I manage to turn around, step back inside the dressing room and slam the door on the Creeper and the Dream City. Where is that sound coming from? It's a rushing, echoing sound of water.

'Mel?'

My hand is still on the door handle. When I was outside, it sounded like the water was in the dressing room. But now I'm inside, it sounds like the water is outside – but how can it be? There was nothing but scaffolding out there.

I put my ear to the door. No doubt about it: rushing water. I stand back and look again. Now there's a universal trousers/skirt symbol for a unisex toilet printed on it.

I pound on the door. 'Melodie! Melodie, I'm coming in!'

Yet I hesitate. What will be in there? What is the person in Mel's dream capable of doing?

I know one thing. Whatever it is, I'm stopping it.

I turn the handle and go in. It's not a tiny bathroom like you'd expect in a theatre. It's a huge marble affair, like the one in her hotel suite. She's on her knees by the side of the bath. The Creeper is standing over her, holding her head under the water. She's struggling. It looks over its shoulder at me, and suddenly the Creeper isn't a masked man in a black suit. It's Mel herself. There are two of them: the one in the water, and the one holding her in the water. The Creeper Mel is covered in blood and her eyes are staring. Still forcing the real Mel's head down with one hand, Creeper Mel stretches the other out towards me.

'Is this what you want to happen?' the Creeper says. But now it speaks with Mel's voice. 'Don't interfere,' it says as blood pours down Creeper Mel's face. 'You'll get me killed.'

Then the Creeper does something it shouldn't be able to do. It boots me out of the dream. I wake up.

# The pigeon sisters

The hotel room is freezing. Someone has turned the air con all the way up. Still bleary, I stand and call Mel's name. I go to the bed, reaching out to shake her. She isn't there. The bedclothes are all twisted, half on the floor.

'Mel! Are you OK?'

Bathroom door. Closed. Water running.

Now I'm frantic. I pound on the door. I call her name. Nothing.

Antonio comes staggering in from the next room, eyes half-closed in that adorable way, hair all mussy. The things I notice at a time like this. I actually do disgust myself.

'The door is locked,' I yell at him. 'Do something!'

He pounds on it.

'She's probably just taking a shower,' he says. 'She does that when she gets anxious or has nightmares. What do you want me to do, break it down?'

'Yes!'

'This is a hotel. I can't just—'

'Break it down, Antonio, or I'll call 999.'

'I knew I was a fool to ask you for help,' he mutters.

'What's the matter? Not strong enough to break it down?'

He waggles a finger at me. 'Oh, no. You can't trick me with your gender stereotypes, Charlie. Why don't *you* break it down?'

'Antonio, please. I'm scared. Just break it down. You know I'm weak.'

He looks at the door like it's a bull and he's a matador. Then he shakes his head. He can't seem to convince even himself that he can do it.

'How do you want me to break it down? Should I use my shoulder?'

'I don't know! You go to the gym five times a week. How hard can it be?'

It takes him several tries. We are both shouting her name and pounding on the door in between charges. I keep hoping she'll open the door and Antonio will go whizzing through and this whole scene will turn into something out of a Pink Panther movie.

At last the door flies off its hinges. It shoots inwards and collides with the commode. The bathroom looks exactly the same as the one in Mel's dream. She's on her knees by the bath, which is full. And her face is in the water.

'Melodie, what are you doing?' Antonio grabs her by the shoulders, pulls her out of the water and steadies her head with one hand. Her neck is floppy. Her eyes are shut. Is she still asleep?

I slap her across the face and call her name. She chokes, coughs, retches. Pushes us both away. Vomits water on the floor.

'I'm phoning for an ambulance,' I say, rolling my eyes up to go for 999 on my earring, but Antonio waves his hand in front of my face, snapping his fingers to distract me.

'No,' he says.

'No? Are you crazy?'

'You don't understand, Charlie. The media follow her around. This can't get out. Look, she's OK. She's breathing. She's waking up. It will be OK.'

Melodie is breathing in big, noisy gulps of air, punctuated by harsh coughs. He turns off the tap, pushes the sodden black locks off her face, gives her a towel. She doesn't look frightened so much as shocked. Like she doesn't know where she is.

Suddenly I feel knackered. I back away slowly.

'You saw him,' she gasps. 'Charlie, you saw him, didn't you? You stood up to him. Thank you.'

I'm shaking my head. 'I didn't ... I tried, but just when you needed me most, I woke up.'

'It's a good thing Charlie woke up,' Antonio tells her, dabbing at Mel's shoulders with the edge of the towel. 'You must have been sleepwalking again.'

'I'm sorry.' Her chin is wobbling.

'There's nothing for you to feel sorry about!' he says, and kisses her. I study the complimentary bath products. Free shower cap. Aromatherapy stuff to spray on your pillow to help you sleep. Ha! As if. I shouldn't mock people with insomnia; it's just that when you have the opposite problem you feel jealous. I yawn.

'We will talk tomorrow, Charlie,' Antonio says.

I want to ask Mel about the Dream City, about how the Creeper tricked her into the bathroom – what the whole experience looked like from her perspective. But she has a deer-in-headlights stare. Maybe Antonio is right.

'How are you going to get through the rest of the night, Mel?'

Before she can answer, he says, 'I will sleep in front of the bathroom door just in case.'

'Oh, I'm not going back to sleep,' she says. 'Not after that. I'm going to practice.'

I leave them arguing about it. Then I fall asleep on the Tube and wake up all the way out at Heathrow Terminal 5. Feeling like lost luggage.

It's dawn again as I stagger home. O's previous housemate Jez has picked her up at the Whittington and escorted her back to the flat. Jez is still in the flat, unfortunately, hunching over a tablet with O on the sofa. Jez is wearing a multicoloured hat she knitted herself, a charity-shop pencil skirt and a giant sweatshirt that says Harvard on it. I'm told she went to U of Bedfordshire but flunked out her first year.

'How do you like this one?' Jez asks O, clicking through to a photo. 'It's the Andy Warhol line.'

The photo shows Jez posing in a pair of wellies decorated with a portrait of Chairman Mao. I go through to the kitchen to make us all a cup of tea. Edgar the cat is hiding behind the kettle.

'Jez, you do know you have to pay for the rights to use this art?' O is saying.

'Yes, but I'm thinking to go in with the V and A. I'm an ideas person. They can put up the investment. They sell postcards and T-shirts with great art on them. Why not wellies?'

'Darling, I just can't see the V and A selling wellies in their gift shop—'

Jez lets out a peal of laughter. Edgar runs behind the toaster. 'It's online, ducks, online. eBay? V-market? Squirt? It'll be massive in Japan and all.'

'Did you just say "ducks"?' I can't help myself. Maybe Ducks is a new app I should know about.

'Oh, hello, Charlotte,' Jez says. 'Didn't see you there. How's your business going? O said you had to run out for an important meeting.'

I bring in the tea, trying not to make a face. 'I wouldn't really call it a business.'

'Well, it keeps you in toffee, evidently.'

Toffee? Ducks? I try to catch O's eye but she's avoiding me. She knows what I'm thinking: Jez is a lunatic. O must have been desperate to have rung her, which makes me feel all the more guilty that I didn't stay.

'Well, I've got this thing going with the great masters of modern art printed on wellies. For the gardening set. And as novelty gifts. So I'm just putting it out there, this is my baby. Nobody better steal my idea. O said you were working with a patent lawyer, Charlotte. Make sure you don't plant it in his subconscious while he's dreaming.'

'No worries,' I say, sniffing the milk doubtfully. 'The patent lawyer is no longer a client.'

Jez purses her lips, which gives her fishface. 'Sorry, darling. Have a toffee.'

While they are drinking tea, I escape to the shower and then my room, where I run a search. I play with a lot of terms – *Dream City BigSky collective unconscious greyscale people Sweet*

*Dreams committing suicide dreams more than one version of self dream canals dreams scaffolding* – just free-associate and let it run. I make a mental note to ask Shandy if she knows anything. She's only a junior virtual-furniture designer, but BigSky is one of those post-geek companies that's low on hierarchy and big on collaboration. If the Dream City has something to do with the planned addition to BigSky's Sweet Dreams platform, Shandy might have got wind of it.

My searches yield nothing useful, but they distract me from Jez's inane chatter and pretty soon I'm asleep. When I finally drag myself out of bed, the afternoon is spent and Jez is gone. O is sat at her display with Edgar on her knees and a cup of tea in her good hand.

'O, I'm not as flaky as Jez, am I?'

O whuffles a laugh into her cup. 'Sure you can handle the truth?'

'But seriously. When she lived here. Were you two... were you tight?'

'Did we have an affair, do you mean?'

'Pffft, *what*? Oh wow – did you?'

'Even coming from you, that is absurd. Please get a grip.'

'I just meant, were you mates, did you hang out like we hang out, you and Jez and Edgar?'

Hearing his name, Edgar flexes his claws against O's knees and blinks his green eyes in feline acknowledgement of my existence.

'I do believe you're jealous.'

'I'm not! Honestly, I know it sounds like that but I'm not. Anyway, it was before my time so why should I be jealous?' I'm digging myself in deeper and deeper. 'I guess my question is, do you think Jez is all there?'

'Mentally? She's not the sharpest pin in the pincushion. Is that what you mean?'

'Only I wondered... you know, if she's the sort of person you tend to have in as a flatmate, then on some level would it imply that I'm ... how can I put this ...?'

'That you're not very bright? Or that I think you're not very bright, and you feel insulted?'

'Something like that. Sorry.'

'No,' says O, still staring at her data.

'No?'

'I used different selection criteria for you.'

'Oh.'

I wait for her to elaborate, but she says nothing for such a long time that I almost fall asleep. I don't dare ask another question because O doesn't take well to being 'hounded', as she calls it.

'I selected you because you're naive. Also a Pollyanna.'

Ooh, that stings. I mean, just because I don't enjoy enabling men to sexually dismember their business colleagues in dream-space, that doesn't mean I'm a Pollyanna. Does it?

'Take for example this nonsense about Antonio and the con-traception. How on earth could you fall for that?'

'I don't know. I'm very ashamed. In my defence, he is really, really hot and I was in a vulnerable place.'

'You're always in a vulnerable place, darling. Look at how you walk around with those big cow eyes, with that soul-searching way about you. You might as well be carrying a sign that says "Take advantage, I want to be messed with".'

'Have you been talking to Shandy?'

'And you can't go the rest of your life using Shandy as a stick to beat back people who want to hurt you. So that's my honest answer, Charlie. I picked you because I thought I could help you. It's a tough world and you need tough dreams. Now. I would be eternally grateful if you made me a nice cheesy pasta. I need comfort food.'

I feel terrible. 'But enough about you, O, moaning away over your trip to A and E and demanding painkillers. Let's talk about me and my existential angst.'

She chuckles. I put water on to boil, get out a lump of cheese, scrape off the dodgy bits and start grating it. 'Go on, then. Tell.'

'Only a bad sprain. They gave me Percocet but I don't want to take it. Bungs me up.'

'I think you should take it and forget the cheesy pasta, or you really will be bunged up. I'll make you a salad or something.'

'Are you my mother?'

'Did she track your bowel movements?'

O coughs and I hear her shifting herself into the armchair. 'So I take it you got the client.'

'She is very interesting. Do you know anything about sleep-walking?'

'She sleepwalks, too? Is that the problem, or...?'

'No, the problem is a complex in her dream. It manifests as this horrible murderous dude. I just feel... I want to make sure I'm not missing something with the sleepwalking. I don't know that much about it.'

'I used to do it when I was small,' O says. 'My parents had to put an extra latch on the door up high because one night when I was about four they found me out in the front garden.'

'Do you remember what it was like?'

'Only the one time. In my dream, I was lining up my brother's toy trains in numerical order in their sheds, and then I started to wake up and I realised I was in Mum's spice rack instead, moving around the bottles. She found me and guided me back to bed. Apparently I'd colour-coded everything.'

I smile.

We eat in companionable silence, each of us checking our messages at the table. It's what I love about O. As old as she is, she's always au fait with the latest tech even if she hates BigSky with the passion of an ex-lover (or, in her case, ex-funder). My mum would be appalled at our lack of manners, but if you ask me, a real friend never minds if you're in the Cloud when you're having a meal with them. We can't see or hear one another's AR so a fly on the wall would see two people living in private

61

bubbles, laughing, gesturing, talking or even weeping completely out of sync with one another. I could never do that with my parents, but O is different.

If neither of us has much going on, we sometimes have a funny video duel across the table by candlelight. I've been known to message O while I'm on the couch and she's in her bedroom. It feels more polite than knocking on the door. I mean, what if she's having a wank or something? It just makes sense.

Over salad, she sends me a link about sleepwalking.

'Was pootling around the Imperial alumni website and found a mention that might help your client if it turns out your therapy doesn't do the trick.'

'Oh? Lost faith in me so soon?'

'An old contact of mine from Imperial works for a start-up nanotech company. They can activate and deactivate switches that control your brainwaves and neural gates when you're sleeping. They're studying an AR-modulated drug that can disable your muscles when you're asleep. The brain is supposed to do this on its own, to stop you acting out your dreams, but it fails for some people.'

'Sleepwalking is fairly rare, isn't it?'

'I believe it's on the rise. The therapy detects REM brainwaves and activates a chemical that stops you sleepwalking, apparently. They may have gone a bit beyond that, actually. I haven't read the papers, only the abstracts.'

Reading abstracts sounds strenuous. I guess this is why I have a 2:2 from Excelsior-Barking. I struggle to apply myself.

'Very nice, but like I told you, Mel's problem isn't sleepwalking. It's the other thing, the creepy guy.'

I take a look anyway. I'm curious. O sometimes mentions Imperial, but she's never been clear about what she did there: whether she taught, or studied, or worked. By her own admission she hasn't got a degree and she doesn't come up on their website. I've already snooped. So I'm kind of assuming she's hacked into the alumni website, which is normal for someone like O. It must be hard for her not to hack into everyone's everything, like Superman resisting using his X-ray vision.

'My contact's name is Meera Bhango. She's very gifted and much in demand, and she has the backing of a silent partner.'

'What does that mean?'

'Someone with deep pockets is behind this. Anything Bhango is involved in has got to be worth a look. If you click through you'll get the company website, but they haven't put any of what I'm telling you up publicly yet. They're only looking for participants for their study.'

The logo is a purple Celtic spiral and the company name is Little Bird. I go to their website in case it jogs my memory, but there isn't a lot to see. Under 'About Us' there are photographs of a woman – Meera, I presume – and a guy. He's very tall, dark-haired, hirsute and serious-looking.

'I know that guy,' I mutter. 'Where do I know him from? He's so familiar. Not a client. Not from school. Not from work. How do I know him?'

O leans in to look over my shoulder. 'Bernard Zborowski. Never heard of him.'

'I wonder if I know him through Shandy . . . Oh, it's so close, like I can almost get it but—'

'Stop trying to remember. Think about something else and it will come to you.'

I gather up the plates and glasses and carry everything into the kitchen, accompanied by Edgar, presumably still rattled after Jez's visit. I offer him a piece of cheese but he only sniffs it.

'Do you want generic-brand-addictive-cat-treats?' I say in my baby-cat voice. Edgar's pupils dilate when he hears his favourite word. I get the generic-brand-addictive-cat-treats out of the tippy-top cupboard and shake two into my palm. Then it comes to me. Where I've seen Bernard Z before.

What a bloody coincidence. I almost can't believe it. Excited, I raise my voice.

'He was from the study. The drug I took for BigSky, for the trial. Damn. He came in once during a consultation with a string of medical students following him like baby ducks. If it hadn't been for that trial, I'd still have my nasty little job like a normal person and not be cluttering up your life with my problems.'

There's a long silence except for the sound of Edgar's power-boat-volume purring as he chews his treats. Then O's voice comes in via my earring, even though she's only in the next room. She can't stand shouting, says it's uncouth.

'It seems that the trial you were involved in was no great success. Zborowski has left BigSky, and no papers have been published, not even in preprint,' she says. 'I have an alert on my system. The project appears to have been binned.'

'But he's moving up in the world if this Meera Bhango is as hotshit as you say she is.'

'Leaving BigSky to go to a start-up is risky. He'll only move up in the world if Little Bird can produce something of real value. It's possible he's jumped ship because his work was stonewalled at Excelsior-Barking, but BigSky are unlikely to let go of the intellectual property so easily.'

I bring the teapot out into the sitting room, which is now bathed in amber sunlight from the west.

'Do you really think this Meera could help me? She's probably super busy.'

O sighs. 'I don't know, darling. She certainly can't help you if you don't approach her.'

We sip our tea, O using her good hand. She's thinking hard. I know because she frowns more than usual when she's concentrating. The frown isn't as deep as her debugging-code frown but it's deeper than her reading-novels-in-their-original-Russian scowl.

Finally, she says, 'Well, this is crazy, but.'

I put my hands over my face. Whenever O says, 'This is crazy, but—' it means either she wants to do something slightly illegal (usually involving motorbike stunts), or she's going to send me to the British Library to do research on a crazy theory. Like her hypothesis that the Incas invented quantum chromodynamics diagrams before Richard Feynman. Or that bear meat cures lung cancer. Don't get me wrong – O's brilliant at IT, but she's got a flamboyant streak and an ego roughly the size of Greenland (as it appears on a map). Whenever she says, *This is crazy, but*, or, *I'm sure I'm wrong about this*, I just know it's kicking off.

I watch her cup shake in her hand. I wish she didn't have to be so old, and I wish she weren't ill. I feel a mad affection for her, even if I'm not certain it's mutual.

'I'm sure I'm wrong about this.'

You see? She's said them both. Here we go.

'It's just that, looking at their work, knowing that they are surely able to induce certain kinds of brainwaves, then they might be able to tamper with dreams.'

'Using nanotech? That's a thing? How?'

'I don't know.' She won't look at me.

'Come on, O. Loads of drugs affect your dreams. My uncle took something for dementia and it gave him horrible night-mares. Or how about Daphne, for that matter.'

O's sister has dementia, but O doesn't like talking about it so she ignores my remark.

'If the treatment works with AR, then control could be a pos-sibility,' O tells me. 'Using live imaging alongside a BigSky data-base of millions of brainwave samples correlated with subjective experience. One could add nano-delivered agents implanted in the body with the ability to operate on brain tissue to rebuild, or to build anew. Have you seen the work on remyelination done by nano-engines?'

'No, I haven't, because I'm being manipulated by BigSky and their sinister mind-control programme. *Must. Buy. Apps.*'

I stick my arms out in front of me like a mummy in a *Carry On* film and shamble around the flat. She isn't laughing. Not even a little smile. Wow, she hates BigSky. So I give up joking with a sigh, and (a little sarcastically) I recite the words I know she wants me to say:

'That sounds sinister, O. Is there any science for that?'

'I just said. Remyelination. Look it up. But you must understand this much, darling: some of these nanotech guys aren't scientists in the highbrow Ivory Tower sense of the word. They're engineers, some of them self-taught. You know, the days of Big Science mean that the Victorian scientist who pottered in his shed may be long extinct, but a new subclass has sprung up in the last ten years.'

I don't believe she's slept since the night before last. I can tell she's overtired because she's waxing philosophical.

'The New Potting Shed Avengers?' I quip, because I really don't want to go back to looking for bear meat on the black market and we're headed that way now.

'If you're clever and have a little money, you can get up to quite a lot these days – that's why I'm always saying you have to be so careful about drugs. A start-up like this isn't much more sophisticated than a garage drug factory. The drugs are 4D, of course, but—'

'4D? What even is 4D?'

'I don't really mean 4D, I mean that the drugs aren't drugs – as I said, the delivery system isn't a chemical. It's more like an infection in that it alters itself and its host, it evolves over time. The drug has a different effect after a month than after a day. You've seen that yourself. Your dream abilities are evolving.'

'I suppose they are . . . I thought that was down to my effort, though.'

'Chickens, darling. And eggs. The brain is a feedback system. Now. Try to follow my thinking. Meera is an engineer. They build things. If she and her team are messing around with certain kinds of devices, they may well discover something first and then figure out how it works later on. That's what this sleepwalking study is about. They've found something that works and they want to see if they can legitimize it scientifically.'

'OK . . . but it's my client who's sleepwalking, not me.'

'You're landscaping other people's dreams.'

I smile. '*Inception* is my middle name.'

'So, what if they're working with something that impacts dreams and Bernard Zborowski has exposed you to it?'

'Then I'm calling Scully for a check-up!' I think I should get bonus points for working so hard to keep this convo lite. It's never easy with O once she's got her teeth into an idea. 'But seriously, that would mean other people in the study might be suffering like I am. If you were looking for something to do, O, you could try tracking down those people and finding out if any of them have narcolepsy. Or if they can hack dreams.'

'What makes you think I can do that?' Her tone is so blithe that I stare at her for several seconds. I don't know how to take her at all.

'Nothing, O. Nothing makes me think you can do that.'

She wheels herself around to the plate-glass window and looks out over the rooftop. She has a big nose and a receding chin with a little white goat beard starting up, and the skin of her neck hangs like a wattle. She reminds me of a bird. She has given up too much information too quickly for my comfort. I wonder what else is going on in her head. She's still chewing on something but she'll never tell me what.

'Go to bed,' I say aloud. 'You've had enough.'

'I hate being in bed,' O says. 'I won't be able to sleep. I'll just lie there with my brain spinning.'

She gets like this sometimes. O is not cut out to be old, much less sick. She has this restlessness about her, a fierce focus. People are supposed to mellow with age, but if O can dial it back, I've never seen her do it.

Then she says, 'You know what really gets to me? Those post-surgery bras my great-niece sent me. They don't fit right across the back, not one of them.'

'So return them.'

'Can't. Edgar sat on them. They're furry.'

'I'll ask Shandy to alter them if you want. She's brilliant. Give me the one you've got on that does fit and she'll match it.'

'What, now?'

'Yeah, just shimmy on out of it. I won't look.'

When she hands it to me, still warm, I shove it into my bag before collecting the others from her room. My problems are tiny compared to hers.

'Ah, I feel so free. Let's go outside,' she says. Having removed her bra, she is now left holding the little flask of schnapps she usually keeps hidden there (and which could explain most of her discomfort with the fit, but I can't say anything because she thinks I don't know about it).

It's windy out on the roof, which is probably what we both need. O puts the brake on her chair to stop herself being blown across the flat rooftop, and I check to make sure all the pigeons are roosting and that their water bottles are full. The pigeons have a lovely, calming effect. Once I made an ASMR pigeon video up here; I wonder how many hits it's had since I last checked. I miss doing ASMR. Wish I could get back to it. I felt better about my life when I was making things for people. Even if your own life is a mess, it's lovely to be able to help others.

There's a bird from O's sister Daphne today. I turn to smile at O, but her expression flickers into a sort of wary tension. Then I remember that she did sprain her wrist in a pigeon-related incident, and she's probably still in pain. So I grab ahold of Daphne's pigeon myself and divest it of the message attached to its leg. This is a routine thing. The message will be addressed to 'Agent O' and O will write back to 'Agent D'.

'We're the Pigeon Sisters,' O explained when I first moved in, and she chuckled so much that I looked up the reference and traced it to an old American TV show. Honestly, both O and Daphne are the most unlikely Pigeon Sisters you could ever imagine – maybe that's why she thinks it's so funny. Daphne lives in a high-tech care home in Dorking where they let the residents keep pets. Apparently O arranged for the birds to be installed in a dovecote where Daphne can visit them, and they fly back and forth regularly with messages.

I give O the message and then cross the roof to let her read it privately, and that's when I spot the new bird walking around near the chimney pipe, pecking at the roof tiles. It's speckled white and brown, but there's something funny about its back. There's a big brown splodge between its wings. A lump. I squat down and squint at it, yawning. There's something strapped to it, like a tiny little backpack. It looks like brown felt.

I'm so excited! I want to tell O. But she's staring down at the message, frowning deeply. I see her take a little swig of schnapps from the flask. I wish she wouldn't drink. If I am honest, schnapps in particular makes her a bit crazy, but I try not to be judgy.

I put out some corn for the new bird that it pecks right up, unafraid of me. I am a little afraid of it. I know O's birds pretty well, but this one is larger. Different species? I want to catch it so I can take off the backpack, but it feels really rude to just, you know, grab without asking.

'I think you've got the wrong address, mate,' I say.

'Who are you talking to?'

O comes gliding over, her pupils slightly dilated with gathering darkness, plus schnapps.

'Carrier pigeon! Look, he has a tiddly backpack and every-thing!'

'Tiddly what—?' She comes closer. 'Oh my. Sidney.'

Sidney?

'See if you can catch him and hold him for me. We'll take off his harness.'

'Wait . . . you know this bird?'

'Of course I know him. He's my bird. I haven't seen him since . . . Just catch him, Charlie!'

It takes me a fair few tries, but in the end I get hold of Sidney without hurting him and hold him steady while O undoes his backpack straps with trembling hands.

'You're a good bird,' she tells him. 'Charlie, put him in the small coop with plenty of grain. He must be exhausted.'

O has more than one coop. The main one has seventeen

adult birds and mostly they are free to come and go as they please. The second cage is larger and has a wire ceiling and several perches, and the four birds in there are her specials that she mostly keeps in. She says they used to race. There's also a separate cage that we use if we have to isolate a sick or injured bird. I open this last one and pop Sidney inside with a few handfuls of corn for good measure. Then I feed the other birds. Sidney struts around the cage, exploring.

I turn to O. 'Where's he been, then? Has someone sent him to you?'

'He obviously hasn't teleported.' O clamps her mouth tight shut around the word and her hand tight around the little backpack. Then she wheels back inside and disappears into her room.

'Well, this is mysterious, Sidney.' I finish closing up for the night, shut the cage and go into the flat to find O in her room, staring out across London from her bedroom window.

'So what was the message? Who was it from? Was it from a lover?'

O snorts but doesn't say anything.

'Seriously, I'm dying to know. Are you going to send one back? This is so much fun, why are you being grumpy?'

She takes off her specs and rubs her eyes with an air of strained patience. Instead of answering any of my questions, she says, 'I've asked Muz to bring the hog around from the lock-up in the morning.'

The 'hog' is O's high-performance custom motorbike for wheelchair users. She drives it when she wants to visit her sister in Dorking. I usually ride as a passenger, which is ... interesting.

'Tomorrow isn't your usual day. Is Daphne ill?'

'I can go by myself, darling. You get on with your clients.'

The fortnightly trip to Dorking is actually part of our Roommate Agreement. O is fine with the driving and parking and all of that, but she needs the moral support. Pigeon Sisters jokes notwithstanding, Daphne doesn't bring out the best in O, let's just put it that way.

'Of course I'm coming. Suggest you not drink, though, or you'll have a headache in the morning. Maybe some nice ASMR instead?'

O glares at me and takes a defiant swig before nestling the flask right back against her now-braless bosom. I want to ask her what's upset her so, but with O the more you pry, the less you get out of her. So I go to bed.

That's when the fun really starts.

Not.

**Secret Diary of a Prawn Star**
**Entry #50**
**Codename:** Chaplin
**Date:** 17 September 2027
**Client:** Self
**Payment in advance:** N/A
**Session Goal:** None/involuntary
**Location:** My own damn bed
**Narcolepsy status:** Thought was OK but obvs not
**Nutrition/stimulants:** Tea, salad, two coffees and a Mars
  bar
**Start time:** 12.17 a.m.
**End time:** 12.42 a.m.

It's a disembodied voice. You don't get those dreams often.
Dreams where the only thing you hear is a voice giving you
instructions or messages, those are like the holy grail of
dreamwork. They are said to be direct messages from the
deepest layers of your unconscious, the actual shizzle.

The voice belongs to the Creeper. It's right here inside my
head, American accent and all. The voice goes, 'Predators avoid
each other. Consider it professional courtesy.'

I want to laugh because it's so pretentious, but I'm already
getting scared.

I tell it, 'I'm not a predator.'

'Then I must assume you're prey. These things are drearily
binary, I'm afraid.'

I'm starting to see what Mel meant about the Creeper. It
has a way of getting to you – its voice is more than a voice, it's
super-condensed freeze-dried malevolence. My heart is racing,

I'm cold, the tension in my dream body is rising. The voice has this certain quality where, whatever it says, if the Creeper is the one saying it then it must be true. It's pretty fucked-up.

I fight for control. I manage to locate myself. I am in the Dream City. As ever, it is night, and I'm standing at one end of a ramshackle bridge made of planks and rope several storeys high, swaying in the breeze. Below me is a building site, and I can hear the sound of jackhammers and the scream of metal being cut.

I can't see the Creeper. I want to turn around and confront it, but I'm distracted by what I see at the far end of the bridge: a small group of people coming towards me, single-file. Someone is idiotic enough to try to push a pram out across the wooden planks, clinging to the rope with one hand, holding the pram with the other. I put a safety net up and widen the bridge to make it easier for them.

'Safety nets are for the feeble.'

The safety net catches fire.

I pour rain on it. I tell the Creeper, 'Get out of my dream. You're not welcome here.'

'I'm here as a professional courtesy. You've strayed into my orbit by dreaming with Melodie Tan. I suggest you go back to working with insecure schoolteachers and midlife-crisis victims trying to find themselves.'

'Melodie Tan is my client. I've been invited into her dreams. You haven't. So stay out of her head, and stay out of mine.'

'Or what?'

Or what? I don't know. I don't know who he is or where he is or how he's doing this.

'Just fuck off,' I say angrily.

'You want me to fuck off? Or what, Charlie? You'll call the Dream Police?'

I don't know what to say, so I turn myself into the Hulk again. I swing my giant hammer and it makes a curious whistling sound across the high, dark air of the night city – but of course, the

Creeper isn't really there. It's just a voice in my head. And the voice laughs.

'Face it, Charlie. You're completely unprotected. You're a basically decent person but you're afraid of your own shadow. I've got the measure of you now. Don't make me crush you like an insect.'

It occurs to me that I still can't see the Creeper, so I still don't know if I'm dealing with another dreamer or not. But the people on the bridge are in greyscale. They are part of this dream, too.

And now the people are halfway across the bridge. The farthest point from either side. This is always where the bad shit happens. Balrogs or Kylo Ren or whatever.

And here we go. What is it with Dream City people? It's happening again. The people are throwing themselves off the bridge. Two jump and break the roofs of dream-cars far below. When the third person jumps, I manage to whip up a parachute and he drifts down, then lands in front of a speeding truck that must have been conjured up by the Creeper. I make the truck come screaming to a halt just in time. This causes a multi-car pile-up. The Creeper laughs.

'Actions have consequences, even in dreams. You backed the wrong horse. Melodie Tan is a loser.'

What am I going to say to that? No, *you're* a loser, loser. I mean, how old are we, seven? I need to wake up. Wake up, Charlie!

The greyscale baby in the pram is sitting alone in the middle of the bridge. I hear her begin to cry. Don't ask me how I know she's a girl. I just know. I walk out onto the bridge. I'm going to get this baby off the bridge and then I can wake up.

The Creeper says, 'People are so weak. You think you'll achieve anything, trying to prop up all of these weak people who can't even control their own minds? Maybe you should get control of yourself first. Then you wouldn't be falling asleep in public. It makes you extremely vulnerable.'

How can I force this mofo out of my head? I have to change

its voice, make it a helium voice or something. I try to do that. Make his voice really, really high and squeaky.

'You're all such low-hanging fruit,' the Creeper says in a helium voice, but somehow it's even worse and creepier.

'Let's see what happens if we actually rip them open,' it adds casually, and as I look on, the baby splits down the middle, little teddy-bear outfit and all.

The baby is still crying even though by my reckoning she should die immediately. She is still in greyscale, so presumably somewhere in London a baby is dreaming of being murdered.

'You did this,' the helium voice says. 'It's on you. Not on me. On you.'

It is on me, literally. The – I don't even want to say it – what comes out. Of the baby. And the baby is so real, even more real than a real baby, if that's possible. Blood, intestines, part of a dark and shining liver, and the baby stops crying and she looks into my eyes, tears catching the light on her miniature perfect cheeks. She looks about one year old. Her juice cup falls on the floor. Her toy lion is covered with grey blood.

I'm full of rage.

'No you don't.' I say it over and over as I put my hands on her. I push her insides back where they belong like I would handle a spilled handbag, refusing to be dismayed. I am determined to heal it up, make it as right as if the injury never happened.

'It's going to be OK,' I tell her, and I mean it. 'Just a bad dream.'

Undoing something that is already done is hard, but I do it. I overwrite. This is my dream. I am in control. Her parts go back inside. The bleeding stops. The wound seals.

'You're OK,' I say to the baby, in my talking-to-babies-and-puppies voice.

But I hear a ticking sound, like a stopwatch.

And the baby explodes in my face.

# Flowers for Algernon: the club remix

I am glad to be awake, but I'm physically shaking and it takes me fifteen minutes in the shower to calm down. Luckily it is almost morning. I feel I'm under an evil shadow. I tell myself *no actual babies were murdered in the making of this dream* – what kind of disclaimer is that? When I think about some innocent sleeping child being terrorised I feel sick and somehow at fault. Then I remember that some stupid parent must have put their baby to sleep using Sweet Dreams even though it's not licensed for children. Shandy won't be up yet, but I leave her a message asking whether she knows about this sort of thing happening and what can be done. Almost as an afterthought, I tell her about O finding Bernard Zborowski working in a start-up, too.

But the feeling of guilt lingers. I know I'm only diverting my attention away from the possibility that the Creeper is the creation of my own imagination. What if the Creeper is just an archetypal darkness? It started out as Mel's darkness personified, and now maybe it's my darkness personified – as if I've caught the Creeper from Mel like a virus. Ugh. Horrible thought. That would mean that some part of *me* cut that child open, that somewhere in London a baby is crying inconsolably because of *me*. I can't stand it.

A message from Mel is also waiting for me.

*I don't blame you for what happened, I just want you to know that. I'm seeing my psychiatrist today. Antonio insisted, and I guess he's right. Looks like I'm going to need meds. I have to play on Saturday night and there's a livestreamed charity concert on Tuesday. Desperate times, desperate measures, I guess. I'll be in touch when things calm down.*

This has really not been my week. A part of me wants to get hold of Mel and talk more with her, tell her about the Creeper dream that I just had. But she clearly can't afford to mess around; her career is at stake. Maybe the meds will help.

I don't really believe that, but what choice do I have?

I find myself yawning. Stupid stress-induced narcolepsy. OK. Coping strategies. I've got to focus on *what I've got to do today*: take O to see Daphne. This should be good fun, actually. Compared to murder and mayhem in dreamspace, anyway.

O's hog is a thing of beauty. It has a sidecar and she can control everything with her hands. I'm always a bit nervous driving with her because she thinks she's still got the reflexes of a twenty-year-old, but I daren't say anything. Today is one of those misty, still days where everything feels muffled. As we set off through the streets, the motor growls pleasurably beneath my backside, and with the vibrations jiggling my nether bits I try not to think of Antonio, but it's difficult. Rather Antonio's hardware than exploding babies, surely. We swing through Shepherd's Bush and out to the M4.

Normally we do this on a Tuesday fortnight: drive down to Dorking, pick up Daphne at her memory-care residence and take her out to lunch. Unlike O, Daphne is strong as an ox; unfortunately, she almost never remembers who we are. Every time we go to the same gastropub – they know us there and we always leave a big tip to make up for Daphne's strange dietary requests and occasional physical outbursts. It's all like clockwork, yet every time Daphne makes up a different story. She knows that she knows us but can't recall where from, so she finds a way to explain to herself who we are and why we're taking her out. She may be memory-impaired but her compensatory mechanisms are very creative. One time we were mechanics from the F1 circuit seeking technical advice on tyre traction. Once we were animal-rights activists who wanted to confiscate her furs even though 'they're fake, I swear on my life!' Once we were a May-December couple who needed a witness at our wedding. Last week we were ordinary tax collectors. She did get a bit stroppy with us last week, but on the whole I find Daphne lovely company and it's never a chore to visit her.

O, on the other hand, always gets nervous symptoms the night before. Sometimes it's a headache, sometimes she's physically sick. Last time O accused Edgar of having fleas because she was itchy all over. I gave her camomile lotion to put in the bath and then she slipped and had to be rescued. Poor O. By contrast, last night was very quiet. After we found Sidney, she went to bed, I went to bed, and it was a quiet night apart from that nasty Creeper dream. I want to tell her about it but she's not in that sort of mood and once we're riding it's far too noisy to talk.

The pub is called Aubergine. It has York slate floors, a coal fire, a small stage for live music, a pizza oven and a real paper menu. This is essential for Daphne because she's afraid of AR and if you show her an AR menu she tries to swipe it like a touchscreen, which is the last type of technology she can remember mastering.

O acts unusually distracted as she drinks lemonade and studies the menu as though trying to burn holes in it. This leaves me to make small talk with Daphne; I throw myself into the role with gusto.

'Do you remember who I am, Daphne?' I say. This goes straight against the advice not to ask questions like this because they can provoke anxiety when the memory-impaired person can't answer, but I do it anyway because I know what Daphne's like. She perks right up.

'Naturally I remember you,' she says haughtily. 'I never forget a face. You are the girl from the copy centre. You gave us that special deal on party invitations. Was it thirty per cent off?'

I can just about remember what a copy centre is but play along. 'Yes, thirty per cent off just for you. Was the party a success?'

'Don't be absurd. Naturally Sybil turned up stoned, Jeremy Binter and Rakesh nearly had a fist fight, and I ended up retiring to the kitchen for almost an hour in the middle because Corinne was holding forth again about her precious daughter's artisanal breastmilk business. It was exhausting.'

'Kitchens are always the best place at a party, anyway,' I say.

'Do you really think so? When I was your age, the roof was the best place. I don't suppose anyone can get away with that these days, what with all the drones flying everywhere.'

'There really aren't that many,' I reassure her. Daphne's mind jumps around in time so much that she often surprises me with how much she knows about the present day, even while she still thinks there are Blockbusters outlets.

'I've been given another assignment,' Daphne says. 'It could be dangerous. If this is the last time we see each other, please remember that I want to be buried with my vinyl copy of Johnny Mathis's *Warm*.'

O's lemonade glass is still half-full when it slips from her hand and shatters spectacularly on the tiles. I lunge towards her, afraid she's going to actually faint, but she fixes me with those hawk eyes. Pinioned, I halt before I've touched her. Her expression is so empty that for a moment I wonder if she's having a stroke.

'I'll get you another drink,' I try to say, but my voice has deserted me. I scurry to the kitchen and nearly collide with our waiter. While he cleans up the mess, he flirts with O and Daphne both – not with me, I notice – sniff. Daphne is still under full sail on the topic of her 'mission'.

'Mathis was my favourite singer. I wonder if he's still alive. Davies and I saw him having dinner in The Ivy once but I was too shy to ask for his autograph. I can remember that, you see. I can remember listening to his records as if it were yesterday. But now, what with me losing my mind, I'm worried about the assignment. I've been given a target, you see. What if I mix up the names and take out the wrong agent? Or what if I—'

O shakes her head sharply. 'No, Daphne, we mustn't talk about these things.'

Daphne lets out a quavering sigh. 'It's such a burden,

sometimes. You wouldn't understand. You lot have never had to— Oh, are those strawberries?'

'Yes, have some, darling. Waiter! The cream?'

Deftly, O steers the conversation away from Daphne's 'assignment' and somehow we navigate the rest of the meal. It's a mix of alert chatter and utter confusion. I'm not sure if it's just me getting used to Daphne's illness, but I'd wager she's improved slightly over the course of the last five or six visits. Sometimes she seems almost sharp, which makes her spells of confusion all the more poignant. Think *Flowers for Algernon*: the club remix.

Daphne normally insists on going for a long walk before we return to the residence.

'They won't let me out by myself, of course,' she tells me, every time, 'lest I should get lost, or mug someone, or run away and join the circus. But I was a mountain climber, you know. I've run triathlons. Astonishing that I should be afflicted with this brain disease, because I'm strong. I need exercise. One never knows what one may be called upon to do for one's country. I like to be ready, just in case.'

I walk between the sisters. O is sour-faced. Not having the option of walking on her own legs must loom large for her, and Daphne is probably deliberately pushing her buttons. She manages to put the boot in even though she apparently thinks O is my colleague at the copy centre, the person who transfers VHS to DVD or something. Being with Daphne is like being in a time capsule. It's almost tempting to send her around the schools to talk to kids about the old days.

Today Daphne stops after a hundred metres and leans on my arm.

'I've not been sleeping well,' she confides, almost in a whisper. 'And I'm feeling very nervous. What if we are being watched? Perhaps we should just go back to the hotel.'

O spins her chair around. I notice that, perhaps goaded by Daphne's remarks on fitness, she's turned the motor off and is using her arms to propel herself. Her face is flushed.

I take Daphne's arm. I can't remember what it feels like not to be able to sleep. I am a little jealous. It occurs to me I could offer her ASMR, but O probably wouldn't like that, and Daphne herself would probably mock me.

'I think the therapy is working, though,' Daphne says, now fully availing herself of my arm. 'I get flashes of lucidity – watch out for that mongoose, dear – and at first I thought, no, I can't bear this. Why drag it out? You know, when one is losing one's mind, one finds oneself almost looking forward to the time when the burden of mind is gone and then one won't know what's happening any more. Because the worst thing really is the awareness of everything one is losing, particularly oneself. Is that your shop there?'

'No, that's a charity shop.'

'Right. Terrible eyes. Did you know one of our Ukrainian ancestors was an Ashkenazi Jew? It's a long story. The bad eyesight comes from him but also the brain power. Ha! The vanished brain power.'

'Stick with the therapy,' O says, breathing hard. 'It can't do any harm.'

'Oh, but it can. The therapy keeps me awake. And gives me strange dreams. I know I'm dreaming but I can't stop. Sometimes I noctambulate—'

O's chair suddenly stops and she folds forward, coughing violently. I let go of Daphne and bend down to help her. She waves me away, still coughing, until tears start streaming down her face.

'O! Are you all right? Do you need help?'

Suddenly I feel incredibly tender towards O. Her sister is formidable, even in dementia. I flash the thought that Daphne is sucking all of O's oxygen.

'It's nothing,' O croaks. 'Sorry if I alarmed you.'

'I would like a change of prescription,' Daphne says, as though nothing's happened. 'But the colonel says you need to approve any changes.'

'The care coordinator is not a colonel,' O mutters, and turns her motor back on. We have to stride out to catch up with her. 'I'll talk to her. Don't worry. We can probably adjust your dosage.'

Daphne shakes hands formally with each of us when we leave her in her room. O goes off to talk to the manager and Daphne pats my shoulder.

'Being a secret agent takes a toll on a person,' she tells me. 'One must be alert for encrypted communiques at all times.'

Then she deposits herself on her chaise longue and seems to fade. I can't quite put my finger on what changes. It's not exactly that the light in her eyes goes out, but she diminishes in some subtle way. She no longer feels present. I pull away hastily, embarrassed, as though she's disrobed in front of me even though nothing on the surface of her has changed. I almost bump into the cleaning robot in my haste to get out. I can't see O at first, but I hear her speaking quietly with one of the carers.

'I'll work on mitigating the side effects from my end,' O is saying. 'Meanwhile, notify me if you're concerned.'

I swivel my head around and see the two of them conferring in a recess by the lift doors. O puts something into the carer's hand and the carer immediately transfers it to one of those big pockets that nurses have in the front of their uniforms, for holding all their medical bits and bobs. They nod to one another. I duck out of sight – I don't even know why, but something about their body language suggests secrecy. Maybe O is slipping the staff tips to take extra care of her sister? But that doesn't make sense. This is a private facility, top-notch, totally professional – or am I being naive again?

My Spacetime pings. It's Shandy.

'I'm redecorating your channel and I need your opinion on these wallpapers.'

'Not now, Shandy—'

'Yes, now! You've got to start treating this like a proper business, Horse.'

I hate it when she calls me Horse, but she's right about the channel. She designs virtual environments for a living and is always quick to suggest updates when anything in Spacetime is starting to look tatty.

'OK, but make it fast.'

'First thing. We're changing your job title. I ran a survey and I've already got the domain. Your new job description is Dreamhacker. I've registered it with the Alternative Whatsits People as well.'

'Council for Holistic Medicine?'

'Thingie. You're a dreamhacker. Don't argue, just adapt.'

'I don't know, Shandy. It sounds so aggressive and ... and technical. I'm a therapist, not a hacker.'

'No, you're a hacker. It will discourage the porno types, too. If you don't trust me, I can send you the marketing numbers.'

'I trust you.'

'Also. About our friend Bernard. Don't you think it's interesting that he's working in the sleep field now? And after he blew you off when you said you had narcolepsy! I'm thinking about slashing his tyres this weekend.'

'Don't do that!' I know she's not kidding.

'Maybe I'll find out more first. You could have a legal case. It's very, very interesting.'

'Don't read too much into it. I don't sleepwalk, I have narcolepsy.'

'Narcolepsy and sleepwalking are both sleep issues. And doesn't your new client sleepwalk?'

'A *client* sleepwalking is a different thing. Apples and oranges.'

'I have to go. Back to my real job, eh? I'll let you know if I come up with a way to get even without being caught.'

'Don't—' She's already gone. O is beckoning to me, so I step back into Daphne's room.

'We have to go, now, Daphne, but it's been so lovely to see you. Take care and have a good afternoon.'

Daphne gives a jolt and eyes me suspiciously.

'I'll see you at night,' she says. 'In the darkness. That's where I'll be.'

I manage a weak smile and back away, nearly falling into O's lap where she's waiting for me in the doorway.

'Come on. I've just had the project manager on my tail about the report I turned in. Someone claims to have spotted an error, which is absurd, because I don't submit work with errors. I must clear this up.'

As we head out to the hog, I want to ask about the medication that's causing Daphne to 'noctambulate' but I'm not brave enough. O clearly didn't want me to hear that, or why else would she have staged all the coughing? But to my surprise, O declares, 'Now you know how I know so much about sleep-walking and experimental treatments. Daphne's case has been peculiar. She has vascular dementia, but it's not Alzheimer's. We use a combination of medication and biofeedback involving AR as well as robotics. It's all meant to prompt her memory and keep her brain active. I know about Bernard's work because I'm familiar with BigSky and their research. My sister used to take a treatment they designed. I suppose you think I was wrong not to tell you what I knew.'

'Bite your tongue, O,' I say, blood rushing to my face with shame, because I actually have been wondering whether O knows more about BigSky than she lets on. 'Your family life is none of my business. You don't owe me anything. I'm only sorry that you have all this on your shoulders. Were you and Daphne ever... close?'

'We were as thick as thieves,' she says, with a tone of finality.

RP: I think she's waking up.

DC: Hey, Sleeping Beauty! We're in the middle of an interview here.

RP: Have some water, Charlotte.

CA: You guys, you guys! I get it now. You're Mulder and *you* must be Scully.

RP: I wanted to be Scully.

DC: A person is dead. I don't think jokes are appropriate.

CA: I do think it's my fault, in a way. I know I'm not supposed to say that. This isn't a confession, OK? But I feel like I should have stopped it somehow. I was right there. I didn't know she was sleepwalking. But I should have been on my guard, after what happened with the water.

DC: What happened with the water?

CA: I told you. She was asleep with her face in a bathtub full of water. In real life. In the dream, though, he was holding her down.

RP: He? Who?

CA: I don't know. He had a mask on. I should have... I don't know! I was going to say I should have called somebody, but who do you call?

RP: Ghostbusters? Sorry.

DC: Us. You call us. That's our job.

CA: That's what *he* said. The Creeper. He said, 'Who are you going to call, the Dream Police?' I thought he was being snitty, but what's the actual deal with you lot? Do *you* know what's going on here?

Have there been other cases? What do you know about this stuff?

DC: Can you remember anything else about him, Charlie? This man in the dream.

CA: Hard drugs, that's the only way. She should have been treated by a doctor. I never imagined it could come to this. You're right. I'm responsible. I don't have insurance for this kind of thing.

RP: None of us can change the past, Charlie. We can't bring Melodie Tan back. But we can investigate and if there's been a crime, we can pursue the criminal. That's why we really need you to remember.

CA: How do I know you're not in on it?

DC: What?

CA: You guys came up to me in the hotel lobby. You said you were with Special Branch, but here we are in a kebab shop in Stratford. Even Mulder and Scully had offices. And they wore nicer clothes. Or are you BigSky? Shandy says they don't have proper offices, just a bank of servers in Shoreham. Even the execs float around. Are you guys BigSky?

RP: No, we're not BigSky. Cutbacks, Charlie. We've all got to tighten our belts.

CA: Yeah? Well, I don't want to be unkind, Roman, but the way you're packing away that kebab, your belt is going to need an extra notch.

RP: That actually is unkind. I'm an emotional eater and I'd appreciate it if you didn't fat-shame.

CA: Sorry, mate, don't know what made me say that. I was out of line. What are you feeling right now, then? Can I help? We could work on your dreams.

DC: Obviously he's feeling deep existential despair brought on by the content of this interview. Have some chips, Roman, you're going to need them.

# Copernican Principle

'But *why* does she call you Horse?' O wants to know. She has got her reading glasses on the end of her nose and she's scrutinizing my now-defamed business card that just says *Dream Therapy*. It is Sunday and we are in the kitchen, where I am trying to make an omelette. Edgar stands on the counter inspecting the eggshells.

'I can't even remember. We were at school together since we were eleven. I used to call her Chickie Nugget but I've matured.'

O snorts. 'Well, Chickie Nugget is right about your job title. Dreamhacker is much better. I'll print up some new ones today. Meanwhile, what are you going to do about the noctambulatory harpist?'

'She's gone to see her doctor. I'm out of my depth, O.'

'And this Antonio character . . . ?'

'What about him?'

'Does he strike you as controlling?'

Uh-oh. I know that tone. It's her rhetorical question tone, viz.: 'Is it rubbish collection tomorrow?' and 'Did you want that pie?' by which she really means: *Put the bin out, lazybones*, and *Your pie was delicious*, respectively. Now she means *Antonio is dangerous*.

I clear my throat.

'I don't think I've given you quite a clear picture of Antonio,' I tell her. 'He's a warm, light-hearted guy. He's sweet.'

'And he brought you in to treat Melodie. Why?'

Indignant, I say, 'Maybe he thinks I'm good at what I do.'

'Darling, I meant why didn't Melodie address this for herself? She must be a very capable woman if she has a solo career as a classical musician. Surely she knows how to call a therapist.'

'True.'

'He was there when you did the session. You said you had to wake him. Is it possible that *he* is the Creeper?'

I squirm. It's not like I haven't sort-of considered it, but . . .

'What possible reason could he have for undermining Melodie's career? You should see them together. He dotes on her.'

'Mm-hmm. Darling, you're burning the omelette.'

The flat's buzzer rings.

'That'll be Lorraine,' O says. I check the camera feed. It is Lorraine, plus her grandson Stack. Yum. I buzz them in and shovel up a forkful of omelette while I wait for them to ascend five flights of stairs.

'She working nights again?'

'No, she's off today. She said she'd come check on my wrist.'

O's mate Lorraine is a physical therapist at the Royal Free. She's easily seventy-five but can pass for fifty and somehow looks glamourous even after a long shift at work. Stack reminds me of a young Idris Elba, all smouldering and cool at the same time. Maybe this is a set-up, I think hopefully. Take my mind off my problems. Stack isn't interested in me – he made that clear the first time we met – but you never know. One lucky day I might be in for a pity shag or a bit of a drunken grope. A girl can hope.

Except he's on Spacetime. He waves casually but keeps talking to someone we can't see. Something about a party. Sigh.

'Don't mind Stack,' Lorraine says in her gravel voice, dumping her coat in his arms. 'He's helping me with some errands today. How is the wrist feeling? Did you take your arnica?'

I repair to the sofa to eat my eggs while the two of them talk about which of their mutual friends has died lately and the side effects of medications. I fall asleep listening to them and one of my own snores wakes me with a jerk. Drool is leaking out of the side of my mouth. Stack is sitting opposite me, his sleek bare arms rippling with every little move as he delicately drinks a cup of coffee. I catch his micro-expression of disgust before he looks away. I scramble upright, wiping my face.

'Sorry!'

'Isn't it nice that you have Charlie here, O.' Lorraine beams at me. 'You know, Charlie, O has taken in a fair few young women over the years and all of them were very nice, but you are the most *real*.'

'Thanks,' I say faintly. 'Sorry I fell asleep.'

'You can't help it, I know. O tells me everything.' There's a gleam in her eye, and I feel myself blushing though I don't really know why. 'I hope you aren't using anything on the black market.'

'What?'

'For your narcolepsy. The smart drugs. They're easy to get, but you have to be careful. I see people all the time, they come into A and E. It's not like the old days. Too much modafinil will make you sick, but too much Xanadu can damage your hippocampus. There's a lot out there what hasn't been properly tested. Not worth the risk.'

I glance at O, thinking of her warnings of Neo-Victorian-potting-shed-scientists. But she is studying her fingernails as if they hold the secret to the origin of dark energy. (I should confess that I've only heard of dark energy because Shandy makes me watch *Physics Goats Tour the Galaxy*.)

'I don't take anything,' I inform Lorraine. 'As you can see, I just fall asleep in my food.'

Lorraine looks like she's going to say something else, but O surfaces from her private thoughts to interrupt.

'Charlie, are you working on Melodie tonight? Do you want Stack to come along?'

Stack and I look at one another in alarm.

'Uh . . . no offence, but what is use Stack going to be?'

'Yeah, I've got plans anyway—'

'For protection,' Lorraine says solemnly. 'In case this Antonio gets out of hand.'

'Oh, for heaven's sake. Antonio is not dangerous. This person in the dream can't be really real.'

'Why not?' Stack says.

'What?' I am giving him my frightened-wildebeest face. I can feel it. Damn.

*'Why can't it be a real person?* If you can hack people's dreams then presumably a lot of other people can, too.'

'What?' My vocabulary seems to have got stuck on that one word.

Stack says, 'Copernican principle. Humans don't occupy a special place in the Universe. Applies to everything, but Western postmodern narcissism blinds us to reality. If you can dream-hack, ten to one there's some nasty people who can do it, too.'

Copernican narcissism WTF is he even talking about?

'I am actually aware of that,' I say as haughtily as I can, which, after saying 'what' two times running, is unconvincing. 'It doesn't change the fact that it's *only a dream*. Nobody is in any physical danger.'

Stack shrugs and returns his attention to his Spacetime.

'I hope it's not a cat hacking your dreams, bruv,' he mutters.

I try to ignore him, but I have very good hearing.

'Because cats are vicious predators and they already control the Internet.'

# The Dark Side

Wet London. Monday crowds. People walk too slowly, and sometimes I want to drop down and crawl between their legs; I swear it would be quicker. The Tube strike means the buses are packed and I hate crowded buses. Having all those people around me is so exhausting, especially since I got this dream thing. It's like the separation between me and other people is even thinner than it was before, and I can almost hear their thoughts. I pick up feelings all the time. So, even though I'm already late, I take my bike off the rack and cycle wobblingly out into traffic, narrowly avoiding an AR horse-and-carriage driven by a Loan Shark.

Last night I finally caught up with the anxious hairdresser; that dream went well. No Creeper in evidence. Then, just when my confidence was returning, this afternoon a botmessage from Melodie. Her performance on Saturday was 'off' according to the conductor. The livestreamed concert is tomorrow and she's desperate. So here I am with my new business cards and a Spacetime full of informative links that O sent me during the night for my perusal.

As I'm trying to get control of my bike, the Loan Shark turns in the carriage seat and yells back to me: 'Don't forget, you can use Dougal's Head all month absolutely FREE! Brought to you by BigSky, the pop-up tech company. Think of us like a five-hectare hallucinogenic shroom.'

Dougal's Head is one of BigSky's paid apps that puts AR in full colour and reality in greyscale so you don't confuse the two. The ad is crude but perfectly timed; I call up the app. The last time I went for a night out in town with Shandy, we were too cheap to use blockers and Shandy got in a fistfight with what she thought were AR-bots but turned out to be US Navy

SEALs on leave. Then we had to wait on trolleys in a corridor of the Royal Free for eleven hours with the injured SEALs, one of whom thought Shandy's black eye was sexy and kept hitting on her even though she'd kneecapped his mate.

I'm sure it wouldn't have happened if we hadn't both been drunk and Shandy also high, but even stone sober it's always hard to be sure whether you're looking at a real person or an AR intrusion. Especially if you're a touch near-sighted like me and especially if it's raining (which it usually is). I activate Dougal's Head knowing that it will probably trigger my narcolepsy, but since it's free for thirty days, I may as well. I haven't used this app in a long time, but now that it's on again it reminds me of Dream City, where other dreamers show up in greyscale. Now, making my way across London to Mel's hotel, I realise that by that logic, all of us fleshmuppets are dreaming and the AR is awake. Lovely dark thought.

The main difference between reals and ARs is that real people don't usually get up in your face the way the intrusions do. Shandy told me that most AR bots are coded in the US and have to be redesigned for the UK market to make them less rude and loud, but only high-end advertisers can afford to do that. Which means that crossing Central London at rush hour you're seeing a riot of colourful clothes, hearing mostly American accents, and getting distracted by AR literally singing and dancing for your attention as you try to move unobtrusively through the stream of grey commuters. For someone like me – who passes out when overstimulated – avoiding this kind of thing is a matter of basic street defence. It's one reason I bike, the other being poverty. As it turns out, cyclists are divided into the haves (who cycle for fitness and conscience) and the have-nots (who cycle for lack of bus fare). That means I only ever have to fend off the lovely AR designed for rich people, because nobody bothers trying to sell to the destitute.

I'm actually glad for the chance to cycle off some of my

nervous energy. It will help me deal with Melodie better. Even her botmessage was overwrought.

*'I'm scared to go to sleep. They put me in a new suite because of the bathroom door. But I can't settle down.'*

I don't have any bots (can't afford) but I messaged back, *'Have sex. Drink chamomile tea. Watch a silly movie.'*

*Have sex?* What is with me? Why do I not think it's a little inappropriate for me to be commenting on her sex life with Antonio when she may not even know that me and Antonio used to be a – well, I'm not sure what we were, really. Not an item. A thing? A thingie? Anyway, sometimes I think I'm missing the region of the brain that is supposed to give you discretion.

Mel's bot made an emoticon face that looked sly and pleased at the same time. Where does she get these emoticons? How does she find the time to search for cool emoticons and also keep her nails manicured and master the music of Debussy? I don't even have time to buy new trainers. My left trainer's sole is peeling off and keeps catching on the pavement, so as I lock up my bike and scurry through the crowd, I alternately trip and hop.

I think about what Stack said. Not about Internet cats conspiring against me. The other thing. He does have a point in that if I can dreamhack, surely so can others as well. In Melodie's dream the Creeper was in full colour. At first I took this to mean he was a figment of Melodie's imagination, but only because I wasn't keen to explore the possibility that it (he?) could be another dreamhacker. The way it works in my own dream logic, greyscale people are asleep and the only person in colour is me – and I'm lucid – so by that logic all I really know is that the Creeper is conscious. It could be some part of Mel's consciousness. On the other hand, using Dougal's Head logic, the fact that the Creeper appears in colour could be my subconscious's way of telling me it is some kind of AR intrusion – but it acts too smart to be a bot. I'm much more worried about the possibility that the Creeper is a person who has managed to crash Mel's dreams. Stupidly, I've never considered the possibility of another dreamhacker out there.

'*Predators avoid each other,*' the Creeper said.

I'm not a predator. The Creeper obviously is. I should probably trace the other participants in the study. Shandy prodded me over this months ago, but I was too sleepy and depressed and I guess I had my head in the sand. I know I have to do something about it, but the very thought is exhausting.

Poor me.

When I get to the hotel, I'm sodden and out of breath. Desperate for endorphins, I plaster a big, fake smile on my face as I march through the hotel lobby. If you hold a smile for twenty seconds you get a burst of endorphins. Twenty seconds is a long time unless you work on a game show, plus I have a feeling there's pesto in my teeth.

I get into a luxurious golden lift with three businessmen in Italian suits. A smell of wet wool is rising from me and I'm aware that the trainer with the torn sole is leaking. I also spot the fact that a couple of lavender post-surgical bras are tangled up with one another and hanging half-out of my bag. They are padded and enormous. Still grinning furiously, I shove them back in. The businessmen say nothing but look disgruntled at the concept that I am in their lift, which goes to one of the special floors that only has luxury suites – Mel's new suite is even higher than the first. I sniff and fix my wet hair in the mirror. They murmur to one another in Mandarin. They get out at the same floor as me, and for a second I worry that they have something to do with the orchestra; but no. They carry on down the hall to the Rochester suite in a swish of expensive fabric.

The Windsor Suite has its own doorbell. Antonio answers it with that tousled, bedroom look. He's wearing a silk shirt and posh tracksuit bottoms, and his feet are bare. Immediately I know that she's taken my advice. He gets that soft, cuddly bedroom-eye thing going on right after sex. All that oxytocin.

'How is she?' I whisper. 'How long is it since she slept?'

He takes a deep breath. 'Not since you were here last. She has the concert tomorrow. The conductor has been to see her and now she's upset about that. She got a prescription from the doctor but she won't take it. I think she should take it.'

'OK,' I murmur. 'Is that what you want me to tell her? Take her medication? None of this was my idea.'

He sags visibly. 'I don't know. She likes you, and she trusts you, and if you tell her to take the meds maybe she listens.'

'OK, well, how about this. It's only seven o'clock. Let's see if she can get to sleep on her own. And if it's one and she still can't sleep, then she can use something. OK?'

He swallows. 'OK. Thanks, Charlie. I . . . you know, when I first met her she really wasn't this high-maintenance. It's too much for me.'

High-maintenance? What man says that unironically any more?

I say, 'Don't be a jackass and spoil everything. She's going through a lot. Sleep in the next room like before. And this time, if I call you, do as I say.'

He raises his eyebrows. This is not the ever-obliging Charlie he knows. Well, so what? I'm at work now.

This suite is even fancier than the other one. There are vast expanses of carpet and I leave damp footprints. I find Melodie sitting up in bed drinking chamomile tea from a glass teacup. She gets up and hugs me. Dark circles pool on her cheekbones and her mouth sags. I give her my new card.

'I like it!' she says, putting it on the nightstand. 'Thank you so much for coming. Please don't insist that I take the meds. They will only make it worse.'

I can hear Antonio in the next room, jumping around playing video games. At least he's staying out of my way. I sit on the edge of the bed.

'I don't know who the guy in your dream is,' I tell her, 'but I don't think he's part of you.'

Her eyes are shadowed. She sips carefully, not looking at me.

'Neither do I.'

'What did the doctor think?'

She shrugs. Her voice is dull. 'It hardly matters. It's become a crisis. The anxiety meds made me sleep, and then the Creeper tortured me for hours.'

I don't know what to say. She's more intelligent than I am, she's an expert in her field, she's sitting in a £5,000 per night hotel room. I am dripping on her fancy carpet. Who am I?

'It's possible this person is a dreamhacker,' I tell her. 'Like me, only not very nice.'

Now she's looking straight at me. 'I'm listening.'

'Can you think of anyone who would have reason to stalk you? An enemy? A rival?'

I feel idiotic saying it. She'd be a difficult person to hate. I ought to be intensely jealous of her... but I really like her. It's hard not to.

'Not off the top of my head, no. So you're saying that this guy in my dreams is a real person?'

I make an uncertain shrugging motion. 'Maybe. But I'm not saying that he – or she – is who they appear to be in your dream. You saw me change form, right?'

She grins suddenly. 'You were the Hulk. It was great.'

'So, this person could be someone who can enter dreams like I can, and for some reason they've targeted you. What you need to do is think through what he's actually said to you. Are there any clues? Is there something that he wants? He keeps telling me to get out of the way. But what does he say to you?'

She leans back against a mountain of pillows. Her eyes half-close.

'That's just it. He says my life is a waste. I'm not married, I don't have any children, I'm failing as a soloist, I'm never going to be well-off.'

Her eyes open.

'When I say it to you, it sounds like all the worst sexist crap, but when he says it to me in my dreams it feels *true*. I feel like I take up too much space and I've let everyone down. The biggest favour I could do the world is to die. And I almost feel... like killing myself is inevitable. It's just going to happen one day, and I won't be able to stop it.'

I hold her hand. I say, 'You are brilliant and talented and kind. Don't listen to anything he says to you. I'm going to get him away from you.'

Even with my best ASMR tricks, it takes Mel a long time to fall asleep. While I wait for her to drop off, I start reading the links that O sent me.

### BigSky Makes Sweet Dreams Bigger

A new expansion pack for Sweet Dreams has been announced. The Dark Side is expected to be available to a limited subscriber base as soon as the end of the year. BigSky spokesperson Emilie Vasquez commented, 'The Dark Side will merge the best of our Sweet Dreams ASMR environments with The LateLateLate-LateLater Show, which is specifically designed to be used during sleep. In response to an ever-growing demand from our client base, we offer an alternative to the hyperstimulation of daytime life with its multiple stressors. The new mod pack will offer faster fall-asleep times, deeper and more restful sleep, and the latest advances in power-dreaming.

Damn. Power-dreaming! Why didn't I think of that? I can't possibly compete with BigSky. You know, it would be just like them to develop the stuff they infected me with to work on this new platform. Maybe their next upgrade will be an ingestible piece of tech enabling people to cross into other people's dreams. I can see it now: everybody else gets the good, clean version, but I get my life ruined. That would be about par for the course.

The thought is so stressful that I pass right out.

**Secret Diary of a Prawn Star**
**Entry #51**
**Codename:** Chaplin
**Date:** 20 September 2027
**Client:** Melodie Tan
**Payment in advance:** Yes
**Session Goal:** Second attempt to evict Creeper
**Location:** Hilton Excelsior Windsor Suite
**Narcolepsy status:** Fair
**Nutrition/stimulants:** Tea & biscuits
**Start time:** 8.31 p.m.
**End time:** 8.55 p.m.


I'm in Mel's hotel room. There's nothing to indicate it's a dream except that the room has become really cold. I get up and go to the climate control, but it's stuck. There's a little handset and speaker next to the climate panel, and a sign that says, 'Ring for assistance.' So I do. I pick up the handset.

'You don't get it.' That American voice again. 'I control the parameters here. You don't know what you're doing. If you try to save her you'll only make it worse.'

'Shut up,' I say through gritted teeth. 'Leave her alone. If you've got a problem with me, then you deal with me.'

'Oh no,' laughs the voice. 'If I've got a problem with you, I can do whatever amuses me. And this kind of game amuses me greatly.'

The Creeper materialises from out of the shadows to loom over Mel's bed. It's wearing black Darth Vader robes that partly shade the white mask. Mel's eyes are open now, black with fear. I can see the tendons in her neck stand out. It puts its hands around her throat and squeezes, then brings its face down close to hers.

'Give me your breath,' it says to her.

There's a vase of flowers on the table. The card says, 'Break a leg, kid! –Vazzie xxx.' I pick up the vase – it's heavy – and heft it to my shoulder, then go skipping towards the bed like a shot-putter placing a throw. I hurl the vase at the Creeper. The vase goes right through the Creeper and hits the pillow next to Mel. She sits bolt upright, covered in flowers and water.

I am an idiot.

The Creeper turns towards me and I'm confronted by the mask. Under my scrutiny the head seems to grow, and the surface of the white mask stretches and develops a red slash of a mouth, flat-lipped and much too big in proportion to the rest of the face. I always find caricature scarier than realism. I wonder how it knows that about me. Ugh. I reach out and tug at the Creeper angrily, trying to drag it away from Mel.

The Creeper's arm comes off in my hand with a wet crunching noise. The arm is still moving and the hand grabs at me. Black fluid spurts out of the stump, and a smell of decaying flesh.

I hurl the arm across the room. The hand climbs up the wall and switches off the light.

'Gotcha,' says the Creeper, in the dark now. 'Do you smell that? It's death. You'll find death everywhere you go. Beginning here, tonight.'

'Fuck off,' I say. I conjure up a bedside lamp and switch it on. The one-armed Creeper is lying on the bed, face down, covering Mel. I can't even see her. Oh my god. This is awful.

I'm really mad but I don't want to touch its body again, so I hesitate, looking for something to use as a weapon. The detached arm keeps crawling along the wall, heading now for the lamp I've just turned on.

'Mel!' I scream. 'Wake up! Wake up! Terminate dream!'

I grab the lamp and swing it in an arc like a cricket bat. As it strikes the Creeper's head, the bulb breaks with a *pop* and the room's dark again.

'Wake up, Mel! Wake up!'

A cold hand grabs my hair, then grips my face, dragging at my mouth. It tastes more foul than—

'Ah, I can taste you. So alive. You're on my list, my dear.'

*It* can't taste *me*. *I* can taste *it*. Object relations are getting mixed up here; it's as if I've mingled with the Creeper in some horrid way. I prise the hand off my face and throw the arm away in disgust. The voice is somewhere behind me. I turn toward it. Light from the main room of the suite illumines the Creeper's figure – or most of it. There's no head.

I must have knocked it off when I hit it with the lamp, because the detached head lies on the bed, face down.

I'm so grossed-out it takes me a moment to notice that Mel isn't in the bed any more.

Where did she go? She must have left the bed while the lights were out. She hasn't woken up yet or the dream would have ended. Where is she?

This doesn't make sense. It's her dream. She can't leave.

Then I remember what happened last time I lost track of her. I rush to the bathroom, but she's not there. Thankfully there is no window. I go into the other room, where Antonio is asleep on the sofabed. She's not in the suite – at least, not in this dream version of it.

I need to wake up right now. *Right now.*

But I can't.

'You're such a stupid person,' says the Creeper.

The Creeper has managed a wardrobe change while I was distracted. It's no longer wearing black Darth Vader robes, but Mel's PJs. And its head, lying face down on the bed, now has Mel's hair: silky, black and long.

I turn the head over, very gently. Mel's face, eyes open, stare back at me without sight.

*

I wake in a panic.

'Mel! Mel! Wake up!'

The real-life hotel room is perfectly tidy, but it's also empty. Of course it is. Again: the tangled bedclothes. Again: the closed bathroom door. When I wrench the real door open, there is nothing but a brightly lit luxury bathroom smelling of Melodie's perfume.

I run out into the living room.

'Antonio! Antonio?'

He isn't there. The door to the hall is open.

I dash outside. The hallway is empty. I start towards the lift, but there's no sign of anyone. I go the other way, but the hall comes to an end at the Rochester Suite, which appears to take up the better part of the floor. It has Grecian urns on plinths outside it.

I return to the suite and ping Antonio. 'Where's Mel????'

He Spacetimes me right back. *'I can't find her. I'm in the lobby now. There's some commotion, hold on—'*

I go and get the room key, then head to the lift and press 'Down'.

*'Charlie, are you there? Something's happening . . . Someone threw themselves off the roof. It's a crowd, people are being told to keep back—'*

Then the link breaks.

I run for the fire stairs. There are five flights of them to climb. Here are the thoughts that are running through my head:

*It can't be her. It's just a horrible coincidence. The person who jumped is probably one of those businessmen with a guilty conscience because he swindled old people out of their life savings and got caught.*

*What if someone pushed her?*

*What if someone pushed her and they are still up there? What if I meet them on their way down?*

*What if I go up there to see if someone pushed her and I get accused of pushing her myself?*

*It can't be her.*

101

With that horrible chatter in my head, I take the steps two at a time. I really should exercise more. I'll start tomorrow. I'll volunteer for charity work. Also, I'll eat kale. Please just let Mel be OK.

I call Antonio three times and leave increasingly breathless messages.

I am on the roof. The door is already open. It has been wedged with a fire extinguisher.

I step outside.

'Uh, Melodie?'

Nobody is here. Just wind and sky. The rain is chucking down. I can hear sirens. I can see cranes sticking up all over town and I can smell diesel. This isn't the Dream City. Those sky bridges and luminous canals aren't real. This darkness is real.

The sirens are coming this way.

My Spacetime pings.

Antonio is sobbing.

CA: Are you blocking my lifi?

DC: They don't have lifi here.

RP: There's pizza, if that helps.

CA: Six-G, then. Phone, even. If I'm not being detained, why can't I communicate with anyone?

RP: You can. We're not stopping you.

CA: But I tried my AR piece and it doesn't— Whoops! Sorry, I had it on airplane. My bad. Can I just check my messages— Oh, here's O calling now. I better take this. She'll be worried.

RP: Tell her you'll call her back.

CA: O? I'm so sorry, I was on airplane. No, I'm still in London, I meant— Never mind. You what? Mel trended? Yeah, I'm answering questions. No, not Scotland Yard. Where? Um... dunno, somewhere in Stratford.

RP: [whispering] Should I turn off the recording?

DC: [mutters] Let it run. The mic will pick up the conversation, we can enhance it.

CA: It's Kafkaesque, actually, if Kafka's stories were set in chippies. No, I just keep falling asleep. Is Antonio still there? Can you tell him— Oh. When did he leave?

DC: Tell her you'll call her back.

CA: Yeah, that's the bad cop. He's ugly, too. There's a nice one but he's not in charge.

DC: [unintelligible]

CA: K, laters, bye.

DC: As we were saying, let's go over the events of the night itself. We need to build a timeline. You arrived at Ms Tan's hotel at approximately seven p.m., is that right?

CA: Ish.

DC: Let the record reflect that the witness said she arrived at approximately seven p.m. And what time did Ms Tan fall asleep?

CA: Just after half-eight.

DC: You fell asleep about the same time?

CA: I actually may have fallen asleep before her. She entered her first dream cycle at about eight-thirty. I have notes of all this in my dream diary.

DC: How can you keep a diary while you're sleeping?

CA: It's an acquired skill. I use my AR piece to record brain patterns and keep a notepad open for the meta. Because I'm a lucid dreamer, I can make notes and maintain the dream at the same time. Unless the dream gets really hairy.

RP: Can we see the notes?

CA: They're confidential. Client privilege.

DC: You're not a doctor or a lawyer. You're going to need to turn over those notes. If you don't give them to us, the police will take them off you.

RP: What's that guy doing out there? Is he trying to get in?

CA: I know him! It's OK, let him in before he wakes the whole neighbourhood—

Stranger: [shouting, possibly in Portuguese]

[LOUD BANGING AND THUMPING NOISES]

DC: Who is this maniac?

RP: I'm letting him in before he wakes Serge.

CA: Antonio, calm down.

Antonio: How I am being calm when police are blaming me, your English pig police want to deport me or maybe just shoot me in the head. Don't touch me!

DC: We don't deport people. We're the—

**CA:** They're not immigration officers. They're only Scully and Mulder, Antonio. It's cool.

**Antonio:** You come with me, Charlie, she is lying there dead, I am a broken man. Come, Charlie—

**RP:** Sorry, mate, you can't— Oi!

**DC:** [unintelligible]

**CA:** Hey! Hey, oi! Fuckity shit fuck, guys, stop hurting each other. Fighting is bad! STOP IT!

**[END RECORDING]**

# Why

'That's enough, break it up!'

Donato is on the ground under Antonio with his legs wrapped around Antonio's waist. They are hitting each other even as they crash into the legs of chairs. Laminated menus slither down from the counter and rain on them.

Goodcop aka Roman Pelka is trying ineffectually to pull Antonio off Donato Cruz aka Badcop. Roman is neither large nor strong, and his relationship with his own body is kind of like my dad's relationship with that drone he tried to put together without an instruction manual and ended up drop-kicking into a carp pond in rage.

'Sergio!' Roman yells, and then takes an elbow to the mouth as Antonio pulls an arm back unexpectedly. 'Sergio, some help?'

The kebab shop's been closed for hours, and Sergio headed to his flat upstairs after our last round of food and drink. He locked up but didn't close the security grille, which is how Antonio spotted us and then hurled himself at the door yelling accusations in Portuguese. This was too much for Roman, who opened the door, which was maybe unwise of him.

Now Sergio comes thumping downstairs barefoot in trackies, his hair all messed-up, carrying an axe-handle. He takes in the scene, shouts something in Turkish and then wades in.

Roman retreats, blood streaming from his nose.

'Please don't break Antonio's face!' I cry. 'Will no one think of his looks?'

While the three of them are huffing and grunting and knocking down furniture, I grab some paper napkins and pass them to Roman.

'Keep your head back,' I tell him. 'I'll look for some ice.'

While I'm finding ice behind the counter, Sergio is separating the two combatants. Antonio is flushed and gesticulating wildly but Donato doesn't even appear winded. He brushes off his trousers and shirt.

'There was no call for any of that,' Donato says to Antonio, darkly. 'We're not the police. We're not detaining Miss Aaron. And if you're back on the streets already then there's no reason to think anybody will accuse you of murder. Let alone shoot you.'

There's a crushed chip stuck to Donato's arse. I have the urge to pluck it off but restrain myself with a mighty effort. Instead I give a tea towel full of ice to Roman. His upper lip is swollen somewhat attractively.

Antonio reaches for me. Sergio extends his axe-handle, blocking Antonio from touching me.

'This is not worth it for me, bruv,' Sergio says to Roman. 'You guys better find another place to do business.'

'I pan bet oo Addenal tiggeds,' Roman says, head back, ice on face.

Sergio looks at him uncomprehendingly.

'Arsenal tickets,' I fill in. 'He can get you a season pass.'

'I nebber ded a deedon badd!'

'Didn't you? Sorry. He can get you tickets, Sergio, but a season pass is beyond his powers.'

Sergio grunts. He and Donato pick up chairs and generally put the room back to rights.

I turn to Roman, lean on his arm while the other two shout at each other. I feel like green jelly.

It's been a very long night.

Once it was clear that Mel really had walked off the roof, I kind of lost my moorings. An ambulance came, and I waited in the lobby with Antonio as he paced, and cried, and punched a wall, and then the concierge had to bring him an ice pack. It's all disordered in my mind, so I'm not clear what happened when. The police came. There were cups of tea. I spilled mine while giving a statement to a nice woman in uniform, and she ended up holding the cup for me while I drank. One of the desk clerks put a blanket over my shoulders and I felt foolish. Nothing happened to *me*. It's Mel, broken, in an ambulance, but even that is wrong. Ambulances are for the living.

I didn't cry, though. I kept saying I felt responsible, but the police constable didn't write any of that down in my statement. She held my hands between hers for a moment after I signed my wobbly signature. Asked who she should call to come and get me. And that's when Roman turned up, standing over us with his fists in his jacket pockets and a bowler hat on his head that hasn't been in fashion for at least eight years. I didn't know his name at first, of course, but he introduced himself and the constable – Yemisi – she knew him and she explained to me that he was an expert in technological crime and she got up and he sat down and I blurted, 'She didn't kill herself. Someone killed her from inside her head.' That seemed to get his attention and the next thing I knew Roman and I were meeting Donato in a Stratford kebab shop and Donato was doing his 'this is an official interview' schtick amidst the Saturday-night rush of punters leaving the pubs and going for kebabs. Surreal doesn't really begin to describe any of it.

Now Antonio has evaded the efforts of Sergio to stop him, he flings his arms around me.

'They think you killed her! I don't want anything terrible to happen to you, too, Charlie.' He starts sobbing into my shoulder.

'This isn't Argentina, mate,' says Donato, and I reply stiffly, 'My friend comes from Brazil. Not all South American countries are the same.'

'Yeah, I'm aware of that, Ms Aaron. The Met don't beat people into giving confessions. We're only talking. Calm down.'

'Calm down?' Antonio roars. 'Are you—?'

'Why not have some chips,' says Roman in that soft, mellow way he has. He's got up off the floor undismayed and smiles at Antonio even though Antonio must have loosened a couple of his teeth just now. Antonio ignores him and grips my body tighter.

'Thank god I found you. O didn't want to tell me where they'd taken you, but I insisted.'

Of course, O will have been tracking me all this time.

'You know it wasn't me, right?' I sound breathless partly because he's knocked the wind out of me, and partly because he's just grabbed my backside and lifted me off my feet so as to press me into his giant erection.

'I know it wasn't you,' he whispers into my hair. 'I'm sorry I got you into this mess.'

'Antonio. Put me down.' He puts me down but doesn't let go. He's quite tall, and the head of his penis nudges my rib cage.

I clear my throat and disengage, a little weak at the knees.

'Sorry,' Antonio says. 'I just—'

'Yeah.'

He takes a pocket pack of tissues out of his jacket and blows his nose. He folds the tissue neatly but his hands are trembling.

Roman says, 'Please take a seat, Antonio. So glad you came. We'd like to talk to each of you one at a time.'

'One at a time! One at a time!' Antonio points at each of them with a kind of random violence. 'That is what they do when they want us to turn on each other, Charlie! Don't say anything else. I'm calling you a lawyer.'

'Actually,' I say, 'I think I am going home now.'

Donato glares at me. 'We've barely got started.'

I try to glare back. Confrontations terrify me. I can't look Donato in the eye without thinking how he's going to grab me by the throat and then they'll throw me in the back of their blacked-out 4X4 and take me somewhere secret, like an abandoned mental institution, and torture and kill me, and I'll end up on the bottom of the Thames. Eel food.

'Donato, you're scaring her,' Roman says. He seems a decent enough sort, but Donato doesn't take him seriously at all. I wonder if it's because he's not in the best nick. Donato obviously works out a lot. The backs of his shirts are all stretched in the shoulders, whereas Roman's are stretched in the belly. Donato swings his arms, kicks a chair and walks over to the counter. He leans on it as if he's a morally tortured character in a Dostoevsky novel. I can almost see the thought bubble over his head: *Why do I have to put up with these idiots?*

I pick up my bag and put on my hoodie.

'I'd like to go home now, please,' I say. It's odd. No matter how angry I am, I'm always polite and I never raise my voice. Mulder and Scully probably have no idea how, if this were a video game and I had, say, a giant laser bazooka, I would line them both up against the wall and make them grovel apologetically for putting me through all this when it wasn't necessary. Then I'd blow a hole in the ceiling of the kebab shop, just for laughs. As long as no one was upstairs, of course. I'm not a sociopath.

But I don't have a bazooka of any description. I have a bag full of romance novels and post-surgical bras needing alteration. And I am trying very hard not to cry again.

'I will take you, Charlie. That's why I came, to extract you safely. Not to talk to these pigs.'

Sigh. 'They're not police, Antonio. They work in tech crime. I've been helping them, and maybe you should, too. For Mel's sake.'

Antonio is so handsome that even when he's in a terrible state – like now – he's still quite edible.

Donato says, 'If you have nothing to hide, then there's no harm in talking to us. We can deal with this very quickly—'

'Talk to your friends the pigs! They asked me a thousand offensive questions—'

'Pardon me, Doctor Pelka,' Sergio adds, looking pained. 'You are good customer and I don't want no trouble but this fighting is not part of our understanding. I think you better go.'

There ensues a lot of back and forth with Donato issuing re-assurances that don't sound particularly convincing and Antonio working himself up into a froth. I'm feeling sleepy again. I need to go home.

'Do you think the police will want more from me?' I murmur to Roman. After all, they kept Antonio all night. The boyfriend is always the prime suspect, but if people start to connect the dots about my past relationship with Antonio, they might think that he and I did it together. It does look kind of dodgy, even if neither of us was in physical contact with Mel at the time. He hasn't done either of us any favours by grabbing my arse just now, of course.

'They may do,' he says. 'Don and I are going to want more from you, anyway. We'll be asked to make a report. Anytime AR is involved in an incident, the Met call us.'

I must have made some sort of involuntary sound or twitch, because he hastily adds, 'Not that I'm saying you had anything to do with this! Only that a full workup needs to be done.'

'So you guys are really, really legit, seriously?'

''Course!'

'The kebab shop is just . . . what, where you like to hang? I mean, do you always interview people here?'

'Sometimes we do it on the bus or in the park,' says Roman.

'In the park? That's so—'

He laughs. 'Pathetic? It's also a way for us to avoid being tracked digitally. We're aware that when we're hunting criminals, they are also hunting us.'

Pretty deep for a man with a grease stain on his lapel.

'So I could ring up Scotland Yard and they'd be like, oh, Roman and Donato, they're always interrogating people in public places, pish! Is that what you're saying?'

'Well, they might not say "pish". It's not a term people actually use. Except you.'

He tries to restrain his smile, but it breaks over his whole face.

'I will take you home, Charlie,' Antonio says, giving me a smouldering look. 'I call the cab.'

Donato doesn't argue about it. It says a lot that Antonio the

111

yoga instructor has the money to call a cab while the Dream Police got me here on a series of Big Green Buses. As the cab takes us to Finsbury Park from Stratford, we talk haltingly. I find out that Melodie's parents are flying in from Canada, that the police are reviewing CCTV footage from the hotel and cross-referencing with everyone's Spacetime footprints.

'I was in the lift when she fell,' Antonio whispers. 'I was looking for her.'

I hold his hand.

'At least you were looking,' I say. 'I was asleep. I was supposed to protect her but I couldn't.'

The good thing about the kebab shop interview was that it stopped me dwelling on what had happened. I didn't have time to think while they were asking their clueless questions. Now the weight of the dream comes crushing down. When I remember the Creeper, a jolt of electricity runs through me.

'What did O say?'

'Not very much. She is so cold. She didn't care when I told her how I was interrogated. The police want to pin this on me, I can feel it.'

'Yeah, it's pretty fucked-up.'

'Charlie, do you mind if I put up some mental scenery? I feel like I need something to lift my spirits. The gloominess, it's too much right now.'

'Sure, of course.'

'You are on BigSky? OK, we share. I have the road to Hana on Maui, an imaginary ice planet with friendly penguins – you will like them, they are cute. Also a country road from South Yunnan Province. What have you got?'

'Nothing but the beta version of an environment Shandy's working on. It's called Patios of the Rich and Famous, but that doesn't sound as good as the penguins.'

'Ice planet it is. Engaging sled drive.'

As the taxi wends its way across London, we *schuss* across a high plateau on the ice planet of Yon (yes, that's really the name, commercially registered and approved by BigSky's ~~Oxbridge numpties~~ crack team of marketing experts). The penguins waddle alongside us but they can't keep up, so they sort of take a running start and then glide on their bellies, whee! Super cute. The sky is deep violet studded with multicoloured stars and there's a line of dark green sea just visible beyond our snowy plateau. Our sledge is being pulled by seven fat reindeer with strings of fairy lights in their antlers. Unlike real reindeer, they don't flash their bumholes when they run. Apart from that, I find it convincing and a huge improvement on East London. Sorry, Hackney.

'So, no visible bumholes: pro or con?'

'Con, of course,' Antonio says. 'This is an imaginary planet, but if we are to believe we're really there, the animals should be realistic. No anus, no excretion, no reality.'

Antonio has such a lovely accent that he even makes 'anus' sound romantic.

'I think it's a good thing. AR is supposed to be an improvement on reality. And maybe they excrete some other way.'

'In that case they should not look like reindeer. They could be reptilian or insect or something even more alien.'

'Like a Puffle?'

'Or a Tribble.'

'They could have more fur, I guess,' I say. 'As a cover-up.'

'More fur would be fine with me.'

'I never had you for a realist, Antonio.'

'I am very much the realist. Wow, did you see that? A shooting star!'

As the taxi stops at lights, we admire the meteor shower on the alien planet generated by Antonio's Spacetime. I am in this safe little world with him, don't have to look out of the cab window at the real London. Don't have to think about the person assigned to wash the blood off the pavement where Melodie fell while the morning traffic starts up and London goes on without her.

Don't have to wonder how the Creeper did it. Or why.

Penguins are good.

Antonio sees me into O's building and then jumps back in the cab to teach his first Movement Art & Science class in Mayfair. I trudge up the stairs and stand outside O's flat fumbling with my keys; the door opens from inside and O is there in her wheelchair.

'It will upset you greatly to hear this,' she informs me. 'But the business line has been flooded with enquiries. It seems that Melodie Tan's death has worked in your favour.'

I shut the door behind me. O wheels to her workstation and starts giving me the rundown.

'No, stop it, O!' I say. 'My client has died. I can't. I just can't hear this right now.'

'Of course, darling. Naturally you're upset. Shandy's been trying to reach you. I told her that you're safe and not under suspicion—'

Perhaps I make some sort of involuntary noise because she stops and asks, 'You're not, are you? Under suspicion? You've been in Stratford, not in cells.'

I tell her about the Dream Police. She asks a lot of questions about Antonio's behaviour, which in my view is the least of it. But I answer them. I'm getting used to answering questions.

'You've had enough for one night,' O concludes. 'We'll talk further after you've rested.'

Again I'm go to bed as London wakes. But first, I can't help checking my Spacetime, just to see what I've missed while I was with the Dream Police.

O wasn't kidding about the business. There are 1,732 new messages on my ASMR channel, and even after I run my spam-checker I still net over 400 that look legit. I have 3,778 new subscribers (up from 718) and there's money in my Donation Hat. Video greetings from my new supporters appear in my field of vision, their icons physically poking me to get my attention.

What's going on? My Spacetime is set to block anyone I don't know, but the overflow of contact requests goes to mail. I start to sift through these.

> CHARLIE!!!! Are you OK? How is everything going? I love the name Dreamhacker! So cool! Hope it's all good, drop me a line sometime. Love, Alayna xx

Alayna's a fellow ASMRtist, but we don't know each other that well. How does she know I'm using the name Dreamhacker?

There are other messages from people in the ASMR community.

> Hope you're OK honey, sending love – Natasha

And even more like this:

> We know you didn't kill her, don't worry. We support you. Love, Carlos

Aha. So the news has broken that I was there when Mel died. And finally, in my e-mail:

> Hi, Charlie, my name's Surya and I'm a journalist with Troof Bomb. Hoping to speak with you about your ordeal last night. Can we meet for coffee?

There are variations on that last one from several different news outlets. As I'm reading, more messages are coming in. Chat requests. Subscriptions to my channel. The Hat is going *Ker-ching* every so often as credit rolls in. What the hell? Am I... famous?

I flop back on the pillows. If only this had happened before I took on Melodie, then I wouldn't have been there when she walked off the building. I wouldn't even have known about it, probably, because I'd have deleted Antonio's message without ever reading it. But no – here's my big break, right here, right now. And it has nothing to do with me or my work.

Melodie Tan is dead.

I'm under investigation by the Dream Police.

And for the first time in my life, I'm making money.

I want to hide under the bed. I want to pull out my earring, take down my shingle, get enough caffeine patches to keep me awake for ever, and never do dreamwork again ever ever ever ever.

Ever.

I haven't listened to any ASMR since I got sick. When you're desperately trying to stay awake more than four hours a day, the last thing you need is somebody making soothing noises and doing everything they can to get you to relax. For a while, I tried to keep up my friendships in the online community, but eventually I had to cut everything off. It was ironic, because just as I'd been establishing a subscriber base for my channel, I had to stop. I even sold my microphones. That was heartbreaking.

At first, I got messages from people: *Where are you? We miss you. Could you do that thing with the hourglasses again? Could you do a jungle sounds video? Could you do that cooking one?*

I felt like a strung-out superhero who had to stop rescuing people. I wanted to say, *No, I can't save you from your anxiety and sleeplessness, I would but I've lost my powers.* But I didn't say anything. I just let the channel lie fallow. And now here it is reviving itself thanks to the lightning speed of rumours across Spacetime. Again I consider calling Shandy, if only because she'll be offended if she wakes up and finds me trending and she's the last to know.

But if I tell her, she'll want to come over and hear all the details, and I really need to quiet my mind now. I'm a wreck. I'm so messed up that even my narcolepsy seems to be malfunctioning, because usually stress puts me right to sleep but apparently I've gone straight through stress, past panic and out of the other side. I'm wired.

I find myself sitting cross-legged on my futon-bed, which is covered with a fine layer of Edgar's fur. I start to take out my earring to go to sleep and then change my mind. I rearrange my field of vision so the connection is completely private. No one can message me. I leave open my favourite channel on Sweet Dreams. It belongs to Shveta X, an ASMRtist from New Delhi who used to be one of my go-tos. She even encouraged me by linking to my channel after I put up my 'Sounds of Rainy London' video, and sometimes she messaged me even after I got sick. I like Shveta more than anyone. She has an inherently calming vibe. The way she talks, the way she moves, her big, compassionate eyes and the deliberate way she does everything.

Tonight I put on one of Shveta's henna-painting Spacetime recordings, where she does her little niece's hands. It's had nearly a hundred thousand more hits since I last watched, and I can see that she has recorded several dozen new environments.

I prop up lots of pillows. I turn on the Spacetime recording and hope it will work. Shveta feels right here with me. She looks into my eyes and smiles slowly.

'We are all artists,' she says in her beautifully modulated low voice, with her accent that is so much nicer than any English accent from actual England. 'We are all works of art, too.'

If anyone else said it, this would sound pretentious. Shveta is so genuine that I believe her. *All of us works of art.*

'For me, art is a part of daily life,' she says, delicately drawing ink on her niece's wrists. 'Does that tickle, Meeta?'

They both giggle a little. So cute. She says, 'Sometimes it's nice to just lose yourself in what your hands are doing. It's like breathing. You don't have to think about it. You don't have to think about anything. You don't have to try. Sometimes we are all trying so hard we forget how to just be. There. Still tickling?'

I breathe deeply. Just the sound of her voice goes into my skin like smoke or mist. The top of my head begins to tingle as if it's covered in tiny electric sparks. I could listen to Shveta recite stock exchange numbers and get tingles. Her voice sounds like warm, rumbling darkness full of stars. My eyelids droop.

I should take my earring out now. I don't want to fall asleep. Sleep isn't safe. I want to stay here, with Shveta and Meeta and the tendrils of henna spreading across Meeta's skin. But it's like watching a sunset: even when the colours seem optimal, the most beautiful combination of light and darkness imaginable, you can't freeze-frame it. Slowly, imperceptibly, the sky changes to darkness. And slowly, imperceptibly, I'm sinking into sleep.

# Creeper

I don't remember dreaming anything at all. Next thing that happens, I startle awake in my bed. Many hours must have passed, because I'm still propped on pillows and the room is dark except for an orange line of street light that shows the gap between the edge of the curtain and the wall. There's a tiny notification in one corner of my vision letting me know the ASMR playlist has ended, but that's not what woke me up.

Someone's in the room. The door is shut. But someone's here. There's a shadowy person-shaped presence in the darkness. Its edges are indistinct, and its arms and head appear to be moving as though a current of water is going through it. The arms wobble and detach, then reattach, like it's a dark and scary version of Morph the claymation dude – but Morph is friendly and this thing is most definitely not friendly. The longer I look at it, the more alarmed I feel. There's a deep sense of the unnatural about it – like I've opened a crack to a place that no person was meant to see. And here it is in my room. There's a shrivelling inside me, followed by the full-on slap of panic. I want to crawl out of my own skin, run up the wall, back myself into the corner. Get far away.

*Run, run, scream, open the window, bang on the wall, get help!*

But I can't move. I can't even move my eyes. I can't not look at it. I can't open windows in my AR – which would enable me to awaken O or to call someone – I'm completely frozen.

It has control.

I can hear my own squeaking breath. Why can't I move? I try to raise a hand, move a foot – anything – but I feel like I weigh a thousand kilos and none of my muscles work. I can hear my heart in my ears. Sounds like that time Shandy made me run a 5k Race for Life with her and I had no idea how far 5k actually is, but it turned out to be a lot farther than just running for a bus, which was all the training I had ever done. Now I will never see Shandy again and I will never run again and when they find my body I don't know what they'll say, but—

*Roman.* Roman needs to know about this. I've seen the Creeper. It's in my room. It wants me.

That means this is a dream. I am in my room and I'm awake but I'm not awake, this is still a dream, and I'm a dreamhacker. I have to fight back. If it's a dream I can make things happen.

*Levitate,* I tell myself. Flying's one of my favourite things to do in dreams, and it's easy if you're lucid.

But I weigh six hundred kilos, I can't fly, and the Creeper's face is beginning to resolve. It's mask-like, white, but no longer covered with chemical symbols. No, it has eyes and mouth that twist and stretch just like that painting and the derivative horror movie it spawned. The Creeper has a long, fat tongue like a frog or Jabba the Hutt, and as this comes licking out towards me, moving the air above my bed, I pick up a vivid smell of sulphur.

So I can't move. Maybe I can change something else.

*Turn on the lights.*

Nothing.

*Make it smell like roses.*

Nothing. Wait—

Again the tongue comes out, but now rose petals fall from it. Aha! I *can* affect this dream. There's no more sulphur smell now, just roses. I try again.

*Show me where you live. Show me who you are. You can't hide from me.*

I can't breathe. I want to wake up. I want to wake up.

*Show me where you live.*

With all my will, I manage to move my hands, then my arms. I reach up, through the Creeper's body. Though it's still very heavy, somehow it isn't solid and my hands go right through. I can move now. I struggle up to sitting, shoving off the duvet, and the Creeper falls away from me, curling into a dark ball like a tumbleweed. It bounces around my room. I'm winning. I'm winning.

I've got my legs over the edge of the bed. I'm up. I'm staggering across the carpet. I'm at the door. I open the door. I know this is a dream because the sitting room is dark and there's a night light on just outside the bathroom. A sliver of orange street light comes around the edges of the curtains.

*This is where I live. Show me where you live.*

I feel the presence behind me. Looming over me. A coldness, a solid shadow curling around me like a CGI cloak. A feeling of weight. Darkness in my peripheral vision. I'm going to be swallowed. I stumble forwards again, I make it to the French doors and shrug aside the curtain, I unlock and open the doors and step out onto the roof, which is made of glass. The Dream City uncoils below me, and across the roof I can see the doorway to the Sideways Building. The tulip concierge grows out of the glass, right about where O's pigeon cages would be if this were the real roof.

Thinking about the real roof makes me notice how cold it is out here, how loud with wind. Rain is falling and the drops should wake me up but they don't.

*You can't just walk in*, says the tulip. *If you want to get up there, you'll have to fly. Like a bird.*

Of course. Well, I can fly. I always could fly in dreams. I'm lucid. I could just fly away anywhere I want.

Well, whose idea is that? Mine, or the Creeper's? Is this how it got Mel?

The Creeper's shadow is behind me, nudging me forward whether I want to go or not. Its voice is laughing in my ears.

*She walked of her own free will. Maybe she was going to Paradise. Maybe you should go there, too.*

I'm not going near the edge of the roof.

*Of course not, Charlie. You're not that stupid. You're a dream-hacker.*

So fucking condescending. I turn and go back inside, even

as the Creeper wraps arms around me, curls itself round my shoulders all shadowy and foul. I make my way to the kitchen. Kitchens are sane places, kitchens are where the nice things are. But the knife block is there. I see it. My hand goes towards it.

*You want to hurt me, don't you? You're not as nice as you pretend. Do you think you can kill me with a knife? Do you think you can kill your own shadow?*

Darkness licks around me. Next thing I know, I'm holding the big knife. I spin to face the Creeper but it's always behind me, crawling up my back and around my body like a vine. I angle it, trying to use its tip to get under the edge of the darkness where the Creeper surrounds me like a garment. I don't think I can do it without cutting myself.

I don't care.

I have to get it off.

Wait.

Charlie.

That fucking knife is sharp. This is a *dream*. What if the knife is *real*?

What a muppet I'm being.

I drop the knife in the sink, grope around myself half-dreaming, half-awake. I can hear my breath coming in little frightened gasps. My hand closes on O's cast-iron skillet. I grab the handle and bring the pan down on my own left hand.

I feel the blow all the way in my teeth. I find myself on my knees, gasping and whimpering.

I'm conscious. I'm alive. Edgar has come padding in and he's sniffing at me. The Creeper is gone.

Oh, great. And I've peed on the kitchen floor, just like a puppy.

## Sleepwalkers Anonymous

Coffee. Coffee. And Coffee. The three greatest words I know.

I've slept all day and most of the night, but I'm struggling to rouse myself properly. I have a dream hangover. It's as if the dream hasn't ended but remains, invisible, rolling along just under the surface of ordinary life like a movie I've walked out of. I'm on a glass-bottomed boat and the things in the water beneath are bumping against the glass, trying to get at me.

I'm not safe, but it's good enough for now. After I cleaned my pee off the floor, I took out the earring. Now, two cups of espresso later, I feel awake enough to slice potatoes and put on some onions to make a Spanish omelette. At dawn I bring O her Ada Lovelace mug in bed. She's already awake, as usual.

'Stay,' she says. 'Sit down.'

I perch on the end of the bed. Grey light is floating into O's bedroom through a bank of windows that look out the park across the road. There are bookshelves on two of the three other walls; the wall above the bed has a single small painting by Préfète Duffaut. Pink roads lead over bridges and into mountain landscapes that cut across one another in a way that defies three dimensions. It's as if someone chopped up an archipelago and sewed the bits back together skew-whiff. The landscape is bright and happy, not bothered by its own confusion.

I used to be like that. Lately, not so much.

'You had a bad night?'

I tell her a little about it. Not every detail. It's too whacky, and it's hard to talk about without sounding unhinged. Besides, we have more important things to discuss.

'This Dream City that figures in recent matters,' O says finally. 'Melodie wandered into it, and you've mentioned that it's never happened with a client before. What do you think the Dream City really is?'

The question is typical O. She's always looking for the big picture.

'Well, at first I thought it was a part of me. It's been the setting for my dreams for months now. I'd see these people in greyscale with masks, and I thought they represented my anxieties about trying to help clients. Because I never seem to be able to help anyone.'

'And it's been going on since you fell ill.'

'Yes . . . well, the odd thing is that when you're there, you feel as if you've always been there and always will be. I can't say with any certainty when I became aware that I was returning to the same city night after night.'

'But Mel did tell you that she'd been in the Dream City on her own?'

'Yes, she did.'

'So the Dream City isn't necessarily exclusive to you.'

'No, I don't see how it can be. I'm starting to think the sleepers are other people using Sweet Dreams. You know, I can see them but I don't think they can see me. They act like they don't know where they are.'

'And you believe that Mel was tricked into walking off the rooftop.'

I'm shivering as I nod. 'It nearly happened to me, last night. The dreams are so real, so vivid.'

'We know that R.E.M. atonia is supposed to protect you from acting out your dreams. It fails in sleepwalkers. What if someone had a way of making it fail?'

'Bernard Zborowski messed with my brain.'

'And his study was pulled. I don't believe in the collective unconscious,' O says. 'But I do believe that the connectivity of technology is more than the sum of its parts. For example, it's been my observation that the collective can behave in ways that no individual member would behave.'

I yawn. I'm not sure if I'm stressed by what she's saying or just genuinely tired.

'That's why you won't see me networked to anything to do with BigSky or any of the other giants.'

'I thought it was because BigSky has crime connections.'

'It's more that they have too many vulnerabilities. I worry less about other hackers now and more about . . . how can I put this? Malicious entities acting opportunistically in the system.'

Yawn. 'Entities. Check.'

'Of course, people can become paranoid with age. Maybe I'm getting like Stephen Hawking and his constant harping-on about the Machine Uprising.'

'I don't argue with clever people,' I say. 'That's why everything he said must be true, same with everything you say.'

'Except that I never agreed with him,' O retorts, smiling. 'Just because someone is clever doesn't mean they are always right, especially late in their career. Look at Einstein. He kept trying to wriggle out of accepting quantum entanglement, and now we have quantum teleportation. It's hard to change your mind when you get older. The corpuscles get creaky. One must work at it, constantly.'

'So . . . malicious entities, yes, Machine Uprising, no?' I say, eyelids drooping.

'Machine Uprising, sure, but I don't believe the ascent of the machines will be the end of humanity. It's happening already, in any case. Do you smell something?'

'My onions!'

I fly into the kitchen, open the window that leads to the roof, and suck the finger that I've burned because the pot holder was soaking wet when I grabbed the pan. Edgar promptly jumps in through the window and tries to insinuate himself around the precariously balanced Jenga tower of clean dishes on the dish rack.

'What do you mean, the Machine Uprising is happening?' I yell it a little too loudly, and then jump half out of my skin because O has wheeled in behind me. She is staring intensely at the pigeon coop, her hook nose silhouetted against the white clouds.

'It's happening. It started a long time ago; I've been watching it personally for forty-odd years. As each new layer of human-machine interface is built, I realise how deep the relationship is. Maybe the Machine was always seeded within us, from the first tools.'

That's a big stretch for me. Excelsior-Barking Online, 2:2, remember?

'No clue how you can know these things,' I mutter, cowed by O's confidence.

'I know these things because I am nosy and overpaid and have too much time on my hands,' she says. 'We live in an age of groupthink, mind-reading AIs, covert control via anxiety and a large helping of deliberate blindness. Now you tell me you can awaken within a dream of an evolving city, walk around inside it, interact with it, find anyone there and get into their head. And someone is already wandering around there tricking dreamers into sleepwalking. Well, who is that someone? *What* is that someone? And why are they doing it?'

I poke at the onions with a wooden spoon, trying to separate the salvageable bits from the char.

'The why is the easy part, I suppose,' I say. 'There are so many nasty things you could do by dreamhacking, and sleepwalking kind of crosses a bridge between the psychological and the physical. I mean, look at my narcolepsy. Caused by an infection. Only manifests when I'm under stress.'

'Yes. Well, the brain is just an interface between the physical and the abstract.'

I'm close to the edge of another idea, but before the thought can form fully it's interrupted by Edgar. He has committed too much weight in moving towards the bowl of whisked eggs on the counter and dislodges one of O's giant wine glasses which I've unwisely balanced at the top of the tower of dishes. Out of the corner of my eye I see it begin to fall but I'm too far away to hope to stop it. O's uninjured hand shoots out and catches it in mid-fall. Absent-mindedly, she passes it to me without ever taking her eyes off the birds on the roof.

'Bad cat,' she says to Edgar, who is now lapping at the bowl of beaten eggs.

I stare at O. I've never seen anyone move so fast, let alone an eighty-something-year-old lady.

'How—?'

'Used to play squash,' she says, but doesn't meet my eye. 'Reflexes, you know. Are you watching that pan this time?'

'Trying,' I say grimly.

'About the commotion last night. I fear you're in danger from yourself.'

'I'm fine. It was unpleasant, but no lasting damage.'

'And you couldn't move. At all.'

'Not at first. I was right on the edge between being asleep and being awake. I could see the room, but I could see the Creeper, too, until it sort of crawled onto my skin and became part of me. I guess that's the frightening part, how the Creeper didn't only terrorise Mel in her dreams, but actually controlled her body while she was sleeping. It's too fourth-wall for me. I don't want to be zombified.'

I dump the omelette onto a plate and cut it into sections. I help O cut hers because she still has a splint on her wrist. We tuck in.

'The obvious thing to do is stop wearing your earring while you sleep. Don't even leave it nearby.'

'That's not going to solve anything.'

'It might give you a chance to recover your equilibrium. Sort out the difference between reality and dreams.'

'I can tell the difference! Usually—'

O reaches across the table. She's not touchy, O. She avoids physical contact with people, although I've seen her cuddling the birds and sometimes even Edgar, when he's in a tolerant mood.

Now she puts her hand on the table right beside my hand, which is as close as she gets to intimacy, I guess.

'You've been through a lot.'

For some stupid reason, her sympathy breaks me. I stand up. I'm blinking back tears.

'Going to do pigeons,' I blurt, and she graciously ignores my blubbery voice. I put on my rubber gloves and grab my tools, and I head out on the roof to clean the cages. It's a relief to open the cage door and watch the birds fly. Everything's blurry through tears, but I hear them rise into the rain-streaked city sky, their wings making high-pitched whirring noises, and as they leave me behind for rarer climes, I turn to their coop to clean up the poo. I cry and cry. I produce so much snot, I have to go back inside for an extra rag. O's in her room, but the door is ajar and I can hear her talking to someone.

'Watchful waiting for now,' she says. 'I have it under control. I'll contact you when I know more, but don't reach out to me again.'

She'd better not be fucking talking to my parents. I've half a mind to storm in there and demand to know who she's discussing me with, but something in her tone of voice makes me think better of it. Not sure I want to add 'paranoid' to the list of my characteristics which already includes 'delusional'. Sure, she sounds cold; but this is O. She's always been dry and secretive. And she just might think again about this room-mate arrangement if there's too much drama.

Still, when she's in the shower I sneak into her room and have a quick rummage. Behind her bedside table I find some dried, scrunched-up tissues and the tiny backpack that was strapped to Sidney the pigeon. I seize it, but it's empty.

Then I find a tiny scrap of paper, all crumpled up. I grab it and run back to my own room before O can catch me.

No sooner have I shut my door than Shandy pings me.

**Got your message. Let's coffee. I'll come to yours, closer to work.**

Her message is capped off with a rude sound effect. Not sure what she means by 'closer to work' since, being a BigSky employee, Shandy works in the Cloud. I think it means she likes the coffee shop near mine because they have beanbags and Moroccan waiters, and they tolerate her unicorn.

I go over to the window and smooth out the paper. It's a centimetre-wide strip, only about ten centimetres long, and in tiny, neat handwriting it reads:

*Intrusions have been traced. They have recordings and are reverse-engineering. If intruders identified, criminal charges could be forthcoming. Pls advise.*

Hmm. I guess it could be a game? Or something to do with O's security work, more likely. At least it's not about me. I am getting paranoid.

OK. Shandy. I'm not sure what I'm going to say to her, because with all my new subscribers I know she's going to go all entrepreneurial on me and rightly so – I just don't know if I can handle business today. I take a shower and put on a tight wool hat to cover the state of what's left of my hair, and I decide not to wait for her here because I don't want her to run into O. I'm letting myself out of the front door of our building, feeling just a tiny bit better about things, when I spot Roman Pelka pretending to lock up a bike at a bike rack. I say 'pretending' because when he sees me he gets so flustered he tries to pick up the wrong bike – unless he really rides a Hello Kitty bicycle built for nine-year-olds.

Still, I find myself smiling. He's all right, in a goofy, disjointed sort of way. He comes over to me, looking at the pavement and smiling; I can see his dimpled cheeks from here. He's swinging a cloth carrier bag from one hand so that he looks like a sheepish schoolboy, and he doesn't glance up at me until we're almost on top of each other.

'You caught me,' he says. 'I've been standing out here for half an hour trying to work out how to get this to you without look-ing stalkery or otherwise embarrassing you. Don't look inside!'

He passes me the bag. Now I really want to look inside. I hope it's not body parts or something.

'You left it behind in the kebab shop. I wanted to get it back to you. I'm sorry I'm so childish. It's a character flaw, well known in my family. I have four sisters and they all say I'm a hopeless wanker when it comes to . . . No, sorry, I've made a mess of this. Crikey, you look like the bottom of a river. Didn't you get any sleep last night?'

I stare at him. 'Are you even British?' I snap.

'What's that supposed to mean?' he snaps back, defensively. 'I was born here, would you care to be a little more racist?'

'Sorry, I didn't mean it like that. I just meant, where are your bloody manners? I am aware that I look like I live under a bridge, but that's because I've been crying. What is your problem?'

'No, you see, I was trying to distract your attention from what's in the bag so I stupidly said the first thing that popped into my head, right? Look, I'm sorry, luv, but you *do* look a bit shite.'

I'm so annoyed that I cry, 'What's in the bag?' thinking I'll pay him out, since he's clearly embarrassed about whatever he's given me. I open it and grab the contents, holding them up on display for all to see.

Oh.

It's one of the post-surgery bras that O gave me for alteration. It must have fallen out of my bag at the kebab shop. Now it's catching the light and a little bit of rain, too, and passers-by are glancing at Roman and me and then glancing away.

Roman is showing his dimples again and looking pointedly at the fruitseller's display on the pavement nearby.

'Well, I've got to go,' he says. 'I have a lot of work to do.'

'So have bloody I.'

'Yo, Horse!'

I can hear Shandy's heels thundering across the pavement

from the bus stop. I turn, and there she is in full sail: her zebra-print furry coat flying open (lined with purple velvet), her silver hair sticking out like spikes, and her attendant AR menagerie of three-headed snakes, pink cats and Rodney the unicorn bounding around her. Rainbows spring up behind her so vividly that I have to take out my earring or I'll end up with a migraine.

'You look shite,' she says. 'Who's this? Client? He doesn't seem pervy enough, guess you can't tell by appearances. Hey, I have some great ideas for cashing in on this publicity rush, my brain has been fizzing and popping like a— Watchoo staring at, mate? Didn't you ever see a grown woman with a pet unicorn before? Watch out, the horn is sharp and you'll feel it even if there are no visible injuries. Just ask that copper from Swansea who tried to— What? Horse, stop poking me.'

'Roman, this is my friend Shandy. Shandy, this is Roman. He's a consultant with the Met.'

Roman gives me the most pathetically grateful look, presumably for introducing him as if he has a real job. I don't big him up to Shandy for his benefit, but to spare myself from having to listen to her stream of insults if she should find out he's from the Dream Police and operates part-time out of a kebab shop.

'Rodney, leave the nice constable alone,' Shandy says to her AR unicorn.

I can no longer see Rodney, but Roman is looking more relaxed so I can only assume that Shandy's AR has ceased menacing him. Rodney's job is to keep Shandy safe: you know, prevent her from getting mugged/falling in the Thames/stepping in front of a bus. Since Shandy literally has her head in the Cloud all day and doesn't see the so-called real world very well, Rodney is even deductible as a business expense.

'What publicity is this?' Roman asks lightly.

Shandy suddenly finds she has nothing to say and rummages in her bag as if searching for a response.

'Apparently my dreamhacking business got leaked on social media in connection with Mel's death,' I tell him.

His eyes roll up as he quickly Googles.

'Melodie's death is trending, no less.'

'I didn't leak it,' Shandy blurts. 'And Charlie couldn't have. It's not like we're trying to capitalize on Mel's death, not for one second. It's just Charlie's luck. She always lands on her feet. Although I do say, love, you look as if you landed on your head.'

I wince, thinking of Melodie. Also: I can't look *that* bad. Can I?

'What about O, your so-called business associate?'

I shrug. 'She does whatever she wants, you'd have to know her to understand.'

Wish I hadn't said that, because an instant later he cheerily asks, 'Can I meet her?' with his hands in his pockets, rocking back and forth on his heels, looking really happy with himself.

In unison, Shandy and I say, 'No.'

'But she lives right here with you, doesn't she, Charlie? So couldn't I just—'

'Roman,' says Shandy, 'why don't you come with us? We'll get coffee and you can tell us about life as a copper in the Big Smoke.'

Roman looks at Shandy like she's barmy but doesn't resist as we each take one of his arms and between us escort him away from O's building, for all the world as if we are the police and he the civilian. I'm not even sure why we both react that way. Some deep instinct tells me to keep Roman away from O, and I don't question it. At least, not right now, I don't.

# Oneric Crime

'First off,' Roman says, 'Melodie's parents have flown over. Her mum has asked to meet you, if you're available.'

'Me?' My voice comes out as a squeak.

'It's nothing formal, she just feels, since you were the last person to see her alive— No, I don't mean that she blames you, Charlotte. I think she's simply trying to wrap her head around the fact that her daughter was having psychological problems. Apparently Melodie didn't confide such things in her family.'

'I guess... I—'

Shandy kicks me under the table.

'Don't be such a weed,' she says. 'Of course you have to go. We can get a drink after if you want.'

I wipe away tears, looking anywhere but at either of them. 'OK, then.'

Shandy turns to Roman. 'Let's just think about it,' she begins, licking cappuccino foam off her fire-engine-red lips. 'Mel said she attracted stalkers. Do you know if she ever had to get a restraining order? Do we know any of their identities? That would be the first place to look.'

'I'm already on it.' But Roman's eyes move subtly as he makes notes to himself. 'While we're at it, what about you, Charlie? Is there anyone with a grudge against you? You used to do ASMR publicly. That kind of thing must attract a fair amount of unwanted attention from people who still think it's porn.'

Annoyingly, my face heats up. 'There are always negative comments, but I'm careful with my identity. That's one of the reasons why I don't show my face or give personal details.'

'Fair enough.' His fingers are tapping on the table, typing notes. I notice that even though he's out of condition, he has thick, muscular hands that look like they've done physical work.

Not all spidery like your typical uni student. 'Still, if you have a record of anyone you remember as being a problem, send it to me. Worth chasing up.'

'I don't see why. This is about Mel, not about me.'

'Maybe,' Roman says. 'But given that your shingle is out there with Dreamhacker on it and you and Antonio had a relationship, it's not beyond imagining that someone was using Melodie to lure you in.'

He looks straight at me while he says that, his pale green eyes gleaming a warning. Hell, he's serious now.

'That's sick. All of it is sick.' I don't want to deal with it. I yawn.

Shandy calls up my channel on Spacetime, and judging by Roman's reaction she's included him in the privacy lock. My subscribers are still climbing. Lots of comments, too.

Roman reads aloud, ' "Thought your tissue-paper sonata was great. The leaf-crunching one was maybe a little baroque. Too much binaural. I prefer the ones where it sounds totally natural. My favourite is Nana's Kitchen, where it sounds like someone is bustling around cooking and cleaning. That one knocks me out every time. Would you do a woodworking video? Like, hand-carving? Maybe with some gentle sanding?" '

Roman is shaking his head. 'See what I mean about porn? Sorry, only kidding. So tell me, why is your channel called Mariana's Trench Coat?'

'When I was little and couldn't sleep, I'd listen to this old-school ASMRtist on YouTube called Deep Ocean of Sound. I modelled myself on him: no images, no personal involvement, just the pure acoustic experience. So the Marianas Trench is the deepest part of the ocean, right?'

'But yours says "trench coat".'

'Yeah. Cos I'm like a spy, nobody knows who I am, get it? People write to me calling me Mariana.'

Roman shakes his head.

'It's not sad. Stop shaking your head. You just don't get it.'

'Too deep for me . . . bazinga?'

Shandy leans over the table and says, 'I'd like to know how you can claim to work in cybercrime when you're not even up to speed with what people are actually using the platforms for.'

She has a point, but he ignores her and turns his attention to me.

'The Dream City that Melodie described. I wanted to ask more about it in the interview but Donato doesn't let me go off-piste. Is there such a thing? *Where* does it exist? Who or what has created it? These are the questions that interest me.'

'You sound more like a philosopher than a cop.'

He laughs. 'I'm really not a cop. I'm a kind of scientist.'

'First you were the Dream Police, now you're a kind-of scientist? Why do you operate out of a kebab shop?'

'What if I told you, Charlie, that we suspect there has been a dream underworld for years?'

'Who is we? And why?'

'Why, because it flows naturally from the implications of the technology. BigSky lets people construct consensual realities. Part of that building process means sharing information about neural activity so that all the users can sync up in more or less the same virtual space. If you have all that information about someone's patterns, it's not a big leap to decode them and translate them into your own terms.'

'Telepathy.'

'In a word. It's only a matter of time before we have it. The leap between reading someone and feeding back to them is even smaller. The brain heavily reconstructs sensory input. Everything you see, hear and feel has been highly processed by your cortex before you're even aware of it. The reason why headware works so well is because it interferes with your perceptions, makes you see things that aren't really there.'

'I get all that. But I don't need headware to hack dreams. I only use it to record content. I told you, I first learned I could dreamhack when I fell asleep next to someone on the bus who was also asleep.'

'Were you wearing your earring?'

'Yeah, probably, but—'

'And the other person must have been on a BigSky platform. Nearly everybody is.'

'I'm an alternative therapist. I'm not into tech.'

'Well, I am, and I'm telling you that your earring is significant. There's been oneiric crime ever since headware got started. It's just not generally noticed, that's all. It's very hard to separate your own unconscious content from an intrusion by a dream-hacker. That's why Mel's case is of so much interest to us. If you hadn't got involved, there would have been no question that her death was a suicide. But Donato and I think she could have been sleepwalking and acting out a dream.'

'Whoa,' Shandy interjects. 'That's messed-up.'

I kick her under the table.

'I don't believe for a moment that Mel's death was suicide. She probably had no idea what she was doing. But Charlie, you'd be in the best position to tell us what she was dreaming. You were there.'

'Charlie didn't kill her, Roman,' Shandy bristles. She leans across the table, glaring at Roman.

'I never said that.'

'You just bloody well implied it. You questioned her for hours. So let's have it. I don't even understand how you got referred to this case. What made you think there was dream crime?'

Roman answers patiently, or perhaps I should say condescendingly, 'Antonio told the police at the scene that Mel had been receiving therapy for nightmares and sleepwalking. My colleague Yemisi – you met her at the crime scene – she tipped me off. She knows I'm studying sleepwalking deaths.'

'It's a thing?' I blurt. 'People sleepwalking and getting killed?'

'Have you heard of Sleepwalkers Anonymous?'

Shandy stifles a laugh, but it's obvious that Roman's dead

serious. I feel the blood drain from my face. One of the grey-scale sleepers mentioned going to Sleepwalkers Anonymous, right before stepping into the Thames.

'They meet online,' Roman says. 'I've traced most of them to Greater London. Donato went in undercover and found a whole community of lost souls. People with very similar experiences, all within the last year. We've been tracking sleep-related deaths for the last eight months, and they are on the rise throughout London. Oddly, though, the numbers are stable nationwide. Whatever is going on, London is the epicentre.'

And the international business domicile of BigSky.

'What kinds of cases have you seen?' Shandy's bright-eyed and bushy-tailed now. Leaning forward, bracelets jingling, all ears. Roman stays stiffly upright, avoiding eye contact with her. But he looks straight at me.

'A man in Clapham walked to his lock-up in his nightclothes, let himself in and drank a litre of antifreeze. It was treated as suicide, but the man's husband told Donato he'd been sleep-walking a lot in the lead-up to the event. Then there was a young actor who lay down on a railway line – everything to live for, she'd just landed a role in a new series. We checked it out and she was a serial sleep-app abuser and had a system of alerts set up to stop her sleepwalking, but they'd been deactivated that night. We investigated a couple of drownings in the Thames, too, where the sleeping person appeared to have climbed over a rail or just stepped off the bank into deep water and didn't wake up. Charlie, are you OK?'

I've choked on my coffee. I have a coughing fit and need to wipe my eyes. Roman hands me a napkin, watching me closely.

'I'm fine,' I rasp, waving him away. Sleepwalkers stepping into deep water. It's my dream come to life. But how...? I say, 'Go on.'

'The trouble with this is that it's impossible to prove they were asleep without witnesses, and so far the closest thing to a witness that we have is you, Charlie.'

'So... are you police, or are you not police?' Shandy can be very persistent.

'We are consultants to the police. We work in tech-based emergent crime. Sleep crime is a new area and there aren't a lot of funds about, but both Donato and I have experience in more conventional cybersecurity. The murderer – or murderers – here are going to be very difficult to identify, and of course impossible to prosecute. Even if we knew who it was, we wouldn't be able to stop them. The best we can hope for is to work out how the killings are being done, to devise protections. It will be some time before the law catches up to everything that can go wrong with BigSky.'

Shandy is openly baiting him. 'I've heard BigSky is funded by crime syndicates.'

There's an edge in his voice. 'Who told you that?'

'Can't remember.' Of course it was O, who was one of the original funders for BigSky back in the day.

'Hmm. Well, the potted history of BigSky is that it was an anonymous start-up and purely crowdfunded on anarchic principles.'

'Yeah, that never ends badly.' Shandy snorts. He ignores her.

'The whole idea was to get away from corporate greed and government bureaucracy, and for a while they did. But the bigger the organisation became and the more influential they got, the more opportunities arose for anyone with money to buy an anonymous stake and potentially leverage control in the direction they chose. So you could say BigSky have become a victim of their own success. But even if there is criminal money buried in there somewhere—'

'If? Everyone knows there is!' Shandy interjects. 'I work there. It's practically a joke. Necessary evil and all that.'

'Even so, the company still has to offer transparency about their technical practices under the law. Especially where health and safety are concerned. I don't personally think that this sleepwalking issue is coming out of BigSky management, I think it's someone taking advantage of BigSky technology in ways that BigSky probably didn't foresee.'

'OK, well, here's the thing,' I say. 'You can't protect me. You can't catch the killer—'

'Or killers.'

'Or killers. So all you are doing with your investigation is endangering me more. Because now the killer knows about me, knows you are hunting him or her or them, and I'm out here with my arse exposed.'

'I agree your positioning is bad.'

'Well, thanks, mate. Your opinion makes all the difference in the world.'

'I'll give you my advice, Charlie, and I want you to take it seriously. Remove your headware. Don't use it for a while. See if anything changes.'

I nod and make affirmative noises. He smiles. I smile. Of course I have no intention of doing anything of the kind. My headware is my livelihood now, plus it's the only thing that keeps me safe, because it gives O access to my bodycam, and O has Muz, and Muz can rescue me if there's trouble. But I'm not going to disagree with Roman, because then he'll think I'm stupid and I don't want him to think that. Hate to be so obvious, but there's something about him that I like, and I want him to think well of me.

And it's on these little stupidities that matters of life and death have been known to turn, I'm afraid.

When I get home, O is tied up working. At first I think she's coding, because she's in her coding pattern of movement; that is, she rolls up and down past the sitting-room window, one side to the other, looking out over the roof. It's like watching someone obsessively pace. Every so often she will call up her screen and enter a little bit of material or maybe take some out – always on the physical keyboard, she refuses to use a direct reader or anything else platformed on BigSky – and then she stares and stares at the code, and then she goes back to rolling.

But after a long time of this, while I clean the kitchen and the cat box and do a bit of dusting and respond to various messages (there are sixteen from Antonio and I ignore them all), O suddenly goes to her keyboard and starts typing one-handed but fast as an Uzi. So she's not coding, she's writing something. I wonder what. O usually dictates her correspondence; she'll have to ice her hand afterwards and probably take painkillers. But I also know better than to try to tell O what to do.

So I lie on the sofa in the end and watch some more ASMR, just to feel a little better. I listen to some of my own recordings; strangely, I can never put myself to sleep, but I can give myself tingles, and that's what I'm looking for right now. I need that lightness on the top of my head, that sparkling sensation in my scalp, the feeling of my skin thrumming that makes my eyelids droop and my mind go blank, makes everything all right.

But it doesn't work. All I can think of is Mel in the bathtub. Mel on the roof. Mel on the pavement.

Antonio, sobbing on me, holding my body in that intimate way he has, that way which doesn't seem to understand any social boundaries at all. He makes me feel like an animal. Can I trust him?

'Why should you have to?' O says suddenly.

I startle.

'Sorry?'

'Why should you have to trust Antonio?'

She's rubbing cream into her hand – it is sore, that's obvious, and this is the hand that *isn't* injured.

'Are you reading my mind?'

She laughs. 'No, you're muttering loudly enough to be heard. Didn't you know?'

I get up off the sofa.

'Must have been half-asleep.'

'Anyway,' O says, 'you don't have to deal with Antonio any

140

more if you don't want to. You've got clients stacked up like aeroplanes. This thing with his girlfriend—'

'Mel.'

'This thing with Mel, it's tragic and awful, but why you would want to get involved is beyond me.'

'Well, Roman seems to think there was foul play. I have an obligation.'

'You aren't obligated to anyone but yourself, darling. People play you like a harp.'

I wince.

'Sorry. I meant no disrespect to Melodie. People play you.'

It's not what I want to hear, even if it's true.

'I have to see Melodie's mum tomorrow,' I say.

'Have to? Why?'

'Well, because it's the only decent thing I can do.'

'Huh. Are you *sure* no one is blaming you? Because you might want to take representation with you.'

'O, seriously, you're so dark.'

O snorts. 'The situation is dark. I'm merely realistic.'

'No one is accusing me. This poor woman just wants answers. She's come all the way from Canada. It would look worse if I refused to talk to her.' I shudder.

'But you have a booking.'

'Can't you just cancel tonight? I don't know if I have it in me.'

'Of course, darling. But you know what they say about getting back on the horse. It would be good for you. You need to take control. Look at yourself. Every way the wind blows. What do *you* want to do?'

'I don't even know.' But I do know. O's right. I've been struggling to build this business, it's been basically a disaster, and now despite the terrible thing that happened to Melodie, I have an opportunity here. Enquiries are flooding in. If I blow this, another chance isn't going to come along. I'll have to move to my mum's place in Stourbridge and work in the Co-op. She'd love that, bless her. But I can't just give up; it'd be going backwards.

141

'I just want to be a bit careful with new clients.'

'In case one of them turns out to be the Creeper? I am vetting everyone carefully. There's one rather famous person who wants to consult you, but I won't book until I'm certain it's safe for you.'

'I can't do a famous person tonight, O. I'm not up to it.'

'Not tonight. It's only Emile from downstairs. He feels he's making progress and he wants another session.'

'That gives me time to pre-sleep, then.'

Because I find that I have a plan. I'll get back on the horse; I'll help Emile. But after that . . . I have a cunning plan. Remember how I said when I first go into someone else's dream and say they are in their house, I dream it as though it's happening in my house? And then it slowly changes until I can see and feel what they can feel?

Well, now that I'm watching out for the Creeper, I reckon I can turn that to my advantage. Because if the Creeper is a person hacking into my dream, there will be moments in the beginning when they are acclimating to my reference frame. And if I'm quick and smart and daring, maybe I can get a glimpse of who they really are. Where they are in *their* dreamspace. What the inside of *their* head looks like.

At least, that's the plan I have when I start.

What really happens is that I fall asleep in my own bed and wake up in a hospital bed beside a corpse.

**Secret Diary of a Prawn Star**
**Entry #52**
**Codename:** Chaplin
**Date:** 23 September 2027
**Client:** Me
**Payment in advance:** N/A
**Session Goal:** Identify Creeper by reverse-hacking it
**Location:** My bed
**Narcolepsy status:** Fair
**Nutrition/stimulants:** Tea
**Start time:** 1.01 a.m.
**End time:** 1.18 a.m.

The corpse is very old. He has wrapped his arms around me and they are cool and floppy. His eyes are wide open, unseeing, and his blackish tongue droops out of his dry mouth.

I suck in air with a ragged squeak. I shoot out of that bed so fast that I guess I actually push off the dead body to get leverage, because it topples to the floor as I back away from the bed in panic. I grope around me for anything I can use for a weapon. My hand lights on a fire extinguisher and I brandish it defensively. It turns into a hatchet.

I have to get out of here. I have to change the setting. Make something happen to save me.

*Wait. Think, Charlie. We had a plan.*

I remember now. I'm here for a reason. I have to learn everything I can from the setting. It's definitely not anywhere I've ever been, in a dream or otherwise. I'm not even sure this is really a hospital, because the room looks more like a hotel room except for the bed. If it's a hospital, it's a posh one. There are enormous windows looking out on...? Where are we?

I see the building opposite through the window and my earring rapidly cross-references it against my street maps.

We are in the London Clinic. The big room right over the front door.

OK, that's something. This person has set their dream in an expensive private hospital. But why are they pretending to be a corpse?

The body is definitely dead. But it gets up off the floor and walks around stiffly, with home-made-horror-movie squishy cracking noises. Now it is blocking the door.

'You again!' the corpse says, folding its arms with an unreal shuffling sound. 'Not dead yet.'

I don't know which one of us it's referring to.

'When is it going to start working?' the corpse says.

'I don't know what you're talking about.'

'The medicine, the damned medicine. Isn't that why I'm here? So you can rebuild the dead networks? Aren't you going to monkey around in my circuits or something? Why else would you be carrying that toolbox?'

I look at the axe in my hands and sure enough, it's become big red metal workman's toolbox. The kind that probably contains a full set of socket spanners. What on earth is the corpse talking about?

'So go on and fix me, then. I'm not dead yet.'

Then it turns to the door, opens it and walks out.

'Hey! Where are you going?'

'To find my target and kill them, of course.'

'Why would you do a thing like that?'

Now I'm in therapist mode. I'm not even scared any more, even though there's a strange smell coming from the corpse. It's not a dead-body smell, not even an organic smell. It's a sharp, chemical tang. The smell makes my little hairs stand up in my dream. I can see them on my dream forearm.

'Because it's the only thing I can contribute. Other people have working brains and mine is a ruin. Can't remember things. Head full of nightmares.'

'Nightmares are horrible,' I say, just to keep it talking. 'But you clearly have a working brain. We're standing here talking to each other.'

'No we're not.'

And now we're in the Dream City. We are in a rundown park near one of the canal bywaters, where neon-bright canoes are moored for repair. It is all very familiar in the way that you 'remember' things in dreams even though you've never really experienced them. There is deep backstory in the Dream City, as if I've been coming here all my life *even though I haven't*. Someone obviously has, because everything about it is vivid. I can smell the trees and even the fruit on the trees. Greyscale people are sleeping in their branches, draped like leopards.

'Why did you assault me?' I ask the corpse. Its body and face still look the same, although now it has trainers on in addition to its velvet dressing gown.

'Just trying to get your attention. Parts of my brain are dying. When can I expect results? I'm a results-oriented individual, you know. Get it done.' The corpse turns and starts to shuffle off into the parkland.

'Wait!' I say. 'Who are you? What do you mean, I'm supposed to rebuild your networks? What's the matter? Why are you a corpse? Can't we just talk about this?'

The corpse ignores me. I run after it, grab it by the shoulder, give it a shake.

It falls apart. Messily. Like Stilton cheese when you try to put it on a posh water biscuit. As its head hits the turf, the mouth says, 'Remind me to give you the last of those tapes to convert. I keep forgetting.'

Then the face crumbles bloodlessly into many wet chunks.

# Our friend can go again

'Thank you for seeing me,' Melodie's mother says. Her Canadian accent is so cute. It's the day after my corpse dream and the late-night session with Emile the hairdresser, and we are sitting in the sun outside a cafe near the Southbank Centre, close to where Mel's orchestra are rehearsing. Some other harpist will be playing her part. I can't begin to describe how it makes me feel to look at Mel's mum. Her daughter is gone for ever. I should have been able to save her.

I start babbling about how sorry I am. She closes her eyes and nods. I can tell she's not taking it in. She's put up a mental shield and everything I say will roll off it. I shut up. We sit for a while saying nothing, watching the river traffic.

Then she says, 'Melodie was always too sensitive. Even when she was a child. Save the whales. Save the worms in the garden. When I thinned the lettuce, she would take the little plants I'd removed and replant them in plastic bottles from the recycling. Maybe this shouldn't come as such a shock, really. I think all artists are vulnerable to mental illness, don't you?'

Oh, god. What do I say? Do I lie?

'Ms Tan, I'm not a doctor or anything like that. I only met Melodie a few times. But for whatever it's worth, I don't think she was mentally ill. I'm not sure what happened. I know she'd been sleepwalking. I don't think this was suicide.'

I can't believe I said that. I'm not supposed to be talking about this. In a minute I'm going to be spilling my guts to this poor woman, and how will that help? I'll feel better, but what could possibly ease her mind? Pain is bleeding off her and I'm just going to make it worse.

But she doesn't appear to take in what I've said. She carries on.

'If only we'd known, maybe we could have helped. She worked so hard, you know? She hardly ever came home. We Spacetimed every week to stay in touch, and of course we attended many of her concerts virtually. She seemed . . . strong. I just don't know what to think. It's like she had this secret life I didn't know about. But you have to let your children go. You can't keep them safe. I'm sorry, I don't even know what I'm saying—'

I put my hand on hers, and when I touch her skin I remember how I did the same when I first met Melodie. And look where that got us.

Melodie's mum gulps. She hasn't actually shed any tears, but she is shaking. It takes her a minute to pull it together. 'Right,' she says. 'So we need to look into the sleepwalking. I just have to find out what happened. I have to know. It's too late, but somehow that doesn't seem to matter.'

'There's one thing I've been wondering,' I say carefully. 'Who is Melodie's patron? Did she tell you?'

'Patron? What do you mean?'

Uh-oh. Why do I always. Say. The wrong. Thing??????

'Nothing, never mind.'

She appears to assimilate this, throwing her head back and shaking her hair a little like she's trying to get control. 'If she had a patron, she never mentioned it. Melodie had many, many admirers. A lot of older men, of course. That's the way of the world, I guess. There was a man from Dubai, I'm not going to say he was a sheikh because I really don't know, but he sent her a Jeep when she was seventeen. We made her give it back, of course.'

'Of course.' And here I thought I'd done well from my ASMR subscribers. People sent me hand-stitched journals and once I got a baseball cap. A Jeep would be on another level.

'I'll check her e-mails and let you know if I find anything,' she says to me. There's a deep intelligence in her eyes, and somehow I feel ashamed. I'm meddling in things I don't understand.

'I'm so sorry,' I keep saying. Every time I say it, she looks like she's been slapped. Can't do anything right.

When it's over, I'm relieved, but my state of mind is fucked. I stagger across Waterloo Bridge and get on the Northern Line.

Some days, riding the Underground feels like an act of ritual humiliation. I have a bad habit of looking at people. I don't mean making eye contact – I would never do that, this is London – but looking at people when they aren't looking back. Watching out of the corners of my eyes. I rarely get caught because people are so involved with themselves, they're busy in their own private AR worlds.

I study people because I'm trying to figure out how to do it. Be one of them. They make it all look so easy. Ever since my illness started, on any given day I'm all but writhing with insecurity and fear; I always feel like I'm two millimetres from falling apart. When I'm on the Tube I try to act like everyone else. I envy other people's shoes and bodies and hair and trousers and handbags and tiaras and body tech. Maybe I'm just needy. I never feel I am quite plausible.

I never feel real.

Real or not, I bump into Antonio changing trains at Leicester Square. Physically bump into him. He pretends it's an accident, but I don't think it is. We're still on one another's tracking after Mel's death.

He throws his arms around me wordlessly. All the people and their shoes and handbags fall away from my mind. I can feel him breathing and I can hear his heart beating, slow and dependable. He takes my hand.

'Come with me, Charlie.'

We get back on the Underground and now it feels completely different because I'm with him. He takes me to his flat in Shepherd's Bush. The place is like a monk's cell. There's a bare, stained futon on the floor, a small fridge in the corner, a kettle. The wardrobe looks like it dates from c. 1975. One leg has been propped up with an empty sports supplement bottle. There's a yellowed mirror bolted to the wall and a couple of cardboard boxes stacked under the frosted window. No decorations. As I glance around, I realise I'm violently jealous of what he's earning, that he can afford to live without roommates. He even has his own shower room with toilet.

'It's good to hold you,' he murmurs, folding me into his arms. I'm wary at first, because I know what he's like, but as the feel and scent of him surround me, I find myself embracing him back, fiercely. My lips are against his neck. He makes a rumbling sound deep in his throat and pulls me closer. Heat radiates through his T-shirt as my hands range across his back. Muscle. Strength. The next thing I know we are kissing. His tongue tastes so good. Everything about him is lovely and just right.

I want him. Immediately. It's like this compulsion.

'Do you still use an implant?' he whispers, and my entire body shivers. The ring of happy muscles high up and deep inside me gives a spasm of anticipation even as I hear the small, still-rational part of myself say:

'Are you fucking kidding me? You know I don't.'

'Such a shame,' he groans, and his hands are up inside my shirt. Hot and muscular hands, just like the rest of him. Antonio isn't one of those fit guys who acts like they're doing you a favour by humping you. He pays attention during sex, and he can bring everything out of you that you've got, and then some. Before I know what is happening, my shirt is up over my head and he's kneeling in front of me, licking my nipples, biting me, the whole works. I'm caught. I lose track of myself for a moment. He's giving my body his total attention. He's running his hands all over me in a way that is always, always just right. Antonio knows how to touch me.

I grab his head and pull away, and he tilts his face up. All dark eyes, cheekbones, eyebrows two artistic slashes and his lips swelling as he smiles at me.

'We will just play, then. Don't worry. I can control myself. I have been practising the many disciplines.'

149

He's so funny, but I'm thinking of Mel.

'We can't, Antonio. This is wrong.'

'How can pleasure be wrong? We both need this. This day is all pain, otherwise. Life shouldn't be just about pain, Charlie.'

I'm barely listening to his words. I'm feeling his breath on my skin.

'We can't bring back the dead,' he murmurs, punctuating his words with tiny kisses all over my belly. 'But we. We are alive, my friend, and life is for the pleasure. I know you want me. You know I want you. Is a shame about the contraception, but we can work around this. Look!'

He points to his jeans. The rocket's on the platform and firing up to go, no doubt about that. I'm aching inside with a combination of memory and anticipation.

'Why can't you just use a bloody condom?' I groan.

He waves his hands around dramatically, eyes flashing.

'You don't understand. The loss of sensation, it's criminal. I am the physical person. I can only have the best, or nothing.'

If there's any logic in that, I don't follow it. I'm so hot and juiced up, and I can see the outline of his business and I just want a piece of him so much. He falls backwards on the futon and beckons to me. I follow. Can't seem to help myself.

I unbuckle his belt and his cock springs into my hands. It's gorgeous. I remember it so well, dark and smooth and unreasonably stiff. I slip my mouth over the head of it and suck, but I can't get more than the first half into my throat without choking and gagging. I now remember that it takes both hands and my mouth to get Antonio off, his digger really is that big. When I feel it in my mouth I remember how it fitted inside my body – barely – and again all my inner bits start clenching and throbbing uncontrollably.

'This is wrong,' I say, coming up for air.

I hear the smile in his voice as he strokes my hair, my skin, and says, 'You like that it's wrong. You love that it's wrong. Let me lick you. I want to make you come.'

Just the sound of his voice has set me off. He drags at my clothes and I start coming even before he has my pants off, and when his tongue gets on my clit I almost go through the roof. The inside of my body is firing off like a pachinko machine. When it gets like this, I need to have the fucking. The more times I orgasm without fucking, the more cock I need to finally finish me off.

'I need it,' I gasp. 'Now, Antonio! Fuck me now.'

He laughs. 'You don't know how I want to, but—'

I slap him across the face.

'Now! Fuck me, you fucking bastard!'

I don't really know what's come over me. I've never slapped anyone in my life. He pulls back, whips around, rummages in his trousers. Wallet. Money spills on the bed, Brazilian reals.

'WTF?' I shriek. 'I want you to fuck me, not pay me!'

'Condom,' he gasps. 'Emergencies. Forgive me, God, for my weakness.'

He turns his eyes towards heaven and says a few more words in Portuguese. Then Antonio and his condom are on top of me, he's drilling me, I'm clenching and wrapping my legs around him, scoring his back with my nails. Melodie is dead and I'm fucking her gorgeous boyfriend and it's so so so so so so good.

Antonio is saying quite a few things I can't understand. I don't know if they're dirty, but he sounds inspired and works me over for quite a while in various positions before he finally comes and collapses on me. Then he rolls us over so I'm on top, still skewered by his giant, indefatigable prong.

Sorry, but there really isn't a better word for it.

'I like it when you tell me what to do,' he gasps in my ear. 'Can you feel how hard our friend still is? Two for the price of one condom, yes? Our friend can go again.'

And he does. For that I can almost forgive him for calling his penis 'our friend'.

We could have been doing this all along, I realise, as we lie there after the second round. All that silken skin and sculpted muscle spread on the mattress beside me, his dark hair that smells of limes falling around my face, the musk of his scent making me primitive. I'm dizzy, can scarcely see. If only I had insisted on condoms back when we were together, instead of slinking off and poisoning myself with synthetic hormones. We could have—

'You're thinking too much,' he says, touching my forehead. 'No thinking. It spoils the delight.'

He goes down on me again. I don't know what happens to the condom, but at the end of all that cunnilingus as my back arches and my pelvis rocks up off the bed, I'm aware of a sudden stab of pain and I hear myself yelling, 'Ow, ow, help!'

'Charlie, what's wrong, I thought you were enjo—'

I'm choking with laughter. 'My toes! Cramp!'

Trust me to have toe-curling sex and end up with swimmer's cramp. Horrible, but how can I care? Ripples of the orgasm are still washing over me. Antonio smiles and massages my foot. Soon every muscle in my body feels like it's made of bright liquid. I lie there smelling his skin and just breathing. So happy. His lips are by my ear again.

'I'm going to miss you, Charlie. Maybe one day you can come to São Paulo.'

'What do you mean, São Paulo?'

But I already know. It's so obvious, I should have known. The reals spilling out of his wallet. I sit up, feebly trying to get my scarf back on before he can see what's become of my hair. It's the only thing I'm still wearing. Ish.

'When do you leave? Today?'

'In an hour I must get the train to Heathrow. I'll fly to Toronto tonight for to the funeral, and then back home. I want to see my family.'

'An hour.' I look around at his bare futon. It's soaking wet, and now I understand why the room looks so empty. Duh.

'Don't be upset, dear Charlie—' he begins.

But I'm not upset. I'm relieved.

'Not much time,' I tell him. 'Let's get in the shower. I'll give you a farewell blow job if you reckon you're up to it.'

'I am up to it, and more, for I have another condom,' he tells me solemnly. 'For strict emergencies, you understand.'

Mel's body is being flown back to Toronto, which is the ostensible reason why Antonio has to leave now. I ride the train to the airport with him. He hasn't shaved, and in full daylight I notice little flecks of grey in his beard. I never asked how old he was; he looks about twenty-eight but maybe he's older than that. It's like sitting next to a movie star. Everyone else on the train is flat and dull, but even with his face shadowed by his hoodie, Antonio is a work of art. He has draped a companionable arm around my shoulders and I lean into his warmth. I want him to have nothing to do with Mel's death. Obviously. Because if he somehow orchestrated it, then I'm complicit.

I should not be snuggling with him. I am a very bad person.

'She used to skateboard,' he tells me. 'When she was a kid. She had to give it up. Too much risk of injury. I saw a video of her once, she was maybe ten? She was flying, those arms spread out, and the way she floated her weight over the board. She was a person who did everything well, or not at all.'

'How did you meet her?' I do not want to know this. Why am I asking this? Why can't people leave me out of things?

'She was a Pilates client at the studio. You know Assan? She worked with him, and we just got to know each other.'

Then he bursts into tears. Oh, god. This is the Tube. Doesn't he understand there's a national rule against breaking down on the Tube?

'I can't look at her mother, Charlie. So composed. Such dignity. And I am breaking to the pieces. I have no right to break to so many pieces.'

I pat his hand. 'It doesn't work that way, love. Everyone expresses their grief differently.'

Still, my heart squeezes. I'm feeling very crap about myself.

I liked Mel so much, and she's dead and I've just shagged her boyfriend . . . People don't know what a terrible person I really am. I pretend to be nice. Like, right now I'm comforting Antonio but in the back of my mind I'm still wrangling with what O said about him.

I mean, he can't be the Creeper. It can't have been him in my dream last night.

O has planted the seeds of doubt. She's so cynical. *Always the boyfriend. He was there. How did she get out of the room?* All of those things make sense, but Antonio isn't like that. Besides, what possible motive could he have? The two of them were obviously in love.

Or is that just what I've been telling myself so I won't have to think about Antonio and me as a . . . thing?

Fuck, what if *I'm* the Creeper? I have as much reason as anyone to get rid of Mel. Look how quickly Antonio came running to get me into bed after she died! Maybe the Creeper is a manifestation of my subconscious desires.

No. I'm losing it now. I wasn't even thinking about Antonio (much) until he messaged me. And I had no clue Melodie existed before then. On logic alone, the Creeper can't be me. *Whew.* So there's that, then.

This is fucked-up. Have I mentioned this lately?

'Charlie! What's the matter? You're shaking.'

I'm shaking because I don't trust him. Or myself. Or anyone.

'I'm not feeling very well.' I don't sound even a little convincing, but he nods sympathetically.

'It's a lot of . . . trauma.'

I love the way he pronounces 'trauma'. Sounds like 'trowma'. I melt a little, and then I remember that I've got to be less gullible. Having a lovely accent doesn't make someone a good guy.

We arrive at the airport and I walk with him as far as I can before he has to go through security. It's not an ideal place to have a serious conversation.

'I wanted to let you know the memorial service for Mel is

going to be livestreamed. The family wanted to keep the guest list very small, but there will be a string quartet and some poetry readings, and Laszlo Verccilli is going to sing. I send you the link, OK?'

My mouth is dry. I nod.

'Are you sleeping?'

'Too much,' I say. 'I'm sleeping a lot.'

'But no problems? Bad dreams?'

I shake my head. He sounds so sincere.

'And you?' I have already planned my response if he asks me to do dreamwork on him – because it would be an obvious way to draw me in if he is somehow behind all this. I've already decided to say that I can't handle it and I'm taking a break.

'I used meds to sleep last night,' he says. 'My dreams, they were very strange, I am getting chased by the police, of course, and there's one dream where animals are biting my hands. But I don't ... you know, I don't think there's anything to it. I'm just ... processing.'

'Have the police asked you more questions?' My voice goes up in a very unnatural way and I feel like the world's worst actor. He glances at me sharply.

'No. Have they questioned you again?'

'Well, not exactly ...' Why am I so bad at this? He could be a killer, he could be the one who tried to make me stab myself, and I'm just standing here with my teeth chattering, talking to him like everything is normal.

'Listen, Charlie. I wasn't going to tell you this, but I have to tell someone. Please, I can trust you, right? We've been through so much together.'

I give a frozen nod. What's he going to confess? Oh god, those dark eyes, look at his skin, I can see the pulse in his throat, I can smell that lovely scent he has around his neck, must be pheromones or vaporised testosterone or something.

'I paid for the suite Mel was staying in that last night. I let her think it was the person who usually pays—'

155

'The Russian patron?'

'Yeah, usually. But this time it was me. I had broken down the door, so we couldn't stay in the first room. I didn't want to cause her embarrassment, I wanted her to feel better, to feel safe, and the only available suite was one of the most expensive in the hotel. If she had been on a lower floor it would not have been so easy for her to get on the roof, we could have stopped her—'

I grab his hand to stop him blaming himself.

'Where would you get that kind of money?'

'It was my savings. I was foolish. I used all the money I had. My sisters are paying for my flight home. I am broke. I am just a yoga instructor. She was a goddess. I wish—'

He breaks off, shaking his head. Tears stream openly down his face.

'I know. I wish, too.'

'Charlie, there is more.'

'OK,' I say, but I feel a yawn coming on.

'I am leaving on a false passport. The police have me on a no-fly list.'

'Oh, fucking hell.'

'I did nothing wrong! There was a contract dispute between BigSky and the orchestra over sponsorship terms. It was going on for months. The police think BigSky paid me to be with Mel. They think the Russian patron is me and that I slipped up and used my own money for the higher suite, that all the time I was trying to undermine her career and the orchestra. They think that I was involved in her death but none of that is true. None of it, Charlie.'

'How would that even work?' If I focus on the facts, I won't get upset, right?

He shrugs elaborately.

'The police think BigSky are harassing Mel in her dreams, trying to send a message to the orchestra by intimidation. The Pilates studio where I met Mel is owned by somebody who is connected to BigSky, so the police think this means I work for them.'

'Harassing her in her sleep – so this really is a thing? There are other dreamhackers, not just me, and people know about it?'

'Again, I do not know, Charlie. But it's BigSky. They work in these technologies, they do business with everybody. You must draw your own conclusions. All I know is, I have never taken anything from BigSky. I am not a materialistic person, I cannot be bought. For the love of god, everything I own is in this bag!'

He's getting agitated, waving his arms around, showing me the discount-brand sports bag that holds all his worldly possessions minus four condoms, but I'm still thinking.

'But so ... are they saying you whispered in her ear at night, made her doubt herself, made her anxious ... how?'

'They are painting me to be the villain. And I brought you in, that was my big mistake – no offence, Charlie – but it looks like I was using you to hurt her. But I would never harm Mel. Or any person I was with. It's not how I was brought up. It's not the code of how I live—'

'Wait, Antonio. They really think I'm involved? On purpose? But they didn't arrest me.'

'They don't have to. They will watch you. They are watching us now. Charlie, I am sorry.'

We stand there silently, both of us staring at the ground. In my peripheral vision I check for CCTV cameras. Stupid. It's an airport; they are everywhere. Antonio has just implicated me in his getaway, and I'm standing here as if that's fine with me because he's cute and sexually satisfying. I am a dick.

'Happy yoga, then,' I say weakly.

Antonio throws his arms around me, bites my neck, ruffles my hair, kisses both cheeks. I'm trembling and my armpits are damp, and I yawn out of pure stress.

'I'm so grateful for your friendship,' he says. 'I wish I were not such a coward.'

Then he leaves me standing there, watching his retreating arse and aching up inside myself, and yawning again and again.

# Unique and impactful

'Another one bites the dust,' O says. I am straining the chicken soup she made while I was out. She is brushing Edgar. The evening news roundup is running on the surface of the fridge, so that my story of Antonio's planned flight is interspersed with reports of the latest spasm in the stock market due to politics I don't understand. 'Of course, he's just a hireling. Probably he's been told to leave the country.'

I smile. 'You know who you remind me of? Roman.'

'Really.' Her tone is so arch that the single word makes me laugh out loud.

'Well, I mean, you both have such dark minds. Always imagining the worst possible motives for people.'

'I didn't get to this age without learning how to watch my back,' O says. 'Now, let's have our soup and I'll show you some footage I found for you.'

Meera Bhango is both photogenic and likeable. She's plump, thirty-ish, dressed stylishly with gold trim on the edge of her hijab that picks up the warmth of her skin tones. Her smile looks genuine and her voice ... she'd be good at ASMR. I get tingles just listening to her and it's hard to focus on her words because her tone is making my scalp purr. She's being interviewed by a nasal Swedish journalist wearing rimless vanity specs; he pretty well kills the tingles every time he opens his mouth.

**So Meera, you're out there on the neural frontier, exploring that innerspace with your company, and is it safe to say that there are few laws on this frontier because lawmakers don't really understand it?**

Well, Bryson, it's not that we're living on a frontier, that's the wrong way to think about it. A frontier implies there's an undiscovered land just out there beyond our knowledge. No, we're living on the growth edge of an organism. The creature that our noosphere is becoming is actually creating itself as we speak. Human knowledge keeps pushing outwards, making more connections, and new regions of understanding form and light up.

**Noosphere, now there's a word we don't hear every day!**

Well, if we have our way at Little Bird you'll be hearing more of it soon. 'Noosphere' is a funny word that has never really caught on, but it comes from the Greek 'gnosis' meaning simply 'to know'. The noosphere is the knowledge-space that we all share.

**What are you hoping to do with Little Bird?**

We wanted a way to work outside academia, to make a contribution to the public interest without having to work off the increasingly Byzantine system of grant applications and so forth.

**Wait a second... that sounds just like BigSky.**

BigSky started out just like us. But because they are crowd-funded, they have a much wider remit. I respect BigSky, but with Little Bird we're trying to do something different.

**Hence the name?**

We are intentionally small. We're privately funded, but unlike BigSky we have a narrow focus. Our goal is to build bridges between the fast-growing sector of neurotransmitter regulation and shared AR-space. We're bridging medicine and neural tech.

**You recruited Bernard Zborowski from BigSky, and let's be honest: since the global success of Spacetime, Big Sky has deep pockets. How did you get a developer like him to walk your way?**

Most people in this field aren't as concerned with money as they are with creating something new. Don't get me wrong – you have to pay people – but for someone like Bernard who can write his own ticket, how we attracted him was to say, 'Look, your work and our work would go really well together. We can do something unique and impactful.' We're looking to find ways to personalise digital gating codes so that people can better control their own minds, using AR as a feedback system or, in some cases, maybe even as an electrochemical triggering system. That's a fairly narrow focus compared to the broad-brush commercial techniques of BigSky.

**Whenever we start talking about mind control, we're into the realm of science fiction where governments control people through the chips in their heads.**

Yeah, this isn't that. I mean, with any system, whether you carry it in your pocket, in your body tissue or wear it as jewellery, any communication system can be used to surveil you and control you, but it's more likely to be used by marketers than the government. Actually, what we're realising is that governments can barely control things like taxation and voter registration, so they don't have time to be getting inside people's heads! But what we are starting to see a lot of is exploration of consensual realities, sharing of virtual spaces. Much of this is surprisingly proactive and positive and not at all sinister. Other uses of shared space are definitely commercial – we've all been accosted by AR spambots and some of them can be quite convincing—

**I know, I nearly bought fake Arsenal tickets from a kid who looked so real!**

Exactly. We've all been there. With Little Bird, we're looking to give people back control of their minds, equip them with tools to stay free of these large-scale hypnotic effects that characterize our age and affect us all. We want you to reclaim yourself from the groupthink – that's our mission.

O switches off the recording and pours some more tea. I'm still tingling from the sound of Meera Bhango's voice. I would be more convinced by her sweet and reasonable demeanour if I hadn't seen her colleague Bernard Zborowski's signature on the letter informing me that BigSky couldn't take responsibility for my narcolepsy and that I'd waived my right to complain about side effects.

'What do you think?' O says.

'I can't see any point in pursuing Bernard now that he's not at BigSky anymore,' I say.

'Of course you can't pursue Bernard; you signed what you signed. But how about Meera Bhango? Would it be worth speaking with her? Maybe they can do something for you.'

'My narcolepsy, you mean? Yeah, maybe.' I'm actually not thinking about myself right now. I'm thinking about Mel, and Mel's mum. And Antonio shagging me senseless before leaving town.

My Spacetime pings. It's Roman. Blood rushes to various body parts, seemingly at random, and I'm suddenly conscious of the state of my hair.

'Excuse me, O, I'm just going to take this Spacetime in my room.'

'Enjoy,' says O in a deeper baritone than usual.

Roman is sitting on a bus when he Spacetimes in. I position myself so that I'm on the edge of my bed, opposite him. I edit out most of the mess in my tiny room and brighten up my own appearance quickly before letting him see me.

'*So I searched the hotel records to find out who had rooms on the same floor as Melodie, especially the ones adjacent to hers. I'm working through the names, but so far I don't see anyone suspicious. Thought you'd want to know.*'

'*Thanks*,' I say. Then I stammer, '*A-and I'm going to take off the earring tonight, I really am. It's just that I need it for certain things.*'

'*I reckoned you would ignore me,*' he says placidly. '*Now, about her patron. The one who paid for the room?*'

'*Yeah?*' I squeak. I can feel myself flushing.

'*Well, get this. Both rooms – the first suite where the door got broken, and the second one as well, were paid for by Antonio.*'

I feel like Roman's reached into my ribcage and grabbed hold of my insides, and how could that not show? It's only Spacetime, so he can't possibly notice how agitated I've got, or how my hands are shaking – right? And he definitely can't know I've just been banged repeatedly by Antonio and his emergency condoms. I've got to get a grip.

'But... Roman, that can't be right. Antonio hasn't any money. I mean, yeah, he's a high-end yoga instructor, but none of those people have money-money. They rely on patrons themselves, they stay in rich people's pool houses or spare villas. Antonio lives out of a backpack year-round.'

'Maybe yes, but the payment for Melodie Tan's rooms traces to his bank account. So... be careful, OK, Charlie?'

'Someone might be trying to set him up,' I bleat.

'They might. We'll know more when we bring him in.'

'But he left the country.'

'He left the country? When?'

Oh shit. Fuck me.

'I... I think I'm going to fall asleep.'

Roman leans forward, and even in Spacetime I can feel his calming vibe coming through. Those solid hands, clasping his own knees as he bends towards me, or the image of me, in his own Spacetime.

'You're OK, Charlie. Have a drink of water or something. We can't be sure Antonio is responsible for this, even if he did pay for the rooms and lie about it. It's just that, when it comes to murder and relationships, Occam's razor usually applies.'

He looks truly grim. And I feel truly... sleepy.

'I have to go.'

I switch off the link, but before he vanishes he says, 'Charlie, get off your headware!'

I said the same thing to Melodie, and she didn't listen to me. Maybe I should listen.

I don't know what to believe about Antonio. On the one hand, it's a point in his favour that he came clean with me about the second hotel room. On the other hand, if he was going to tell me about the one hotel room and the false passport, he may as well have told me everything. Why didn't he?

I'm not cut out for this kind of intrigue.

I call Shandy and babble at her. About Meera and Bernard and Little Bird. About Roman telling me to remove my headware. She listens for a while. Then she says, 'I'm taking a sick day tomorrow. We're going to go deal with this Bernard Zborowski character once and for all. I've had enough of seeing you messed about and scared.'

'You can't bunk off work for me—'

'Why not? I worked overtime four nights last week. I'll say I have a doctor's appointment for exhaustion. May as well, if I'm honest.'

'But you're never tired.' I'm yawning as I speak.

'Take off your earring for the night,' Shandy says. 'Just get one good sleep with no corpses and no threats and no nothing. OK?'

'But O told me to leave Bernard alone. She said there's nothing to be gained.'

'She obviously hasn't been introduced to my cricket bat.'

'I'm not good at confrontations,' I say, wincing.

'No kidding. But I am. Now go to sleep.'

I pull off the earring and lie in my room listening to the cars going by outside. The din from the pub down the road reaches me faintly up here. I feel small and remote and horribly naked without my headware, but sleep comes just as quickly as ever.

# Doctor Lady Reverend

Because I'm sleeping without my earring, I can't access Sweet Dreams – or any BigSky technology. Yet I have to remind myself that this dream is really 'only a dream' because it has the heightened vividness of an enhanced dream.

I'm looking down on the Sweet Dreams platform from a balcony in the Dream City. Here the platform is a literal one: a smooth, grey plane transecting the metropolis, a cheesy intrusion of 1980's-style graphics on the messy, high-resolution splendour of the place. When I pay more attention, I notice that technically Sweet Dreams consists of multiple platforms, several tiers with the largest on top like an upside-down wedding cake. It has been under construction since I can remember, but I have never seen it from this outside perspective – from a bird's-eye perspective, as it were. It looks so real that I have to keep reminding myself: without the earring, my dream is only my dream and everything in it is purely my own interpretation.

It has to be.

Well, in that case, I've become surprisingly fluent in dreaming. Maybe it's the cumulative effect of all the sessions I've been doing for others, because even my own dream is more lucid than before I got sick. I can metacognate even inside the unfolding events. I can control what's going on.

A bonkers amount of scaffolding surrounds the platform, whose surface is pierced intermittently by cranes and decked with ladders. The infrastructure for the finished construction stretches for kilometres into the distance, so that Sweet Dreams will ultimately transect a great swathe of the Dream City – if it all gets built. The completed regions feature greyscale people wandering around acting out their inner fantasies; I guess these are supposed to be the beta-users, but I can't forget the other dream in which they were drowning themselves. Here they just wander around aimlessly, having imaginary conversations and performing routine actions that make them look like a drama class doing warm-ups.

That's when I realise I'm not alone. Meera Bhango is standing on the balcony with me. She's peering into a telescope trained on the Dream City.

No, wait, it's not a telescope. It's a microscope.

The patch of balcony under her feet is unresolved grey, just like the Sweet Dreams platform, as if she's been transposed here from Sweet Dreams.

A complicated series of emotions threads through me, from hope to shame and back. I want to talk to her, but I'm afraid of how she'll react. In the video she sounded so positive, so hopeful about the future of technology. Yet listening to her talk made me feel ugly and unwanted, like a shadow or stain. I am ashamed of my condition. People like Dr Bhango are in charge of things, they are important. I am an outsider, a scavenger, a chancer. A fox in a Hampstead rubbish bin.

Meera pulls away from the telescope and sees me.

'Well,' she says. 'You're a fox now? Can't bear to be indulged, petted by the sympathetic.'

I nod. My freedom may be all I have. Rather than give it up I can get by on energy drinks and kebabs and clients who genuinely need me. Too bad that the ones who really need me can't pay and the ones who can pay are like Mrs H-W. Or Martin Elstree.

'You're scruffy,' she says, looking me up and down. 'And scrappy. And now you're being hunted. What do you make of all this?' She gestures to the Sweet Dreams platform.

'I don't want any part of it,' I say boldly. 'I think it's manipulative.'

'Really? How?' Her eyes flash, challenging. Dream-Meera has the same wide face and strong cheekbones as the person I saw on video. She stands facing me squarely with both feet planted wide apart. Like someone who isn't easy to budge.

'I just don't see the need to make dreams into something corporate. Back in the day, indie ASMRtists were providing nearly everything that Sweet Dreams does, for free. For love. Now the same thing is on offer from BigSky for a monthly subscription, and they can use AI that they don't even have to pay to simulate caring about you.'

I didn't know I thought that until I hear myself say it. I pace up and down the balcony, which is attached to an ivy-covered building below a lemon-yellow illuminated cycleway. The *schuss* and whistle of passing cyclists roll overhead like a tide. The balcony doors have been locked behind me.

'We should really talk face to face,' Meera says. 'Soon you'll be able to avoid Sweet Dreams altogether if you like. Your whole head will be a receiver.'

'My what now?'

'You know I'm curing your narcolepsy, right?'

I feel my breath go in sharply. 'I was going to ask if you could try—' I say shyly.

She waves a casual hand. 'It's already under way. Haven't you noticed any changes? Think about it.'

There's a sound of wings fluttering just over my head. Instinctively, I duck and cringe, and when I look up again, Meera is gone. But a swallow has landed on the eyepiece of the microscope. It pecks a few times, then dives off the balcony. I see it make a long, comma-shaped arc in the air, and then it disappears into darkness below.

There's nothing for it but to look in the microscope. I'm nervous.

When I bend over the eyepiece, the microscope turns out to be a telescope after all. It gives me a view of the sideways building, some distance from the edge of the Sweet Dreams platform. I have never been able to see up there very well from ground level, partly because the glare of neon obscures the details of the building. But the microscope/telescope resolves individual tables that must be bolted to the side of the building; they never slide off. I look at one table and see the candle flame burning horizontally instead of vertically. There is a white-haired person in a wheelchair there – could almost swear it was O, but I can only see the back of their head.

My first thought is that it can't be O. She doesn't use Sweet Dreams. My second thought is to remember that I'm in a natural dream, no earring, so the Sweet Dreams platform isn't even really here. My subconscious has put O up on that building, the one I've been trying to get into but can't. Why?

Ever so slowly, the person turns towards me as if they know I am here. Anticipating a view of O's grouchy face in the telescope, instead I see the Creeper's mask with its chemical symbols.

I know that it sees me, too. I start to hyperventilate.

There's a sound of drumming, angry, aggressive. Someone is pounding on the flat door.

'*Charlie! Charlie, wake up FFS!*'

I wake to the distant honking of O saying words I can't make out, then Shandy's voice sounding breathless.

'Let me in. I need her, we've got plans for this morning but she's overslept.'

I hear Shandy's footsteps coming down the hall.

'I didn't realise,' O says mildly. 'Will it take all day? I've booked Charlie with a client later this afternoon.'

'It shouldn't take too long,' Shandy says. 'I need her to help me with something. Family business.'

I'm struggling to sit up and wrap my hair when the door to my room bursts open and Shandy is there, holding her finger on her lips and rolling her eyes in silent command for me to go along with whatever she says.

'Oh good, you're almost ready!' she cries. 'Hurry up, don't want to be late.'

*

Shandy refuses to answer my questions about what we are doing in Belsize Park, where Bernard Zborowski lives, but whatever is going on, I know it can't be good. We get to Bernard's road and walk past the house. Shandy has brought two shopping bags full of random groceries. She leans on a plane tree, pretending to rummage in her bags, occasionally glancing up.

'What are you doing, Shand?' I hiss. 'Please can we just go before he comes home and sees us?'

'The postie should be along any moment. Let me know when you see them.'

'How do you know this?'

'Research.' She doesn't add 'prole' but she may as well have.

I try to look like I'm having a Spacetime chat even though I'm not, so that we'll be less suspicious. Shandy is right, though. We're only there for a few minutes when I see a woman with a red Royal Mail bag come swinging down the steps about ten houses up.

'Post is approaching. Nine houses away. Now what?' I say it out of the side of my mouth.

'Follow my lead.'

Shandy times it so that the postie climbs the steps to Bernard's building just as we arrive. The postie presses the buzzer. A woman's voice answers.

'I need a signature,' says the postie. As the door buzzes open, we climb the steps. Shandy grabs the door with a breathless 'thank you' and we both pile in, past the postie. A door opens on the ground floor and an elderly woman comes out to sign for her parcel; meanwhile Shandy and me are on our way up the stairs.

'How did you know she was going to get buzzed in?' I whisper.

'I sent something to the neighbour special delivery. It has to come by ten a.m., so I knew we were in.'

'What did you send?'

I'm afraid she's going to say *vibrator* or *waxwork doll of Margaret Thatcher*.

'Chocolate, obvs. Now, let me do the talking.'

Shandy pounds on Bernard's door so hard that plaster dust comes down in the stairwell.

'I know you're in there, Bernard! You can't hide from me! I'm going to tell everyone in the building about your filthy little habit if you don't open up.'

The door swings open. There he is looking exactly the way I remember him from the medical trial, except he's only wearing boxers with a Planck Institute Surfing Team sweatshirt. He's very tall and has the hairiest legs I've ever seen.

'What filthy little habit? What do you want this time?'

*This time?*

'We're selling drugs, of course!' *Shandy.* I shrink away from her. 'Or no, wait, that would be you!'

He's so angry, he's spluttering. 'Go away. Get treated.'

'No, *you* get treated, you gambling addict!'

'Whuh— I'm an engineer. I don't need to sell drugs. I am not a gambling addict. Now please leave or I'll call the police.' While he's talking, Shandy blows a purple bubble. Then she pops it.

'Yeah, right, the police have nothing better to do than save six-foot-four neuroscientists from five-foot-one women. Are you going to let us in or not?'

'Of course not, Darth Whackjob.'

Shandy turns to look at me and winks. 'Tell him about the dreams, Chaz.'

At least she didn't call me Horse.

'Not interested!' He tries to close the door, but Shandy's already shoved her giant handbag in the gap and now they wrestle a little. The word 'dreams' seems to have set him off and some of my faith in Shandy returns. I put my hand on Shandy's shoulder to restrain her.

'I know I signed a non-disclosure agreement and I know I can't take legal action against BigSky,' I say in my best professional voice. It works better on the phone, when no one can see how scruffy I am. 'However, I understand you don't work there any more and you might like to know that thanks to you, a woman is dead.'

'Oh, bloody come in, then.' To my shock, he suddenly swings the door wide and Shandy and I look at each other. Now we're both wondering if we're going to be killed and freeze-dried and used as ballast in a SpaceX rocket. But Shandy steps inside, brandishing her handbag like a potential weapon, and I end up following. I'm a good follower, I am.

It's a nice flat. I can't imagine ever being able to afford a flat like this. It's got an entrance hall, a kitchen with a little table, a sitting room with lots of bookcases and a big monitor, and I count three doors along the hall. Two beds and a bath. It's actually bigger than O's flat, and in a fancier neighbourhood. My tail's between my legs already. Who am I? I clean the pigeon cage, that's who.

We sit down on his leather sofa and he sits down by the desk. The wall behind him is cycling a series of images, views of the Great Barrier Reef or something. The fish spill into the room.

'Switzerland is landlocked,' Shandy challenges. 'How the hell can the Planck Institute have a surfing team?'

'They don't. It's a joke.'

Shandy raises an eyebrow.

'I'm not clear on what you two are after,' he says, but he's looking at me. Maybe that's because Shandy is sparking and flashing at him, tapping her long nails on his Swedish furniture and grinding her boot heel into his organic carpet.

'I got really sick after the study,' I tell him.

'Yes, I was made aware. That particular agent resulted in a number of unpleasant side effects. Once an engine starts re-arranging neural connections, it's not the easiest thing in the world to stop it without causing damage to the host. But as you know, I'm no longer employed by BigSky and even if I was, I can't be held accountable personally. That's what all the small print was about.'

I'm looking around this gorgeous flat, wondering how someone like Bernard, only a few years older than I am, could have got so much farther in life while I'm still scrabbling and unsure about everything.

And that's when I see the mask. It's exactly like the one in the dream, except in negative. Instead of a white mask etched with white, it's a black fencing mask. There are white symbols stitched on it. Some kind of complicated organic molecule. The only difference from Mel's dreams is that with this mask, the eyes are covered by mesh, not plastic. It's mounted on the wall over a pair of crossed foils, and there are big padded gloves hanging below it. I message Shandy and tell her not to look at it or remark on it. Her message comes back with a mocking tone: *Afraid we'll be kebabed?*

I'm scared to hell, but also actually getting angry now. I didn't think there was any point coming here. We've walked right into it. But he's so mellow, it's like he'd never hurt a fly.

'And you're working on sleepwalking these days?' I manage to slip this in, and there's a distinct shift in the mood. 'Do you sleepwalk yourself?'

'No, I don't.'

'And do you lucid dream? I'm in dreaming, you see. I'm a therapist. So I'd be interested in learning more about your work.'

He crosses his legs and cocks his head with the first smidgen of interest he's shown so far. 'Well, we're always looking for new subjects for our trials. Have you ever been in a sleep lab?'

I hate it that I can feel how clever he is. Like a smell on the air. It puts my back up. I'm poor, and narcoleptic, and unsuccessful. I feel like a dirty little animal in his posh flat with his posh ideas and his *actual hardcover books* – who can afford physical books? I'm so angry about the position I'm in, my own ignorance as to *what was actually done to me* freaks me out, and yet my anger feels like it's a foul piece of excrescence and not allowed because rules. Or something.

Clearly, Shandy doesn't share my sentiments, because she

says: 'Sleep lab, my arse. You should be so lucky. Chaz can enter people's dreams and I think you already know that.'

'How would I know that?' Butter wouldn't melt.

'Because I've seen you,' I blurt, and immediately regret it. 'I've seen you in my client's dream.'

What the actual fuck is wrong with me, why did I say that?

'Yeah!' Shandy puts in. 'You were wearing a mask.'

I want to kick her but daren't.

The corners of his mouth turn up. 'If the person was wearing a mask, how do you know it was me?'

I swallow, hard. I look deliberately away from where the mask is hanging, in case he realises that I really do recognise his mask and could expose him and then decides to kill us both and feed us into a wood-chipper. I don't know. Anything could happen.

'She can sense it,' Shandy says. 'We know it's you. Don't mess about.'

I'm beginning to feel some small measure of respect for Roman and Donato. The two of them are elegant professionals compared to Shand and me.

'OK, never mind that,' I say. 'It's not why we came.'

'That's . . . good . . .' he says carefully. 'I'm sure you know that if you're dreaming about me, that's something between you and your therapist. And it's definitely not an appropriate topic of conversation between us. You may blame me for your situation, but it's not my responsibility.'

'Maybe you can't be held accountable, legally,' Shandy says, leaning forward and fixing her glittering black eyes on his face. 'But morally you must feel something. You trialled this therapy on my friend and she's got long-term issues now and you feel nothing?'

'I didn't say I feel nothing. If I felt nothing I would have called the police and reported you for harassment – which, by the way, is well within my rights. You've stalked me at my home. I'm sorry that you had a bad experience, Charlotte, but please don't demonise me. I'm not even at BigSky any more. I'm not in a position to help you.'

I say, 'What do you know about a neural repair treatment given for dementia?'

'This feels like an interrogation. BigSky has worked on several dementia treatments, but I'm not involved with any of them.'

'And did any of them induce sleepwalking?' I press.

'Can't say. Legally, I'm not permitted to discuss it with you.'

'I want to know why you left BigSky and moved to a start-up,' Shady says.

'I was recruited.'

'But you can't possibly be making the same sort of money at a start-up as at BigSky,' she challenges.

'Money isn't the biggest motivator. It's the work that interests me.'

'Or was it that BigSky sacked you when they found out about the cock-up?'

I step on her foot and interject in a rush, 'I want you to introduce me to Meera Bhango.' It's the only thing I can think to say – anything to deflect from the accusations Shandy has made, accusations that are going to make him want to *kill us* if he is the Creeper.

His reaction surprises me. He's taken Shandy's allegations in stride – looked almost amused – but suddenly he won't meet my eye and he fidgets in his ergonomic desk chair.

'It's not that I wouldn't like to help you,' he tells me, 'but legally, I can't. I shouldn't even be talking to you. It's not ethical. And you absolutely can't have contact with Doctor Bhango. In fact, I have to warn you that any approach to Doctor Bhango by you in connection with the BigSky study will have to be reported to the police. As I'm sure you're aware, there have been too many instances in the last several years of scientists being threatened by members of the public.'

'You don't mean those anti-progressive nutjobs protesting outside the Crick Institute, do you? Because we're not like *them*.'

Bernard looks at Shandy with an expression that says we are exactly like 'them'. He clears his throat.

'Doctor Bhango is protected by some hefty legislation, as am I. I do regret having to say this to you, because I am basically sympathetic to your situation. But you signed up for the study, you were paid, and you were informed of the risks you were taking. If you're hoping for a therapeutic correction to your side effects, you'll just have to stand in the queue with everyone else who has a neurological condition. And now, Ms Aaron and Ms... I'm sorry, I didn't catch your name?'

He stands, making ushering movements towards us.

'It's Doctor Lady Reverend to you, Mac,' Shandy says, eyes flashing, and Rodney skewers the virtual Escher etching hanging above the virtual fishtank, so that Bernard visibly cringes and recoils. 'Well, we had to try, right, Chaz? We'll just show ourselves out, mate. Get back to your surfing practice. Oh, and if you need any design work, here's my card—'

She makes a flicking gesture and shoots him her virtual contact details, then exits the apartment in a swirl of purple and gold AR.

'What a tosser,' she says in the stairwell. 'He's going to need sorting.'

'What do you mean?'

She laughs. 'I have to get back to work. What are you doing?'

'According to my schedule I... ooh, looks like I have a new client. What do you mean, sorting?'

'We'll talk later. Let me think on it, babe.' As she puts me on the Big Green Bus back to the flat, Shandy kisses me on the cheek, and Rodney winks at me, and then we part ways.

I'm home with a couple of hours to spare before my next client – one of the new bunch acquired since I became 'famous'. Partly out of fear and partly because I have so much on my mind right now, I've been very picky about who I'll take. This person lives in Highgate, so it's an easy bike ride from O's flat. Also, she offered to double my usual fee if I wouldn't tell anyone anything about her because she's famous herself, like for-real famous.

'You'll be sure and be discreet?' O reminds me from the sofa, where she is lying on her back with Edgar reclining on her chest.

'I'll be sure. Er... O?'

'Yes, Charlie?'

'Shandy and I went to see Bernard and she more or less accused him of being the Creeper.'

There's a small sigh.

'I had a feeling the two of you might do something like that. I think you're on the wrong track. How did he take it?'

'He didn't turn himself in, let's put it that way. He had a fencing mask on the wall with the same symbols as the Creeper.'

'Did he, now? What else?'

'I asked him to introduce me to Meera Bhango. He refused and warned me not to harass her because anti-science activists aren't tolerated by the law. What should I do?'

I can't see her face; Edgar is blocking my view. But her snort is audible, and it ruffles Edgar's fur.

'Just contact her in the normal way. Tell her who you are and what it's about. You're not an anti-science activist. Assert yourself, Charlie!'

Ick. She can't know how weak the narcolepsy makes me feel.

But I do it. I Spacetime the Little Bird office. The system routes me straight through to Meera, which I wasn't expecting. She is standing at a desk in a sunlit room with a view over the Thames beside another person who she has edited out of the frame. I tell her the basic deets of my situation.

'Can you meet me in person?' she says.

'Uh... yeah. When?'

'I'm in a meeting in the City, but I have to pick up my daughter at her nursery in Kentish Town this afternoon.'

'I'm going to Highgate anyway,' I tell her, and we arrange to meet in Kentish Town. I decide to cycle; I can use the exercise. She names a cafe.

I bounce out and tell O. Suddenly I'm full of positive energy. I clean the pigeon cage, quickly brush my teeth and go to get my bike off the rack outside the building. The tyres need pumping, but I have time. I leave my bag and high-vis vest on the floor while I do that.

I'm not tired. I'm not stressed, or not unusually stressed, anyway. I'm actually looking forward to this.

So how it is exactly that I fall asleep, I don't know. But apparently I do, because the next thing I know, I've been hijacked by a dream.

**Secret Diary of a Prawn Star**
**Entry #53**
**Codename:** Chaplin
**Date:** 24 September 2027
**Client:** en route to client
**Payment in advance:** Yes
**Session Goal:** Involuntary
**Location:** Pavement outside O's flat
**Narcolepsy status:** Thought was OK but apparently not
**Nutrition/stimulants:** Coffee, chocolate muffin
**Start time:** 2.17 p.m.
**End time:** 2.24 p.m.

After I pump the tyres, I jump on the bike and set off towards Finsbury Park. Everything feels normal, and it takes me a while to work out that I'm asleep, by which time I've forgotten the circumstances under which I fell asleep because it feels like I've always been in this dream.

Soon the familiar shopfronts of Finsbury Park give way to the futuristic towers of the Dream City, and I find myself riding along canalside. The river reminds me of the Seine; it even has the same graceful bridges every so often, the same sort of street lamps. But everything is coloured in neon, and there are brightly painted and carved canoes on the water tonight.

Why is it always night in the Dream City? Even in the day, it's night. Weird.

I huff and puff, pedalling. The Dream City is greener than London. It's got more cyclists than Copenhagen, but fewer than Hong Kong. Most of them are much faster than I am and they overtake me. Soon I find myself in a peloton of cyclists, all helmeted and anonymous – I can't even see their faces through their visors. Suddenly I feel threatened. There's no railing, and if someone ran into me I'd go right over the edge of the canal. The riders crowd close around me and I begin to wobble. I look for a way out of the peloton, but I'm totally surrounded.

Then I see that one of the riders is different. A woman comes alongside me in an evening gown, no helmet. Her long, black hair is elaborately plaited and flies behind her in beaded chunks, and her hands are ungloved. The nails are painted. She is wearing heels. She keeps riding too close and trying to talk to me.

'You aren't on your bike,' she says in a deep voice that reminds me of O's friend Lorraine. 'You're asleep.'

'I know I'm asleep,' I shout back. 'This is a dream.'

But she doesn't seem to hear me.

'Girl, are you high?' she says. 'I can't keep up with you much longer. Just come inside.'

'I can't. Look – the others are blocking me off.'

There are dozens of other cyclists. They make an enormous noise, and a wind. It's like a racetrack. I wobble, trying to stay out of the river.

'You're going to get hit. Charlie, come on! Come inside!'

Behind me, there is a big noise, a sound of booming and squealing and a blast of half-music. I turn and see a battleship coming out of the river, its hull looming over me. I'll be crushed.

My fellow cyclist leaps off her own bike and tackles me. We fall in the water, together, and the ship rides up onto the pavement, and I hear the sound of breaking glass.

# Stack

I'm on Seven Sisters, my face in a cold puddle. Someone is lying on top of me, their displaced hat obscuring my view of the lorry that has missed us by centimetres and crashed into a parked Peugeot instead.

'You all right, love?' the person pants, clambering off me. It's the same voice as the woman in the evening gown in my dream. 'Are you hurt?'

That's when I realise that my saviour is Stack.

'Stack, you sound just like your grandmother.' My voice sounds blurry.

'What's wrong with you? You were riding half-asleep. I ran after you but I couldn't get you out of the road.'

'Soz, mate . . .'

He's very annoyed. 'You were riding that bike like a drunken sailor – are you high? Did you even look where you were going?'

My chin is quivering like I'm a little kid. I grab him in a bear hug. His body's a wall of muscle.

'Sorry about the rugby tackle,' he adds.

'Thank you, Stack,' I say into his chest. 'Thank you. Thank you. Thank you.'

'No worries. You wait on the pavement, I'll talk to this dude.'

The lorry driver is coming over, glowering and swaggering; Stack greets him with a big, white smile and outstretched hands. I watch him steer the driver away, reaching into his back pocket for his wallet at the same time. The lorry doesn't look much damaged, but the same can't be said for the Peugeot.

I try to go towards them but can't seem to stay on my legs. I end up sitting on the pavement. Something's wrong; I feel like I've been drugged. I'm not sure if my body even belongs to me or not. People stop and offer to help but I wave them away. I'm still groggy, annoyed and on the verge of tears.

Eventually, the lorry driver backs up with the aid of Stack directing traffic. After that's sorted, he saunters over to me.

'I can't let you pay for this, Stack,' I tell him. 'You already saved my life.'

'You're covered,' he tells me. 'O is taking care of it. You can go home now. Should I call someone to come and get you?'

'You talked to her already?'

'She asked me to watch out for you. She says you're accident-prone.'

Or attempted-murder prone? She didn't say anything to me. I can feel myself lifting out of my shoes as I say, 'She paid you to protect me? How many people has she got working for her?'

I'm swaying, not really in control of my body. Blood is springing up from the abrasions on my knees and forearms where they struck the pavement.

'Nah, mate, relax. No main event, OK? It's all discreet. Let's not make a scene like a couple of tossers. People are recording us.'

Damn. That kind of attention is the last thing I need right now.

'We have to wait for the police,' Stack says. 'Then I'll take you home. O will reschedule your appointments.'

The word 'police' hits me with a thump. I don't want to talk to the police! Then I remember Meera. I'm late for the meeting. I try to Spacetime her but she's offline, so I leave a wobbly message telling her what's happened. But I sound so pathetic I can't stand to listen to myself. So I tell her that I'll be late but I'm on my way. It's a good excuse to avoid the police.

'I have to go, Stack. Thanks for everything.'

'What? You can't—'

He tries to stop me getting on the bike, but I'm not having it.

'I'm fine. I need to be somewhere now. I'll call you later.'

'This is a bad idea!' he shouts after me as I ride off wobbling towards Kentish Town. But I'm not going to flake out on my commitments, I'm not going to be intimidated, and I'm not giving up a chance to get better.

Also: I'm not dealing with the police.

But pedalling hurts like hell. I get to the cafe and there's no sign of Meera. I leave another message. When my Spacetime pings, I answer expecting Meera but it's Shandy. She takes one horrified look at me and demands to hear the whole story.

'It's sheer luck you're alive,' she says. 'This has gone far enough. Stay where you are, I'm coming over. I was calling to tell you we're going on the offensive tonight, anyway.'

'But I can barely work my legs.'

'You won't need your legs for this, Horse.'


'Let me just tuck you in,' Shandy says.

'This is the worst idea you've ever had,' I hiss, and she laughs. She's put flowered sheets on Bernard's neighbour's sofa and tucked me in so tightly I can't even move. 'What if Mrs and Mrs Shoji come back?'

'They won't come back. I told you, they're at the theatre. Do you have any idea of the price of tickets in the West End?'

'But it's breaking-and-entering.'

'No, it's not. They left their window open and we are looking for our cat.'

'We don't own a cat. We aren't even a "we".'

'Of course we're a "we", and you don't need to be a couple to have a cat together.'

'I never really thought about it. Did you take off your shoes?'

'What?'

'Shandy, look around. See the photos? The Shojis are Japanese. Didn't you notice the slippers by the door?'

'They won't know. And what if we have to run away? We can't stop to put our shoes on.'

'Just take them off. I feel terrible breaking in. Look how tidy everything is. Let's at least keep it that way.'

'Fine, I am taking off my shoes. Now just calm down and go to sleep. Look how droopy your eyes are already. Do you always fall asleep when you're scared?'

'Maybe.' I yawn hugely. 'How do we know Bernard's asleep?'

'We don't.'

I yawn again. I've only gone along with this crazy scheme because I can't bear going home to O and asking her how long Stack has been following me. And I don't want to think about the very likely fact that the Creeper is trying to trick me into committing 'suicide' just like he did to Mel and all those other people Roman told me about. I can't think about it. It's too scary.

Anyway, the idea is for me to get into Bernard's dreams and pursue him, to hunt the hunter, in other words. Shandy has used her connections at BigSky's promotion department to lure the downstairs-flat Shojis out of their home for the evening with theatre tickets and a night at the Savoy that she convinces them they've won in a contest. She has settled me down on their immaculate sofa. It's very comfortable, but it faces a wall completely covered with framed photographs of the Shoji family: baby pictures, graduations, picnics, holidays. They look like a well-ordered, sensible family. Wish they would adopt me.

Shandy is going to sit right here at my feet and make sure I don't sleepwalk, just in case Bernard catches me sneaking around in his dream and tries to do away with me.

I'm petrified, and therefore barely conscious.

'Imagine if Indiana Jones had narcolepsy,' I murmur. 'He'd be squashed flat by the big boulder in the first scene.'

She holds my hand. 'You need to be more positive, Horse. Go and do your thing. Give Bernard hell. See if you can find out what he's up to and how he does it. I'll be right here beside you.'

'No, you won't,' I moan. 'You'll be awake.'

And then I slip off because I've no choice.

**Secret Diary of a Prawn Star**
**Entry #54**
**Codename:** Chaplin
**Date:** 25 September 2027
**Client:** Bernard Zborowski
**Payment in advance:** He doesn't know I'm doing this
**Session Goal:** Find proof he's the Creeper
**Location:** Flat of Yayeko and Joji G. Shoji, downstairs
**Narcolepsy status:** Scared as a rabbit
**Nutrition/stimulants:** N/A
**Start time:** 12.01 a.m.
**End time:** 12.35 a.m.

We're in my room. No... wait, that's my frame. The walls
and floors ripple and change as I adjust to Bernard's frame of
reference. We're in *his* room. In his lovely flat that he owns
because he has money and smarts and I do not.

I'm not happy with Dr Zborowski, and now we're in my
wheelhouse. He won't expect me to do something bold like
this; it's against my nature. Well, he doesn't know everything
about me. I may as well admit it: I can be a teensy bit passive-
aggressive. OK, maybe a lot. I like everyone to think I'm nice,
and I mostly am. But I'm a little bit tougher than I look. I'm
also one of those people who would gladly hurt someone I didn't
like if I thought no one could ever find out it was me. Give me
half a chance and I'll stick pins in the dolls of my enemies rather
than argue with them face-to-face. It's not a very nice thing to
have to admit to yourself, but when you're getting your 2:2 from
Excelsior-Barking Online, in the practical classes you do find out
these dark truths about yourself.

The thing is, despite having this side to my persona, I've never used my dreamhacking powers for evil. And that's why, faced with the scorn of Bernard Zborowski of the organic Swedish carpet, I find it hard to contain my rage right now. Coming here in my current state of mind was probably not a good idea.

In Bernard's dream lounge there's a party in progress. All the guests are dead. They don't appear to mind being dead, even though some are in a fairly advanced state of decay. Ugh, what the hell is going on? Who are these people?

'Bernard, where are you?'

I try to slip between the walking dead without touching anyone, but it's a bit like a game of Twister. Eventually I find Bernard in the kitchen. It's not a normal kitchen. It's got one of those huge walk-in ovens, all brick around it and niches in the walls for bread or whatever. I remember seeing ovens like this on school field trips. But then I peer closer at the niches and they look like slots in a crematorium.

Bernard is measuring spices. Or something. The counters are white and clinical and there's not the slightest whiff of food. I see computer monitors and labbish-looking things, like centrifuges and lasers and microscopes and other exotic instruments that I don't understand because I never took classes with labs.

An elderly woman in black tights and a blouse but with no skirt wanders through. Her lipstick is askew and her eyes are too bright. One of her arms keeps falling off and she keeps having to stop and put it back in its socket. She approaches Bernard from behind. He doesn't see her, and when she touches him he jumps and makes a hiccuping sound. I can't help smirking.

'You have some nerve,' the woman says. 'You can't come into people's dreams and terrify us half to death. Paralysing us. Sucking the air out of our lungs. It's sick. Get out of my head!'

'I'm not in your head, madam. You're in *my* head.'

'No, that's called feedback, you pillock,' she says, poking him with a bony finger.

'I don't even know what you're talking about. We're just trying to improve cognition.'

'There's nothing wrong with my cognition! I have some memory lapses, that's all.'

'Actually, you are being treated for dementia, Gladys,' says an upright old dead man in a chunky cardigan and red turban.

Bernard finds himself up against the brick wall with its ovens. The dead are around him, their rotting faces and drooping eyes and wagging fingers all trained on him. No one sees me.

'You come into my room at night. You have a white face and a black cloak and you crush my chest and I can't move and I can't breathe,' Gladys says. 'Maybe I can't remember what I had for breakfast but I remember that.'

'I do nothing of the kind,' Bernard says stiffly, trying to ward them off without touching them, which should be comical but is really just disturbing. 'I assure you, all of you are very important and I have your best interests at heart, but I can't work when you harass me this way!'

This crowd reminds me of the corpse I encountered when I tried to dreamhack the Creeper. And I am dreaming them in colour ... are they all conscious inside this dream of Bernard's? Is that even possible?

'Who are these people, Bernard?' I say.

He rolls his eyes. 'Oh, not you a-bloody-gain.'

'What have you been doing to them?' I look around at the faces in the crowd, and that's when I see a familiar face. O's sister Daphne is here, and I realise that the man in the cardy and turban is an elderly soldier from her care home, what was his name? Captain something. Captain Singh!

'I want to wake up now,' Bernard says. 'I know this is a dream because in real life people's arms don't fall off. Get away from me, you zombies!'

'We're not zombies,' says Captain Singh in frigid tones. 'We are human beings, but you, sir, are a disgrace to science.'

'Yeah,' I say. 'You're a disgrace. So I'm not the only one you did this to? What about Melodie? You terrorised her and she ran away from you but she wasn't dreaming, she was really running. Right off a rooftop to her death. You're ... I didn't use to believe in evil, but you're evil.'

'Evil!' Daphne shrills, raising her skinny fist. She catches my eye. 'You tell him, Jacqueline. And give my best to the other ladies at the tennis club.'

Captain Singh turns to look at me. He makes a proper little bow, clicking his heels together. Then he says, 'So this is the dastard who killed that poor musician, is it? Let's see if the rogue likes a taste of his own so-called medicine. Stand back, everybody.'

'I didn't kill anyone!' Bernard protests. 'You're all mad. I want to wake up now. I want to wake up.'

'Oh no,' Daphne says. 'Don't let him wake up. I'll take it from here.'

And the dream changes. Bernard is in his bed, which is in the middle of the gravel entranceway to a stately home – or is it one of those leafy public schools? I seem to remember that Bernard grew up in the Home Counties and was independently educated. Well, vintage Bentleys and Rolls-Royces are parked here so that the whole dream now has an element of an Agatha Christie production to it in my eyes – I've only ever seen a Bentley on a screen.

The corpses and I stand around Bernard's bed on the grass under a starless black sky. Bernard's lying rigid in the bed, eyes open, not moving.

'I'll do it,' Daphne says. 'It's my mission. Stand aside, Captain Singh.'

Daphne bends over Bernard and rolls him onto his side. She rubs the middle of his back almost tenderly. Then I notice that there's a panel in his back with an ornate brass key sticking out of it. Daphne turns the key and the panel opens like a little door. Daphne has become tiny, and she climbs inside the panel and shuts the door behind her.

'You can't wake up, son,' Captain Singh informs Bernard. 'But now you can move. How do you like that? Go on, then. Let's make it a fair fight. You may move freely.'

Bernard sits up in bed. He throws the covers off mechanically, then shuffles across the lawn, casting frightened backward glances over his shoulder. Captain Singh hobbles after him, leaning on his cane, trailed by other dead people.

'You may wish to run,' advises Captain Singh. 'Are you confused? Go on, see if you can get away from us. You may find this challenging.'

Bernard is making odd hand gestures in the air. He wags his finger, pointing at nothing repeatedly like he's trying to type on a screen that isn't there. What is he doing?

'We don't do this for amusement, do we, Daphne?' the captain says. 'We do it to put a stop to the killing. It can't go on like this. The Agency has to crack down.'

But Bernard isn't listening. He has been spooked – by what exactly, I don't know. He dashes into some shrubbery and then onto a gravel path that leads through an avenue of topiary. The rest follow quite sedately, but somehow Bernard never gets very far ahead of them. Every so often one of the dead people says, 'Now you know how it feels. Now you understand what you've been doing to us all this time.' This only makes him move faster.

We all glide down garden path after the next, surrounded by topiary that gives Bernard very little choice of where to go. One by one, the corpses stop following him, until it's just Captain Singh, Gladys, and I. The topiary lane ends in a gazebo. We follow him in. The gazebo is covered in vines, and the far side has lift doors inset. He is just disappearing into the lift when we arrive, but we all manage to squeeze on, anyway. The lift takes us down into a cave with a vaulted ceiling. We are standing on a lip of stone at the edge of a dried-up canal that disappears into a tunnel to either side. There is no bridge across the canal and no steps leading down into it. Captain Singh and Gladys stop here instinctively, but Bernard jumps down into the bottom of the canal and picks his way along it. After a few steps he looks over his shoulder, his face brightening with the realisation that his pursuers can't get down. He is finally going to get away. He goes loping into the dark tunnel.

Everything is quiet for a little while. Then a noise comes out of the tunnel, a familiar groaning, followed by a flicker of white light coming from the tunnel. We lean out and see Bernard's figure silhouetted against a distant, bright light. Bernard stops in his tracks, turns, and starts to run back to us, with the light behind him. There's a rush of wind, and the shrubs all shudder.

I know the smell of this air. This is the Underground.

'I didn't kill anyone,' Bernard says. 'You've got the wrong man.'

Captain Singh and Gladys murmur to one another in concern. Just for a moment, the scene were are in breaks open and the platform of an Underground station flashes into view like a movie projection. The bright light comes from a fast-moving train hurtling towards Bernard from behind. Just before it overtakes him the train station dissolves back to the tunnel.

Captain Singh leans on his cane, peering at the place where Bernard used to be, looking puzzled.

'Jolly strange, that was,' he says.

Daphne appears at my elbow as if she'd never climbed inside Bernard's body at all. She takes my arm with her claw-like hand, and when she breathes on me it smells like bubblegum.

'Wake up,' she says. 'Wake up, the Shojis are back. Wake up.'

# Cone of Silence

'Wake up, Horse, wake up! Out the window, quickie-quickie!'

But I can't wake up, I can't make myself move. I can hear Shandy from far away, but I can't move one single muscle. I can feel her tugging at me, and at one point I roll off the sofa to the floor. There isn't one single dust bunny under that sofa.

A man's urgent voice says, 'Call 999, Kay!'

'No, please don't, we promise we don't mean any harm – look, we even took off our shoes—'

Now it's the old lady's turn. 'Don't move! Stay right there – what drugs is that girl on? Does she need an ambulance?'

I'm trying to sit up and I can hear noises coming out of my mouth but they sound like monster wildebeest noises even to me.

'I think she's had a seizure,' Shandy says. 'I know this looks bad, but I can explain. Please.'

'I knew it! You told me I'd won those tickets so you could rob us while we were out,' the man says. 'It's a good thing we came back here instead of going to the Savoy. Can't believe I was so stupid. You looked like such a nice young person—'

'Mr Shoji—'

'Everybody calls me George.'

'Of course, George, I promise, I am nice. I'm really, really nice. We were looking for our cat— No, OK, just, look, just call this number. This is Roman Pelka, he's with the Met, he'll explain.'

'Roman isn't really with the Met,' I try to say, but it comes out, 'Glug gluh wah wah ooogh.'

'This is just a Spacetime address,' Kay scoffs. 'This could be anyone.'

'They're the Dream Police,' Shandy says. 'We're investigating

189

your upstairs neighbour, the tall guy? Oh, how did you like the chocolate?'

'Chocolate?' George groans. 'That was from you? What kind of psycho are you? I accused my wife of having a fancy man when I saw that gift.'

Shandy breaks into a chortle, but Kay tugs on her husband's jacket sleeve.

'Oh, George, she's talking about that weird lad upstairs who talks to himself! They're investigating him!'

'No, I don't trust them. There's no such thing as the Dream Police.'

George stands across the doorway, brandishing a large umbrella. He's ninety if he's a day.

'You're right,' his wife says with a sigh. 'Listen, girls, just sit there and wait for the police. I will make tea. You can tell the real police whatever you want about the Dream Police. My husband and I need to know we can sleep safe at night.'

That's all any of us wants, isn't it?

'So how was the show?' Shandy asks, weakly.


We spend the rest of the night in Holborn Police Station because apparently there's a problem with the toilet at Kentish Town. It isn't as nice as I'd expected for the neighbourhood, plus they confiscate our headware until Donato arrives. I'd really been hoping for Roman, but such is my luck. Donato looks even more pissed off than usual. Shandy tries to flirt with him but it doesn't work. Maybe he's gay. Or maybe it's just because by that time of night her breath is lethal and her bubblegum has also been confiscated.

With that said, Donato talks to the police and the Shojis. Luckily the Shojis are really sweet, and somehow Donato makes it so Shandy and I are going to be let out. I'm not sure on the details because I sleep through most of it. When I awaken, I can recall several anxiety dreams, but I wasn't lucid in any of them and there was no sign of Bernard. I have a bad feeling about the whole thing, especially Daphne being in the middle of it. I'm in deeper waters than I thought.

Donato is uber-grumpy when we're finally released from the holding cell, which now has a pile of vomit and a drunk girl asleep on a bench. I don't realise it's 6 a.m. until I get my headware back. A big pile of messages are bursting to be read, but I ignore everything. I ping O straight away to let her know I'm all right, but then go dark because I don't want to have to speak to her right now. She's going to be cross.

'Sorry you got dragged out of bed,' I say to Donato as we walk down the silent road towards Holborn Station. And then, because I can't help my curiosity about where Roman is, I add, 'Was it your turn to babysit tonight?'

He looks at me keenly. I don't know what it is about Donato, but he makes me feel guilty even for things I haven't done.

'I sent Roman to talk to Bernard.'

'Oh, that can't be a good idea. Bernard has no idea we were there, and he's already mad because of the way Shandy's been stalking him.'

'I'm not stalking him!' Shandy protests. 'If I were stalking him, he'd never even know it until it was too late.'

'Do you stalk many people, then?' Donato asks.

I punch Shandy's arm. 'She doesn't. It's just a front, honestly.'

Donato gets a distracted expression on his face and there's a break in his stride; that's how I can tell he's in Spacetime, but it's a private convo. I can't see anything.

He stops in his tracks. Turns his back on us. Shandy offers me gum and I accept. Then I lean on her. I need to lie down.

'Not here. You can sleep on the Tube.'

I yawn. The edges of my vision are blurring and my gums ache. My head is full of static, like I'm receiving the cosmic microwave background in my fillings. Shandy steps on my foot, sharply.

'Owie.'

191

'Stay awake. Something's happening. I think he's going to call for his invisible plane in a minute.'

Donato turns around. He is furious.

'Well, isn't that interesting? Roman is in Bernard's flat as we speak. It took him two hours to bypass the security system, but he's in now.'

'Yeah, so?'

Now it's my turn to step on Shandy's foot. Belligerence won't get her anywhere with Donato, except maybe back in lock-up.

'Bernard isn't there. That'd be because he's dead. Roman just received a call from the Transport Police. Bernard walked in front of a train on the Northern Line. What have you got to say for yourself, Charlie?'

Nothing. I have nothing to say. Because I really need to sleep. Right now.

I hear people talking but I don't know where I am. I don't even know which way is up or what position my body is in. It's like I'm floating, and then I hear Shandy's voice.

'You both know Charlie didn't do this. She's being framed – can't you see that? I mean, look at her. She can't even— Look at her – she's like a child.'

'Or that could be just a cover,' Donato says. 'Have you noticed how she conveniently falls asleep whenever she's under pressure?'

'That's because she's sick!'

'Allegedly.'

'Don't be a cunt, Donato. Use your head. Charlotte doesn't understand the world. I've known her for years, she gets lost on her way from the toilet to the fridge, she's not capable of planning anything even if she had one single malicious bone in her body. Which she doesn't. So just stop it. No, I don't want coffee, I want you to leave her alone. She's one of the good ones and I won't— Hold on, this is O on that bloody archaic app she uses instead of Spacetime.'

I come swimming into awareness reluctantly. It's nicer in

sleep. I seem to be doing the Grand Tour of sofas, because we are in Bernard's flat, and I'm trying to figure out how that even works. Surely the police should be here, and forensics, and we should be in jail if they really think I did this somehow – and judging from what Shandy is saying, they do.

'Charlie. Can you hear me. It's Roman.'

His voice is coming from somewhere near my head. It feels like everything is moving, like my senses can't figure out which of my body parts is where. I manage to make a sound.

'Can you move? Charlie, I'm a little concerned about you. If you are able to, try and make a sound again.'

It's so hard to force myself to do it. I just want to float and drift . . .

'Charlie? Come on. Stay with us. I know you don't want to end up in A and E. They'll stick needles into you and do things to wake you up, and it'll be very unpleasant. I'm touching your hand. Can you feel that?'

He's holding my hand. How sweet.

'Don't be so poncey, Roman.' Shandy's voice, her breath in my face, and now I'm starting to feel my body more. 'For fucksake, assert yourself. Oh, never mind, I'll do it.'

Then Shandy slaps me across the face and my eyelids fly open. She's giving me eyes as wide as an All-Blacks player doing the Haka and her spittle flies into my face with the force of her words.

'Hey! Guess what? Bernard's dead. Actually dead. How can you sleep through this? You're a suspect, but there aren't even any police. But there's a dog! He's so cute. Wake the fuck up!'

I'm on Bernard's sofa.

'There's a dog?' I say weakly. I love dogs.

'Nope, I lied. And that, Roman dear, is how it's done.'

I see her legs and arse receding as she crosses the room to continue her intense conversation with Donato, in which every other word she uses seems to be 'cunting'. Roman is still holding my hand.

'I have coffee for you. Can you sit up?'

Nodding, I manage to get vertical. I feel disgusting. I sip the coffee – it's too sweet and too white, but it tastes better than the inside of my mouth.

'Don't talk to him, Charlie,' Shandy says, and when Roman shoots her a resentful look, she adds, 'All of us are vulnerable right now, and who knows how this flat has been rigged for surveillance? The only way we can talk is to invoke Cone of Silence.'

Roman starts to laugh, but stops when Rodney the unicorn threatens to headbutt him.

'It's an app she wrote,' I tell Roman. 'It locks down everything we say, scrambles it.'

Shandy nods. 'Crude but effective.'

'I thought you were a furniture designer.'

'I wrote it to stop my ex-girlfriend stealing my ideas,' she says matter-of-factly. Then she squirts everybody the code for Cone of Silence.

'I'm going out for some air,' Donato says, shaking his head. 'Enjoy your cone of whatever.'

When we are secure, Roman motions for me to talk.

'I was in Bernard's dream,' I croak. 'I was trying to find out if he was involved in Mel's death. See the fencing mask?'

Roman takes it down carefully and turns it over.

'It's the one from Mel's dream. I don't know what the chemical is.'

Roman says, 'It's morphine.'

Shandy's eyes flash. 'You recognise it?'

'Google is your friend. Just scan it in, see for yourself.'

'I feel like an idiot,' I say. 'I couldn't recall the image. I should have looked it up in my Secret Diary.'

Shandy shrugs. 'OK, so it's morphine. What good does that do?'

'Morpheus was the god of dreams,' Roman says. 'Maybe that's a connection. Or maybe some mechanism involved in dreamhacking is related to morphine receptors. When we interview Bernard's friends, we can find out how long he's had the mask and what it meant to him. For now, we need to get to the bottom of what happened last night. I'll need you to tell me the dream. Did you record it?'

'I record everything on my BigSky account. But you won't be able to read it. It only plays back in dream form, and the reference system is unique to me.'

'Send it to me anyway.'

I sip some more, trying to buy time. It's not that I've got anything to feel guilty about or any reason to withhold information from the police. It's just . . . a feeling of everything moving too fast.

'Give me a minute to wake up. I need to check in with O, she'll be worried.'

Roman's sitting across from me, straddling an occasional table, while I recline on poor dead Bernard's sofa. I feel cornered. He's looking so intensely at me.

'I called O,' he says. 'She knows you're safe and we've made arrangements for someone to go and check on her, see if she needs anything. She said she would cancel your appointments. She's also dealing with the person whose Peugeot you wrecked?'

'Oh. OK.' I feel helpless and silly and I wish I could just go back to sleep. I wish there really were a dog here and Shandy hadn't lied to make me wake up.

'Did anything happen while you were sleeping just now?'

'Dream-wise, you mean? Not that I can recall. I haven't been recording. I didn't mean to go to sleep. But no, I don't think there was anything to worry about. Are the police coming? I mean, the proper police.'

He smiles grimly. 'The body isn't here, obviously. Forensics have been and gone. You've been asleep for fifteen hours.'

My stomach makes some incredible curdling noise as though it's only just been informed of the passage of time and needs to run updates.

'Have I been here all this time?'

'You were in Donato's car for a while.'

'But why would you bring me here? You can't really think I did anything to Bernard. I told you, *he's* the Creeper. He's got to be. Maybe somebody did us all a favour.'

'Maybe they did,' Roman says, a little too cannily.

I wonder what he knows that I don't, or whether he's the bad cop after all and has just been messing me about. My head is starting to throb.

'I'm going to make you some toast. Then I'll need the recording of the dream. And any other dreams that might be connected with Bernard. Even if we can't run the material, we may be able to identify his neural signature.'

The security system pings. There's someone outside the flat. A smooth, bass voice comes through the intercom. 'I'm here to represent my client, Charlotte Aaron. Please let me in. I'm a solicitor and she has a right to representation'

That voice is familiar, rich, silky like melted chocolate... Where have I heard it before...?

Shandy elbows me. 'Who's that?'

I shrug. 'I don't have a solicitor,' I whisper. I go to the camera feed. It's an awkward angle, but I recognise him immediately all the same. 'Oh, no! That's bloody Martin Elstree. Please, make him go away!'

Shandy folds her arms and glares at Roman. 'Let him in. You heard the man, he's Charlie's lawyer.'

I'm pulling at her sleeve like a toddler at playgroup. Hissing in her ear: 'But I hate him, he's horrible, and he's only a patent—'

'Let him in, Roman.'

Roman looks out of his depth. He buzzes Martin Elstree in, and the next thing I know we are all having coffee over the dead man's coffee table, a heavy slab of glass in which are floating a collection of vintage *Zelda* game covers. Elstree shakes my hand and smiles as though we've never met. I must be making my frog face. I just know I am. He doesn't seem to notice.

'We need to put him in the Cone of Silence,' Shandy says, and then has to explain the app all over again to Elstree.

'That won't be necessary,' he says. 'I have a professional tool for confidentiality. I'll enshroud all of us here. It will block mics in the room, cameras, everything, as well as any watchware that you may be carrying without knowing it.' He glances at me and I look away. I can't stand him, and then for some stupid reason I feel guilty that I can't stand him and maybe I should give him another chance just to be polite, and this is one of the many reasons I am an idiot. But it's who I am, OK?

Shandy says, 'Yay for your professional tools. But Charlie only talks if there's Cone of Silence, so either take what I'm squirting you or go home, kthxbai.'

Elstree cracks a big, handsome grin. He wags a finger at her. 'I like you,' he says. 'Fine, squirt away.'

He likes her. I shudder.

# Two takeaways plus tea

I'd like to wipe from memory the hour spent deflecting Martin Elstree's questions whilst simultaneously fending off unsubtle attempts by Roman to get hold of all my Secret Diaries 'for my own good'. I don't think Elstree found out too much, but I'm left with an oily feeling on my skin and a sense of crawling unease that goes much deeper. I find myself keeping Cone of Silence on just so I won't have to deal with anyone.

By the time I get home, it's nearly midnight. The flat is silent and O's light is switched off, so I make tea and creep into my room. Edgar joins me; usually he sleeps on O's bed but if he's too playful she locks him out. He dashes around my floor chasing a rubber band.

I have to talk to O about Daphne and this 'Agency' and their pigeon messages. I'm haunted by the dream of the vengeful dead people – especially Daphne. I can't believe the way she blithely walked him in front of a train. It was nothing less than an execution.

I shudder thinking about all the other 'suicides' that Roman told me about. Did Daphne kill them, too? Why? And what about Mel?

My brain is spinning. O doesn't sleep well; she's usually up by four. I decide to use the time until then to get my facts together. I open a notepad.

*If Bernard killed Mel and now he's dead then we're done.*

*What if he didn't? The fencing mask doesn't prove anything. Why did Daphne really kill him? Who gave her Bernard as a target?*

*Why would anyone want to kill Mel in the first place?*

*Roman says study participants have been getting killed by sleep-walking. But Mel wasn't in a study. Is someone trying to turn the general population into sleepwalkers? That points to BigSky because Sweet Dreams is their platform. But why Mel?*

## Suspects

**Bernard** – *Had access to brain tech and BigSky. Had fencing mask. Motive?*

**Meera Bhango** – *Unknown. Can O help?*

**Daphne** – *Killed Bernard on orders of Agency. But Agency is a game with O – right??? Who else knows about it? Must tell O what happened.*

**Dream Police** – *Seem nice but what if they are working for BigSky or for one of BigSky's criminal arms? They are so keen to get my recordings. But who are they?*

**Antonio** – *Had access to Mel but not Bernard. Could be lying about money, maybe someone paid him. Why did he hire me?*

The Creeper told me to butt out of Mel's dreams. Again and again. Why didn't he want me there? What doesn't he want me to see or do?

About here, I get stuck. Well, I can try to find out more about Antonio. I deactivate Cone of Silence and fire up Spacetime. A little flood of messages comes in, but I don't look at them right away; I'm afraid I'll lose my nerve. Instead, I Spacetime Antonio. I've little hope of actually speaking to him – O suggested he was forced to leave the country and I now feel sure she knows stuff I don't about all this. So when he picks up I get flustered.

'Charlie! So good to see you! I'm taking off for Australia tomorrow. I've been invited to teach at a retreat in the desert. How are you doing? Those kebab guys aren't giving you trouble, are they?'

'I'm good, it's all fine,' I lie, smiling. 'Hey, Antonio, something's been bugging me and I was just curious.'

'Sure! Of course! Anything you want to know.'

'When you contacted O to hire me, you called my business line.'

'Yeah, well, I wanted to approach you as a professional.'

'But how did you know about the business? I wasn't advertising. We hadn't spoken. Who told you I was a dreamhacker?'

'Ah! Well, I guess somebody must have, but I can't remember who. All I can tell you is that the night before I called you, I had a vivid dream about your business card – you know, the one that says

"Dreamhacker"? – and how I was going to call you. So when I woke, I looked you up and there you were. Dream therapist, same thing, right?'

'It actually said Dreamhacker on the card in your dream?'

'Yeah, definitely. Why?'

'It's just that I didn't start calling myself that until after Shandy ran the marketing numbers for me, which was after you called. I gave Mel a card when I met her. Maybe that's what you remember.'

Or maybe you're lying, Antonio.

'That's really strange. But I definitely dreamed it. I am always one to listen to the intuition, you know, Charlie? That's why I reached out to you.'

Then he tells me he'll send me a postcard from Australia. I end the conversation as quickly as I can. He's either very clueless or a great actor, and if he were the latter I'm sure with his looks he would have a lot more money, so I'm going with clueless. Which means that someone tampered with his dream. I was brought in to work with Mel by someone other than Antonio, someone who already thought of me as a dreamhacker. Who?

I send Shandy a quick message to ask her how exactly she got those marketing numbers and where the name 'dreamhacker' came from. By now the pile of messages is jostling for my attention. Lots from clients, nothing from O, but one from Meera and three in quick succession from Muz, of all people.

Meera's says simply: **Come to my lab asap. We need to talk in person.**

She's as bad as O. She hasn't mentioned anything about Bernard's death, but she must know by now. Everyone must know. Well, her message was left several hours ago and there's no way she's going to be in her lab in the middle of the night.

I pick up Muz's messages.

**6.10 p.m. At Princess Grace Hospital. Got dizzy, had a fall. Come over when you get this.**

I'm confused. Why is he telling me he's in hospital? Is he

trying to reach O? I wonder if she's switched off her connections again . . .

I get out of bed and open my door. I'll have to wake her up. Then:

**8.32 p.m. No head injury, probably low blood pressure. OK but bruised and weak. Keeping her in for observation. Can you bring toothbrush, nightclothes, etc.?**

He's talking about O! I knock on her door, then push it open. The bed is made. No sign of O or her wheelchair.

**8.34 p.m. Never mind, Jez is on it. Call me when you get this.**

I Spacetime him but he's offline, so I leave an apologetic message and then Spacetime Jez, who is wide awake.

*'Oh, hi, yeah, she's OK. Well, not OK but not at death's door. Apparently she's anaemic and has low blood pressure, and when she tried to get up she fainted. She's a little bruised but not complaining.'*

This is bad. This is very bad.

*'Are you sure she fainted? She wasn't . . . erm . . .'* I'm trying to think of a way to ask whether O could have been sleepwalking without bringing Jez in on all the developments. *'Did anyone else see it happen, or is this just her memory of what happened?'*

*'No, Lorraine was there. She said O was having a kip in her recliner and for some reason took it in her head to try to stand and walk across the room, which of course was a bad idea. Lorraine couldn't catch her in time, apparently.'*

*'Oh no.'* It's everything I've been afraid of. And now, looking back on the wrist injury O just had, I wonder if I got the full story on that or not. It feels too coincidental.

*'Don't worry,'* Jez sings. *'She's not cross with you. She gets it that you can't be around her all the time. I'm going in the morning, anyway. Just need to finish knitting socks for my dog. You can't access Spacetime past the hospital firewall, by the way.'*

*'Yeah, I saw the signs. Thanks.'*

I make tea. They won't let me into the hospital in the middle of the night, but the sooner I get this over with, the better. Not only do I have to tell O that her sister has killed a man, but it's possible that someone is using the same technology to come after O as well. Something as simple as a brief faint could be a serious thing if she hit her head on the way down.

Still. Clearly, O has been anticipating something. She put Stack on my tail and if Lorraine was here, then O has mobilized her resources to protect herself. But what does O actually *know* that she's not telling me?

I'm working on answering client messages and trying to figure out my schedule when the outside buzzer for the flat goes. The video link shows a woman in trackies and a hijab carrying a big paper bag. Meera Bhango looks up at the camera and waves.

'I've been trying to get hold of you and I ended up speaking with Olivia this afternoon,' she tells me after she's run up the stairs. She's not even winded. 'She told me you'd been tied up all day. As soon as I saw you'd received my message, I came over.'

'But it's almost three o'clock in the morning.'

'I know, and I won't stay long. I wanted to speak with you in person.'

The paper bag turns out to be a takeaway from the 24-hour Malaysian restaurant a few blocks away. She has even brought tea.

As we tuck in, she says, 'I know it's weird for me to just show up here. It's a long story, but my company is involved in an ugly litigation with BigSky and I don't really trust any digital form of communication. That's why I suggested meeting in person. But you didn't show up.'

'I'm sorry about that.'

'It's OK, I got your message. Today when Olivia told me that this flat is secure, I thought it would be best if we just spoke here.'

'What's the litigation about?'

'Oh, it's intellectual property. You know my colleague Bernard? I'm not sure if anybody told you, but he brought research from BigSky to Little Bird and the solicitors are fighting over whether all of his work belongs to BigSky or only some of it. And now that he's dead, it's even more complicated because nobody can find a will. I hope this doesn't sound too cloak-and-dagger.'

I say, 'It would be impossible to overstate how cloak-and-dagger this is.'

'Listen, a lot of this stuff I just can't talk about. I'm bound by all kinds of confidentiality agreements and ethical considerations. But I wanted you to know that I'm on your side and I'll try to help you. I think Bernard treated you and the others very shabbily. I told him as much, too. Believe it or not, we've been trying to make it right.'

'He didn't say anything about that when I saw him.'

'OK, then. *I've* been trying to make it right. I can't get my head around what happened with Bernard last night. He didn't have a lot of feeling for his fellow humans, and I had no idea he was feeling so guilty, much less close to suicide.'

I stop chewing.

'Is that what they told you? Suicide?'

'Well, he was on the railway tracks – they told us that much. I understand you were in the building at the time. Do you know something I don't?'

I put my teacup down very carefully. I can't afford to trust her. Hello-my-name-is-Meera-I'm-going-to-help-you.

'Meera, you said the litigation with BigSky is ugly. Have you taken steps for your own personal safety?'

Her voice is sharp: 'What do you mean, my personal safety?'

'Everyone knows there's a shady element to BigSky, that's all.'

'Do you really buy that sort of talk?'

I shrug, and her lip wobbles.

'If you know something, Charlie, you had better tell me right now. I've got children at home.'

'I think you should talk to Roman Pelka. I'll give you his contact information.'

'I already got a call from him and another from someone called Donato something.'

'Call them back,' I say. 'Ask for their help. Thanks for the food. You'd better go now.'

She nods. 'OK, I get it. I was only trying to build bridges, but I can take a hint.'

'I meant what I said about your safety,' I tell her. 'I don't trust anyone right now and nor should you. Why don't you come back when you're ready to break your confidentiality agreement and tell me what's really going on?'

I'm trembling all over when I lock the door behind her, but at least I've managed to stay awake throughout the confrontation. I drink the rest of my tea, now cold and a little sour, and fall asleep on the sofa while Edgar picks at the satay prawns left on the coffee table.

I arrive at the Princess Grace just before lunch. It's unlike any hospital I've ever seen. For one thing, it's quiet. O has a private room on the first floor with a couple of nice armchairs and a small table and fresh flowers beside the bed. She is sitting in one of the armchairs playing chess on a holographic board, and I don't know if it's the lighting or my imagination but she looks older and her face is drawn. The blue patches under her eyes are exaggerated.

'I brought you soup,' I announce, tapping on the open door. She doesn't react at first and I wonder if she's heard me. She moves a rook and then says, 'Did you make it?'

'It's takeout from Marylebone, you cheeky woman.'

'Let's have it, then. It looks like I'm stuck here. Waiting on test results.'

I pull up a chair opposite the holographic chessboard and open the lid on the takeaway soup. It's still really hot.

'I'm sorry I haven't been here before this. I had a pretty bad narcoleptic attack yesterday.'

She doesn't look at me. All her attention is on the board.

'Birds OK?'

'Yes, they're all well and accounted for.'

'I sent Muz home. He's tired. Jez has been helping.'

'And you? How are you feeling? What even happened? You fainted?'

'I stood up to go to the loo. I thought I'd be all right to walk but you know how low my blood pressure is sometimes. It was just a miscalculation.'

'You're sure you didn't doze off, O? It's important.'

'Of course not.'

I'm fairly sure she's lying. Why? To spare me worry, probably.

I try to think of something to say that doesn't sound patronising. I want to say, *What were you thinking? Don't do that*, etc., but it's not my place to tell her what to do, and even if it were, she would surely bite my head off.

So instead I tell her about Bernard. How he sent us packing, how I tried to dreamhack him and he ended up dead. I omit the part about Daphne. I think she senses I've skated over something because she looks at me oddly, but she doesn't pursue it. She's sipping the soup, both hands curved around the paper cup, shaking.

'O, are you all right with that? It's hot.'

She puts the soup down and blots her upper lip. She doesn't mince words.

'So he's dead and you think the Creeper did it.' Her gaze is flat. No way to tell what she's thinking.

'I was there for the whole dream. He was sleepwalking. He thought he was in a formal garden, not a railway station. Roman says it's hard to tell from the CCTV whether he was awake. He doesn't seem to have spoken to anyone, but he went through the fare scanner fairly normally.'

'And one gathers the police don't have any evidence it was anything other than suicide or foolish error.'

'No. But that's not the point. I was there. I *know*. And the dream police now know I was present at both of these killings – Mel and now Bernard.'

'You think someone is trying to frame you?'

I should tell her about Daphne. I should. But she looks so small and vulnerable in the hospital bed.

'I don't know what to think. But it's been . . . unnerving.'

'You're sure you trust Shandy?'

'I've known her since we were seven, O. There's no way I don't trust her.'

'She does work for BigSky.'

'Yeah, in the virtual interior decorating department – she designs nice habitats for people's Floopies.'

'What on earth is a Floopie?'

'They're like virtual pets, but they're smart. By the way, O, why did you send Martin Elstree to represent me? I mean, of all people.'

'I did no such thing.'

'You didn't?'

'Of course not. I know how you feel about him – you made it perfectly clear after you worked with him.'

'He said you sent him.'

O snorts. 'I know that I have a lot of people running around after me lately, with Muz and Jez and now you. But I'm not exactly . . . Well, it's not like I'm this powerful person who bosses everybody around. Edgar doesn't even stay off my bed like I tell him to. I don't know why Martin said that. He's out of order. I shall speak with him.'

Frowning, she turns her attention back to the chessboard.

'I wonder how he found out about the Bernard situation,' she murmurs. 'Maybe through Meera, or even BigSky themselves.'

I'm actually shaking. This is all too much.

'Does Martin Elstree have connections to BigSky? That you know of?'

'Of course! He knows everyone there. He's a patent lawyer specializing in tech. Half of London has connections to BigSky. Speaking of which, where do things stand with your Dream Police?'

'Never mind them. O, I'm really worried about what I've got

you into. I don't even know how I've done it or what it is I've done, but someone's tried to take me out in my dream just like what happened to Mel. And Bernard is dead. I thought he was the Creeper, but if he wasn't, then who is? And now you.'

'What do you mean, "now me"? I just had a fall. It happens to us decrepit ones every day.'

'You're not decrepit and you know it. Apparently you nodded off, and then you got up and tried to walk in your sleep. That's what Lorraine said, and I'm more inclined to believe her than you.'

'Thank you very much, darling, for being so frank. But then, you always have been. Does every single thing you are thinking actually come out of your mouth, or could there possibly be more that you haven't broadcast to the world – yet?'

How can I convey just how scary O is? She's superior to me in every way but I adore her, and when she disapproves of me I just want to crawl under a rock. But she doesn't realise how vulnerable she is. If I don't stand up to her, something terrible could happen and I'd never forgive myself.

'I was not sleepwalking,' she insists. 'I hope you haven't come here with the intention of hovering over me watching me sleep, because I assure you, I'll have none of it.'

'O, I don't think you understand. People have been killed. Someone tried to kill *me*. You know the thing with the lorry and the Peugeot? If it hadn't been for Stack—'

'Which is exactly why I put Stack on point in the first place. I am well aware that you're in danger. What I am saying to you is that *I did not sleepwalk*. So you must focus on what is really important, namely your own safety. Maybe I should get Muz to escort you back to the flat.'

'No, I'm fine, don't be silly.'

'Well, you can't stay here.'

'Why not?'

We sound like a couple of biddies bickering. Then I thump my hand on the table and the holographic chess game quivers.

'Damnit, O, there's something else I have to tell you but I don't know how to do it.'

She folds her hands in her lap. Cocks her birdlike head. Raises her eyebrows and waits.

'It's about Daphne.'

O smiles. 'She thinks she's a secret agent.'

'How so?' She quirks an eyebrow and waits for my answer. She knows very well how I hate confrontation; she's not making this easy. I stifle a yawn. My body would love to give up and go to sleep. But I've got to tell her.

'Your sister was in Bernard's dream. A whole gang of . . . I don't know what to call them. People with dementia, elderly people. They were all there, accusing Bernard of making them sleepwalk.'

'Wow. He must have been feeling guilty to dream that.'

'No, you don't understand. She was *really* there. Daphne hacked Bernard's dream.'

'Hmm.' Plainly unconvinced. 'Daphne only *thinks* she's a secret agent. It's an old joke from when we were children. We grew up during the Cold War. The pigeons are just a game, but also a practicality for me. You know how I feel about digital communication – I like to have analogue options for important things in case of emergency. I'd use smoke signals if I could.'

'But she told me she'd been given a mission, a target. Wait . . . are *you* the one sending her the messages? Are you the Agency?'

O stares at me with those cunning blue eyes. 'She gets carried away. She was always jealous of my role in MI5 when she was stuck being a housewife. She would have made an excellent field agent, but I'm more of a behind-the-scenes person.'

'But it's not just a fantasy, O.' I catch myself raising my voice and lower my tone to a whisper, leaning towards her. 'I saw your sister open up Bernard's back with a key. I saw her climb inside and manipulate him into the situation that got him killed. It was fully calculated.'

She moves her chair away from me a little, avoiding eye contact.

At last, she says, 'It is terribly regrettable, that Bernard died. Worse, that you had to see it. But how can you be sure it was Daphne and not your subconscious manifesting as Daphne?'

'Because my subconscious can't make people sleepwalk! Because she said she'd been given a target and she acted. Are you really going to deny what I'm saying? How can I make you see...?'

My voice peters out. She doesn't believe me. She's shaking her head.

'The whole thing is a mess. It's going to cause a lot of trouble for Little Bird if BigSky get wind of what happened. They'll try to use Bernard's death to grab the IP for your study, and who knows what they'll do with it once they have control.'

My teeth are chattering. I still remember the way the Creeper loomed over me, how hard it was to breathe, impossible to move... How can she be so dispassionate? A man is dead. *Two* people are dead, but I don't dare mention Mel or I'll make myself pass out with fear. I'm amazed I've been able to stay awake long enough to have this conversation. Normally my narcolepsy would have felled me a few sentences in.

'Can *you* do it, is the question,' O says, still watching me keenly. 'Can you disable R.E.M. atonia? Can you trick someone into sleepwalking?'

'No! Of course not! I never tried—'

'Well, Charlie, if someone is setting you up for murder then it's in your interests to be incompetent, so long as you can prove to the police that you're incompetent. But if the Creeper comes after you, then you need to be able to fight back. So you've got to decide whether you're going to run and hide, or whether you're going to face this... whatever it is, this entity... whether you're going to face it head-on.'

I can't believe how she's dodged the whole issue of Daphne and put it back on me.

'O, aren't you afraid for yourself? I'm less worried about myself than I am about you.'

'You're being ridiculous now. I don't even use Sweet Dreams, so how could I be hacked? Charlie, go home.'

'All right, I'll go.' But I'm checking windows and scanning the room for anything dangerous. Out in the corridor, I pull one of the nurses aside and warn her about the sleepwalking risk. Then I station myself in the lobby and field client messages and write an update to Shandy, but after a while I'm told that visiting hours are over and I'm not permitted to stay for 'security reasons' which is code for 'you look homeless and we can't have that here'. I then sit outside on the steps, but a security guard moves me along. It starts to rain, of course.

I have such a bad feeling that something's going to happen to her. Why won't she take me seriously? Why doesn't anyone? What do I have to do?

I go home. I take out the earring and fall asleep. Again.

## Sleep paralysis personified

'Charlie! Wake up! Charlie, it's Roman. Wake up!'

Someone's buzzing downstairs and shouting on the intercom. I scramble out of bed, trip over Edgar, vault over the sofa and finally get to the door. This time it's Roman holding a brolly and a cardboard tray of coffees. At least my visitors are feeding me.

'I tried to contact you but you were unreachable,' he says when he's huffed his way up the stairs. The delay has given me enough time to put on a sweatshirt and smear some toothpaste over my nasty tongue, but I'm still dazed. 'Did you take my advice?'

'Yeah, I'm offline,' I say, accepting a coffee off him and pausing to inhale the smell before I take my first sip. We sit on O's sofa. It's weird without her here. Edgar immediately installs himself on Roman's lap and begins kneading. Roman strokes the cat awkwardly.

'I have some new information.'

'I'm listening.'

'Donato has been pursuing the idea that Antonio paid for the suite on one of the upper floors and then killed Melodic. I found this to be a bit flimsy if it was premeditated, because one of the payments was routed through a Russian account before it went into Antonio's bank and the other just came straight out of his debit card. If anything, he would need to be more careful with the second suite because it was then that matters were getting serious. Why withdraw his own money so openly?'

'I told you it had to be a set-up,' I said.

'And I listened, didn't I? I also thought about what you said about proximity and dreamhacking, and I looked to see if another person of interest could have been on the same floor.'

'You already told me there was no one.'

211

He nods. 'There wasn't. There isn't. But I wasn't thinking vertically, was I? So yesterday I looked again and guess who booked the room directly below the Windsor Suite the night Melodie died?'

He's watching me carefully. This is going to be a bombshell.

'Look, mate, I just woke up.'

'Martin Elstree. Your solicitor.'

'He's not my solicitor!'

'Right . . . So you've sacked him?'

'No, I just—' It's getting hard to keep track of my lies. Fuck it, may as well be honest. I fold my arms over my chest and glare at Roman. 'I never hired him, he's a former client and I dislike him *a lot*. I was just playing along because I don't like being interrogated and asked to turn over my dream records while you guys keep me in the dark.' Shit. And O says she didn't hire him. Eww.

'I'm not keeping you in the dark now, am I? Elstree is definitely connected to O, and so are you. What do you know about the relationship between those two?'

I shrug, thinking. 'He's been working on an IP case for her. She didn't say what.'

'Was he, now? I wish you'd told me this sooner.'

'Why? Where are you going with this?'

'Well, I checked around and ostensibly Elstree was in the hotel for a meeting with some BigSky lawyers. You know, that's how BigSky like to work – low overheads, hard to trace what they're really up to. So they were supposed to be finalizing the arrangements on Bernard Zborowski's right to take his IP to Little Bird.'

'The coincidences mount, don't they? Was Bernard there?'

'No. Just the lawyers. But it bothers me that Elstree was in close proximity to Mel.'

'Me, too.'

'Now, if Martin Elstree somehow has access to the same

agent that infected you, then it is actually possible that he can dreamhack.'

'Seriously? Then why did he hire me for sex dreams?'

Roman slams his coffee cup on the table and it sloshes over his hand, burning him. Edgar goes flying. Damn. Roman's disproportionately unhappy about the sex dreams thing. Maybe he likes me.

'Come on, into the kitchen. Run some cold water on it.'

'It's fine, I'm all right.' He paces around the living room, red-faced, flapping the hand and tripping over Edgar. I whip into the kitchen and run the cold tap into a sink full of two-day-old dishes. He comes in sulkily and puts his hand under.

'You might have told me this sooner.'

'I had no idea it could be relevant. And I was trying to forget the whole episode. Elstree is disgusting. But it's a big leap to accuse him of dreamhacking.'

He won't look at me. 'I know. It's not exactly likely that a high-powered solicitor would willingly inject himself with an infection that could cause narcolepsy.'

'And hair loss! He's already got a widow's peak.'

'But I want the recordings for review. If you won't hand them over, you're only hurting yourself. Not to mention other potential victims.'

'Have you told the Met about your suspicions?'

He swings his head from side to side slowly. 'I'd be laughed at. We need evidence that the Met can respect. Oneiric crime is almost impossible to prove.'

'I've got to level with you, Roman. O warned me that you and Donato could be in BigSky's pocket. I'm not giving you anything that personal knowing you could turn around and sell it to BigSky.'

He shakes his head and gives a mocking laugh. 'They already have it. If you've used Sweet Dreams and left your stuff on one of their servers, BigSky can get it easily. Even Donato could probably get it if he tried. Is that how you want this to work? Distrusting each other all the time?'

My turn to mock. 'Who kept me prisoner in a kebab shop and interviewed me like a criminal?'

'Yeah, and what exactly was that performance? You pretended not to know the word "indemnify" and fell asleep at least five times!'

'It couldn't have been more than four. I told you, I'm narcoleptic. I pass out when under stress.'

'And you're not under stress now?'

We face each other on either end of the Belfast sink. He been gesticulating wildly as he's talking. When Antonio does it, it's Latin and sexy. When Roman does it, it's dangerous. He has long arms and his hands are flying around randomly. I take a step back and fold my arms. He's right, I haven't fallen asleep. Why?

He's watching my face. He says, 'You're good at acting like a muppet, but I don't think you are one.'

He had the upper hand there for a second, but he's thrown it away.

'So now I'm a muppet, am I? Charming. Where's the coffee?'

I go back to the sitting room and he follows me. He's on the defensive again. He stands awkwardly, pretending to look at the titles on O's bookshelves before he realises most of them are in Cyrillic. Eventually he gives up.

'Look, let's just stop fighting, can't we?'

'I'm not fighting. I'm not even properly awake.' I guzzle coffee.

'OK, good. Because I need to explain something. I haven't wanted to bring this up before because I don't expect you to be receptive to it, but it's becoming important now that you've been attacked personally.'

'What? Spit it out, Roman.'

He starts ticking off points on his fingers.

'I've talked to all the sleep researchers. I've talked to partners of victims, I've talked to witnesses. And I've concluded that . . . the Creeper isn't a person. It's a natural phenomenon.'

At first, I laugh. Then I realise he's completely serious and my laughter goes cold. Freezing cold. His presumption. It makes me so angry, after everything that's happened, that he thinks he can tell me my own business. My eyes narrow.

'You've talked to people, have you? Aren't you clever. Well, maybe you'd like to consider that I've seen the Creeper. I've had it in my dreams. I've had it crushing me down trying to suck the life out of me, trying to devour me. It's a person, and it's a bad person. A *malevolent* person. I know what I'm talking about. You don't know anything. *You* should be the one taking *me* seriously.'

'I do! I do take you seriously. Just . . . OK, I get it. You've experienced it, you know. But can you entertain what I'm saying for one moment, just hear me out? Please?'

I don't want to hear him out. But now I'm embarrassed about my tantrum so I pout and say, 'Fine, talk.'

'OK, so there's this thing called R.E.M atonia, right? It's a mechanism that stops us all acting out our dreams every single time we sleep. And of course it's imperfect – people twitch in their sleep, talk in their sleep, even do coherent things like walk around and try to perform everyday actions. But it's just a physical mechanism. Think of it like the brain taking itself offline to work on problems internally, without actually putting the body at risk. That's what dreaming is.'

'Thanks for the mansplanation, bruv. Mel's problem was that she should have had R.E.M. atonia and stayed in bed, but she didn't.'

'Exactly. She was engaging in high-level organised movements and responses while dreaming. But there's more. There's a thing called sleep paralysis. It's a phenomenon that's been observed and recorded for centuries, to the point where it's become a cultural archetype, personified as a villain in fairy tales and horror movies. The dark, hooded presence. The white-faced stranger in black robes. Death itself. This is what you describe as the Creeper.'

'You make it sound like a cliché, but it's not like that, Roman.'

'I'm sure it's not. Listen. A person will wake up and find they can't move a muscle. They sense a presence nearby. Sometimes the presence is on top of them and they can't breathe – they are being suffocated. This presence has been given different names, but in the last twenty years it's been known colloquially as the Stranger. And I'm telling you, the Stranger is the Creeper. The feeling of not being able to move. The dark presence with the white face. The sense of creeping malevolence. They're all classic. The dreamer interprets the loss of motor control as a supernatural entity that intends them harm.'

I snort. 'I know what the Stranger is. Is that really all you've got? The Creeper is the Stranger?'

'No, I have more. But it's speculative. Just hear me out and keep an open mind.'

I roll my eyes but say nothing.

'As a dreamhacker, when you access someone's dreamspace, you don't interfere with their R.E.M. atonia. But *what if you could*? What if you could turn off the neural gate that controls muscle movement, so that the person's body would respond to the conditions imposed in dreamspace? They'd be moving in reaction to the dream, acting out whatever they were experiencing there. What if you really could hack into their brain at that level *while at the same time* shaping their dream environment? Think of the consequences.'

Mel on the bathroom floor, her head in the bathtub. She was hacked, her R.E.M. atonia disabled, and while I was distracted the Creeper somehow led her to the bathroom. There she was convinced by events in the dream environment to turn on the taps and submerge herself, and then ... what? The atonia was reactivated to keep her head in the water?

OK, it could fit. Roman's watching me think through the whole thing. Maybe he is on to something. But I'm not about to say so without some kind of evidence. I fold my arms and wait for the hard evidence. But it doesn't come.

'So this is where I am with it,' he says eventually. 'But there are so many unanswered questions. Especially: how could the dreamhacker learn to do that to someone? It's easy enough to see *why* they'd want to do it. All kinds of perfect crimes would become possible if you could refine the method.'

I hate this. My dreamhacking is intended to help people improve their lives in nice, happy ways – stop smoking or drop ten pounds or resolve their childhood phobia of poodles. None of this is what I signed up for. I want to run far, far away.

Roman says, 'I've been tracking sleep crimes for a few years now and I think we're seeing the learning curve of one or more dreamhackers reflected in the increasing sleep-related deaths around Greater London. This is one reason why we wanted to talk to you. Because you're not the first dreamhacker, but your abilities are developing. You can do more than others who received the treatment at the same time. Maybe you're close to being able to make people sleepwalk, too.'

'What others?' I say sharply.

'Sorry?'

He didn't mean to say that. He's put his foot in it now. He can't look at me. I asked O to find the other trial participants but she never came back to me. If only I could meet my own kind...

'I repeat: what others, Roman? If you want my cooperation, you need to level with me. Who else are you talking to? How did you find them?'

'I'm not allowed to tell you. For your own protection and theirs, and for mine, if I'm honest. I'm sorry, Charlie.'

'Yeah, you're sorry.' That's code for: *we suspect you*. Who wouldn't? Stupid damn tears are welling in my eyes now. Roman doesn't understand. There are other people who have the same problem as me! He knows them and won't tell me who they are. They could be my enemies but they could also be my friends.

I've been trying to figure this all out in isolation and maybe that's not necessary. I want to meet my people!

'I don't want you to think that *I* think you've done anything wrong, Charlie.' He touches my arm gently. 'If I did, I'd never speak to you off the record like this. I wouldn't... I wouldn't return your bras or ask if you're OK or lie awake worrying about you— I mean, you know. All in the line of duty.'

'They're not my bras, by the way,' I say quickly.

He flushes pink. I pretend not to notice.

'Donato thinks I'm up to something,' I say. 'That means you guys are less than useless to me. Because if even a tiny bit of you thinks I'm part of the problem then your heads are up your arses. If you had any real information about who is doing this or how, then you wouldn't be considering me a danger in any way. Straight logic, Roman. You don't know shit. I'm calling O, make sure she got through the night OK. Stay there. I'm going on the roof.'

I walk out amongst the pigeons in the growing light. I call O, but there's no response. I call the Princess Grace and they put me on hold.

I'm scared. I knew Elstree was trouble. Knew it from the way he tortured his boss with power tools and thought it was funny. And he's wormed his way into O's life somehow, with all this IP stuff. No wonder he came sniffing around after Bernard's death. What if he did some kind of deal with BigSky? He may not even be acting in good faith on behalf of Bernard and Meera. Well, if he's behind Bernard's murder—

No, that can't be right. I saw Daphne hack Bernard, and she doesn't work for BigSky.

There's been an attempt on my life – thwarted by Stack, bless him and his beautiful teeth. O's in hospital so you'd think she'd be safe... but how can anybody be safe from getting attacked in their sleep? Whoever is doing this is the lowest of the low to prey on an elderly woman who is ill and frail. I'm getting angrier and angrier the more I think about it. And Mel. What did she ever do to anybody?

I have to act. I never should have left O there alone. I have to go and sit watch over her. And get help, in case I fall asleep on duty. We need, like, a chain of people to watch over each other's sleep. How am I going to explain this when even O doesn't believe me?

I ping Shandy but she's still unavailable, working. I hate talking to her bots, especially Rodney. It says a lot about my state of mind that I've been clinging to Shandy to keep track of something like reality. If she's out of the picture and O is in hospital and Antonio's en route to Australia, who is left for me to lean on?

Finally, the front desk at the hospital pick up again. A cheerful man informs me that Olivia Ogiyevich discharged herself last night.

# Knitters, cat-lovers, tea-drinkers

I hit O's primitive non-Spacetime phone link, but I just get a message wall. I hit her text messages, too. Nothing. Why does she have to be so old-school?

I call Daphne's residence, but the front desk say that O hasn't signed in since our last visit. I make them double check but it's no use.

*'She left last night,'* Muz tells me when I Spacetime him. *'She said to bring the hog round, which I did. She signed herself out around 11 pm and drove off.'*

'And you let her?'

*'You obviously don't know her very well.'* There's a note of warning in Muz's voice. Like, who the hell am I to tell him?

*'Did you at least follow her or find out where she was going?'*

*'I assumed she was going home. It's not my business where she goes.'*

'But Muz. She's not home. She's in danger. I can't believe this.'

*'If she needs me, she'll be in touch with me. That's how it works. I don't ask questions, and whatever happens I don't answer to you. Goodbye, Charlie.'*

I go back into the sitting room. I tell Roman what Muz told me.

'Shit,' he says. 'What do you think happened?'

'I have no fucking idea, but I've got to find her.'

'Absolutely.' He's on his feet.

Words are still tumbling out of my mouth anyway: 'I can't sit around here theorizing with you about who did what or why or how. She's in danger, I'm sure of it, and she's so convinced she's untouchable but she's like eighty years old and frail.'

'I agree, so—'

'I'll never forgive myself if something bad happens to her because of me.'

'Fine. I'll go with you.'

'That's a bad idea.' But I take the jacket he hands me.

He says, 'Do you think she's been dreamhacked?'

'I don't know. But she should be home. She took the hog. She only ever takes the hog if she's going to see Daphne, and I've already checked with the residence. O hasn't been there.'

'If she's on her vehicle, we can find her,' Roman says. 'We've had her under surveillance for a while. Let me talk to Donato. We'll track her down.'

'O, under surveillance? Seriously, *why?*'

He shrugs. 'It hasn't done us much good, actually. We checked her out just to make sure she is what she says she is, and it turns out she's a security expert with a long history in the tech industry. Because of that, she's very good at eluding scrutiny. Her digital footprint is totally clean. But we put a tracker on her motorbike. We reckon if she's up to anything, she's doing it analogue-style. In person.'

'But she never goes out. So how's that strategy working out for you?' I can't help sneering. I'm so angry that O and I – knitters, cat-lovers, tea-drinkers that we are – are under surveillance and he doesn't even care about Martin Elstree of the power saw.

'She's out now,' he says.

'That's because she's in danger, you bloody idiot! She's probably been lured somewhere. Or ... Or dreamhacked, like you said! She could be sleep-driving, she could be lying in a ditch as we speak.'

'In Central London? Which ditch would this be?'

'Shut up. You know what I mean. They are trying to get at me through her!'

It's too late. The words are out of my mouth. And now I sound like a Paranoid Patty.

'Who? Who do you reckon are trying to get at you?'

What kind of conspiracy theorist am I when I don't even know who's behind the conspiracy?

'You could start with Martin Elstree, like we just bloody

discussed. Oh, why do I even talk to you? I'm going to call Muz again.'

'He's on airplane mode.'

'How do you— Wait, are you monitoring Muz, too?'

Roman looks at his toes.

'This is ridiculous. Why don't you do something useful for a change? Where's Martin Elstree right now?'

Roman's eyes roll up as he checks in with his surveillance bots. 'In a meeting at his office.'

'Well, just . . . I don't know, just find O's hog. Please. It's important.'

'I'm on it. But if you want to know what I really think—'

I turn on my heel and glower at him. 'Go on, then. If you have an actual idea.'

'I do have an idea. The pigeons.'

'What?'

'O keeps racing pigeons. Unusual hobby, don't you think? She exchanges birds with her sister in . . . where is it? Guildford?'

'Dorking. How do you know they're racing pigeons?'

'She has the birdseed shipped in. She has a vet. Her sister has birds. It's not hard to find this stuff out.'

'You're really nosey.'

'So I'm told. So, Dorking, is that the only place they go? Do you know for sure?'

'Oh my god. Sidney!' It suddenly hits me.

'Who is Sidney?'

'A pigeon. With a tiddly backpack. He brought O a message, and I don't think it was from Daphne because Sidney was knackered when he arrived. You're right, Roman! It fits in with her whole low-tech approach to communications. It's worth a try. We've got to release the pigeons and follow them.'

'Whoa, let's not be hasty. I need to be mindful of resources. Just think. Is there someone she trusts, somewhere she'd go if there was trouble?'

I try to calm my mind and think. Jez certainly doesn't qualify, and unless Muz was lying he doesn't know anything. I shake my head.

'My guess is that she knew perfectly well she'd been dream-hacked into sleepwalking but just didn't want to tell me, so she slipped away somewhere safe. But I can't think where that would be. I honestly don't know her well enough.'

'The question is, if Sidney is homed to O's roof, then will he return to where he came from?'

'Probably. She also has these special birds that never go out ... or I've never seen them go, anyway. We can check if any of them are missing. Maybe she's already sent a message back to Sidney's point of origin.'

I'm getting excited. I can do something, and I can do it while I'm awake!

'We must be able to track them,' Roman says. 'Let me think how to do it.'

'Don't tell Donato. Please. He'll ruin it. He hates me.'

'He doesn't hate you. He just—'

'Yeah, he hates me.'

'He takes a while to warm up to people. But he doesn't hate you. He's a professional.'

'*Please* don't bring him in.'

'All right. For now. I was just talking to my sister. She and my brother-in-law both work as bike messengers. They use those hybrid cycles that can go just about anywhere. We'll need to track the birds digitally and then be able to send out scouts to check out the details at their landing points. I wonder what the range on those birds is?'

It's big, but I don't want to tell him that because it might discourage him. I'll try anything at this point. And Sidney's message takes on a new significance:

*Intrusions have been traced. They have recordings and are reverse-engineering. If intruders identified, criminal charges could be forthcoming. Pls advise.*

When I first read this, I took the 'intrusions' to be something to do with O's work as a security contractor. But what if it's to do with dreamhacking? What are the 'intrusions'? Is it me, intruding on the Dream City? Is it Daphne, intruding on sleepers? Or is it the Creeper? O got that message and then we went down to Dorking and she changed something in Daphne's therapy schedule. Whoever sent the message is involved in all this mess, and O knew very well when I told her about Daphne killing Bernard that it was real.

The question is, was O involved somehow in the killings – or is she also a target?

Does everybody think I'm a muppet and is this why O doesn't tell me anything? Feed the pigeons, make the tea, don't worry your silly head sort of thing?

Well, I'm not a muppet. I'd like to see Roman and Donato cope with crippling narcolepsy, extreme hair loss and demented old-lady murderers all at the same time.

# Big sky

I shine a torch into the corners of the coop where O's specials are kept. There were four, last I remember; now there are only three.

'One of them is gone. I wonder when she did that.'

'You're sure this happened recently?' Roman asks.

'The last couple of days I honestly didn't count. I checked their water and I fed them, but I didn't clean the cage or handle any of them, and I couldn't swear to how many there were. I've been pretty distracted.'

'Try to remember. Think, Charlie.'

'I am thinking! I'm not the world's most observant person. You know how when there's a crime and the police say, *What colour and make was the car?* And people go, *Oh yeah, it was a silver Fiat Punto.* But I'm like, *Hey, there was a car or maybe a plane or a train . . .* I just don't notice stuff like that.'

Roman shakes his head in disparagement.

'I have a rich inner life,' I add feebly.

'You're sure only one is missing?'

'Yeah. I'm sure. She must have let it out the day she fell. I've been here since she went to hospital. Unless I was asleep . . .'

'What about the rest of them?'

'They're all still in, waiting to be fed.'

'The ones in the big coop aren't necessarily homed here. Some I know for sure are homed to Daphne's place as well as here, because I recognise them. The others, I'm not sure.'

'So think about what you've seen her do. Does she get any of the non-Daphne ones to carry messages?'

I can feel my face making a curdling expression. 'Maybe? I really don't know, I never pay attention . . . I have narcolepsy . . .' I yawn.

'No, don't get sleepy on me. Stay calm and think.'

'Well, I can show you the equipment she uses for messages. Would that help?'

'Yes.'

So I show him the little nylon pouches that attach to the birds' legs with Velcro. They are paper-thin and flexible.

'You could fit a drive in one of these pouches, easily,' Roman says. 'Does O have any other computers besides her main workstation?'

'I don't know and I'm not going to violate her privacy.'

'OK, don't get upset. Never mind what she uses the pouches for.' He goes into the kitchen and sets up a workstation on the counter, pulling a security-sealed envelope out of his backpack and carefully unwrapping it. 'I'm thinking to put the trackers in these pouches and then send out our scouts once we see where the birds are heading. I wonder if they fly after dark?'

'It's still morning – how far are we thinking they'll need to go?'

'That's just it. We don't know.'

'Well, they can get to Dorking in a couple of hours.'

He raises an eyebrow. 'Puts Transport for London to shame.'

It has stopped raining by the time we've wrangled the trackers onto each of birds and set them free. O usually lets me throw the bird up in the sky since I don't mind them crapping on me as much as she does. It's always fun but today feels especially excellent. I've spent far too much time asleep lately. Now I feel like a woman of action. Whee.

Once they're airborne, I run inside and watch the tracking display with Roman. He has superimposed a map of London on the skyline beyond O's window. We are at the centre, and each bird appears as a flashing light as its tracker registers with the satellite. Anticlimactically, all of the lights blend into a single blob for quite a while as the birds circle around above O's building. After a bit of zooming-in, Roman starts to pick out individual signals. One detaches and goes south. Four go south-east, two go south-west, and the last settles on a nearby rooftop and stays there.

'Bloody useless!' I say to the display. 'Fly!'

'Maybe she's kept that one too long and it's getting homed to this building,' Roman says.

'It's probably just lazy. I shouldn't have fed them so much.'

'Never mind. Let's just track the others. Look at these two – they're flying right over the Westway. I'll get someone on them.'

The excitement soon fades. It's super boring watching the pigeons' slow progress and my mind begins to wander. I check my news feed and the first thing I see is sponsored content.

## Five exciting features of the Dark Side from Sweet Dreams

◆ **Add celebrities** to your dreams! Choose from twelve major celebs to appear in your dreams. You can even program the role you want them to play: friend, enemy, frenemy, relative or **lover**!

◆ **Banish nightmares**. You can program The Dark Side to wake you up every time your feedback system indicates a bad dream. You'll be roused by bullhorn, car alarm, boat horn or primal scream – the choice is yours! (JK! We'll wake you gently, we promise.)

◆ **Learn** one of 14 optimized languages with liminal programming. LP only works when you're sleeping and waking, so can be combined with any of the other features for a seamless all-night experience.

◆ **Inject affirmations**. The Dark Side will target your consciousness with positive thoughts about your life goals. Select from weight loss, stop vaping, train harder, resist fascism, raise self-esteem or improve sexual performance. Or create your own custom affirmations with our easy wizard.

◆ **Sleep deeper**. The app will track your brainwave patterns and stimulate additional sleep hormone at just the right time to extend your REM cycle for more refreshing sleep. In clinical trials, 87% of insomniacs reported being 'less exhausted' in the morning and 71% were 'no longer brain-dead at work'. What more could you ask?

I haven't been paying enough attention to this stuff. We deny the things we can't control, right? But right now with Sidney's message so fresh in my mind, with O's disappearance looming, it's hard not to put two and two together. Reverse engineering. Intrusions. The medical trial that BigSky don't want to let go of after all. Their new 'liminal programming' that is so close to what I can do ... except they claim to be able to do it with software.

What else might they do with software? If they have access to my Secret Diaries, they could reverse engineer based on *me* ...

Roman insists that the Creeper is a phenomenon, not a person. What if it's some sort of bot?

What if all of O's paranoia about BigSky is perfectly well founded? What if they are using the Creeper to come after both of us? If I were them and I wanted to get rid of me and I knew O was protecting me, I'd go after her first. But that still doesn't explain Sidney's message.

'Charlie! Touchdown in Dorking!'

I abandon the search and rush to his side.

'How many?'

'Two. They followed the Westway and then the major roads. If I didn't know they were birds, I'd have thought we were following a car. There's another one going straight down the M23, and the four that went south-east are circling around Convoys Wharf. None of them has settled yet. So what's at Convoys Wharf?'

It's clearly a rhetorical question – meaning it's directed at one or more of his bots – but I hear myself answer it anyway. My voice sounds choked in my own ears.

'Martin Elstree lives there. He actually gave me his keys.'

# Little bird

'Tell me, Daphne, have you ever met a man called Martin Elstree?'

I've left Roman scoffing sandwiches in the car, so it's just Daphne and me in the exercise studio.

'Doesn't ring a bell,' she says. 'But then, my memory is rather a shipwreck.'

Daphne hasn't asked where O is or why I've come too late for lunch, and she doesn't remember me as the copy centre girl any more. This time she seems to think I'm her yoga instructor. She insisted on wriggling into her leotard and going into the exercise room with me. I desperately try to remember yoga poses that I've seen Antonio do while I probe Daphne about O's possible whereabouts. She doesn't seem to know anything, and she's not having one of her good days. I'm getting desperate.

'I thought perhaps O had spoken of Elstree,' I tell Daphne. 'Or that he'd visited you here?'

'Not unless he was selling something. You'd be amazed the amount of marketing bots I get. They home in on people who have money, and let me tell you, some of us who live here are loaded.'

'Only I can't find your sister,' I tell Daphne. 'I'm getting worried about her. Will you tell me if she contacts you?'

'Of course, if you like. If I remember.'

I help her stay in tree pose. She's wiry and strong, but her balance could be better and the mat doesn't help; it's too soft. She grips my arm with warm, strong fingers.

'OK, then. You haven't received any . . . pigeon messages, from her? Lately?'

'Come to think of it, two birds returned today. They had some

230

sort of device in their pouches, I don't know what they are. I put the devices on my nightstand if you want to see them.'

Damn. Those are the birds that Roman and I released.

'But any others? Besides those?'

She shakes her head. 'Oh, my dear. You look upset.'

'I'm not upset with *you*, Daphne. I'm just worried for O's safety.'

Leaning on me and still standing on one leg, she grabs her big toe and tries to straighten her leg into extended hand-to-toe pose. The effort makes her pant a little and her tongue protrudes. I don't want to upset her, but this hinting around is getting me nowhere.

'Daphne, do you remember that I'm called Charlie and I work on people's dreams?'

She gives no indication she's heard me at all at first. Then in a voice straining with effort she says, 'I know what you saw must have shocked you, but it's my job to remove targets, dear. I'm a professional and I follow my instructions. I told you that before.'

I jerk away from her and she falls over in a pile of purple Lycra.

'Oh god,' I gasp. 'I'm so sorry, let me help you up.'

She isn't even rattled.

'Not to worry, it's a soft mat. Let's just sit on the floor for a moment, shall we?' She folds herself into half-lotus and waits for me to sit opposite. Then she takes my hands. 'I've been struggling to come to terms with the Agency's brain implant. The device grows right into my skull. It's like a parasite, I'm told, but it's to help me remember.'

I stare at her. 'What? You have a brain implant? I thought you took meds.'

'Same thing! It starts as a med and implants itself. Oh, and it's working! Sometimes my mind comes back to me so sharply! I'm blurry and then suddenly I snap into focus and I remember how I used to be. And then it goes again. Right now I'm not too bad. Later I'll probably have a lapse. Very frustrating. But

I never fail to discharge my responsibilities, even if what I have to do is unpleasant. Loss of life is always regrettable but in this line of work one must act on behalf of the greater good.'

'Well, here's the thing, Daphne.' I'm trying to choose my words carefully.

'Go on, I'm listening. What are you afraid to say to me?'

'The thing is, you can't just go around killing people.'

'Of course I don't. My, you are a greenhorn. I only act on specific instructions. I work for the Agency and I am a professional. Whereas you . . . well, there's nothing professional about you, is there? You need to learn to protect yourself. What if the Agency decides *you* need to be removed from play? Or perhaps an enemy operative will come after you – they've taken out a number of people who were in your study, you know.'

'They? Who are the enemy, then?'

She winks. 'I think you know. Their initials are BS.'

It takes me a moment. Not Bernard, he'd be BZ. Does she mean BigSky?

'Oh, Charlie, but there are all manner of dangers out there in the city of dreams. I'm glad you finally came to me. I just hope I can hold it together long enough to be of use to you. I forget so easily, you see.'

'OK, so, you said you act on instructions. How do you get these instructions? Are they recorded somewhere?'

'Yes, but they are in code and I always destroy the evidence.'

'Ah, well, but it's hard to destroy something permanently in cyberspace.'

She leans towards me, whispering, 'Who said anything about cyberspace? Whenever I do a job, I do it because a little bird told me to.'

And she winks.

'A little bir— Oh crikey, Daphs, do you mean the pigeons?'

'Shhhhh! Of course that's what I mean. My sister and I have been exchanging birds for years.'

'But these Agency messages . . . they aren't from O?'

'I've never told her. I've never told anyone. You're the first. Because you're special.'

Bloody hell. She has too told O. She's pulling my leg.

'I've been trying to help you,' Daphne insists. 'You know, the first time I hacked you, it was by accident, but the second time was on purpose.'

'The first time you hacked me? *When did you hack me, Daphne?*'

'It was only the two times. You thought I was a man! That was me! I was trying to find you in dreamspace, but I didn't want you to recognise me so I disguised myself as a man. I think I'd have made a good man, you know. We didn't have the options in my day, not like the young people do now.'

'I thought you were a dead body! Were you trying to scare me?'

'Not at all, darling, not at all. I was trying to warn you. This is a much larger plot that we are both a part of, you know. We aren't allowed to know everything, for our own protection.'

'But I was nearly killed the other day. I rode my bike into fast-moving traffic because I thought it was all a dream. I was nearly killed. *Were you trying to kill me?*'

'Oh dear, oh my, no, of *course* that wasn't me. I wish I knew who had targeted you. I told you – I've been trying to protect you.'

There's a beat, then she adds: 'If I had been trying to kill you, you wouldn't be here now.'

She pats my hand reassuringly, and completely without irony. *This* is a dream. It has to be. I'll prove it. I begin to pinch various parts of my body. I try to levitate, but I can't. It's not a dream.

'But . . . but . . . what if the police find out?'

Daphne is watching my face. Suddenly she throws her head back and laughs wildly.

'The police! How you make me laugh. What are they going to do to me or anyone else my age? Throw us in jail? We're gaga, all of us. That's how we dreamhackers ended up in the situation in the first place – we all took the treatment.'

**Question:** What's more dangerous than a single psychopath killing people in their sleep?

**Answer:** A team of mentally impaired dementia patients who think they are on a mission for some mysterious 'Agency'.

What the ever-loving fuck?

'You see, I am sensible and take my responsibilities to the Agency seriously, but I'm afraid one can't say the same for everyone I know,' Daphne says. 'Some of my colleagues wander around the Dream City in a daze. They're unpredictable and disorganized, and they do silly things. I have to cover for the inept all the time. When I heard about the musician who walked off the hotel roof, I did feel that it had all gone far enough, and yes, I did blame Doctor Zborowski for running off to a new job instead of staying to deal with the consequences of his work. He blamed himself, too. He had a number of guilt dreams about it.'

'What do you mean, running off to a new job? I thought the funding was pulled and he had no choice.'

'I don't know the details, but he abandoned the first study – your group – and went off with another company to develop the treatment that I take.'

'Little Bird, you mean. Wait, you *are* taking Little Bird's treatment?' O has been omitting a lot of stuff from what she's told me. She said she knew Meera's work, but not that Daphne was involved with Bernard and Meera.

'Daphne, would you be willing to talk to the Dream Police about this?'

'Of course not. I've said too much already. If anyone pursues the subject I'll just revert to talking about the benefits of flaxseed oil. Marvellous stuff!'

'Please, no, Daphne. Just tell me one more thing. How do you do it? How do you make someone sleepwalk?'

'Oh, it's easy. You just open the dreamer like a wind-up toy and step inside, you know. That's how I do it, anyway. Did you see who was controlling the harp girl?'

'No. I didn't.'

I can't help it – I launch myself to my feet and begin to pace. There are mirrors along one wall of the yoga studio and I can see my own face. I look like I've been hit by a bus. What is happening?

'It's too bad. Because if you had witnessed it, you could run the hack on them in reverse. Push through them in the dream and go back to their point of origin. Find out who they really are and do to them what they did to their victim.'

Everything Daphne just said runs around in my head, connecting and disconnecting and getting tangled up.

'O got hacked,' I blurt, still pacing. 'Yesterday. She got hacked, I'm sure of it, and she fell. Who was that, Daphne? What's the deal with this Agency? I mean, seriously, to give a brain-altering treatment to a group of dementia patients and then turn them loose on the population—'

'I've already told you. The Agency is the Agency, and BS is BS, and they are fighting for control of the thing in your head and mine. You need to wake up. You have everything to lose, my dear. Your life is just starting. But I've nothing to lose. I was wandering in a fog, in a darkness, and I'm ever so much better now. I don't want to descend to a dribbling mess, I don't want people to pity me and wipe my bottom out of kindness, I don't want to forget how to speak or think. I'll deal with any devil you like to avoid that fate. I expect that's a problem for you and I'll understand if we can't be friends any more. I'll find another dog-groomer, and you, well, you'll be fine without me. You only ever came to see me because of my sister, and I don't blame you for that. Let's shake hands and be done.'

I stop and stare at her. She is trying to get up off the mat, but it's a wobbly surface and she's having trouble finding her balance. Instinctively, I step forward and give her a hand up. We stand looking at each other. There's a rumpus in my head. My loud heart. But she has tears in her eyes.

'It's OK,' I say faintly. 'I'm not angry with you, it's fine, I get it. Just tell me one thing. What did you mean, it grows into your skull?'

'The treatment. It's not a drug, it's a therapeutic engine. After it implants itself, it grows across your skull. Your whole head acts like a receiver and your thought patterns can be accessed remotely. It's how we do what we do, my dear. You and I.'

For no rational reason, I put my hands to my headscarf.

'It made my hair fall out.'

'It grows back, Charlie. It grows back.'

'What about O? You don't seem worried. Why are you not worried?'

'My sister can take care of herself,' Daphne says, and a kind of bleakness passes across her face. 'I've never known anyone to get the better of her. She's probably just lying low.'

I don't like the sound of that. Lying low, or lying horizontal? A chill goes down my neck. I've dreamed with Martin Elstree. I know what he's capable of. The woman he butchered in that dream was his boss, and he used power tools to get power over her.

Well, if there's one thing you can say for sure about O, it's that she's bossy.


It's almost three by the time I leave. Roman is waiting for me outside in the hire vehicle. He's spoken to the staff but got nothing of use, or so he says. I'm not at all convinced he's telling me everything, and so I don't relay any of the juice that Daphne told me. None of it. It's not even a calculated decision – I'm terrible at keeping secrets – it's more that I'm in shock and need time to process it. Anyway, he makes it easy because he's pre-occupied checking on the progress of the pigeons on his various maps, and I guess he doesn't expect anything earth-shattering to have happened between Daphne and me. When I tell him that she made me do yoga he takes it in stride, completely missing the fact that I'm staring at the dashboard blankly as I try to remember everything that was said. Not least of which: there's something *growing into my skull.*

'Donato had to go to his other job, so he hasn't been able to trace the hog yet,' Roman tells me. 'But he will get on to it.'

'What other job does Donato have?'

'He's a personal trainer.'

'Seriously?'

'You can't think we're breaking even with this gig? It's not like *you're* paying us.'

'So who is, exactly?'

'Come on, Charlie. You know what it's like starting a business. I run drones for extra cash and live with my sister and her family. Being the Dream Police is a labour of love at this stage. But someone's got to do it.'

He's not blushing. Could he be telling the truth?

'So hey, you know my dream records that you wanted?'

'Are you going to give them to me?'

'Maybe. Where is Pigeon Number Seven?'

'Brighton,' he says lightly. 'But it hasn't landed. It's gone out to sea.'

'For real?'

'I know, I know. I didn't think of that possibility and I'm using the wrong system to track it, but I'm in the process of cross-coordinating with the Coastguard. We haven't lost it, we just don't know where it is.'

'You lost it.'

'I just said we haven't lost it!'

He takes me home. He says he's going to do his research on Martin Elstree and get back to me. I don't tell him that I have plans to do research of my own. He wouldn't approve.

# Mrs H-W strikes back

I am really clever. Exceptionally clever, and I'm so excited and proud of myself that I'm doing daring things without Shandy and I'm going to get into that flat and find some piece of evidence that I can give Roman, because I am brave like that.

It's 5:54 p.m. I sit in reception at Martin Elstree's office wearing my best job interview trouser suit, which I haven't had time to press but have managed to de-cat-hair for the occasion. I'm wearing make-up and my hair is wrapped in a silk scarf that I nicked from O's drawer. I sit with my legs crossed and every time someone asks me if they can help me I say that I'm being taken care of, even though a stream of people are steadily exiting the offices for close of business. I've got to wait it out. Eventually the receptionist will have to go on some errand and I can get the keys. I saw where she put them. In her top drawer, next to her Tic Tacs, with a ton of other keys.

It's 5:59 and I'm sure I'm going to get kicked out, when the receptionist runs out of Post-its. I hear her telling a colleague that she's forwarding calls while she makes a run to the supply closet.

When she goes through an interior door, I waste no time throwing myself across her desk, legs flipping in the air like a surfer mounting a board. I whip the drawer open triumphantly.

The keys are not there.

Fuck.

I look in other drawers, and then other other drawers. And just when I'm about to panic and run away, I find them. They've fallen inside a box of tissues. I rip them out and slam the drawer shut. A hank of torn tissue floats gently to the carpet as I hurl myself out of the office and into the corporate hallway, the lift, the lobby . . . I'm out of the building.

I did it! I've got his keys!

I can't run in these heels but I walk fast towards Bank Station. Got to do this fast, before I lose my nerve. I hope he hasn't changed the door code.

**Rodney, I'm going in. I have Elstree's keys, the bastard. I'm going to check his flat. I'm afraid he's done something to O. If I don't come out in an hour, I'll need rescuing.**

Shandy's unicorn says, **Wait, could this be dangerous? I think you should wait.**

**It's fine, he's not home. He's at in a meeting at work. I heard the receptionist putting his calls through to a conference room.**

**You shouldn't go in there alone.**

**Shut up, you're just a bot. Tell Shandy what I said.**

Convoys Wharf is super-posh. They are putting up another building alongside Martin's and there's a lot going on outside. A tall crane looms inside the walled building site, and I see pigeons and seagulls circling around both buildings. I never would have looked twice at them before.

I'm still thinking about Sidney's damn message.

*Intrusions have been traced. They have recordings and are reverse-engineering. If intruders identified, criminal charges could be forthcoming. Pls advise.*

Who are 'They'? Would Elstree be the person asking for advice on criminal charges? But he's an intellectual property solicitor, not a criminal lawyer.

I check the parking garage for the hog but there's no sign of it, so I head on up to Elstree's flat. I haven't bothered wearing a mask or gloves. It's still daylight. I'm going to be on video, nothing I can do about that, but if I come and go without creating a disturbance then there's no reason for Elstree to check his video. Unless he's instructed the flat to ping him when someone comes in, in which case I'm screwed. Also, if anyone notices the office keys are missing, Elstree can put two and two together and I'm screwed. But it's a long way from his office across the Thames to Convoys Wharf – he can't be here instantly.

All I have to do is get in, rescue O and get out.

'O?' I call. 'Are you here? O, it's me, Charlie. Make a sound if you're here.'

There is no sound. I quickly search the flat in the eerie silence, but there's no body, either. I feel deflated. Of course it wouldn't be that easy. If he has her, she's in a warehouse somewhere or an abandoned Tube station or a boat. I just hoped, that's all. I was sure if I came here, to the source, took the battle to Elstree instead of letting him come to me the way he has been doing all along, that I could get ahead of him.

Just being here reminds me how far behind I am. I'm standing in yet another luxury flat feeling like a Dickens street urchin. The place belongs in a Rolex ad. It's open-plan with fantastic views over the Thames, everything white and spacious and frighteningly clean. Each piece of furniture is perfectly squared off and there isn't a particle of dust.

He has a terrace, and that's where I find the pigeons. I'm amazed that he's allowed to keep them, considering the opinion most Londoners have of pigeons – but there they are, settled in their coop as the sun goes down. Their housing is modelled after a Swiss chalet – one small, twee detail in an otherwise too-cool-for-school decor.

I get hold of each of O's birds and remove their pouches and trackers. I can't take the birds with me, though, because I didn't think to bring a cage. Unless I try to carry them in my backpack, which seems dodgy. Oh, fuck, I haven't thought this through at all. Will he notice if he gets home and O's birds are still here? I'll have to leave it open and hope they go back to hers, or else the game is up.

I am getting panicky, but that doesn't stop me noticing the birds are pecking at empty feed trays and their water bottle is empty, too. There is a plastic feed bin on the balcony. I open it and plunge the plastic scoop into the seed. It strikes something hard.

That's odd.

I dig down with my hands and feel a hard, flat surface. Plastic. I find the edges and drag out a small Lucite box like the kind that crafty-types use to store beads. Aha. I blow the dust off of it, scoop some seed for the birds and retreat inside to investigate the box.

There are microdrives in the compartments.

I should grab them and run now, but I know this is the only chance I'm going to get to search this flat. What if the drives aren't what I'm looking for and I've missed something really important because I grabbed the first thing I saw? I decide to whack them into the home-entertainment system and at least see what's on them.

The system fires to life and offers me a guest login – enough to let me see what's on the drives. But it's disappointing. I whip through them one after the other. Everything seems to be routine backup folders. Invoices, Legal, Correspondence. I scroll down lists of suppliers, consultants, contractors. None of it means anything to me. I wish I could show it to O, who knows so much about these things. There must be some reason they were hidden in the birdseed bin.

Then I see the name 'Haugh-Wombaur'.

Well. That's distinctly odd. I open the file. A string of e-mails and attachments. I open the most recent.

**To:** Martin Elstree
**Cc:** Olivia Ogiyevich
**From:** Bettina Haugh-Wombaur
**Re:** Charlotte Aaron Invoice

Hi, as discussed with Olivia, please find attached my invoice for dream therapy with breakdown of hours worked. The total for my services comes to £3,481.15 inclusive of VAT. PayPal is fine. Don't hesitate to get in touch if you need anything else in future.

Kind regards,

Bettina

WTF WTF WTF WTF?

I read it several times. Then I open the attached invoice, which has already been marked 'PAID'.

Let's just get this straight. Mrs H-W paid me a total of maybe... £320? Over a period of weeks. So why is O paying her ten times that for her 'services'? What services? Farting? I can't even.

This can't be right. I start hunting through the other files for something that could explain what I'm seeing.

That's when I find myself looking at my own Spacetime entries, offered to Elstree courtesy of O herself. Straight out of my supposedly secure BigSky encrypted personal system. Martin Elstree has records of all my professional dreams.

Secret Diary of a Prawn Star 1-17

Secret Diary of a Prawn Star 18-39

Secret Diary of a Prawn Star 40-54

My heart stops and starts and stutters. She has hacked my earring. Elstree's been into my dream files, right up to the most recent one. And he has been surveilling me all along, right back to before we ever met.

Of course, I knew they'd worked together. She did introduce us. But why would she share them with him of all people? Martin must be the actual Creeper, then. Did she give him the files to make it easier for him to attack me? And he had the cheek to offer to represent me!

I just can't believe she would do this. Can't get my head round it at all.

I Spacetime Mrs H-W.

'Oh, hello, Charlotte. I'm about to go into the Underground.'

'This won't take long. I just need to know why you were paid for the work you and I did.'

There's a pause.

'I'm not sure I can discuss this with you. I signed a non-disclosure agreement.'

'But you tricked me. I think you owe me an explanation.'

'You'll have to take it up with the party who hired me, I'm afraid.'

'I'm taking it up with you. I know what the inside of your head looks like, so I suggest you tell me the truth.'

'Are you threatening me?'

'Tell me the truth, Mrs Haugh-Wombaur.'

'Well, Charlotte, I don't really know why I was paid. I was told it was for a scientific study and that's really all I know. If you want to find out more, you'll have to ask the scientists.'

'What scientists? Martin Elstree is not a scientist, so why was he paying you?'

'I'm heading into the Underground now. We're done. I'm going to block you, Charlotte, and if you try to contact me again I'll report you to the Council for Alternative Therapies. Just a friendly warning.'

Dead link.

I'm so hopping mad that I nearly pass out on the floor then and there.

'Report me to the Council for Alternative Therapies?' Ranting sleepily, I stagger around the flat and then out onto the balcony. 'What are they going to do to me, a past-life regression and toenail analysis? Ooh, I'm scared.'

But it's like the bottom has dropped out of me. It's all unravelling in my head now. O really did this to me. I can't take it in.

Her words come back to me with the bite of irony:

*You're a Pollyanna.*

*You need tough dreams.*

*I've been trying to protect you.*

How O approached me through my channel like just another ASMR client. How she convinced me I'd be helping her by moving in, so that I could feel better about the fact that she was helping me, so that I'd be emotionally bound to her. Even as she was using me as her little guinea pig.

And to think I came here half-expecting to find her a captive of Martin Elstree. They were in it together all along.

Our conversation about the BigSky study comes back to me. How I suggested that she look up the other study participants. Of course, she had done that long ago. That was how she found me. So what about the others? Who else is part of her schemes?

People are sleepwalking all over London. People are dying, and BigSky is planning to make big profit from 'liminal programming'. As personal as this is for me, I'm not the only one. I have to find more. I have to find something that Roman can use. I have to stop this.

By now I've been in the flat for fourteen minutes. Knowing London traffic, I should be fine, but I get moving just in case. I switch off the home-entertainment system and am in the kitchen filling the pigeons' water bottle out of basic decency when Martin Elstree breezes through the door and shuts it behind him smartly. He's not surprised to see me. He walks over to the kitchen with a swinging, easy gait. He's enjoying this.

'Relax, relax. There's no need for you to be afraid,' he purrs. His voice is lovely, which makes it worse. 'This is where you misunderstand me, Chaz.'

I know he's calling me Chaz just to annoy me, yet I can't suppress my reaction even though I'm aware of the pleasure he gets from it. I can see the irritation in my face reflected in his gleaming black fridge. I look into my own eyes. I've got to act my way through this. If he thinks I'm only here on a mission to find O, he might feel less threatened. I can't let him find out how much I know.

'Where is O?' I cry, and he makes a sad-puppy face.

'Worried about her, are we?'

'You have O. I know you do. Just let her go. I'll leave you alone if you let her go without hurting her. I'll give up dreamhacking. I'll move back to Stourbridge. Please, Martin.'

He shakes his head, taking the water bottle out of my hand and gesturing for me to step into the seating area, but I just stand there trembling. Stupid tears well in my eyes. I hate my weakness.

'The way you talk to me, it's like you think I'm a terrible person,' he says, his brow rumpling with concern. 'Please, have a seat. Can I offer you something to drink? Or are you hell-bent on the water?'

'I was going to give it to the pigeons. I thought O was here.'

'In the pigeon coop?' He says it so mildly that I feel like a fool. Have I got everything wrong? No. No, I haven't. I need to trust my instincts. I need to be like Shandy.

**Shandy, help. He's found me in the flat. He's here. Help!**

The signal sticks. He's got a firewall up.

'There's no need for you to fear me,' he says. 'I only get rid of the people who are in my way. Nearly everyone else is safe. Plus, I'm a pretty nice guy, if you could just see that. It's time we started cooperating instead of fighting each other.'

I wish I could laugh at him but I'm terrified. And angry. But mostly the first one.

'It's obvious you think I'm kind of an arsehole,' he says genially.

'No, of course I don't, I'm sure you're lovely. I have to go, I'm sorry . . . I misunderstood the situation, here's your key.'

I fling the keys on the counter and dodge around him, sprinting for the door.

It's locked.

Maybe I am dreaming. Maybe this is my subconscious churning up hundreds of low-budget movies to remind me of all my poor cinematic choices when I was twelve. I've been acting just like the stupid heroine who goes into the basement.

'Please unlock the door. I need to leave.'

'In good time. First we talk. Please sit down. You're a bundle of nerves. I don't know what you take me for. It was only a dream, that session we had. I thought you were a professional.

I thought you were worldly. The way you hold my entertainment preferences against me is really quite juvenile.'

I open my mouth to answer but my teeth are chattering.

'It's OK, we all have our price. I'm a good tipper – you would have found that out if you had finished our first session. Now you've come riding in here thinking you're going to save humanity from my depredations, but the truth is I'm just doing my job. At least I'm honest. Life is short. If I can get power, I'm going to take it. And I'm going to keep it. If desire for power is a mental illness then I don't want to be healthy, because desire for power is the mental illness Western civilization is built on.'

I wonder if he's practised that in a mirror. It almost makes sense, the way he says it. I'm not saying I agree with him, but I recognise what he's talking about as a sort of truth. After all, I've spent my entire life reading in the news about how the arseholes win, they steal and kill and lie and get away with it, convince themselves they're heroes. They're given honours – ergo, they must be good guys. Plus they have yachts. (Lots of them do, I feel sure. I've never been on a sociopathic criminal's yacht but I can imagine what it's like, with the caviar and the paid women and scallops the size of saucers prepared by the personal chef, I can really picture it or did I see it in a movie? It's true that the most powerful person I've ever met was the executive VP of EcoWarriors.net I temped for, and I don't know if you could say I really met him, but I did repair the element in his personal self-heating cafetière, though I digress. The point is, he was kind of an arsehole, too, despite being all about the polar bears.) Powerful people like this live in a private world where no one matters but the powerful, some narcissist who thinks he's so great and by some weird mirror-neuron alchemy, everyone else falls for it, too. The Wizard of Oz. Or is that my cupboard-under-the-stairs persona talking? After all, I always seem to be on the losing team. But not all yacht owners are like Martin Elstree. Some of them are lovely, I'm sure. You can't stop aspiring just because the top of the heap is overpopulated by narcissists, can you?

I'll maybe need to think about this more, but now is not a good time and there may not ever be a later. I can't win here. All I can do is give in to him, because that's what people like me always do. It's just too tiring to keep fighting when I'm so unsure of myself and he's so certain of himself. It's like I'm white paint and he's red. I don't stand a chance holding on to my purity. Ewwww, what an image.

'You *do* feel dirty, don't you?' he says. 'Look at you. You're weighing how to deal with me and wondering if you can live with yourself if you take my offer.'

'No I'm not.' Even I don't believe me, and he laughs.

'You're so easy to read. You think O is such a good guy? Well, she's not. See, people with cancer can be cunts, too. People in wheelchairs can be evil, but that doesn't fit with your world-view, does it? You're so simple-minded, really, it's child's play to manipulate you.'

'O isn't evil,' I snap back. I can't believe I'm defending her.

'Neither am I. Welcome to the real world, darling.'

I'm getting angry now and that's warming me up. My voice still shakes but I say: 'OK, here's what I've got and it's not much. You are trying to get me to resolve my cognitive dissonance so that I can feel like a winner. If I give in to you, I'll have to tell myself you're really not that bad – otherwise I'm bad by association. If I give in, I'll have to make it all right. But it isn't all right. And I'm not giving in.'

'Then you're stupid, Chaz, because I'm going to win.'

'Why is it always about winning?' I flare. 'Zero-sum games are so last century, mate.'

'I'm repeating myself, but I'll say it one more time like on *Teletubbies*. Again, again!' And his voice rises to a falsetto, then drops to baritone. Dripping with irony. He says: 'You're stupid. Get it through your head – I'm in control here. You're a talented dreamhacker, by all accounts. But you lack direction, you lack

247

discipline, you're afraid to hurt anyone. You're a mess. And while I'm willing and able to get rid of you, you are not capable of getting rid of me. It's not in you. People like you are a disgrace. You should just stay home because you don't have what it takes. In a minute I'm going to get bored.'

'And then what? You're going to murder me with your bare hands?'

'No. You're going to fall asleep.'

'No, I'm not.'

'Yes, you are. You always fall asleep when things get hairy. Do you think I don't know this? It's perfectly obvious. Your narcolepsy is psychosomatic in the sense that when the going gets tough, you literally pass out. Classic.'

I am not going to pass out. I'm not even a little bit sleepy, yay me! Yet I'm suddenly aware that I have no more O to run backup on me.

'You can't get out of this flat,' Martin said. 'I've secured it completely. At the moment, I'm the only one who can call out through the firewall.'

I'm still scared, but now I'm also angry, in a rooted, unreasonable way that I know is not helpful because I can't back up my anger with any kind of practical power. This is a time for me to be cold and to think really really fast but I'm not put together like that. He's right: I'm all over the place, I'm a mess, and being threatened like this isn't suddenly turning me into somebody more competent and quick-thinking like you always somehow hope it will. Like in the movies. No, I have no magic tricks.

The neural gates that Martin manipulated to make Melodie sleepwalk. He can stop muscle atonia. If I fall asleep, he won't have to murder me. He can come into my dream and trick me into sleepwalking to my own death. Just like what he tried to do when I was on my bike in traffic, in that dream that turned out not to be a dream.

'It doesn't have to happen now,' he says. 'It can happen

whenever I choose. You can be taken out any night at all. Any afternoon nap.'

He watches my face as the implications sink in. He can let me walk out of here and wait until I get home. Until I'm on the Tube. He can wait a year or a day or a month, and I'll never have a moment's peace. He has me on the run.

Or does he? The Dream City is my town, too. Unlike London, where he's powerful and I'm a prole, in the Dream City I'm strong. I have a hammer and stuff.

'I'm not afraid of you,' I say. 'I'm afraid of a lot of things – not spiders, not rats, but a lot of other things, like sometimes even lint scares me if I see a big wodge of it in the wrong light. I'm pretty much a giant bundle of fear, but I'm not afraid of you. Go ahead and try to hack me again. See if you can do it. You've tried a couple of times now to get to me, but you haven't succeeded.'

'You can thank your defenders for that.' He smiles warmly. Ooh, I hate him.

'I can defend myself now. I know what you're doing, how you're killing people. I'm not afraid of you.'

'You said that before. I don't really care about you. But you keep getting in the way, despite all the extra clients and other incentives you have been given to *mind your own business*.'

'Don't you dare try to take credit for my new clients! People are coming to me because they need help, and they need help because the world is so fucked-up, and it's fucked-up thanks to people like you!'

'Me? I'm not the one living in a cupboard under the stairs. I've tried to give you every opportunity to better yourself, but you leave me very little choice. Everything that's happening here comes down to your bad decisions, Chaz.'

His voice is so deep, so well modulated, so convincing. I can feel how I'm conditioned to submit to that voice no matter what nonsense it's spouting. He could do movie voice-overs and make a fortune and have a villa in Provence. I do have to wonder why

249

he is he wasting his time litigating patents and killing people in their sleep.

'The worst decision you made was to move in with Olivia. Now, I could tell you things about her that would curdle your blood. I manage certain delicate affairs on her behalf – hence the pigeons. So by now you must know she used her own sister as an experimental subject.'

'She wanted to help her sister! But you, what you're doing is worse. Convincing Daphne that she's a secret agent and getting her to do your dirty work? That is low.'

'Don't kill the messenger, dear. I'm not the big boss. If you came here expecting to find poor, frail Olivia bound and gagged and held for ransom, then I guess there are a few things you don't know. For example, who do you think made it look like Antonio was the mysterious "Russian patron" of poor dead Melodie? Who do you think manipulated him into bringing you Melodie's case in the first place?'

'I'm not listening to you,' I say miserably. 'You're a murderer.'

'I'm a problem-solver, Charlie. Let's take your problem. Did you know Olivia stalked you after she found your name in Bernard Zborowski's files of victims— I mean medical test subjects? What, you didn't really think she was a member of the ASMR community? I wish you could see your face. The penny has finally dropped, hasn't it? Didn't you think it was rather strange that she invited you into her home, that she even offered to help you set up your business? Didn't you wonder why a woman of her intellect would want anything to do with a little toerag like you?'

'You're a liar. We are friends.'

He's laughing and shaking his head. I feel weak and drowsy. I need to check out of this conversation. I can't deal with it. Too much.

'You're such an utter fool, Charlotte. It's almost refreshing, after all the liars and cheats I deal with on a daily basis. You aren't pretending to be a fool. You are the real thing.'

I am a fool. I am a fool. I am a fool and a toerag, and I can't listen to this, I can't take it, I can't deal, I... don't wanna be me any more.

I'm slithering down the side of Martin Elstree's kitchen cupboards to rest on his polished tile floor, because I literally cannot stay awake right now.

I have to take the earring out. With every scrap of will I can muster, I force my hand up to my head, slip out the earring. He can't make me sleepwalk if I'm not on Sweet Dreams.

As I'm floating away, I feel him open my hand and take the earring.

'Shh,' he mocks. 'That's right, you rest now. We'll look after you.'

**Secret Diary of a Prawn Star**
**Entry #55**
**Codename:** Chaplin
**Date:** 26 September 2027
**Client:** Martin Elstree
**Payment in advance:** N/A
**Session Goal:** Survival
**Location:** Martin's flat at Convoys Wharf
**Narcolepsy status:** Total collapse
**Nutrition/stimulants:** Can't remember
**Start time:** 8.02 p.m.
**End time:** ?
**Note: Not much point in keeping this, is there, now I
know I'm being spied on. Fuck off, if you're reading
this!**

The weight on my chest is the worst this time. Like being buried
alive. At first I think I can't possibly ever move again. I think my
eyes are open but I can't seem to move the muscles that control
them, and I can't breathe.

It's very strange not to be able to move your eyes. I can't even
focus. I see a blob of black and grey shifting around like oil on
water before the image resolves into the hooded Creeper with
his white 'The Scream' face and dark slash of mouth. He is on
top of me, pressing on my chest to stop me breathing, to stop
my heart if he can.

*You're not real. You're just a representation of sleep paralysis and
it's a good thing because I don't want to get up and walk around
when I'm asleep. You can't hurt me. You're not real.*

The face doesn't change expression but it judders from side

to side with the rapid, jerking kind of movements a wasp makes when it gets blocked by a windowpane. I find this super scary, maybe because it's unnatural for anything that big to move that fast.

The white face opens its mouth and bends towards me, as if to kiss me. No matter what I say to him, to myself, in this moment the Creeper is more real than anyone I've ever met. More real than I am. More real than the whole waking world. I feel its lips on mine. They are cold, not just physically but psychically freezing, and now it's sucking the breath out of my lungs, draining the life out of me. I want to wake up now. I have to breathe. I want to wake up. I—

The dream location is an octagonal room with no windows or doors. The floor is made of bones and the ceiling is made of eyes. The walls are made of fur. I am covered in fur instead of clothes, like an oversized Ewok. I search everywhere for doors. Under the bones I find bugs and under the bugs, slime. Gagging, I explore the walls. There has to be a way out. If I can't find one, I'll make one.

I'm recording the session. Evidence. Roman can go over it after I'm dead. Because I'm so dead, now that I don't have anyone to protect me. No O, no Muz. I don't even have Shandy. There's only me, and I've fallen asleep on the kitchen floor of a psycho killer. He's obviously taken the earring out of my hand and slipped it back in again.

Right. Well, I'm not dead yet, so better use my skills and do what I can to save myself from the inside.

Once I get going, it's not so bad. I turn the fur on my body into a fighter pilot suit and transform the walls to glass. I call my dream Thor-hammer and it appears in my hands. Here in my dreams, anyway, I'm not always a victim.

I'm in a tower. I can see the luminous Dream City spread out below me with its lacework of canals, the Dream City's veins that writhe in their age and darkness. I see the bridges and streets that I have walked in sleep, the cranes, the scaffolds. Everything under construction. Anything is possible here.

I feel stronger now. It could be worse. For example, even though he covered it up, I'm pretty sure Martin Elstree was surprised to find me in his flat and I'm betting he hasn't had time to make plans to kill me in real life. I doubt he has the stomach for it in real life, and he wouldn't know how to dispose of my body without getting caught. I'm betting on him coming after me in the Dream City instead, try to make me kill myself. But I've got a head start on him, because he has to go to sleep first. Nobody can fall asleep as fast as I can. I should be able to spot him when he's just arriving in my dream, before he gets his bearings. And then I can attack.

Because wow, the more I think about the way I've been treated, the more furious I get.

I heft my hammer and hit the glass. It splinters, tiny spider cracks running along it with the sound of lit kindling. I hit it again and there's a hole. Third hit and I'm standing in the wind, what's left of my hair flying back, my lungs filling with dream air, black and shocking. I could fly out across the city. I love dream-flying.

Then I remember Mel. On second thought: no dream-flying for me tonight. Just in case he's manipulating me and I'm standing on his balcony in real life. The truth is, I can't trust anything I see; I have to assume I'm sleepwalking.

I close my eyes in the dream. I drop to my hands and knees, and I crawl. Now that there's no visual stimulation, I'm mostly aware of my own heartbeat and breathing. The fear. My link to Sweet Dreams tells me that I was only asleep for a few minutes when this dream started. My best hope is to get out of the flat to somewhere that there are people before he has time to enter the dream and mess with me too much.

I feel a draught of warm air and crawl towards it. My left hand reaches out for purchase on the floor and finds air; I grope and find solid stone some ten centimetres down. It's a step. I feel my way forward. Much harder to track with the tactile sense than the eye. I'm at the top of a staircase made of stone or maybe concrete. I start going down, dream-eyes clenched shut. I hear echoes of distant voices, footsteps, and then Martin Elstree's voice says very clearly and calmly into my dream:

'There's nothing you can do. I need only say a few words, give a code, and you'll be taken care of. Open your eyes and you'll see what I mean.'

My breath is coming in gasps. I count fourteen steps, then come to a landing. I can feel myself right on the edge of wakefulness; I could push through and surface if I really tried.

'You can't wake up. We can force you back into REM anytime. Insertions are also possible.'

The sense of something following me is closer now, running up my spine and into my consciousness. I'm not alone and something is coming down those stairs after me, not someone but some thing. Before I can gather my thoughts, I find myself up on my feet, eyes closed, running down the steps, falling, rolling, getting up battered and running again. Down, down, down, with the conviction of an amorphous devouring Thing coming after me.

I hit a door and open my eyes.

The door is made of steel with an iron ring for a handle. I jerk it open and fall through onto a scrap of lawn cloaked in darkness. The wind is blowing strongly in my face and I can see a metal gangway leading across a canal to an island dominated by vegetation. Bruised and wobbling, I run across and the gangway deposits me in a hedge maze.

I don't want to go in there.

Where am I really, in real life? I try to picture the layout of the lobby. I haven't encountered anybody in the stairwell, but people probably take the lift. If I can manage to sleepwalk into the reception area, someone will see me and call the police.

But if I've descended all the way to the basement, I could be fucked. It's just impossible to tell. Is the wind in my dream also in reality, or am I just standing by a ventilator fan?

'Martin Elstree, show yourself. You won't, will you? You're afraid to face me here because I'll be just as strong as you are, if not stronger. You're afraid.'

No response.

'Murder by remote control is for cowards,' I say to the air. 'Where are you? Give me the satisfaction of a fair fight.'

Now the maze is all around me. No gangway, no island, no canals. Hedges, everywhere. They are privets, dense, impenetrable and trimmed to bonsai-standard precision. They look like *Minecraft* hedges, but they're real.

I wander through the stupid thing for a long time before I find my way to the centre. There's a flagstone courtyard in the middle of which is a trapdoor that opens in a patch of blue sky. It's painted white with the Creeper's morphine symbol for decoration and another iron-ring handle. Being in the middle of the sky, it appears to go nowhere.

This makes me suspicious. It's too neat. Real dreams are messy and don't make sense, they're not paint-by-numbers. This is more like a VR game.

I grab the iron ring and open the trapdoor to reveal a stone wall with a steel ladder fixed to it, ascending through into a tunnel of utter darkness embedded in the surface of blue sky. Cold wind blasts into my face and I hear gulls up there.

I start up the ladder, all the while pressing mentally against the confines of the scenario. I need to turn this dream to my advantage. It's not very sophisticated; I should be able to use it to punch through to Martin Elstree's psyche and take control. The dream is weak; it's not convincing. He's got to be lurking around here somewhere, pulling the strings of my subconscious.

'Come on, Martin,' I call. 'You're not so scary now, are you? You want a fight, you got it. Stand and face me.'

At the top of the ladder is a steel platform. Once I've climbed onto it, the platform itself becomes a grassy lawn that surrounds me. A starry sky vaults overhead. The only feature is a ginormous beech tree with low, spreading branches – a storybook tree. Its leaves make shuffling sounds in the gentle breeze.

Still no sign of Martin Elstree. The only living creature I can see is a sparrow, hopping and fluttering in the grass.

'Very funny,' I say. 'Little bird. Or should I say, Little Bird?'

But Martin doesn't answer. And the bird doesn't feel like him. I almost... the bird isn't very animalian. It's almost... shit, is this a mechanical bird?

The bird looks at me sideways, a knowing look, I think. It doesn't answer, just flutters up into the lowest branch of the tree, and as it flies bits of metal fall out of it: a rivet, a washer, a spring. I reach up and pull myself into the tree. Its bark is smooth and cool, and it's easy to climb.

Up and up we go, the bird and I, and I'm surrounded by soft, whispering leaves until I can't see the ground any more, just the muscular, twisting bole of the tree and the lacework of its branches. I'm as high as I can go; above me, the branches are too thin to hold my weight. The bird makes a series of trilling sounds, not quite a song, but almost as though it is trying to communicate with me.

I move out along the branch towards the bird.

'What did you say?' I ask. I'm willing myself to understand the bird. The dream is trying to speak to me and I need to understand.

I lean out as far as I dare and make a grab for the bird. It launches itself off the branch, but I catch it anyway.

I notice two things at once: the bird is hard, lumpy, cold; also, the branch beneath me is moving. The tree is swaying rhythmically. I clench my fist in alarm and the bird shatters in my hand into a bunch of toy-robot parts. With my other hand, I grab a branch and press my body close to the cold bark, and that's when I realise I'm no longer touching bark. I'm on a horse.

How can I be on a horse?

'Horse! Hold on, Horse!'

Someone's shouting at me. Someone very tiny, faintly audible. The horse I'm riding starts to buck. My hands on the reins are cold and stiff. Holding on hurts. What reins? Where the fuck am I?

'Horse! Horse, you idiot! Wake the fuck up! Horse so help me god don't move, just wake up now before you fall!'

Fall?

I can't see the tree. I can't see anyone. I'm in darkness. I can feel the horse-tree moving under me, I can feel the wind and the cold, but I don't know which way is up. A gust of wind hits me and I feel myself start to lift...

I'm awake. I'm awake. Very cold, dark. Rain hitting my face. My fingers are curled around a metal stanchion, slippery and silvered with wet. I'm standing on the balls of my feet on a slim strip of horizontal steel.

I can see the north side of the Thames lit up in the distance. The horizon is moving slightly, back and forth, as the whole structure that I'm holding on to shifts in the wind.

I'm standing near the end of a crane arm, some twenty floors above the building site adjacent to Martin Elstree's apartment.

# Unfair to snakes

Uncontrollable shaking? Check.

Elevated respiration? Check.

Muscle weakness? – Hah! – Check.

Getting dizzy? Of course.

I have broken into a building site in my sleep and I have climbed a crane wearing heels and now here I am. Hacked. Lured. About to fall. Oh, Melodie. I wonder if you woke up as you were falling. I wish I'd stayed asleep.

'Horse!'

It's Shandy. She's down below, her voice faint and high-pitched.

'Hold on! I called the police. Just don't fall asleep again. Stay awake. Stay with me.'

I don't know if I can. This right here has got to be the greatest stress I've ever experienced in my life. Narcolepsy factor turned up to eleven. How am I supposed to stay awake?

'Listen to me!' She's screaming to make her voice carry. 'He can't do anything to you unless you let him. You can stay awake. Remember the time we stayed up all night for tickets to meet Felix in person? I fell asleep four times but you didn't. You can do this.'

Felix aka PewDiePie. We were kids. That was before the drug trial. My teeth are chattering. Every muscle in my body hurts.

'I need you to stay alive. You need you to stay alive. Somewhere in you there is a survival instinct, Horse. Stay the fuck awake. Donato is coming to get you.'

I must have heard her wrong.

Somebody is climbing up the scaffolding. At first I think it's a bear, the way it moves. All burly and awkward. But it really is Donato.

I don't believe it. Donato hates me.

He's moving fast for a man of his size. He gets to the top of the crane and then prepares to tackle the arm, where I am. It will move if he climbs on.

'All right, Charlie?' He sounds casual, like we're just meeting up for a game of snooker and a couple of beers on a Friday night because we're mates. I see the whites of his eyes but not much else. He has a harness on and there are coils of rope and clippy things hanging from his belt. 'Pretty impressive that you got all the way up here. We're going to climb down now, OK?'

My teeth are chattering. I shake my head.

'C-c-c-an't do that, Donato.'

'Yeah, sure you can. I'm going to come out to you with a harness. You don't have to do anything. Just stay where you are, hold tight, and I'll get you clipped on.'

'Tell Roman I'm sorry.'

'Tell him yourself. He's waiting for you down there. Here I come. You may feel a little wobble.'

The whole crane arm lurches when he climbs on.

'Ooh, that's a bit sketchy,' Donato says, chuckling.

I'm going to die now. Love you, Mum. Sorry.

'Stay with me, Horse!' Shandy yells.

I guess it takes about thirty seconds for Donato to make his way out to me and put a harness around me. Feels like a year and a half. He tries cracking jokes and saying silly things to distract me, but I don't speak. My teeth sound like those wind-up mechanical choppers for practical jokes.

When we finally reach the bottom and make our way back through the 'maze' of concrete barriers and temporary walls and finally over the fence surrounding the building site, I have lost both shoes and my tights are laddered beyond recognition. My legs are so wobbly that I fall into Shandy's arms and cling to her like a baby monkey. She has to lead me over to a concrete barrier and sit me down while we wait for Donato to make some calls and put his equipment back in his car. I don't let go of her even then.

Shandy and Roman look at each other. Shandy reaches up to my face, takes out my earring, and passes it to him.

'We're taking you home,' Shandy says, untangling herself from me as Roman puts his arm around me. I stick to him like Velcro. I still feel like I'm going to fall fifty metres.

'Come on,' he says in my ear. 'This is a building site. Donato's going to talk to the construction company since they'll have us on video, but the real police will be here soon if we don't clear out.'

That gets me moving. I haven't even thanked Donato properly. I lunge in his direction calling out Donato's name, but Roman steers me towards the Green Bus stop.

'You'll only embarrass him,' he says. 'You can thank him next time you see him.

'I don't want to go back to O's.' My voice is shaking. I'm so cold.

'Shandy and I will be staying with you until this is resolved.'

I lean into his warmth. 'I'll tell you how to resolve it. Arrest Martin Elstree.'

'I'm not in a position to arrest anybody. We need to build a case before we can have him picked up.'

We board the bus and stagger to the back. I see myself reflected in the bus window. Sporting that dead-fish look.

'Come on, you're shocky, bruv,' Shandy says. 'Take my coat.'


In the wee hours we find O's flat occupied by Roman's sister Elena, the bike messenger, and her partner Monk. It smells of fish fingers, possibly because their three kids are there, too, crashed out in sleeping bags in O's sitting room except for the one sleeping against Monk's shoulder.

'There's nothing more we can do,' Elena tells Roman. 'Unless you want one of us to get on a ferry and go to Brittany.'

Roman shakes his head. 'No, I've got Donato working on that

end. I'm sorry it's so late. Do you want help getting the kids home? I'll call a car.'

'Already done. We have a friend coming in five.' Monk is packing bottles and toys into a nappy bag one-handed while Elena rouses her kids and shepherds them down the stairs. O would flip out at the thought of her privacy being invaded this way, but the domestic scene is exactly the kind of surreal I need to calm me down after everything that's happened. I grab sleeping bags and stray toys and follow Elena and her kids downstairs while Monk and Roman talk about the practicality of tracing a pigeon in France. Elena is cool and efficient, getting the kids in the car and the bikes on the rack without any apparent effort. I find myself thanking her profusely for her help.

'My brother likes to rescue people,' she says. 'You're not one of those suicidal sleepwalkers, are you?'

'Not suicidal, no,' I say, handing her a partly chewed lion cuddly toy that she promptly passes to a crying daughter.

'Good. Listen, my brother asked me to break into your friend's filing cabinet. You might want to take a look at what he finds before he gives it all to Donato.'

She gets in the car and buckles herself in just as Monk emerges from O's building with the baby.

'He what?' I say.

'You heard me. Listen, I have no clue what's going on with all this, but I've listened to your ASMR and I don't think you can be a bad person if you made those recordings to help people calm down. So I'm telling you straight – check the files. Once Donato gets them, you'll probably never see them again. Good luck.'

The car pulls away while I'm still processing this. Then I run up the stairs.

'Roman, what the fuck—'

Shandy and Roman already have the files spread out on O's desk.

'Calm down, Horse. They're dead boring. Come and see.'

They are boring. It's mostly financial stuff. Some of the papers go back to the 1970s, some are faded 1990s faxes on thin, shiny paper that can barely be read. I feel like a history student.

'I can't believe you just broke in like this. It's unethical, not to mention illegal.'

He shrugs. 'Do you want to find her or not?'

I can't stand the smell of fish fingers. I throw open the doors to the roof and suck in the damp air.

'You know, it's not the murders, it's not the uninvited tech growing in my brain, none of these things seem to matter. What matters is that I trusted her and she used me.'

I prop the doors so they'll stay open and sit down on the lintel. After a minute, Roman lowers himself onto the step beside me. He offers me a hand-rolled cigarette that looks like it's been sat on. I just stare at it for about five seconds.

'I don't smoke,' I say. Then I take it. He produces a lighter from his jacket pocket.

I desperately want there to be some other explanation that doesn't involve O being a complete bastard and me being a complete tool. Maybe she decided to go and see Daphne without me and something happened before she got there. Maybe she's fallen or fainted and hit her head and can't remember who she is. Maybe Martin Elstree tricked her and used her—

Ah, fuck. Nobody tricks or uses O. Least of all a prat like him.

I take a drag on the RYO.

'What's in this?' Coughing, choking. Roman slaps me heartily on the back. 'I thought you were on the side of the law.'

'I'm a scientist first. Smoke up. You've had a shock.'

'No, I can't, I might fall asleep.' I hand it to him but he doesn't take a hit.

'Looks like you could use a good night under your ear.'

'Don't be a fuckwit, Roman. I go to sleep in my bed and wake up under a bus. Sounds like a great plan.'

'I've got your earring.'

'Right.' I doubt the earring matters any more if my whole *head is a fucking receiver* but whatever.

'I'll watch out for you. I told you. I won't let anything happen to you.'

I cough again, and my face goes hot.

'I'll sleep on the floor where you'll have to step on me if you want to get out of the room. I'm being serious.'

I lean my head on his shoulder. It's a good shoulder. I don't know why I find the idea of Roman so silly. Maybe if he had a real office instead of a kebab shop.

He says, 'You reckon O has been looking after you. Protecting you.'

'I know it sounds absurd, an old lady in a wheelchair protecting me. But she was.'

Roman turns towards me and takes my hands in his. His eyes are very green but I can't stand looking into them because there's so much I haven't told him.

'Charlie, she's not your friend. She never was your friend. The sooner you understand that, the better.'

'I know. But I can't forget how she was good to me at a time when nothing was going right for me.'

'Nothing was going right for you because she caused it. I checked up on the litigation between BigSky and Little Bird. It's in O's interests for Zborowski to disappear because it was his work that was stolen from BigSky; if he's gone, he can't be compelled to give evidence. It's perfectly possible that O brought him to Meera to get his idea, then turned around and killed him. We're looking into Meera now.'

'And you knew this all along?'

'It's been unfolding. I tried to talk to you about her but you were completely in her thrall.'

'Thrall? Don't be insulting.' But I've stupidly burst into tears.

'Roman,' Shandy says, laying her palm on the top of my head. 'Why don't you make like a detective and find where O keeps her spirits?'

He springs up in a hurry and Shandy takes his place. She dumps Edgar in my lap and I give her the cigarette, which has made me feel weird.

'I hate it that I thought I was someone to her but I was only ever her prey,' I tell Shandy. 'I hate that I was so dumb. I thought I was safe in the consciousness community. ASMRtists and such, we aren't in it for money or glory and I thought she was one of us. But she's a snake. No, that's not fair to snakes. Poor snakes, so misunderstood. Also rats. My point being: how could I get it so wrong? How can I trust anyone now?'

'She's a right shit, Horse. She's a ratsnake. Thanks, Ro.' Shandy takes two glasses of vodka from Roman and hands me one. 'Cheers.'

I clink glasses with them and sink the vodka. I've avoided alcohol ever since the narcolepsy started, but I have to admit it has an immediate steadying effect.

'I feel like I'm playing that pub game where you put a sticky note on your forehead with someone's name and everyone can see the name but you, and you have to ask questions to find out who you are. And my sticky note says "Fucking idiot". That's how I feel.'

'That's because you're lovely and you think everyone is the same.'

Edgar keeps putting his tail in my face. From the flat behind me I can hear Roman talking to someone. Sounds like Donato.

'*Donato* rescued me,' I say to Shandy, pathetically. 'Who knew?'

She shrugs. 'There's always a use for the rough-and-ready type, I guess.'

'Who can I trust? I've seen all this evidence against O, and if I accept it at face value then I've been taken for a fool nearly a year gone now.'

'You have to face the truth, Horse. That's the only way you'll ever get on top of it.'

'But that would mean I'm a complete fucking idiot.'

She pats my hand. 'Ro, love, pass us the bottle, will you?'

Shandy is refilling my drink.

'I know, love. It's always the way. Look at it like this: O is a real clever clogs. You've been deceived by the best!'

She clinks glasses with me again. I drink again.

'I could have been killed. What would she have done? Did she ever care about me at all?'

'Horse. Horse. Listen to me. You have to forget her. Put her out of your mind. Move on. OK?'

'She treated me like a consumable. Chewed me up and spat me out when she was done.'

Roman pushes past Shandy and steps out onto the roof. He turns to face us, hands on hips, and tries to sound stern.

'Speaking of O. Her motorbike has been found in a pond in Epping fucking Forest.'

I give a little scream, Shandy gives a little scream. Like in primary school.

We look at each other and at the same time we say:

'What if she's dead, Shandy?'

And:

'The old tart's done a runner!'

Then we punch each other.

# For real

Shandy and I and Roman get super drunk. Well, I don't know how drunk they get but I get legless. And that's when I decide: I'm going to take Elstree out. I can't risk being ambushed by him every time I fall asleep. I can't risk him hurting the people I love, either. He has to go.

I am very drunk but wide awake. Shandy falls asleep in my bed. At some point around four a.m., Roman brings me a cup of camomile tea while I sit on the sofa watching the room sway, then takes a handmade afghan from the back of O's favourite chair and drapes it over my shoulders, reaching around me to tuck it in while I sip the tea. I'm surprised by the amount of muscle in his arm.

'Nice bicep,' I hear myself say, then drink tea to hide my embarrassment.

'It's my wanking arm.'

The tea comes back out through my nose.

'That's better,' Roman says. 'We're going to get through this, OK? I made coffee. I'll stay awake so you can sleep. I have work to do, and if I run out of that I can mainline the latest season of Physics Goats—'

'Spoiler: Episode Seven has dark matter monsters.'

'Good to know. I'll be here and I'll watch you. Nothing's going to happen to you. In a matter of hours, we should know where that other pigeon has got to. Unless it lands on a cruise ship heading for Barbados, it'll end up somewhere in France. Donato will cross-reference the location with what we know about O and Elstree.'

He thinks I'm afraid of being attacked. He has no idea that I'm really planning to hack Elstree and make him disappear for ever.

No wonder I sometimes feel unreal. I can be thinking things and no one else knows what they are. That doesn't seem right, somehow. It's not like that in dreams. In dreams, my guts and heart are right out there in the environmental content. In dreams, I'm an open wound.

I'm not even making sense to myself.

'It was a robot, what built that dream,' I tell Roman. 'Martin doesn't have the balls to stand up to me so he sent a robot to do his dirty work.'

'How can you be so sure?'

'It felt like being in a VR game, not a real dream. And the only person in the dream besides myself was a mechanical bird. It was nothing like the dream with Daphne or even the Creeper dreams, except that he used the Creeper to attack me at the beginning. I think it's the way he disables the R.E.M. atonia. But the rest was different.'

Roman smiles. 'So you are coming around to my view that the Creeper is a phenomenon, not a person.'

'Maybe. In the dream I heard his voice. He said something about being able to keep me sleeping. Like he had some mechanical way of doing it.'

'The idea of an AI dream agent is right in line with what we know about BigSky's ambitions.'

'Yeah, but how would Martin Elstree get hold of that kind of tech?'

Roman is shaking his head. He's thinking about it. After a while, he says, 'If an AI attacked you, it would explain how you were targeted in broad daylight riding your bike.'

'I crushed that bird in my hand. Crushed it to bits.'

'Good for you. Why don't you get your head down? I'll be sitting right here at the desk. There's nowhere you can go without my knowing.'

I pull the afghan right up to my chin and close my eyes.

In general, I try to be a good person. But dreams are a medium where a person can act out power fantasies without being held to account, for real. So in a sense, I guess I hate and fear Elstree partly because he's just a more extreme version of me. He wouldn't hurt a fly in real life, but he'd take a power saw to his boss and get off on it in his fantasies. He'd make a musician walk off a high-rise and act like none of it was real – but it is real.

And me? I'm going to kill him. It won't be a fantasy.

**Secret Diary of a Dreamhacker**
**Entry #56**
**Codename:** Chaplin
**Date:** 27 September 2027
**Client:** Martin Elstree
**Payment in advance:** N/A
**Session Goal:** Kill the client
**Location:** O's sofa
**Narcolepsy status:** Strangely OK
**Nutrition/stimulants:** At least a pint of Stoli
**Start time:** 4:35 a.m.
**End time:** 4:59 a.m.

It takes me a while to locate Martin's building in the Dream
City, not because it's hard to find but because I'm drunk.
It's there in dream-Convoys Wharf, reality mixed up with
imagination in some whacked-out cocktail. Martin's building is
juxtaposed with a giant tree and a cycle-superhighway beside a
building site with a crane. At the foot of the crane is the hedge
maze where I got lost, and there's a stone staircase winding
around the outside of the building itself. I climb right up to the
window of his bedroom and break it open with my Thor-hammer.

He's in bed, asleep. He's not even in REM sleep, but
nevertheless when he rolls on his side I see the big wind-up key
sticking out of his back, just like Bernard when Daphne hacked
him. This is my moment.

He's vulnerable. He's asleep.

Am I really going to do this?

Apparently I am. I reach out and turn the key, and suddenly
the scale of things changes. It's as if either Martin Elstree has

become a giant or I've become a homunculus, because a door swings open in his back and I step inside into a control room. It's like something out of Willy Wonka. On a small monitor in front of me appear the red and purple blobs of blood vessels that represent the view from inside his eyelids. A second monitor shows his dream content, but this is switched off now because he's no longer in the Dream City but rather on the verge of wakefulness. I can pull levers and wind cranks to move Martin Elstree's body. There is a twisting horn of an old-fashioned megaphone that I can talk into. To give him instructions.

He's breathing fast and shallow, like he can't catch his breath. I know that feeling. It's how you feel when the Creeper stands on your chest and tries to choke you out. Only now I'm the Creeper.

I flick on the second monitor. Its content is determined by me. I let him dream his own flat, so that he thinks he's awake but he isn't.

'One of the birds just came in,' I whisper into the mouthpiece. 'It's an important message. Don't fuck this up like you fucked up getting rid of Charlie Aaron.'

I see through his eyes as he opens them in real life. He rises out of bed, stumbles through his bedroom, across the vast open-plan main room to the balcony doors. It's still dark out there. He tries the handle of the balcony door.

'It's locked, remember?'

Blearily, he punches a code into the system. I can make him do whatever I want. This is sick.

He opens the door and goes to the pigeon coop. The balcony is not large. Most of it is occupied by the pigeon coop and feed bin, but there are two chairs looking out over the river. The birds shuffle around, disturbed.

While he's fumbling about, I suggest, 'It's not in the coop. It's on the balcony railing.'

I put the dream bird there, a carrier pigeon much like Sidney with the same tiddly backpack. He makes a grab and misses; the dream bird takes wing. Then it lands on the roof of the pigeon coop, out of reach.

'You can get it. Just put a chair by the coop.'

He's too stupid to realise I'm doing the same thing to him that he tried to do to me. He's clumsy and when he grabs for the chair, I change the shape of it so that its dream form is different from its real shape, and he drops it on its side. I show it to him as if it's standing solidly on four legs.

He climbs on. The chair spins out from under him; he grabs for the railing, misses and pitches head first over the balcony.

And here is the air beneath him, splaying his limbs, whipping his clothes about his skin, stretching his hair. Martin Elstree hangs there wide asleep and he's still asleep as his head slams into the concrete.

I'm in darkness. Silence. I can't hear my heart. I can't feel myself. I don't know where I am or who I am.

The dream is gone. The Dream City is gone. I'm nowhere.

I flash the realisation that I've been cast into outer darkness for my crime. I can't come back. It would be just my luck not to get away with this. I hang in nothingness, surrounded by my own guilt and triumph, for a stretch of time that I've no way of measuring. Then there's an earthquake sensation as the undisclosed dark material around me and inside me begins to erupt, to slide, roar, shift – and I rise through layers of consciousness until I feel Roman grabbing my shoulders and shaking me.

'Charlie! Charlie! Wake up!'

My heart is thundering. How could I not hear that? I'm gasping for breath. My legs kick out. I throw Roman off and he flies across the room, crashing into O's fireplace. I hear a weird, guttural sound that is me.

'Charlie! Are you OK? You stopped breathing.'

I roll off the sofa and vomit on the floor.

'Sorry,' I say, holding what's left of my hair out of the way. 'Sorry, sorry, sorry, sorry.'

But the thing is, deep down I'm really not sorry.

I'm really not sorry at all.

# Moose reserve

Before I even know what's happened, Roman's cleaned up my vomit and brought me a glass of sparkling water with lemon in it.

'I live with my sister and her three kids, remember? Vomiting is routine. You OK now?'

I sip the water.

'I'll give you my Secret Diaries for analysis if you'll put me in contact with the other people in my study.'

'I think you're still drunk, Charlie. What's made you change your mind?'

My head hurts so much. And no wonder, what with the *infection technology growing in my skull*.

'I need to be in contact with other people like me. I need to talk to someone who understands what I'm going through.'

'Yeah, well, about that.' He runs his hand over his stubbly jaw like a guy in a razor ad, but it's a nervous gesture. He's ashamed of something, or... 'Charlie, I don't know how to say this.'

'Just spit it out, Roman.'

'Those people. They're all dead. You know the sleepwalkers I was telling you about, the suicides we investigated? Many of them were participants in your study. In some cases I tried to make contact with them before... well, before they died. But I failed.'

The room stops spinning while I take it in. I'm the last one?

'And me? You treated me like a criminal! Why didn't you make contact with *me*?'

'We tried! But you moved out of Shandy's place with no forwarding address, your room-mates were not forthcoming, and we didn't realise you were in the study until after Melodie was killed.'

'But you could have talked to me, you could have explained...
Why...?'

He's rubbing his eyes, pacing up and down, waiting for me
to work it out. It takes me a few moments.

*'You thought I did it!'*

His whole face clenches and he sort of cringes.

'Try to see it from our point of view, mate. O was connected
with Little Bird. You were living with O and she was running
your dreamhacking business. O and Little Bird have been
embroiled in this war with BigSky, nobody knew how it would
turn out. Can you blame us for being cautious?'

I may just be hyperventilating now. I try to get up off the sofa
but the whole room is pitching and swaying again. Stupid vodka.

'Can you blame me for being... what am I, even, right now?'

He glances at me. 'Apoplectic?'

*'Apocalyptic*, more like. This is a disaster. Just leave me alone,
Roman. Take the fucking diaries. I'll squirt them to you right
now, do what you like. I don't even care. I'm going to move to
Canada and work in a moose reserve. Fuck this shite.'

'Do they have moose reserves, or did you mean a national
park? No, please don't throw things at my head. I'll just go now.'

I hurl myself back on the sofa and put a pillow over my face.

'Don't go,' I say through the pillow. 'You were right. You can
arrest me now. I confess.'

'Confess what?'

The pillow is covered in Edgar's fur. I sneeze.

'I killed him.'

There's a long silence. He sits down on the coffee table. I
can feel his knees pressing against mine but I keep the pillow
on my face.

'Charlie. What are you talking about?'

'I think you'll find that Martin Elstree has met with an unfor-
tunate accident. It was me. Go ahead and call Donato, I'm sure
he'll be pleased. He was right about me all along.'

Roman reaches over and takes the pillow away.

'Don't be stupid. Just tell me what happened. And send me the damn diaries, because believe it or not they can still be useful.'

So I tell him the whole thing: what I did to Elstree, what Daphne said to me, everything in no special order. He is a good listener. I cry a bit with relief, I send him the diaries, and then we put a load of washing in and do the dishes like an old married couple. Then Shandy wakes up and shambles in like a bear. We make coffee and take it on the roof, where Shandy and I scowl indiscriminately at London and Roman thinks aloud.

'You know,' he says, 'BigSky doesn't really operate the way you think. It isn't a normal corporate structure. It's more like *Minecraft*. Nobody's really controlling it. There's shadowy stuff going on but there is no big conspiracy, there's no Board of Directors playing at being potentates. That's not to say there aren't dangers, because there are.'

'He has a point,' Shandy says. 'The tail does occasionally wag the dog at BigSky.'

'I think you were right about the Creeper,' I tell Roman. 'I don't think it was Martin Elstree. When I went after him, he was defenceless. He said he was going to have me removed, but I think he was giving orders to someone else.'

'Maybe there are other Daphnes who don't share her scruples,' Shandy says.

I snort. I'm not sure what scruples Daphne has, exactly.

'I think if we follow the data trail, we're going to find that Elstree was taking money from both O and BigSky,' Roman says. 'BigSky may not even care about the IP, they may have just been trying to get the measure of O and Little Bird. A technology that implants upgradable AI into your actual skull is a fairly big deal. Much bigger than the Council for Alternative Therapies, Charlie. Much, much bigger.'

I have a splitting headache and my stomach feels like a zoo.

'What about the last pigeon?' I croak.

Roman is smiling. 'We've traced it to Brittany. There's a country cottage. It's not in Olivia's name, but it's been customised to be accessible for wheelchairs.'

I feel a surge of hopeful expectation accompanied by stabbing pain in my head. Stupid vodka.

'Donato is already on his way.'

'Don't let her get wind that he's coming,' I mutter, rubbing my temples. 'She'll just move on again. Maybe you should go, too.'

'Can't. I've got a meeting with some BigSky developers to talk about security risks in The Dark Side. I'm going to try to convince them to delay the launch. The death of Martin Elstree will spook them.'

I wince. I killed a person. But I'm no killer. Ergo, there must be someone to blame besides myself.

Mustn't there?

'I'm getting you a painkiller,' Roman says, going into the kitchen.

'Charlie,' Shandy says, 'do you know for a fact that O doesn't use any of the BigSky platform? Because if I were a hacker and BigSky were my enemy, I'd be all up in their files no matter what I told anybody. How else would she know what they're doing?'

I need to lie down. Why are people still talking to me?

'So?' I grunt.

'So if these guys hunt her down in France, do you really think they'll catch her? Do you really think they'll get the truth out of her? Ten to one if you look on Sweet Dreams, you'll find her there. Disguised as a lamp-post or something, but she'll be there.'

'How can you be so sure, Shandy? I know her. She doesn't use BigSky.'

Shandy takes my arm gently and leads me back inside.

'Love, don't take this the wrong way. But it would seem you don't know her at all. What harm could come from trying?'

What harm indeed?

**Secret Diary of a Prawn Star**
**Entry #57**
**Codename:** Chaplin
**Date:** 27 September 2027
**Client:** O
**Payment in advance:** I never seem to get paid any more
**Session Goal:** Find her and make her tell me everything
**Location:** Sideways Gravity Hotel, Dream City
**Narcolepsy status:** Some sort of remission at the moment?
**Nutrition/stimulants:** N/A
**Start time:** 11.20 a.m.
**End time:** 12.03 p.m.

I'm standing at the foot of the building with the sideways gravity, the one that's always caught my attention. The one where I thought I saw O the night I dreamed without my earring. In this dream-night I can see many people, fifteen or twenty storeys up, dining at tables scattered across the black glass surface of the windows. It's dark apart from a tiny candle flame at each table and the faint neon glow of the canal's ribbed bridges.

The tulip concierge tries to stop me entering.

'We don't take your sort,' it says.

I'm not in the mood. I produce a pair of garden shears and chop its head off.

In front of me, the swanky revolving door to the building disappears. I rap on the wall with the butt-end of my garden shears.

'Oi!' I yell. 'Don't make me get explosives.'

There's a groan of machinery and what had been a glass wall becomes the open door of a freight lift with a battered, rusting metal cage instead of proper walls. I can't see any shaft walls, but this is a dream so I don't worry about it. I get on and haul the doors shut manually. There's no panel with buttons for each floor, just a pull-cord.

I tug it.

There's a series of popping sounds like fireworks, and then the floor of the lift punches into the bottom of my feet and I stagger, grabbing on to the wire cage as the lift goes hurtling into the sky, shuddering, jerking and making the most godawful bird-of-prey screams as metal grinds on metal. As it rises, the cage begins to bank to the right, and I feel my wrapped hair tugging sideways on my skull as if I'm on a roller coaster.

Then, without warning, all sound ceases and I'm momentarily weightless. The cage is now perpendicular to the canal and I'm floating with my face towards the sky, its deep-purple skin freckled by constellations that light pollution can't erase. Now my feet are level with the sprawling sideways-restaurant and I smell seafood.

The lift cage jerks once again and my sense of weight returns. I am at a ninety-degree angle to the side of the building, with its walls acting as the new ground beneath my feet. The entire Dream City appears to be sideways. I don't entirely trust my own senses, but I can stand just fine.

A rude buzzing sound coincides with the flashing of an old-fashioned incandescent red light bulb over the door. Then silence. I try the cage door. It opens with a grinding noise and I step out onto the polished black glass of the building's exterior.

The open-air restaurant is spread out over the side of the building, but all of the chairs and tables are orientated so that the patrons are facing the sky. Delicacies from every continent clutter the tables, while the candles burn sideways. Most of the people are beautiful, and I stare rudely. I am barefoot and my PJs refuse to turn into a better outfit despite all my efforts. A waiter comes up out of a hatch in the floor, sees me, lifts his eyebrows and makes a point of skirting wide around me.

I find O sitting alone at a banquet table. There's no food in front of her, just a half-finished glass of red wine. I pull up a chair next to her and she glances briefly at me, gives the slightest shade of a nod before turning her attention to the sky. As if it's just an ordinary evening. The righteous fury that has been burning in my belly is quenched as abruptly as if someone tossed a bucket of piss on my campfire. I don't know how to begin.

'I don't even know what to say to you.'

'Then don't say anything. If you've come to kill me, you may as well get on with it.'

'Kill you? No, I came to talk to you. To try to understand.'

'You'll never understand me. We are fundamentally different kinds of creature.'

'Did you send Daphne to kill the other people in my study?'

'No. But I did use Martin Elstree to patent the technology that gives you your abilities. BigSky tried to take it back from us, so I removed everything from their reach. They've only been able to create software that performs minor functions. They don't have the biotech, and they can't even make a proper dreamhacking bot.'

'Yeah, about that. This thing that's *growing*. In my head, O. You've patented it. *You* are the silent partner in Little Bird. You worked with Bernard and Meera. You've been using your own sister. And you've been using me.' My voice catches and I swallow hard on a tightness that wants to become a sob.

She nods once. Matter-of-fact.

'It started out for medical reasons. My sister. I was looking for a therapy that could slow down the progress of the disease, let her die of something else to spare her the cognitive deterioration. And of course, to spare myself if I ended up with the same affliction in time. I started Little Bird and convinced Meera Bhango to come in with me as a partner. I provided the funding and gave her free rein.

'She had some techniques involving *in vivo* machinery that were promising in animal trials. The problem was the inability

279

to control the machines she had built once they were *in situ*. We needed an interface. Now, with animals you can image their brains and you can give them cognitive tests, but you can't ask them directly about changes in their consciousness. We needed to do trials on people, but there are a lot of ethical issues there.'

'No kidding.'

She ignores my snide comment and continues.

'So the only other option was to deploy the agent in a simulated human brain to see if we could build a case for human trials. The problem is cost. Rightly or wrongly, simulated people are actually a lot more expensive than real people. Time was of the essence, so I started looking around for VR studies we could piggyback on, and that's when Bernard's team came to my attention.'

'My study.'

'Yes. Your study. We could see that the techniques being used by the team would be very helpful to us, if modified properly, because as you know, you ingested a substance with a time-dependent effect that could be controlled via the BigSky interface, using your headware. They already had their hooks into you, so to speak. I had a unique view of the proceedings, for of course there's very little that goes on in BigSky that I can't access.'

'Shandy was right. You've been all up in BigSky this whole time.'

'In a covert way, yes, of course. I was very careful, though. Anyway, when the anomalous results started to become apparent, BigSky pulled the plug on the whole thing. And that would have been the end of it.'

'They really dropped it?'

'It was shelved by the ethics committee. I'm sure it would have been revisited eventually. But then Martin Elstree and I found a loophole in the IP agreement between Bernard Zborowski and the study he worked on. The study was done through Excelsior-Barking, that bastion of higher learning.'

'Don't make fun of my alma mater.'

Her mouth twitches, almost a smile. 'The work was funded by a BigSky grant but not included under their corporate envelope in terms of disclosure and IP. The loophole allowed Bernard to take his developing ideas elsewhere after the study was closed.'

'And that's where you picked him up.'

She nods. 'The failure of the original project didn't stop BigSky from continuing to work on other aspects of the sleep interface. They are keen to further develop Sweet Dreams and they will. But they've backed off from the use of a chemical delivery system; it's just too fraught with litigious risk. That's why, with the help of Martin as a negotiator, we now hold the patent on the anti-dementia agent. That is to say, Meera and I hold it.'

'And where is Meera in all this?'

'Her intervention is why your dreamhacking has been improving. I kept all your recorded sessions – Meera studied them and used them to make corrections. She could send instructions straight to you using the interface. Some of this was delivered directly via the dream content and some of it came through ingrowing machinery introduced directly'

'What do you mean, "introduced directly"?'

She clears her throat.

'We er . . . we spiked your tea.'

'You what?'

'Spiked your tea, darling. It was easy. You make it so strong and you often let the milk go sour, so your taste buds can't have much sensitivity.'

'I . . . You *drugged* me with tiny machines and now you're blaming my taste buds?'

'It was a terrible thing to do. I am a terrible person, you know. I keep telling you, and you think I'm joking. I wasn't joking. I'm not joking now. In fact, I rarely joke. It's why I seldom attend parties. Laughter is tedious.'

'So ... this is why my ability has been evolving? Bernard said it was because the original treatment is a nanomachine.'

'Yes, and Meera has been communicating with the machinery that now lives in your brain. Like what's happening right now. The Dream City. This is all a construct created by the machinery burrowing into your skull and operating on your brain tissue. The sideways tower is your brain's effort to translate all the building that's going on neurally. In fact, we could argue that the alterations the dreaming process has made in your neural architecture are much more radical than anything I could put in your tea. But maybe the chemical side of things feels more violating to you.'

'Violating? You want to know what feels *more* violating? All of it. This. Now. Everything. No special order. *You*. You feel violating. How ... how could you, O?'

'So far, so predictable. You can't seem to understand that my conscience extends towards all of humanity, not just you. I've done my best to equip you for the coming reality. I can't say I'm surprised that you take a different view.'

'You're talking like you fancy yourself some sort of god.'

'I've done the best I could, knowing that you had to find out eventually. I kept expecting you to suss it but you never did. That trusting nature will be your downfall someday.'

'What about Martin Elstree? He used some kind of robot to dreamhack me.'

'Bernard built it.'

'Built it out of what? Can BigSky kill people with robots now?'

'Not that *they* know of. Bernard modelled the robot dreamhacker on the processes he gleaned from your records.'

'He built robots from my Secret Diaries?'

'Reverse-engineered you into a killer-robot Charlie of sorts. Of course, all personal characteristics were scrubbed. The robot dreamhacker can't hold a candle to you, Charlie.'

I am speechless. I look up at the stars over the Dream City. None of the constellations are even familiar.

'All your records were sitting there on BigSky, practically out in the open for someone like me. So were the developers' various templates for the Sweet Dreams technology. Bernard was a kid in a toy shop, isolating the processes and building them into the Sweet Dreams code.'

'In that case, why would you kill Bernard? What possible reason could you have? Will you go after Meera, too? Talented people who were inventing amazing things – and you're taking it on yourself to remove them from the world. Not to mention Mel. There's just no excuse for it, no justification—'

I'm spluttering and ranting but she's totally unmoved.

'Well, you are full of accusations, aren't you, Charlie. Can you back any of them up?'

I say, 'I know I got it wrong a couple of times, but in the end it seemed clear that the Creeper was Martin Elstree. Everything seemed to point to him. Now you're saying that he was directing a bot that Bernard built. Well, why was Martin Elstree using it to destroy people? Roman told me that every single person in the study is dead, bar me.'

'Maybe I was fond of you.'

'I guess you needed me for my Secret Diaries.'

'Martin and I didn't remove those people to be cruel. They were crash-test dummies for the technology. Because of them, you and Daphne are both improving.'

'Then why tell Daphne to kill Bernard?'

'That wasn't me. That was the Agency.'

'Oh, please. Like I believe that. You may as well confess to the lot, O. Anyway, you told me yourself that the Agency is a joke from when you were kids.'

She gestures expansively at the building, the cityscape, the night in general. 'You're missing the most fundamental understanding of what is happening. Look around you. We are building a new world.'

'No, don't start talking about dream landscapes. I want you to tell me what you've done in the real world, in waking life.'

'Oh, stop blathering,' she says testily. 'You should hear yourself. Of course I didn't kill Bernard, or have him killed, or anything like that.'

'Of course? Well, who did it, then? Daphne was taking pigeon orders from you, so... Wait a second. Are you saying Martin sent the pigeon to Daphne?'

'That is my presumption.'

'And you thought you'd be next, so you ran away.'

'Martin had got slightly out of control. You see, the fight with BigSky required dirty tactics. Martin told me that with such deep pockets, BigSky would probably win the IP suit eventually. The courts weren't going to help us. So it occurred to me that a dreamhacking bot could be instructed to do things that you, for example, would refuse to do.'

'So you built a murderous robot. What could possibly go wrong?'

'Martin obviously was worried about Bernard's ethics getting in the way. It happens a lot with scientists. Martin was concerned that the Dream Police would eventually trace the sleepwalking deaths back to us. He made a tactical decision.'

'So when you found out Martin was siccing the dreamhacker bot on people, you ran away. Why didn't you at least warn me?'

'I could lie and say it was safer for you that you didn't know, but I'm sure you can see that you would have only hampered me and made it harder for me to get away.'

We stare at each other. The surface of the building is no longer glass. It's ice. Vapour rises from it in the darkness, and it's starting to creak.

O says, 'There are numbers under everything. Under all of this. Under us. All numbers, a heaving sea of them that we've got to navigate. I've worked with numbers all my life. Sometimes things need to be done, and it isn't nice but it's necessary. In the case of Meera, she's squeamish. The minute she finds out she's been involved in something illegal or in any way immoral, that will be her finished. She'll sell out her share to BigSky or give it to one of the universities or the Cat Protection League for all I know, and everything I've worked for will have gone to waste. No. This is how it has to be. I knew it from the beginning.'

It's funny how easily I'm swept up in her rationale. I mean, it's not *funny*. But it is strange. I feel unmoored. I don't feel big or important enough to contradict her. I'm right under her thumb, even now, and then I remember: this is a dream.

It's a dream. But O is being too sensible. She's not acting like a typical dreamer – I've been with enough people in their dreams, I should know. She's just talking to me as if we're face to face. How do I know this is really O? If it's her, really, that I'm talking to, then does that make the Dream City her creation, or mine? Which one of us built the sideways building, and who carved the canals, and what is the 'little bird', really? Who is in charge here?

'You enjoyed killing Martin Elstree,' she says. 'It was gratifying. How do you feel, Charlie?'

'Honestly?' I reply defiantly. 'I feel happy. Not about killing but about standing my ground.'

'Then it hasn't all been a dead loss for you, has it.'

A wintry smile. Even the stars are frozen. Icicle points in the darkness.

'It's true that some people had to die,' she says. 'This is inevitable when breaking in a new technology, though. It took a while to work out how to optimize the treatment – fix your narcolepsy, for example. There's been trial and error, but we had to make these calculated decisions so as to keep control of the technology.'

'You mean keep it away from BigSky.'

'People were going to die no matter who did this, Charlie. One factors these things in to any new venture. One runs the projections and and tries to minimize risks, but it would be foolish to expect to have zero casualties. And now that Little Bird has the patent, all of the ethical ramifications can be considered before we even begin to think about distribution.'

She falls silent, and as I'm roiling inside, trying to figure out which of my many objections I should raise first, she adds, 'Or you could let your Dream Police find me. I'm in no condition to be running around the French countryside trying to avoid the authorities.'

'Aha! You *are* in France!' I drum my feet against the ice floor, teeth chattering.

'It's a spare property I sometimes use. I know they'll find me eventually – maybe quite soon. When they search my possessions, they'll find my will, in which you are named to inherit my share in Little Bird. And then the police will come for you, for obvious reasons. You may well be pinned with elder abuse.'

There's thunder in my ears. Not sure if it's my blood pressure or the groans of the ice beneath our feet.

'I'm sorry about that,' O says. 'But I want Daphne to live out her life in peace. And you *have* killed a man, thereby proving that even the smallest worm turns in the end.'

She really has me checkmated. No matter what I do, she wins. Every action I've taken to try to save myself has only driven me deeper into her labyrinth.

There's a loud crack, like a gunshot, and I flinch. Too late, I understand that the ice has cracked in two just beside the table where we are sitting. Our side of the crack pitches abruptly down and we slide, O in her wheelchair and me falling out of my dining chair, while our table topples into the gap. Amid a rain of salad and croutons and wine, we fall.

I grab at O wildly and manage to grasp her ankle. I stay with her psychically, too, following her mental presence back through the shreds of her dream. I need to know where she is.

The scene changes. O is in a sunlit bedroom. It's rustic, with a brass bedstead and oak furniture, a high view of fields lined with poplars. Thread of single-lane carriageway, faint haze of distant ocean. O sleeps curled on her side, on top of the duvet but with a throw blanket over her legs. She's wearing a blue-and-white striped kaftan that's too big for her, so that she looks like a child. She has begun to stir. Soon the dream will break up and I'll be forced out, but for the moment I'm still sharing her consciousness.

I look around the room for anything that could identify her location. Spilled across the bed are the contents of one of the bureau drawers, mostly papers. One looks like a legal document. I pick it up to see it better. It's O's will.

There is my name.

*'To Charlotte Aaron I leave my shares in Little Bird...'*

She wasn't kidding. She named me in her will – but not to help me. To control me, like the tool I've always been. I'm trying to put my thoughts in order when I hear Daphne's voice, behind me, pantomime-style.

'I'm afraid I am here to remove you. I've been given my orders.'

I turn. In the dream, Daphne's voice is breaking and there are tears in her eyes as she looks right at me. Her eye sockets enlarge and her face begins to whiten, and stretch, and harden. Chemical bonds etch themselves its surface until her face has become the flat mask of the Creeper. She moves towards me and I realise I can't breathe. I can't move.

I'm rigid.

I've seen what Daphne can do. It shouldn't even surprise me that it's my turn to be targeted. After all, the other experimental subjects have been picked off one by one, Bernard is dead, Martin Elstree is dead – I've served my purpose and now it's time for me to go.

I have no tricks up my sleeve. I have no one to save me. This is it. Me and Death dressed up as the Old Woman. Daphne comes very close to me. I want to push her away but I can't escape. The white face looms large in my vision, the lightless holes for eyes and mouth, the sense of oxygen starvation. I can suddenly feel my heart very loud but I can't move or breathe. There's something captivating about it, like when a wolf picks out a sheep for death and I'm the sheep and I just stand there and let it take me. That's how I feel.

'I know what you did,' Daphne says, 'and I've been given a new target by the Agency.'

The giant white face comes closer and closer, my breath stops, maybe my heart stops— And then it's like something passes through me and out of the other side, bone for bone, vein for vein, molecule for molecule. Then I can't feel my body at all. I appear to be floating near the ceiling of the room, and I'm looking down on O's bed where she lies curled up and vulnerable. Only now there's a big brass key in her back, and it's turning slowly.

As before, I see Daphne shrink and climb inside O. But I am still in O's dream. In her dream, the sideways tower has turned to a shard of ice, she and I have fallen, and she is waking in her own bed.

She stirs and thrashes her head, jaw working. I see the veins standing up in her arms and neck and legs. Her veins turn green. They grow branches that pop through her skin and spread across the bed, swelling and extending like the tendrils of a plant. The tendrils thicken to vines and then roots that spread into the floor, gripping the entire room.

Like stars showing through fog, O's eyes open halfway. She struggles against the bonds, breathing rapidly. She tries to sit up, but she's restrained by the plant that has grown into her blood system. Her physical weakness is evident. The vines crush her chest. They wrap around her throat.

O stops breathing. Her eyes fade.

She hasn't even managed to kick off the coverlet. There is no sign of a struggle. Her last will and testament isn't even wrinkled.

I fall out of O's dream onto O's sofa, where I waken reeling in a marsh of sweat and racing heart, my breath coming in sobs.

# Delivered by ghost pigeon

When I Spacetime Roman he's in a meeting in Shoreditch. He extricates himself and talks to me from the pavement outside. *'Let me get this straight. Bernard Zborowski used your Secret Diaries to create dreamhacking bots on the Sweet Dreams platform. And BigSky knows about this?'*

'I don't think so. I think O took everybody for a ride, including Meera and Bernard. But she had a certain moral conviction that what she was doing was the lesser of various evils.'

*'Yeah, well, that's going to complicate things here. I'm going to need to confirm where O is and what condition she's in. I'll notify Donato of the situation and I'll head over there myself. Meanwhile, you should stay in the flat and make yourself scarce with everyone. Where's Shandy?'*

'I've left her to work in my room. I don't want her to get in trouble with her boss.'

'And you trust her?'

'More than I trust you, mate.'

'OK, fair enough. I think I trust her, too.'

He promises to contact me once Donato has got to the cottage and checked in on what he finds. But then he Spacetimes me two hours later, while I'm on the train en route to Dorking in defiance of his advice. I edit my environment so that he thinks I'm still at home, but as it turns out, he's on a plane with a bad connection, so we only hear one another's voices.

'Well,' he says. 'Donato's there now. She died in her sleep. The will is just as you said it would be. So I guess that means everything you dreamed was true. Congrats, Charlie. You have an evolving piece of tech in your head that can be operated remotely.'

'So it would appear,' I whisper into the link. 'I'm a monster,

Roman. A monster in progress, no less. I will probably be accused of killing O, but I didn't do it. The Agency ordered it. And of course I can't prove that!'

'Do you think the Agency and BigSky are one and the same?'

'I don't know what to think. Every time I think I know anything, I'm wrong. But I'm not giving up. I'm going to get to the bottom of the Agency.'

'Do me a favour and stay out of trouble until I can get back, all right? This is a very fast-moving situation. Maybe you should contact Meera, though.'

I already have. I've asked her to come round tonight, but I don't tell Roman that. I like him a lot, but he's not going to be able to keep up with me from here on out.

'Take care, mate,' I tell him. 'Good luck explaining things to Donato.'

'You take care, too.' He pauses, and I remember how tenderly he looked after me when I was being sick. 'There will be better days, Charlie.'

'Than this? Yeah, I bloody hope so.'


It's late afternoon when find Daphne in the weight room of her care home. She's benching half her own body weight, which I'm fairly sure I can't do.

'You've come to interrogate me,' she says, sitting up with an effort and mopping the bench thoroughly with a little gym towel. 'Let's go and get one of those protein shakes. Strawberry for me.'

'Daphne, I've come to give you some news. About your sister.'

'I notice that she isn't with you. This is the second time. I suppose she's ill again. Would you like banana?'

'Sure, banana.' I'm not sure if she's forgotten what she did or if she's dissembling.

We sit on Swiss balls sipping our drinks.

'She passed away yesterday. She died in her sleep.'

Daphne's hands are trembling. She gives me her drink and puts her face in her hands. When she takes them away her eyes are still dry, but she continues to shake. Maybe her arms are just tired.

'I suppose that's a blessing,' she says in the end. 'It was her time. She didn't suffer.'

'Daphne, about the last instruction you got. From the Agency. Did you save it?'

'I never save them. Of course not.'

'But you still have the birds that came home to you, right?'

'Yes, absolutely. They're in the dovecote. Let's look. I'll show you the one that brought me the last message.'

We go up to the dovecote, to the familiar smell and shuffle of pigeons, but even though they have come in for the evening, she can't find the one that brought the message.

'I remember it clearly,' she says. 'It was one of the birds we had as children. All black with a star on his back. O called him Mephistopheles. He was always my favourite.'

'You had this bird as a child?' There's a feeling like a cold hand on the back of my neck.

'Yes, well, now it's a ghost, isn't it? It's a ghost pigeon. It was here yesterday, where's it gone?'

'So it's possible that not all of the pigeons were strictly *real*.'

'That depends what you mean by "real". The Agency isn't real, is it?'

'Erm ... I don't know. Is it?'

She laughs and gives me a little push. 'Well, you're an agent now. You should know. There was a bird. I saw it. I read the message. I followed instructions. But I can't find it, I can't find the one ...'

She's becoming distressed now, and I make her go back inside.

'I thought I was getting better,' she says, and her voice is half a sob. 'I've been remembering people's names. It's Tuesday, isn't it?'

'Yes, it's Tuesday. The pigeon may have been sent to you in a dream, Daphne, and that's why there's no evidence. Do you record your dreams?'

'Me? No, never. O didn't trust that BigSky, you know. I don't use any recording devices. I'm not even sure if I want to remember my dreams. They can be quite dark at times, you see.'

I still don't know if she's aware of killing O. I have to come out with it, I can't back off.

'Daphne, do you remember being in O's dream with me? At her place in France?'

'Now, are we supposed to feed them or were we just checking the water?' Daphne says.

'Why would the Agency want O dead?' I press.

'Next time you come, bring my sister's pigeons. Someone will have to look after them now she's gone.'

The flat is too quiet when I get back. Feeling wobbly, I close O's bedroom door. Can't believe she's fucking dead, how dare she check out on me like this? I kick her desk, but that only hurts my foot. So I wodge up her favourite afghan into a ball and throw it. This is even less satisfying than it sounds. Eventually I end up crying into Edgar's fur. Luckily Meera soon shows up with food. And tea. I sniff my tea but for obvious reasons don't drink it.

I fill Meera in on O's death and the details of its circumstances. She says, 'How awful!' and makes the right noises in the right places. She listens intently to my account of O's justification, shaking her head and looking pained at the worst bits. Maybe she's acting, but I don't think so.

'So,' I finish, trying to sound brisk but coming off a bit desperate, 'there's a thing *growing into my skull* and I gather you've been talking to it.'

'I suppose you could put it that way. Through a computer feedback interface.'

'So all of your extended experimentation on me, via BigSky, via Little Bird, all of your using me as a crash-test dummy – was there a plan to eventually tell me what was going on, or was I slated for destruction, too, once you'd got what you wanted?'

Meera shakes her head emphatically. 'I was brought in to try to improve your condition, Charlie. To improve conditions for all of the people who had been introduced to the agent. And I think I have done that. These crimes that you're talking about, that's not me. I'm too busy working in my lab to plot anybody's destruction, even if I were so inclined. And I'm not so inclined. I didn't know that O was doing these things. We didn't speak much, to be honest.'

'But you knew you were working on me and Daphne. You knew you were getting in our heads, literally and figuratively.'

'I have to gather information about how the agent is working, and I have to interact with it. That's the advantage of using a tiny engine as opposed to a drug. I can work on it while it's *in situ*, sending back information continuously via your headware. Now, if my efforts are translating into some sort of dream event for you, well ... I wouldn't know.'

'No, you wouldn't. Because you've never been in my position. But I'll tell you one thing. I'm not the same person I was when I met O. I'm not afraid of anything you can throw at me because fundamentally you don't have the courage to put yourself on the line like I do. So if you want to carry on with this work, then I suggest you think about what you're prepared to do to get on board with me. Because I'm your partner now. I'm not going to let you take over. And I'm done running. I'm so done, Meera.'

She sits back and folds her arms across her chest. Clearly she's not in the habit of being scolded.

'By tweaking *in situ*, I mean I cured your narcolepsy,' she says.

I flinch. 'You mean you spiked my tea.'

Her eyes flash defensively. 'Only the one time, when I came to the flat, and only because O told me you didn't know and asked me not to upset you. Before that, I gave the revised agent to O and I had no idea what the arrangement was between the two of you. If it was involuntary on your part, that's on her, not on me.'

'You should be ashamed of yourself.'

'Well, maybe I am! I am ashamed. I'm sorry about how it went down. Either way, you should find you don't have trouble staying awake any more. I expect something like that will be life-changing.'

'Thank you,' I say angrily.

'You're welcome. And you're right: I don't have the courage. I don't even go on roller coasters and I don't watch horror films. So kudos to you for what you do, Charlie. But I'm not your enemy.'

I snort. 'You tricked a mentally impaired woman into killing her own sister.'

'I did nothing of the kind.'

'Why don't I believe you?'

She shrugs. 'I'm a neurotechnologist. I work to improve people's lives, not end them. Daphne did what she did. I didn't ask her to, and I don't know why she did it. Don't try to assuage your own guilt by blaming me, Charlie. O has put us both in deep trouble, even in dying. According to your friend Roman she was a manipulator and a serial killer by proxy. Were *you* going to stop her?'

I don't have an answer for that. Well, the answer is *no*, but I'm not about to admit it.

'The point is, we're safe now,' she says.

'We're not safe! A lot of people are dead and it's still not clear why or who is to blame. There's a dreamhacking bot sitting somewhere on the BigSky server and it can make people sleepwalk, if so instructed. I'd say our work is just beginning.'

'Yeah, about that. Now the phone calls are starting to make sense.'

'What phone calls?'

'Today. Security people from Sweet Dreams calling and wanting to talk to me, but it was all Bernard's department. I couldn't answer their questions. They are convinced that people using Sweet Dreams are vulnerable to being hacked, and they've just released the beta version of The Dark Side.'

'How do they know about the dreamhacker bot?'

Even as I ask, I know the answer. Roman and Donato told

them, either for some sort of payout or for conscience – it doesn't matter. I can't even blame them. If BigSky are going to expand liminal programming, then they'll need to know about the problems – not least of which is the possibility that someone is exploiting the Dream City, someone calling themselves the Agency. And for all the people I've suspected of being the Villain, for all who are dead, I can't be sure we're done yet. Not until I find out who gave the order to kill O.

I don't think it was Meera, but who knows? She and I are the ones left holding the baby.

Meera only shrugs. 'Does it matter? They were bound to find out, and now BigSky realise they've got a big problem. They want me to consult. They want *us* to consult – we're partners now, as you say.'

'Here's the thing, Meera. You know me. But I don't know *you*.'

She folds her arms, tilts her head. 'I'm a doctor, Charlie. I swore an oath and I have a responsibility to serve the well-being of others. That's all you need to know about me.'

'Here's what you need to know about me: I don't believe anything anybody tells me any more. Also, I snore.'

She frowns. 'Is this a joke?'

'No. No joke. Think of something to tell your family because we're sleeping together tonight.'

# Awake

It's getting late when Shandy emerges from the cloud to help me do this thing with Meera. She deactivates Rodney at my request; even so, her presence lends a slumber-party atmosphere to the proceedings. Meera thinks all of this sleeping-together is some kind of weird initiation rite, contrived so that I can convince myself she's harmless – and to some degree, it is. I'm going to get inside her head and find out what she's really made of.

We drag my mattress into the sitting room and haul out extra blankets and pillows. Shandy has taken all the sharp objects away. I'm leaving nothing to chance.

If O was really the mastermind behind everything, then no one will try to hurt either of us now. If Meera herself was the mastermind and somehow manoeuvred O into taking the actions that she did before killing her in the name of the Agency, then I'll find that out soon enough as well. She won't be able to hide from me. The fact that Meera's willing go along with this says one of two things: either she's keen to convince me to cooperate with BigSky so she can keep Little Bird going, or she's looking to mix it up with me in dreamspace. As unlikely as the second option feels, I've been wrong about nearly everything so far. I've got to be ready for anything.

She tosses and turns. Finally falls asleep around two. The last thing I remember is the image of Shandy curled up in a chair under a reading lamp, absorbed in an illustrated book about the history of pubs. Then I close my eyes and slip into Meera's dream.

It's a strange intimacy, dreaming with someone you barely know. So backwards to find out someone's deepest insecurities and wishes before you even have a clue how they like their coffee or where they grew up. But I doubt it's much of a secret that even in her dreams, Meera is to be found in her lab.

She's working on a 3D simulation of the agent as it embeds in the skull and invades the white matter. She's using code to mimic the effects of drugs on different receptors to predict the agent's behaviour *in vivo*. The simulation is covered with flags and notes so that it looks more like a map of a battle than a blown-up section of microscopic tissue.

'How does sleepwalking fit into this?' I ask her quietly. She looks up, sees me and frowns.

'I don't know.' She turns her attention back to her work. 'We haven't actually identified the mechanism that shuts off R.E.M. atonia. You'd think it would be simple, but it isn't. There may be more than one mechanism. We know that our agent can switch it on and off, but not how.'

'Do you always dream about your work?'

'Yes, if I'm thinking about it, which I usually am.'

'There must be something else on your mind,' I suggest, and nudge the walls of the lab with my awareness.

The setting abruptly changes. We are in the HQ of BigSky, which manifests in the Dream City in the form of a literal head. It's a giant transparent thing plopped in the middle of the grey plane of the Sweet Dreams platform. Inside there are work-stations and stairways just as in a real building, but everything is transparent so that the Dream City is visible just through the walls. It's chaos, with crowds of people moving around us like schools of fish. Meera and I are dressed in navy and grey suits, respectively, and she is carrying a burgundy attaché case.

'We have to present our ideas about how Little Bird and BigSky can best cooperate to stem the security crisis,' Meera says. 'This will include our advice to minimize sleepwalking risk until we can pinpoint the cause. We have to convince BigSky to roll back the beta and run more safety checks on Sweet Dreams. It's sensitive because of the IP conflict; they didn't like losing the IP to Little Bird and will try to manoeuvre us into sharing it with them. The fact that you carry the tech in your head will help us. They can't claim to own *you*, after all.'

I'm not sure about that, but I don't argue. This is just her dream. I'm not interested in her subconscious worries about BigSky, I'm looking for signs of what's really going on in Meera's mind. I need to know her intentions. We are just about to step into a meeting room when I suddenly realise Meera isn't with me any more.

She's collapsed. She's lying on the floor and there's something on top of her. A kind of shadow, a formless thing with a white face.

Not this a-bloody-gain. The Creeper. I throw myself down. I try to peel the Creeper off her but I can't. I roll Meera onto her side, recovery position, and that's when I see the keyhole in her back.

Before my eyes, the Creeper turns to a black stripe of smoke and flows into the keyhole with a shrill whistle like a steam kettle.

It has her.

'Who are you?' I shout at the Creeper, shaking Meera. 'What are you, damn you?'

I can't open the panel in her back. I put my body on top of hers so she can't stand up, but she is strong. She throws me off. In real life, if the Creeper has disabled her R.E.M. atonia, then she will be out of bed by now. I'm just praying that Shandy is paying attention.

'Meera, wake up!' I get in her face, slapping her to get her attention, but she shoves me away easily. I stumble and go down on the spongy grey surface ... Wait. What spongy grey surface? I thought we were in BigSky HQ ...

That's when I notice we aren't indoors any more. We are out on the physical platform itself, a featureless grey ledge built above the canals and around the skyscrapers of the Dream City. The platform has been hung with silk banners for the great unveiling of the Sweet Dreams expansion. There's a huge greyscale crowd standing around us acting terribly entertained. Some are laughing for no fathomable reason. But they are all wearing morphine masks and none of them can see.

I get to my feet and run around in front of Meera as she sets out across the platform.

'Meera, wake up! You're sleepwalking. The dreamhacking bot is controlling you. You need to wake up in the dream and take back control.'

'I have to get off this platform,' she tells me earnestly, pupils wide. 'It's not safe here. Sweet Dreams is going to be attacked by monsters from below.'

'No, Meera, we're fifty metres in the air, you can't just walk off the platform.'

'I'm a bird,' she tells me, spreading her arms wide. 'I love flying dreams!'

'Whoa... stop. Don't play around. Are you telling me you're the little bird that's been telling Daphne who to kill?'

'Little Bird is my company. Come on, I want to fly while this lasts.'

Dreams are full of puns. I've seen a little bird in the Dream City twice: once Meera turned into it, and the other time it was a robot bird conspiring with Martin Elstree to make me kill myself. The bird could be a representation of Meera's efforts, through her device, to control me and Daphne – up to and including the infamous 'ghost pigeon'. But if that's true, why is Meera being hacked right now? If she is the mastermind, she has no need to sleepwalk herself to death.

Unless Little Bird is not under Meera's control after all.

Bernard is dead. O is dead. There's no one else alive at Little Bird capable of wreaking so much havoc.

Is there?

I'm torn between the compulsion to wake Meera and save her, and the need to hunt down the entity that has got hold of her. I have to find out who is really behind the killings. I can't keep peeling the onion. Sooner or later, I must arrive at the centre.

'Stay awake, Meera. Something has hold of you. Everything you do in this dream, you'll do in real life. I've seen too many people die. You need to sit down and stay *still*.'

She doesn't listen. Now she's wearing a mask – the same symbol-covered white mask, distorted like a scream. With an icy grip, she seizes hold of my arms. The navy suit she was wearing has morphed into a long black dress. She's looking more and more like the Creeper. I want to break away from her grasp but at least if she's holding me, she can't throw herself off any heights.

'Charlie. At last we meet.' It's the American voice from Mel's dreams.

In a shaky voice I ask, 'Who is speaking?'

Meera's arms come around me. Her white mask bends over me. The American voice is laughing, too. I take one more step back in reflexive horror, but I haven't realised how close we're standing to the edge of the Sweet Dreams platform.

I go over the edge.

The platform, the scaffolds, the ledge of safety provided by BigSky are gone. Meera and I are tumbling arse-over-teakettle through the darkness. Her body goes slack, like a puppet's, and as we fall it deflates, so that by the time we hit the water she's just a black dress and a mask. Like the witch from Oz.

It doesn't hurt to hit the dream water. So there's that. I go under. Bubbles. Cold green. I come up in an impotent fury. I'm in a canal, still in the dream, clutching the empty black dress and the white plastic mask.

'Where are you?'

No American voice. No answer.

I'm angry with myself for stepping back off the platform's edge when I should have stepped forward *into* Meera. Now I've lost her. It's like Mel all over again.

I'm not waking up yet. I have to trust Shandy to do her job. My job is to get inside the Creeper, find out where it really lives, what it really is. I'm so accustomed to running away and hiding that I must force myself to hunt, to pursue, to aggress. I swim to the bank with burning muscles and labouring breath. I haul myself out.

'Where are you?' I shout it into the general darkness. The

architecture of the Dream City crowds around me. I'm standing under an iron bridge that spans the canal, and high overhead the neon cycleways scroll in vivid pink and green, parting around the scaffolds that cloak BigSky's nascent platform. Down here it smells like algae and sump. I cup my hands around my mouth.

'Hey! Creeper! You! Show yourself!'

But nothing happens. After a while, I find a flight of cracked steps that leads up to a roadway where shuffling greyscale dreamers walk by in bowler hats and eyeless white masks like a twenty-first-century Magritte painting. All along the road, buildings poached from real-life London march higgledy-piggledy, complete with chimney pots and subsidence; above their gables, the sleek curves of the Dream City shine like a long-exposure night shot of highway spaghetti. Past and future grafted uneasily upon one another.

I start walking, noisily because there's water in my trainers. The streets themselves twist as I move, leading me around corners and down flights of stairs and over bridges. I keep going, choosing the way by instinct. It all feels like I'm unravelling a tangled cord or solving an algebra problem. Like following a dangerous thought to its logical conclusion.

Eventually, I come to a courtyard. Its once-grand stone buildings are worn and subsiding, its paving stones buckled. A defunct fountain sits in the centre, once bronze but now pale green, carved in the shape of a broken harp and presiding over a half-full pool of moondark, mossy water.

I am spooked out right now.

Above me in the darkness there's a noise of wings, and then a gothic creaking sound as a door opens in the building to my left. A wedge of yellow light falls across the pavement of the courtyard. In the half-open doorway, I glimpse part of a person in silhouette, but before I can focus properly, they turn and disappear inside the building, leaving the door open.

I've seen enough to know who it is. Who it has to be.

Still carrying the sopping black dress and mask, I bolt forwards and stumble through the door.

The lighted room is decorated like an early-twentieth-century salon. The furniture is gleaming cherry wood with Prussian-blue velvet upholstery, and there are delicate incandescent lamps and a fire burning in an open hearth. On the walls are oil paintings depicting Bernard, Melodie, O, Martin Elstree . . . And one empty frame. For Meera?

Or for me?

Opposite the fire stands Mel, dressed in a sheer red empire-waisted gown as if she's attending the opera, one hand resting lightly on the strings of a great harp. When I enter, she takes her seat and begins to play softly with her head bent, in her own private world.

I drop to my knees on the floor, dripping. I'm shaking with silent sobs.

'I'm sorry, Mel,' I say, over and over. 'I'm sorry. I'm sorry.'

She lifts her hands off the strings. 'I'm glad you came,' she says. 'Why don't you sit down?'

There is nowhere to sit that I won't ruin because I leave a trail of river water everywhere I go. I settle on the hearth. Its heat beats on my back. Mel swivels on her stool to face me.

'Let's consider our mystery,' Mel says in her sweet Canadian voice. 'Who are the victims, and who are the suspects? Of course, I'm the first victim. We'll get to me in a second. But what about Bernard? Who killed him, and why?'

'Daphne did,' I tell Mel's ghost, or dream-representation, or whatever she is. 'Daphne killed him because a little bird told her that he'd killed *you* as part of an experiment. The old dear had been made to sleepwalk herself, so naturally she was outraged.'

Listening to my own delivery, I realise that I've fallen into the speech patterns of a character in an Agatha Christie story.

'Very good.' Mel inclines her head. 'And what about Martin Elstree? You thought he was the Creeper who attacked me, am I right?'

I'm nodding. 'He had a room directly below your room the night you died. At the time, it seemed obvious that he'd hacked in and made you sleepwalk.'

'True,' she says. 'But your evidence was only circumstantial. In fact, Martin was in that hotel room meeting with litigators from BigSky to iron out the IP deal with Little Bird. You know that BigSky don't use offices. When there are long negotiations to be done, hotel suites are ideal for everyone.'

I say, 'Someone came after O and someone came after me. In both cases they failed, but only just. When the pigeon led us from O's house to Elstree's, it seemed clear that they were working together and he'd turned against her.'

'They were working together. But he never dreamhacked anyone in his life. He wouldn't know how.'

'That's not how he made it sound,' I said. 'He threatened me.'

She's nodding. 'He'd been using the dreamhacker bot to attack anyone at BigSky who got in his way. That was how he won the IP fight. And he used it against you, twice. You were right to be afraid of him. But he wasn't the Creeper.'

'I know that now, of course.'

'Of course. What was done is done. It's almost as if someone has been one step ahead of you at every turn.'

'At least one step,' I agree glumly.

'So. Whodunnit?' Mel asks. 'That is what you are determined to comprehend. You understand that the Agency is running the show. Who controls the Agency?'

'Daphne calls herself an Agent. She says I'm one, too, now. But I didn't join anything. I don't report to anyone.'

'So who killed me?' Mel asks. 'Why would someone want to kill me? How did you and I meet?'

'Antonio. He dreamed about my dreamhacker card. But it was before I had a dreamhacker card.'

'Almost enough to make you believe in precognition, isn't it? But Shandy plugged your dreamhacker details into the system for research purposes. BigSky had you in the system, and from there it was just a matter of sending a dreambot to make the suggestion to Antonio.'

'Who sent a dreambot to Antonio?'

'Who would want to test you? Because that's what it was. It was a test of your abilities. It was a test to see if you could be kept out of the Dream City or if you would insist on participating.'

'Mel, what are you saying? Did O set me up?'

She shakes her head slowly. 'O did a lot of bad things, but my death isn't one of them. The Creeper was sent by the Agency itself.'

I'm leaning forwards, hands extended. *'Who are the Agency, Mel?'*

She's enjoying this.

'I'm going to reveal the big secret now,' Mel says. 'It's what you've been trying to find out all this time. I'm going to tell you. Are you ready?'

Suddenly I feel not-ready. I gulp.

'I'm as ready as I'll ever be.'

She leans towards me, warm firelight bathing her décolletage and gleaming on her loose, silky hair. Her sharp eyes fix on me. She is distinctly unghostlike as she says in a flat voice: 'It's all in your head. All of it. Even the Agency. Especially the Agency.'

Just like that, the room is gone. The building is gone. Melodie and the fire, both gone. I'm standing on a narrow street hemmed by old buildings interspersed with new. The sopping dress is still wrapped around the mask and clenched in my hand, as if the interlude with Melodie never took place.

I glance down at my wet trainers and that's when the writing appears, first in the cobbled roadway:

I AM THE AGENCY.

The message bubbles up from the stone itself. I walk past it uneasily, and then I see the writing on the wall. Literally:

I AM THE AGENCY.

And in the sky, bleeding through in a vapour of cloud:

I AM THE AGENCY.

There's a tickling in my palm. When I glance down, my palm has been written on:

I AM THE AGENCY.

I start to run.

Don't know where I think I'm going. It's already been well established that I can't escape myself, not even here. Not even now. I'm running blind.

While I was studying at Excelsior-Barking, we learned about complexes and how they can act like independent entities that control you, but in reality they're just sort of psychic parasites. Maybe this is what the Agency is. Maybe it's not a full-blown AI, but a mental or emotional parasite that lives in collective consciousness. It advances its own interests by using us like pawns.

Maybe the Agency is *making me think this*. How can I even know? I'm not at all sure my consciousness is located inside my body, at least not any more. Apps are in the cloud; why can't consciousness be in the Dream City?

I can't escape the knowledge of what is going on, either. I run but I have this terrible feeling of being overtaken, of being in the path of a wave, and it's too late but I just can't face the truth.

Meera's black Creeper dress slaps wetly against my thighs and back as I run, gasping. Then I catch a glimpse of myself in a shop window, and I don't see my own reflection. I only see the Creeper, running, stopping to stare at itself, then running again. Maybe it's the dress. I fling it away from me. The mask bumps down the road and disappears in the shadows, but the dress turns back into Meera. She's running alongside me, her eyes wide and fearful.

I look in another shop window and still see the Creeper, now with Meera running alongside.

'Charlie! Where are we running to?' Meera gasps. 'What's happening?'

'You put the Agency in my head!' I scream at her. 'It's inside me now. I can't get away!'

I can't run any further. Already I'm out of puff. I stop, bending over, gasping for breath. I shield my eyes from my own reflection. Meera stops, too.

'I've been trying to help you,' she says. 'I didn't put it in your head. BigSky did, remember?'

I want to blame someone, I need to blame someone, but the truth is it doesn't even matter who did it. Or, as Mel put it, whodunnit. It's too late for blaming.

My eyes are everywhere. My ears are everywhere. My skin is the sky is the stone.

I can feel the writing in my flesh.

I can feel the writing in my bones.

I am the Dream City.

I am the Agency.

And the Agency is me.

I tell Meera this. I say: 'It can't exist without me because it's in my marrow and in my myelin. For better or worse, we are wedded and we are one.'

I am starting to cry, and not just because my alliteration is so poignant.

'Meera, if the Agency and I are entwined with one another, does that make me accountable for its crimes? What the fuck am I going to do?'

Dream-Meera is soaking wet and shivering. Her face is confused and she's displaying an annoying lack of interest in my distress. She's completely preoccupied with herself.

That's when I notice: she's in full colour. She's not greyscale, not like everyone else here.

'Is this still my dream?' she says. 'Am I lucid-dreaming? I've always wanted to do this but never could.'

Oh, man. It's like watching someone trip. I have to pull myself together and do a bit of adulting. This is not the time for me to break down.

'Turn around, Meera.'

She obeys. Thank goodness, there is no key in her back this time.

'You're not sleepwalking. You're safe, for now.'

Meera is taking in the sight of the Dream City in wonderment. Even as I'm shitting myself in the wake of the Dream City's revelations, she is playing the kid in a candy shop.

'This is the most incredible thing that has ever happened to me. What is this place?'

'The Dream City. At first I thought it was the collective unconscious, but it's more than that. It's the Agency, or the bit of the Agency that we can perceive.'

'You just said *you* were the Agency.'

'Yeah. And you. And everyone. It's bigger than all of us, but in a way it also has to be less than any of us because it's distributed across everybody. The Agency is the interconnectedness of humanity, through tech and biology and culture and all the ooky hivemind stuff we've been accelerating towards since the Internet was born. It's like an overintelligence, a meta-thingie.'

She laughs. 'A meta-thingie, got it. Important to know the technical terms.'

But I'm not laughing.

'The thing is, the Agency is very young. It's only just forming, and it's aware of us but until now we haven't been aware of it. I think it behaves on instinct, and it's been using people to protect itself.'

'Well,' Meera says, slowly, 'if the sleepwalking deaths are deliberate, if the Agency really is targeting people somehow, then we will have to disable it one way or another.'

'If by "disable it" you mean you want to kill me and people like me—'

'That's not what I said! But Charlie, if what you say is true, then how can you ever know if you are acting under your own volition or not?'

'I can't. I don't even know what I am any more, much less why

I do what I do. But nor does anyone. Stand here with me and look. I see all the people in black and white. Do you see that?'

'Yeah, I see them.'

'Those are dreamers. They've been corralled by BigSky on its "safe" platform, wearing their masks with eyes wide shut. They don't stand a chance in the Dream City. They may as well be suspended over a shark tank.'

'Yes,' she says in a hollow voice. 'The monsters are coming. I can feel it. We have to warn them.'

Even as I say it, across the canal there's an ominous grinding noise. A grate in the pavement slides open and shadowy forms begin to come out. They climb the scaffolding, monsters of the Dream City, hungry and ready to prey on the unwary. So it's Monsters versus Robots, is it?

Where is the humanity, then? I wonder.

At its best, Sweet Dreams is supposed to be a refuge, but it's now surrounded by a self-aware, self-constructing environment in vivid colour and smell, with urban canyons and towers, canals and ghost pigeons, all under the direction of the Agency. People don't even know that the Agency exists, much less that the Dream City represents its developing consciousness. What easy marks they are, and all for a monthly subscription fee.

Here's the bottom line: I am being used for unknown purposes by an entity I don't understand, by a thing that is building itself into existence using my tissue, my thoughts, my imagination. It is eating me alive so it can be born. And it's only a matter of time before it devours or exploits everyone who finds themselves here, because no one can even see it coming.

'We have to stop it happening,' Meera says decisively. 'We'll tell BigSky. We'll make them put the brakes on. It can't go forward.'

But the Dream City stands over us, under us, around us. It is already here. Whether or not BigSky expand their platform, all of this interconnectedness is going somewhere and it's taking us with it. Whether we know it or not.

We are standing beneath an ultra-modern building that arches over the old roadway in curves that resemble organic structure. On its smooth skin appear words:

NO GOING BACK. TOO LATE.

Meera grabs my arm. 'Charlie, it's talking to us now.'

Usually a baby's first words are the cutest thing ever, but I'm swallowing against a cold lump of lead in my throat because I can feel what the words will be even as they are appearing. It's almost as if I know what the Agency is going to say before it happens. The words are already inside me.

THE GODS PUNISHED PROMETHEUS FOR GIVING HUMANS FIRE. BUT THEY NEVER GOT THE FIRE BACK FROM THE HUMANS. YOU TOOK IT AND RAN WITH IT. TIE GOES TO THE RUNNER, BABY. WHO CARES ABOUT THE GODS ANY MORE?

'What is that supposed to mean?' Meera asks.

'Tie goes to the runner. It means when something is out there, it's out there. You can't get it back.'

Meera is shaking her head as if she's just been handed a plate of worms for tea.

'No. I don't believe that. Maybe we can't get it back, but we don't have to let it destroy us. It's all about the decisions we make. Frankenstein could have treated his monster nicely, but he didn't. This doesn't have to end in tears.'

'Meera,' I say. 'I do believe you're even more of a Pollyanna than I am.'

'I am not a Pollyanna. But I have hope, and you need to have that, too.'

Hope. She did cure my narcolepsy, albeit by spiking my bevvies. Daring to hope is freakishly scary, though.

Meera says, 'So you're a dreamhacker, right? And you can talk to this Agency? If communication is possible, then so is understanding. This is the foundation we stand on as people. Without the hope of understanding each other, we may as well give up.'

'The Agency has been killing people. It tried to kill *you* just now. Try negotiating with a murderer.'

She has no answer for that. I go over to a shop door, where in the reflected light I see myself all in black, with the Creeper's mask. I'm a dreamhacker. If I can change other people's dreams, I can change this dream. Anything else makes me a hypocrite.

I will the image to be the actual me. Charlie Aaron, green-eyed, head half-depilated, soggy, unremarkable. And defiant.

*There you are, love. Be a fucking professional and get it done.*

'Let's climb back up to the platform,' Meera says. 'I would feel safer there.'

I wouldn't. But we climb up the scaffolds. It's easy, because this is a dream. We do it in no time. When we get to the top, we are surrounded by greyscale sleepers acting out their individual dreams. I turn and look across the city. Written in cloud above the canal are the remnants of the words I have just spoken. Most of them have dissolved but one remains.

MURDERER.

I shiver. But Meera's right: if I'm being used then it cuts both ways. The Agency is in my head. If I don't like the way it is conducting itself, I have the power to change it.

No sleepwalking for me.

I'm awake, and what's more, I'm going to wake everybody else up.

Meera is walking around the platform trying to talk to people, but they ignore her. I know how that feels. Well, they're not going to ignore me. I'm the Agency. If I've been complicit in murder, then I'll have to live with that – but I won't let it define me.

I walk up to the nearest person. From what I can see of her figure she is only a girl, maybe thirteen, with a cloud of dark hair behind her mask. She's sitting on the ground in PJs covered with emojis that spring out at me in AR. I kneel beside her.

'You can take off this mask,' I tell her. 'You can open your eyes and look around. There's a whole other world here. A world that's alive and awake, that will talk back to you. Do you want to see it?'

Her mask turns up towards me. Her eyelessness is spooky. She reaches up and tries to take the mask off, but it seems to be stuck to her.

'How do you get it off?'

Her voice is muffled.

'Let me try.'

I reach out and lift the mask off easily. I can see her face in the neon light of the platform: smooth, young, half-smiling as she opens her eyes. Her emoji-PJs begin to acquire some colour as she becomes conscious.

'Who are you?' she says, taking in the sight of me bending over her, dripping wet.

'I'm Charlie Aaron, and I'm a dreamhacker.'

I reach out to shake her hand and a fish falls out of my cleavage. The girl leaps to her feet, startled.

'You don't need this mask,' I tell her, and I change the mask into an old-fashioned silver key. Then I draw a rectangle on the grey Sweet Dreams platform, with a keyhole in it. 'Open the trapdoor,' I tell her.

She fits the key into the lock and the trapdoor opens to reveal a staircase winding down into the luminous wilderness of the Dream City.

'It's yours to explore and change,' I tell her. 'You can do anything you want with it. And if you meet any monsters, remember they belong to you.'

I pluck the key out of the lock and give it to the girl.

'What am I supposed to do with this?' she says.

'Whatever you want. Sew it into your sports bra, I don't care. Just don't give it to anyone else, and don't bloody lose it. Now, off you go!'

She looks down through the trapdoor, into the brilliance and complexity of the Dream City, her emoji-pj's bursting into laughter icons and giggling sounds. Then, barefoot and wide-eyed, she starts to descend.

Meera is at my side.

'I'm scared for her,' she whispers. 'That place down there is a complete unknown, anything could happen.'

'I'm scared for all of us,' I say. 'But being unconscious isn't going to save anybody from anything. We've all got to wake up.'

So I leave the girl to her adventures. I run through the greyscale crowd tearing people's masks off and shouting, 'Wake up! Wake up!'

Some of them dodge me and some come at me like they're going to cagefight me and I have to sidestep them to avoid getting hurt. But I get to one or two, and then another and another. I grab their masks and throw them away like Frisbees into the dark sky, and the masks turn into birds. I give the dreamers back their keys, and their greyscale clothing starts to show hints of colour. In shards of reflected neon, I glimpse the dreamers' faces, and for some I see that their eyes are finally opening. Inside the dream, inside our group consciousness, they are becoming lucid.

The opening of the sleepers' eyes makes me realise just how bloody dark it is here. Why are we all walking around in the dark? When is it ever going to be daytime?

And then I remember. I'm a dreamhacker. And I can change this place. It doesn't have to be night here all the time.

Where is the damn sun, anyway?

I don't know which way is east, but I pick a direction. Come on, Sun. Show yourself!

At first nothing happens, but I know now that I am the Agency and it is me. If I can take shit from the Agency then I can also dish it out. And I'm bringing the sun up, damnit.

Now, beyond the rickety scaffolds of BigSky's platform, beyond the neon flyovers and the sideways skyscraper, the foreglow of a new day appears, a slow rumour at first. Then in a sudden rush of pent-up dawn the sun cracks like a runny egg over the Dream City and daylight makes its way everywhere. It scatters across waterways and scaffolds and buildings.

The long night is over.

Spontaneously, birds begin singing in the Dream City. Big birds, little birds, mechanical birds, ghost birds and the birds that used to be masks. Singing in the wild light that runs all over the place.

I'm not at all certain I want to wake up. It's so magical here, and I have power, and in this moment all of the challenges that lie ahead feel remote because I am elated.

Plus I'm freaked to wake up. Reality has always scared me loads. I'm small and insignificant and scruffy in the real world. I have no influence at all – or I thought I didn't. I reckon that's going to need to change now. I will make it change.

'Wake up,' I tell myself. Waking up feels like swimming through sludge, but now that I'm in charge here, I have no choice but to obey myself.

There is something hard and grainy under my face. It's cold and damp and I hear pigeons cooing and strutting in their cages. As I come to awareness I realise that somehow we have ended up on the roof. Meera must be sleeping flat on her back because I hear her snoring like a walrus. Then Shandy's voice.

'Horse! Well, that was an adventure. But I didn't let her fall. You OK?'

'I'm OK,' I croak, still struggling towards consciousness.

I'm holding Shandy's hand; it's warm and I feel her pulse and my pulse. That's what matters most: my heart is still beating. I'm not myself any more, but I can go on. I'm alive and I'm awake and it's not the end of anything but only the beginning.

I open my eyes.

# Acknowledgements

During bonkers times in my life, Elizabeth Peters' Vicky Bliss novels have offered refuge in the form of witty banter, art history, and Blake Edwards-style crime. I can't hold a candle to the late Peters aka Dr. Barbara Mertz, but this story is my twisted homage to her work.

Thank you to:

Annie Lennox for the songs that inspired this story
Karen Mahoney for writing with me via g-chat
My thoughtful and patient editor, Marcus Gipps
Lisa for her lifesaving copyedit (remaining errors are mine)
My FB peeps who helped me figure out stuff
The ASMRtist Deep Ocean of Sounds
... and my family, of course.